Thicker than Water

A MERCY GALE NOVEL

ROBIN JAMES

Copyright © 2025
All Rights Reserved

No part of this book may be reproduced or transmitted in any form or by any means, electronic or mechanical, including photocopying, recording, or by any information storage and retrieval system, without the written permission of the author or publisher, except where permitted by law or for the use of brief quotations in a book review.

This is a work of fiction. Names, characters, businesses, places, events, and incidents are either the products of the author's imagination or used in a fictitious manner. Any resemblance to actual persons, living or dead, or actual events is purely coincidental.

Thicker than Water

A Mercy Gale Novel

Robin James

CHAPTER
One

"Unless you can walk on water, I don't think you're gonna make it, lady."

At the ripe age of twenty-eight, had I already graduated to being a lady? My Uber driver was probably twenty-one at best. He had shaggy brown hair and wore a Nirvana tee shirt with the sleeves cut off. A nice kid though. Not too chatty. And he never asked me why it looked like I might have been crying when he picked me up at the airport.

"Well, that's his boat there," I said. The driver parked at the end of the pier. In the distance, I could just make out the small island tucked into the protected cove of Little Traverse Bay. As I remembered it, the house faced west so you could see the sunset over Lake Michigan every night. A 1957 Chris-Craft Runabout was moored to the first slot. I remembered loving how fast it could go, cutting through the waves on a lake so vast it felt like the ocean.

"You sure this is where you want me to drop you off?" the driver said. His name was Kobe. I didn't ask him who he was named after. I imagined he got that all the time. So did I. Mercy. It's the kind of name people question. "If the boat's there, it means he's in town somewhere."

"Do you know him?" I asked.

Kobe's face changed. It was subtle. Just the widening of his eyes. A tilt to his head. "Sure. It's a small town."

Small town. The smallest. Helene, Michigan. Population 2,007 the sign said when we passed through the city limits.

"I mean I could take you to his office. It's just a few blocks. Too far to walk with your luggage. I won't charge you extra or anything."

"Okay," I said absently. It would be like him to get distracted. Buried in work. Forgetting that he was supposed to pick me up at the airport over two hours ago. He would apologize. He might even mean it.

I climbed back into Kobe's Honda Civic and buckled my seatbelt. Two minutes later, he parallel parked in front of a small, white office building on a corner lot. The name of the office was painted in gold letters on the window glass.

E. Thomas Gale
Attorney at Law

Kobe popped his trunk and pulled out my two matching vintage Louis Vuitton suitcases, the ones my mother was going to throw out. I saw a similar pair go for $2,000 at an online auction last year.

"You want me to wait?" Kobe asked.

"I'm fine, thanks," I answered.

"Do you work for him or something?" Kobe's tone turned dubious.

"Why do you ask?"

Kobe shrugged. "I mean...did you fly all the way out here for some job with him? You look like the type."

"What type?"

"Like a lawyer, maybe."

It was in me to ask him what he meant by that. I was overdressed. I wore a navy-blue suit and three-inch heels. Not the most comfortable thing to wear for air travel. I just knew I wanted to look nice today. No. It was more than that. The suit was armor.

"Maybe," I smiled, thinking that would satisfy Kobe's curiosity.

"Well," he said. "Good luck." There was emphasis on the word luck that made it sound like sarcasm.

"Is there something you think I need to know?" I asked, feeling defensive.

"No. It's just...well...good luck." This time, the phrase came off more genuinely. I thanked Kobe again. He hopped into his car and drove off.

In the middle of the afternoon, at the height of Northern Michigan tourist season, downtown Helene bustled. Tucked between the more popular Charlevoix and Petoskey, not as many people had discovered Helene. That's the way most people liked it. It was changing though. Even I could sense it. The harbor was full of expensive boats, even a few yachts. The outdoor patio of a restaurant across the street looked packed with people waiting on the sidewalk.

The downtown area itself comprised a single long boardwalk with a state park on the easternmost end. To the south, behind the main thoroughfare, the streets inclined sharply. A bluff overlooked the shops. From here, I could see the largest building at the top. A sign built into the side of the hill read "Helene High School."

I tried the office door. Mercifully, it swung open. I didn't expect what greeted me inside. No one sat at the front reception desk, but it looked like someone had set off a paper grenade. Files were strewn all over the floor. Every drawer in the wooden cabinet against the wall was open.

"Dad?"

I stepped through the reception area. He kept an office in the back. I knocked on the door. No answer. I called him at least half a dozen times. Texted too. A little pit of dread formed in my stomach as I gripped the brass door handle. This building was old. One of the originals built when Helene was established in 1867. My footsteps creaked over the wooden floorboards.

"Dad?" I said again. I opened the door.

If I thought the reception area looked like a tornado hit it, the inner office was worse. I could barely find a clear patch of floor to walk on. He had more papers, notepads, and files thrown everywhere. The receiver of his ancient desk phone hung off the hook, touching the floor. I picked it up and put it back in the cradle.

Closing my eyes, I could vividly remember the last time he'd brought me here. He'd seemed so big then. Important. Gruff but with kind eyes, and he let me sit at the smaller desk against the wall. I remembered a crystal paperweight that shone like a prism in the sunlight.

The smaller desk was still there, buried under more paperwork. I picked up a yellow legal pad. I recognized my father's looping cursive. He wrote so hard, a few of his capital letters had punctured through to the next page. These were meeting notes dated two years ago. Sensitive financial information that shouldn't just be lying out for anyone to see. I put the pad down.

Dad had glass shelves along the back wall. Despite the chaos and disorganization, the items on the shelves did not show a speck of dust on them. Photographs. Mementos. A shadow box containing the medal I knew my father was most proud of. His Navy Cross. Beside it, a picture of my father. He had to be close to my age in it. He stood next to his F4 Phantom, his expression stern. But God, he was handsome with a thick head of dark hair and devilish cleft in his chin. He had a booming baritone voice, and the room would shake with him when he laughed.

I put the picture down. At the very top of the shelf, just out of reach, an iconic gold statue glimmered. He let me hold it just the once. That booming laugh vibrated through me as I stood in front of a mirror and thanked the Academy as I held my father's Oscar. He told me someday he'd let me have it. At eleven years old, that had seemed to me the greatest prize of all.

The ancient desk phone rang, jarring me. Instinct drove me and I picked up the phone.

"Law offices of Tom Gale," I answered.

"Violet? You don't sound like yourself."

"Um...what? I'm sorry. This isn't Violet. To whom am I speaking?"

"Who is this?"

I cleared my throat. "This is Mercy. Mercy Gale."

A pause. "Well, Mercy Gale. This is Crystal Cline over in Judge Homer's courtroom. If you're looking for your father, you better get down here right away. His Honor's about sixty seconds from throwing Tom in jail."

It wasn't hard to find the courthouse one block over from Helene High School at the top of the bluff. Just a five-minute walk from my father's office at the center of town. Once inside, a middle-aged deputy sheriff pointed down the hall.

"You must be Mercy," he said.

It seemed in a little over thirty minutes, all of Helene knew I'd arrived and who I was. My heels clacked as I hurried down the hall. The heavy oak double doors to Judge Vincent Homer's courtroom were shut, but I could hear my father's big voice coming from inside.

"I am not gonna let you railroad my client today, Whitney!" Dad shouted. "You know damn well Deputy Smith didn't properly serve this warrant. This tree is so poisonous it's gonna rot right through!"

I opened the doors. My father, the great E. Thomas Gale, stood at the lectern, red-faced and shaking his index finger straight at the judge. My heart fell straight to the floor. I'd never seen him like this. His thick head of hair, now pure white, stuck out in peaks and cones. He wore a faded gray tee shirt and a pair of Dockers shorts. I looked around the courtroom. One attorney sat at the prosecution table, another at the defense table, but whatever proceeding he'd interrupted, my father clearly had nothing to do with it.

"Tom," the Judge said. "Why don't we talk in chambers?"

"Is he coming?" My father pointed toward the prosecution's table.

I stepped forward. "Your Honor, my name is Mercedes Gale. I'm from...this is my..."

"Mercy?"

I came down the rows and went up to the lectern to stand beside my father. His eyes clouded for a moment, then snapped back into focus. "Is it Tuesday?"

"Yeah, Dad," I said. "It's Tuesday afternoon."

"I need to go," he said, scratching his head. "Mercy needs me to pick her up from the airport."

I felt my cheeks flush. Though there were no public spectators in the courtroom, the concerned eyes of the two attorneys at the tables, Judge Homer and his court reporter, seemed judgmental enough. Every protective instinct in me flared. I just wanted them all to stop looking at my dad. I wanted to get him out of here.

"Head into my chambers," Judge Homer said, his voice kind.

My father looked down. He ran a hand over his wrinkled tee shirt. All at once, he seemed aware of his surroundings again.

"Leslie," he said to the female attorney. "Sorry. I didn't mean to take up your time."

"It's okay, Tom," she said.

I took my father by the hand. His posture shifted, going rigid. Proud. He walked with me through the doorway to the left of Judge Homer's bench.

"We're adjourned for a half hour," Judge Homer said as he came in behind us and shut the door.

Dad went to the leather couch against the wall of Judge Homer's chambers.

"Do you have a glass of water?" I asked the judge. Vince Homer peeled himself out of his robe and hung it on his chair. He reached into a small cube refrigerator at the side of his desk and pulled out a bottle of water, tossing it to me. I unscrewed the cap and handed it to my father. With shaking hands, he drank it down. Slowly, the color came back into his face. He rubbed his eyes.

"You feeling okay now, Tom?" the judge asked.

"I missed lunch," he said as if that explained everything.

"It happens," Judge Homer said. "Why don't you just put your feet up and finish that water? I'm gonna have a word with Mercy here if that's okay with you."

Dad nodded. I didn't want to leave him. But Judge Homer didn't seem inclined to give me a choice. He gestured for me to follow him through the second door to his inner offices.

A blonde woman sat at her desk as Judge Homer closed the door to his chambers behind us. "Jesse," the judge said. "This is..."

"Mercy!" she beamed. "So glad you got here safe. Tom's been telling us all about how you're coming up for a visit. That's all he could talk about last week."

"How long's he been like that?" I turned to the judge.

Judge Homer took a sharp intake of air. "Today's particularly bad. Most days, he's just fine. Today..."

"He came in ranting about the Sweeney suppression hearing," Jesse said. "Accused me of not sending him a revised notice of hearing."

"When is the hearing?" I asked.

Judge Homer and Jesse exchanged a look. "Honey," Jesse said. "Your father represented Dale Sweeney ten years ago."

"Like I said," Judge Homer said. "Most days, he's just fine. Today he's just having a bad one. But you're here now. Can you get him home?"

"I think I can manage," I said.

"Well, anyway," Judge Homer repeated. "You're here now. It's about time."

I stopped myself from telling him I didn't think things had gotten this bad. No one had told me. But I said none of it. Judge Homer looked me up and down.

I felt my back go stiff. Once again, my protective instincts kicked in. I didn't like that these people who I barely knew seemed to know more about my father than I did.

"I'll take care of him," I said. "I'll get him home. I won't need any help."

Judge Homer smiled. "You sound like your dad. Mercy? Let me give you a piece of advice." He put a hand on my arm and leaned in. "Do your dad a favor. Hurry up and pass the bar exam, for all our sakes."

CHAPTER
Two

"Dad, are you sure?" I stood on the dock as my father started flinging the ropes off the boat.

"I know how to drive the damn boat, Mercy. You wanna get in or are you planning on getting a room in town?"

I felt a lump in my throat. Was this him telling me he didn't want me here? A million childhood emotions flooded through me.

This isn't a place for you, kiddo. Girls should be with their mothers. I promise I'll be at the next concert, okay? You know how crazy things get when I'm in trial.

My father's face softened. "Get in the boat, Mercy. It'll be dark soon. I'm tired and I'm cranky. Hand me one of your suitcases."

I'd almost forgotten I had them. I picked up the first one and heaved it over the side of the boat. My father grabbed the other and tucked it under one seat.

"Unhook that last rope," he instructed me. Then he held out his hand to steady me as I stepped into the boat. He gave us a last shove and revved the engine. My father stood as he steered away from the pier then executed an arcing turn heading straight for the little island in the center of the cove.

Everyone had thought him crazy for buying it. My mother screamed about it for days. Two million dollars. Dad said it was a steal. She worried it meant there'd be nothing left for me by the time he was gone. But as the waves beat against the side of his wooden hull, I saw it with fresh eyes.

It was beautiful here. With blue waters stretching to the horizon, you could think you'd come to the edge of the world. One side of the island stayed natural, with thick red maples and ancient oak trees on a high bluff. On the other, Dad had renovated a hundred-year-old cabin spending just as much as he had on the property.

He slowed as he came to the dock on the east side.

"Keep your fingers inside," he cautioned me like he'd done when I was eleven. He carefully aimed for the boat lift under the covered dock. He cut the engine and let the wind take us the last few yards. Before I could help him, Dad hopped onto the dock with almost athletic agility and cranked the winch, raising the boat up out of the water.

I grabbed my suitcases and stepped out of the boat. Dad took one of them from me, heaving the strap over his shoulder. It was a long walk uphill to the house. But Dad didn't head for the tiered stairway. Instead, he hit a button on his key fob and a garage door opened on the side of the hill.

"That's new," I said, marveling at the hidden tunnel it revealed. "That's...what are you, James Bond now?"

I could hear my mother's voice asking him how much *that* had cost him. But I could appreciate the genius of it. A set of motion lights kicked on as I followed my father into the tunnel and up a ramp. It led straight to the mudroom on the basement floor of the house.

"I told you I was gonna die here," he said. "Can't very well do that when I'm too old to take those stairs, can I? And you can be damn sure I'm not letting anybody put me into a nursing home."

"I wouldn't dream of it," I said. He'd omitted the incident in Judge Homer's courtroom. He never asked me what the judge said to me when he led me out of the room.

"Your room's just like you left it," he said. "I figured if you wanted to change it, you could do that yourself."

The mudroom led into Dad's enormous kitchen. He'd kept that mostly original, with black granite countertops and oak cabinets that went to the ceiling. He had a few dishes in the sink, but otherwise everything looked organized. I didn't know what to expect after seeing the state of his office.

"I've moved into the room downstairs," he said. "Renovated it five years ago."

The show-stopping feature of the main floor was a massive fieldstone fireplace in the center of the room. Dad's trophy buck was mounted just above the mantle. He had green Mardi Gras beads hanging off "Bucky's" antlers.

I inhaled the powerfully familiar scent of the place. It took me back fifteen years to that last day I was here. Mom and I weren't getting along back then. But my father was ill-equipped to deal with a sullen teenage daughter.

"It's good to be back here," I said. "Have you eaten anything all day?"

Dad stood in the middle of the room, regarding me. He was handsome still. That thick hair and anvil-sharp jaw. He had a devilish dimple in his left cheek when he smiled. The warmth of that smile when he focused it on you felt like sunlight, potent enough to reach through a camera lens.

Wattage. That's what my mother had called it. That smile had made Dad millions as a legal commentator on cable news back in the nineties. He'd blazed a trail that made the careers of every legal pundit who came after him. But E. Thomas Gale had been the original.

"Do you remember where it is?" Dad said. "First door at the top of the stairs?"

"Of course, I remember where my room is. But you didn't answer my question. Have you eaten anything today? Violet said you never remember to eat when you're in court."

"Violet," Dad said as if the name left a bitter taste in his mouth. "She knows nothing."

"Where is she, Dad?" I asked. "Your office was empty when I got there."

"You'll have to ask her," he said.

"I would. But I don't know where..." I let my voice trail off. Whatever was going on between Dad and his long-time secretary clearly had him agitated. I left it there and headed for the fridge. Dad had foil-wrapped casserole dishes stacked on the middle shelf.

"Garlic chicken," I read the bold lettering on the top written with a black Sharpie. It looked like Violet's handwriting. I knew it well from every birthday card my father sent me over the years. She'd put today's date on it and instructions to heat it at 350 degrees for forty minutes.

"Smells good," I said. Dad had moved off and sat in his leather recliner in front of the fireplace. He switched on the flat screen TV and started watching the news. I turned on the oven and slid the casserole inside. Wherever Violet was, it looked like she'd prepared meals for Dad for the entire week.

"I'm just going to freshen up," I said.

"Suit yourself," he said. I went to him, putting a hand on my dad's shoulder. We hadn't hugged since I got here. He hadn't said he was happy to see me. But he reached for me, putting his hand over mine as he stared at the TV. For now, I met my dad where I found him. He squeezed my hand. I turned and went up the winding staircase to the second floor.

He wasn't kidding that he'd left my room as it was. I was eleven years old when he let me meet with his decorator. I'd chosen pink and green for everything and a garish canopy bed. Pink walls. Green chiffon drapery. The entire room looked like an ice cream cone to me now. I put my suitcases in the corner and sat at the large vanity dresser with what I'd called "Hollywood Lights" surrounding the mirror.

I ran my finger over the top of the dresser. It came away clean. As far as I knew, nobody had slept in this room in fifteen years. Dad's housekeeper still came out once a week. Violet arranged for that too, probably. Where in God's name was she?

My phone buzzed. I'd left it in the side compartment of my purse. I didn't need to read the screen to know who it was. Mom had called me no less than six times since I stepped off that plane. But I wasn't ready to talk to her. I didn't have the energy for another argument about the direction of my life. She didn't want me to go to law school. But now that I'd dropped out, she was furious. I took out my phone and texted her back.

> Safely landed. I'll call you in a couple of days. Everything's fine.

It wouldn't totally placate her, but I knew she'd respect my boundaries at least that much.

I went to the window. This room faced east so I could watch the sunrise over the little town of Helene. When I was eleven years old, I could imagine I was a princess, and this was my castle tower. I had wanted to stay forever. Now, it felt hard to breathe. Dad was isolated out here. It's what he wanted. His words echoed through my mind.

"I mean to die here."

After today, I worried my father might just get his wish sooner than he meant.

∼

THE CRANK of the winch woke me up out of a dead sleep. Light stabbed through the green chiffon curtains and for a moment, I thought I was dreaming. This wasn't real. I was just fifteen years old again and Mom would show up ready to haul me back to Florida.

"Dad?"

I wiped the crust out of my eyes and ran to the window. He was down there on the dock, about to put the boat back in the water. I turned the crank on the window and shouted down.

"Dad! Where are you going?" He seemed disoriented for a moment, wondering where the sound of my voice came from. Then he looked up and stepped into the light.

"Good morning, Lazy Bones!" He waved.

"Christ," I muttered. Grabbing my phone off my charger, I read the time. It was almost nine o'clock. Still in a tee shirt and boxer shorts, I slipped my feet into my flip-flops and ran downstairs.

Dad was about to climb into the boat. "Where are you going?" I shouted.

"To work," he said. "Where else would I be going?"

I looked behind me as if someone might magically appear to talk some sense into him other than me. "I thought you agreed you'd take a few days off while I was here?"

Dad straightened. "Days off? Why would I do that? The work won't wait. But if you wanna head into town with me, I'll wait a few minutes."

"I'm not even dressed. Haven't had my coffee."

"The pot's still warm in the kitchen. Grab a cup and come on down. You can get breakfast in town. The bakery next door makes these chocolate eclairs that'll send you into orbit."

I knew I'd get nowhere trying to argue. "Just...give me ten minutes." Dad tapped his watch as I cranked the window shut.

I scraped a toothbrush over my teeth and twisted my hair into a knot. Lord. Would he try to go back to court today? I tossed out one of my suitcases and picked something that could pass for courtroom attire in a pinch. My purse sat on a chair against the wall. The crumpled letter I brought with me peeked out of the side pocket. I shoved it back in, slung the bag over my shoulder, then ran down to the dock with high-heeled shoes in hand.

Water sprayed my face as Dad took the boat up to full speed. I won't deny it was an exhilarating way to drive to work. But I worried about what he did when the lake froze over in the wintertime. I hadn't planned to stick around long enough to find out.

As he docked the boat at the pier, the town of Helene came to life. Dad got waves from a dockhand on the adjacent pier. Two ladies walking their dogs called out to him.

"Better hurry!" one of them said. "Connie's had people trying to buy the last of her eclairs. She said she's saving them for you, Tom."

Dad fixed his killer smile on all of them as we made our way up the street and back to his little office on the corner of Main and Harborview. He unlocked the front door and flipped the little placard hanging in the window, so it read, "Come On In!"

The disarray of the office struck me again as it did the day before. Dad didn't seem to notice. A pile of mail had been dropped through the slot and landed on the floor. He picked it up and tossed it on the reception desk.

"You can use Violet's desk for the time being," he said.

"When is she coming back, Dad?" I asked. He shrugged but didn't offer me an answer. I went to Violet's desk and put my bag on it.

"I've got some client calls to return. You think you can take care of yourself for an hour? If you want more coffee, Connie makes that too. Go shopping. The company credit card's in that little box under Violet's chair."

"You keep it there?" I said. "That doesn't seem very secure, Dad." But he was already down the hall to his office. I knew by the purpose in his gait, I might as well be invisible now. Again, I heard my mother's voice in my mind.

I could run naked through the street with my hair on fire and he'd never notice. That's how he gets when he's working, Mercy.

Fine. Maybe I could try to make sense of the chaos in the front office. At least I could make it look less like an episode of *Hoarders: Law Office Edition* if someone were to come in.

I heard my father's muffled voice through the walls as he took the first of those client calls. As far as the mess of papers strewn all over the desk, there seemed to be no sense to them. I found appointment notes. Random copies of pleadings. Receipts. Billing statements. I decided to just start putting them into various piles. If Dad ever came up for air, I'd make him sit down and talk to me about it.

I lost myself in the task for a little while. Hearing Dad's voice soothed me. He had a gravelly tone and spoke with authority. When I was a kid, I thought he knew everything. Thought there was no problem he couldn't solve. No answer he didn't have.

But this? This was nothing like the man I knew. Things were falling through the cracks. The courthouse staff had seen it. They were worried.

I heard the phone slam down. My father still refused to use a cell phone within the confines of his office walls. He said he'd never give a client his personal cell phone number. Boundaries, he said. Though it felt hollow. E. Thomas Gale worked twenty-four-seven, even through his only daughter's school plays.

"I can't find it, Vi," I heard him shout. "Violet? Where did you put my appointment book?"

I started down the hallway. "Dad?"

I knocked on his door. When he didn't answer, I cracked it open.

Dad was gone. He had a back door into the alley through his office. "Shit," I said. "Dad?" I peered down the alley. He'd already disappeared.

I heard the front door chime go off. Relief flooded through me and I headed toward the sound. But it wasn't Dad. Instead, a middle-aged woman with jet-black hair and the weight of the world on her face walked in.

"May I help you?" I said. But I wasn't completely focused on her. I was watching the sidewalk, hoping to see my father walk down the street.

"I'm here for my appointment," she said. "Are you new?"

"I'm...sort of," I answered. "My...Mr. Gale had to step out. Is there something I can help you with?"

She cocked her head to the side, reminding me of a confused puppy for a moment. "I'm at my wits' end," she said. "I told him the last time my next stop was the Attorney Grievance Commission."

"Why don't you have a seat," I said, gesturing toward the conference room next to the reception area. I had a moment of panic as she brushed past me, realizing I hadn't thought to check the state of that room yet. Luckily, the chaos of the rest of the building hadn't crept in there. Dad just had neat stacks of law books on the shelves and a cheery plant in the corner. The woman took a seat at the table and plopped her heavy purse down in front of her.

"Um. Can I get you anything? A glass of water or..."

"No," she barked. "You can just get me Mr. Gale."

"He had to step out. But I'm working with him. Maybe you can tell me what we can do to help."

She gave me that confused puppy expression again. "I've been loyal. But things aren't the same around here. I will not be brushed aside."

"I'm sorry. Maybe you can start from the beginning." I took a seat opposite her, grabbing a pen and blank pad of paper from the center of the table. She looked annoyed with me, but it didn't stop her from talking.

CHAPTER TWO   21

"You don't know who I am, do you?"

"It's my first day," I said.

"What's your name? Or maybe I shouldn't even bother trying to remember it. They never last long around here."

"My name? It's...I'm Mercedes."

Her eyes widened a bit. "You're the daughter, then. Well, I don't suppose he can run you off as easily."

You'd be surprised, I wanted to say, but bit it back.

"Well, he's very proud of you. Told me about it when you went to law school. He was beaming. Just beaming. I was a little jealous. And I'm not proud of that. It's just...my Jeremy wants to go to law school, too. He wants to do a lot of things."

Jeremy. I kept my face neutral.

"Jeremy Holt," she whispered. "My son. He's in prison, Ms. Gale. I would have thought your father told you that."

I hesitated, feeling my pulse quicken. "Even if he had," I said. "It's better if you tell me what we can do for you in your own words. I'm a fresh set of ears."

"What you can *do* for me? Jeremy is my son. He's in prison for a murder he didn't commit, Mercedes. Your father promised he'd get him a new trial. Now, he won't return my calls. Your father has taken a lot of money from me. Money I didn't have. And I'm now starting to believe he has no intention of really helping us."

"Mrs....Holt..."

"Benning," she snapped. "Diane Benning. You remember that. Jeremy still has his father's last name, not mine. But I'm talking about twenty thousand dollars, Ms. Gale. That might not be a lot of money to you or your father. But it's everything to me. And it's everything to Jeremy. I want a full accounting. I've given him names. Witnesses. There's a girl who can tell you where Jeremy was when they say he killed that girl. I want to know why your father won't talk to her. I have more than enough to file a complaint with the State Bar. Jeremy believes in your father. But I have to protect my son."

"I understand," I said. "Let's reschedule this, okay? Give me a week. Do nothing for a week. I'll get you some answers. I promise."

She sat back, eyeing me with suspicion. Twenty thousand dollars. And Dad's doing things like leaving the company credit card lying out at the front desk.

"Do you keep your promises, Ms. Gale?"

"Yes," I said.

Her shoulders dropped. "Okay then. I'll be back in a week. But I'm only doing this because I know Jeremy would want me to. If it were up to me alone, I'd have your father in front of the State Bar or maybe in jail himself. You understand?"

"I understand. And I'm sure whatever's going on, my father is doing what he can."

She got up and held her purse in front of her. "I want your father to do what he promised my son. He's going to die in prison if he doesn't. He's only thirty-five years old. He's been rotting in that place for sixteen years, Ms. Gale."

She turned on her heel and stormed out of the conference room. As she let herself out, Violet Tamblyn, my father's missing secretary, walked in. Her face registered pure shock as Diane Benning brushed past her.

I got to my feet. "Mercy," Violet gasped. I couldn't tell if she meant to call me by name, or if it was an exclamation of exasperation.

"You talked to her?" she said. "You talked to Diane Benning? Alone?"

Anger boiled through me. "Do you see anyone else around here? He's alone, Violet. Why didn't you tell me?"

"Honey, you do not know what you just walked into. That woman has been in here every day this week and half of last week. For the love of God, tell me you didn't promise that woman anything."

My mouth was still hanging open. I clamped it shut not knowing what else to tell her. I was only trying to help. But I had the sinking feeling that I'd just done the exact worst thing.

Violet went to the front door, she locked it and flipped over the closed sign. I went to her desk and grabbed my bag. I reached for the thick envelope sticking out of the side pocket. It had brought me here as much as the rumors I'd heard about my father.

I shoved the letter down farther so Violet couldn't accidentally read the return address. I did though. I ran my fingers over the thick black letters.

Jeremy Holt
Ionia Correctional Facility

CHAPTER
Three

I HADN'T SEEN Violet Tamblyn since the last day I spent on the island years ago. She stood with her hands on her hips, surveying the disarray in the front office and throwing me a withering gaze.

"When did you get here?"

"Yesterday evening. Where have you been?"

She took a step back; her face falling. "Are you accusing me of something?"

"No. But it sure feels like you're accusing me."

"Mercy, please just tell me you didn't promise Diane Benning anything."

"She's threatening to file a grievance against my dad. And from what I've seen in the last twenty-four hours, she might have valid reasons. Where have you been? Did you know things were getting this bad?"

Violent didn't answer me. Instead, she charged down the hallway headed for my father's office. Along the way, she slammed file drawers shut. "Where is he?"

I had to practically sprint to keep up with her. Violet had to be sixty-five years old. She'd been with my dad since before I was born. She wore a long, flowing floral print duster and flat shoes. She stood over six feet tall and had been one of the few people I'd ever known who could cut my father off mid-sentence and get him to listen.

"I don't know where he is," I said. "He took off."

Violet whipped around. "And you let him? He left you with Diane?"

"Stop. Just. Stop. You're the one who's been here. I'm doing the best I can. Things are bad, Violet. You should have told me."

Her face softened. "They're not that bad. He's just…he gets a little scattered sometimes. That's all. We're managing."

"You're not managing. Look at this place! Was it like this when you left? Did you know?"

She closed her eyes, finding her inner Zen. "No," she finally answered. "The place didn't look like this when I left it. He must have been looking for something. I had a few texts and missed calls from him but I told him I was taking two weeks off and I would not pick up my phone. My therapist told me I needed to set a boundary. So I did."

"What is it? What's wrong with him?"

Violet reached for me, putting her hands on my shoulders. "Honey, he's just old. He's been under a lot of stress for far too long. It's just caught up with him a little bit. It's been tough since your Uncle Lloyd retired. He enjoyed having a partner."

CHAPTER THREE

Lloyd Murphy had been my father's law partner since the early eighties. He handled civil cases while my father dealt with anything criminal. For many years, Lloyd carried the practice without my father when he focused on his cable news career.

"You or Lloyd should have called me," I said.

Again, her expression felt accusatory.

"Mercy," she said. "That was his choice. Not mine. He just wasn't up to it. And he was afraid to tell you. He didn't want you to worry. But maybe two years ago, Tom had a stroke. A minor one, the doctors said. But it's been a struggle for him since then. He's managing, don't get me wrong, but..."

"Things have been falling through the cracks," I said. "That's what Judge Homer told me. He said a lot of people have been covering for him but it hasn't been enough."

"Well, Vince Homer doesn't miss much. I've been on Tom to retire for a while. He won't hear of it. Still thinks he can work just as hard and as long as he did forty years ago. He thinks that's the way to beat this."

"Beat what? Does he have a diagnosis?"

"He won't see any doctors. If he has his way, he'll drop dead some day in the middle of a closing argument."

"When I saw him in court yesterday, I thought he was about to get his wish."

"That must have been very frightening for you, honey. I'm sorry. I mean...not sorry about not being here. I hadn't taken a vacation in five years. I needed a break. I went to visit my son Glen, in Denver. It was nice. I'm going back the entire month of December. Tom's not going to like it, but what's he going to do? Fire me?"

She put her arm around me and led me back to the front room. "Lord," she said. "He really made a mess of things out here. It's going to take me all week to put it right."

"I can help," I said. "I've been trying to help."

"How long can you stay?"

That was the question. How long could I stay? How long did I want to stay?

"I don't know," I answered. "Not long. I have to…"

"Have to what?" she asked. "Mercy, I know you dropped out of law school. Your mom called me."

"She shouldn't have done that. It's my business."

"She hasn't told your dad. And I won't either. But you should."

"I don't want to hear it. He'll just get angry. He'll lecture me. I don't need that. I'm almost thirty years old."

"Right. High time for you to make a plan for your life."

"You sound just like him."

"Well, whatever your plans are, I'm glad you're here now. And so is Tom."

I felt a painful lump in my throat. He hadn't said that to me since I got here. I didn't expect him to.

"He forgot to pick me up from the airport," I said. "He never showed."

"Oh, dear. I left him several reminders. He must have just gotten busy with something. You can't take it personally."

"I've been hearing that my whole life, Violet. It's his work. It's who he is. Don't take it personally. And now?" I couldn't finish the sentence. Couldn't let myself fully think it in my head. If my dad was sick, what kind of person would it make me if I blamed him for that?

"You should talk to him," Violet said. "Your dad loves you. He's been excited about you coming to visit this summer. Even if he's lousy at showing it."

"What about all of this? Violet, this can't go on. Why do I feel like Diane Benning is just the tip of the iceberg? What's going on with her anyway?"

My eyes went to the letter on the outside of my bag. I'd shoved it back facing inward. Violet couldn't read the return address. Maybe I should have shown it to her. Maybe I should have shown Diane Benning. I couldn't. Not yet.

Violet's expression turned grim. "Diane Benning is a special situation. And your dad can't really help her or her son."

"Why not?"

"Honey, trust me. That's a can of worms you don't want to open."

"The woman didn't strike me as a kook. She seemed sincere. And I believe her that she's headed for the grievance commission. If someone takes a hard look at what's going on with Dad, it could be a problem."

"Tom's not going to file a motion for a new trial for Diane Benning's son. He can't."

"Why not? What happened?"

"Mercy, Diane Benning's son is Jeremy Holt. Did she tell you that?"

"Yes."

"Honey, your father's not handling Jeremy Holt's criminal appeal. He's the one who defended him at trial sixteen years ago. Defended him and lost."

Jeremy Holt. His trial had been the convenient reason my father wouldn't let me stay with him when I wanted to leave my mother's house and live with him when I was thirteen years old. Now he was the reason I came back.

It had been the only murder trial the great E. Thomas Gale ever lost.

"What if she claims her son had ineffective assistance of counsel? Violet, if she digs into what's been going on with Dad..."

"We won't let that happen."

"We? How are we going to stop it? If he won't retire. If he won't stop taking cases, he's not equipped to handle..."

A door slammed behind me, sounding like a gunshot. I jumped. Violet jumped. My father came in through the back door.

"How dare you?" he yelled. "Violet, what the hell have you been telling her?"

"Tom," she said. "Just calm down. You're taking things out of context. Mercy's just worried about you. She's your daughter. She has a right to—"

"Get out!"

It felt like my guts had just spilled out onto the floor. He was talking to both of us.

"I don't need either of you to tell me how to run this practice," he hollered. "What the hell have you been telling people behind my back?"

"Nobody's telling anyone anything. But you're tired, Tom," Violet said. "You need to take a break. Pace yourself a little better. You know what the doctor said about—"

"You think I won't fire you? Is that what you said? Consider this your last day, Violet. I mean it."

"Dad, stop. Violet's just worried about you. So am I. Look around? This place is in shambles. You were off your game in court yesterday. Something's going on. We're just concerned."

"Get out," he repeated. "Both of you. I won't have you telling me how to run my life. I've done everything you asked of me, Sandra. Everything. You wanna bleed me dry!"

It was as if a thunder crack went off inside my head. Sandra. He was looking straight at me but calling me by her name. It was an argument I'd overheard them have at least a hundred times. *You wanna bleed me dry, Sandra?*

"Tom," Violet said, her voice soothing. She stepped between me and my father. "Tom. This is Mercy. This is your daughter. Stop yelling. Mercy doesn't deserve that. She's trying to help."

My father blinked. His face was ashen. "Mercy," he repeated. "I damn well know my daughter, Violet. *My* daughter. I don't need advice from you about how to treat her. You worry about your own kid. Glen could use it. Mercy doesn't."

Violet's face fell. This wasn't my dad. "You called me Sandra," I said. "I'm not...I'm not Mom."

A muscle jumped in his jaw. For a moment, the man I'd known as this fierce force of nature just looked scared. He recovered quickly, squaring his shoulders. "I'm done talking."

He turned on his heel and went back down the hall, slamming the door to his office and clicking the lock behind him.

Violet waited a moment, then she turned to me. "He didn't mean any of that."

I held a hand up. "I know. Don't take it personally."

"Mercy..."

But I didn't want to hear anymore.

I FOUND my way back to Dad's island. One of the fuel attendants on the pier ferried me over. It was odd being there in that big house without my father in it. He refused to come out of his office after his blow up. Violet stayed, even though he'd technically fired her.

I took out another of her casseroles from the fridge. Lasagna this time. I didn't bother to plate it and ate it straight out of the dish. As with everything Violet cooked, the thing was delicious.

Three more missed calls from my mother. I couldn't bring myself to call her back. I just didn't want to hear her bashing my dad again. Whatever problems there were between us, let them stay that way.

I set my fork down and walked into Dad's study off the living room. It was just like I remembered. Knotty pine-paneled walls. An old-fashioned mahogany desk. Pictures of Dad with the famous people he knew. The NFL player he'd successfully defended against a murder charge. National news anchors. And that night at the Oscars when Dad won as a producer for Best Picture for the movie they'd made out of his most famous case of all.

My mother had been there that night, though she'd tried to stay in the shadows, not wanting to be photographed. She hated the limelight my father thrived in. I saw no pictures of Mom on these walls. She'd always said she thought she was my father's most prized trophy.

My phone rang. For a moment, I expected it to be her. But as I read the caller ID, relief flooded through me.

"Christian," I said.

"Mercy, thank God. I was beginning to think you were dead."

"Don't be so dramatic."

"Please tell me you've come to your senses and are coming back to school with me in the fall. How the hell am I supposed to handle Consumer Law without you? Ripley's class is supposed to be impossible."

"You'll do fine. You'll probably book it."

"What's wrong," he said.

Christian Foley had sat next to me at first year orientation at the University of Toledo Law just fourteen months ago. When they told us that the person sitting next to us probably wouldn't graduate, Christian grabbed my hand and blurted out, "Thank God it'll be you, not me!" We'd been joined at the hip ever since.

"Nothing's wrong." But in the short time we'd known each other, Christian became better at reading me than my own mother.

"Liar. How's your dad?"

That odd protectiveness flared. Only I knew it wouldn't work with Christian. Not even over the phone. He knew too much.

"Lousy, I think."

"You think?"

"He's not himself. I don't know. He sort of had an episode in court yesterday."

"An episode? What's going on, Mercy? Is it what you thought? Alzheimer's?"

"I don't know. His secretary says he won't go get a diagnosis. But there have been some...signs."

"Well...shit. I'm sorry. So Holt was right. And your mom didn't know?"

"They don't talk. And when they do, they yell. She's been mad at him for twenty-five years. This isn't going to change that."

"So, what are you going to do?"

I took a beat. What was I going to do? What could I do?

"I'm not sure," I said. "I think I want to stay long enough to make sure he's got what he needs. You know. That things are in place."

"Yeah. Mercy. I don't mean to be crass. But you hear things. When people get dementia. Erratic behavior. What if he tries spending everything?"

"I'm not worried about his money."

"Somebody should be. You sat right next to me in Trust and Estates. You've heard all the same horror stories. Does he have advanced directives?"

"I would think so."

"People say lawyers make the worst clients. You should really check into all of that. What about your brother? Where's Everett in all of this?"

"You know we don't talk. He and his mom think she was just the trophy wife and I'm just some spoiled brat she had to trap him. As far as I know, he's still in New York working for that big law firm and raking in millions of his own. I don't know."

"While you're going to UT because you're too stubborn to take his money. Mercy, come on. You gotta make sure he's being taken care of. Or that *you're* being taken care of. Financially. From everything you've said, Everett is exactly the kind of snake that will move to cut you out if he can."

"I've never wanted a penny from my dad. That's all my mom's deal. I watched money tear them apart. Let Everett have it all. I don't care."

"That's shortsighted."

"My father has been absent for most of my life except for a few fairly formative moments. And now...now that I'm a grown woman, I can put some of that behind me. I can finally get to know him one on one, without my mom interfering or their relationship interfering or just...any of that baggage. I come here and he's going. Christian, I can feel it. And I hate that I think this but I'm so damn mad. I have so many questions. So many things I want him to account for, you know? Things he deserves to be held accountable for. And now...he's got dementia?"

"Well, if you won't come to me, then I'm coming to you. I've got six weeks before school starts."

My heart soared. I wanted to tell him not to come. But sitting there, I couldn't think of a single good reason.

"You don't have to do that," I said.

"Well, I think you need an ally. If things are as bad there as you've said, maybe your dad could use us both this summer. Wouldn't be the worst thing for my resume. You think you could help me find a place to rent for a few weeks?"

"Okay," I said, swallowing past a lump in my throat.

"Good. I thought you'd fight me more. What about the other thing?"

The other thing. It was still tucked into the outside compartment of my purse. I'd read it maybe a hundred times. I knew it by heart. So did Christian.

Should I tell him that Jeremy Holt's mother came into the office today? I felt that odd sense of protectiveness over my father. Even though Christian knew every fear I had.

"I haven't brought it up to him yet."

"You think he'll give you an honest answer if you do?"

"I don't know."

"Well, it's gonna get out, Mercy. If Jeremy Holt is writing *you* letters, he might be writing them to somebody else too."

"I know. I know."

I should have thrown his letter into the trash unopened. Instead, I reached for it and held it.

"You okay?" Christian asked.

"I will be. And I love ya," I said. "If I leave now, I'm never going to get to know him. If he throws me out again...well...fine. But at least I'll always know I'm the one who tried."

Christian laughed softly. "Well, shit, Mercy. That sounds entirely grown-up of you."

"I know. I promise not to let it go to my head."

"Well, I'll see you soon. I'll be up there in a couple of days. Should I buy a parka?"

"It's May, Christian. This isn't the Arctic Circle."

Christian seemed unconvinced as we said our goodbyes. A shadow passed over the wall. It was then I realized I wasn't alone in the house. I hadn't heard my father come back in. But he stood there in the hallway. I don't know how much he'd heard, but his eyes shone in the dim light. He gave me a soft smile.

"I'm sorry for yelling," he said.

"I know," I said. "But you should also apologize to Violet. You started getting pretty mean. You said something kinda rude about her son."

He tilted his head to the side. "About Glen? I didn't mean it."

"She knows that."

"I'll say something to her. Although, those kids of hers have never been told no a day in their life. They take advantage of her. Bronny used to keep them in hand. Violet's a pushover."

"Violet has taken pretty good care of you. I'm on her side."

He grunted, but didn't argue the point. He looked at me. "Are you sticking around, do you think?"

I drew my shoulders back. "If you think you could use the help." Had he heard me tell Christian I wasn't going back to school?

"Yes," the legendary E. Thomas Gale told me. "I think maybe I could use some help."

He tapped his knuckles against the doorframe, then turned and headed back to the kitchen.

I exhaled, still holding Jeremy Holt's dog-eared letter in my hand. The one that had brought me here to Helene after all these years. Smoothing it out on the desk, I read Jeremy Holt's words once more.

CHAPTER
Four

Ms. Gale,

I have rewritten the opening to this letter at least a hundred times. Trying to find the perfect thing to say. The one thing that might get your attention and convince you to keep on reading. My name is Jeremy Holt, and I know you probably think I'm the one who took your father away.

I don't know how you'll take this. Your father has been like a father to me, too. I thought if someone like Thomas Gale could believe in me, then the rest of the world would. Your dad had more faith in me than mine did. I know he spent more time with me than you. He told me he knew taking my case would probably wreck his marriage to your mom.

But he tried to help me anyway.

I did not kill my sister. People have been lying

about it for sixteen years. I want you to know that, but it's not why I wrote this.

Something's happened to Tom. If it were my father...I would want to know. I would give anything to have just one more day...one more hour with my dad. Mine died of a broken heart believing I was a murderer. That is the hardest thing to live with.

Your father visits me on the last Friday of every month since I was sent here. That's fifteen years of monthly Fridays. Six months ago, he stopped coming. No warning. No contact. But I knew something was wrong for a long time.

He forgets things. Sometimes it seems like he lives in the past. I am writing this with affection in my heart. But I can't let those feelings be the reason I sit here in prison for one day longer than I should. Your father knows the truth. But I'm afraid his mind is going. When it does, any hope I had of getting exonerated might go with it. So please, help me. Help him.

He loves you. He's so proud of you. He talked about you every time he visited me. Please don't wait too long. For your dad's sake. And for mine.

Jeremy Holt

CHAPTER FOUR

"Are you sure you're okay with this?" Violet stood in the doorway of my father's file room looking doubtful. I'd spent all morning hauling his various banker's boxes and loose paperwork in there and set up three folding tables. On each table, I'd taken an empty file folder and written labels in thick, dark ink.

Active. Closed. Archives.

My father stood next to Violet, his expression stern. "It has to be done," he said.

"Right," Violet said. "And I've been telling you that for two years. I'm glad Mercy could finally talk some sense into you."

"She needs a summer project," he said. "Consider her our intern."

"Better be a paid one," Violet answered. "This is some mind-numbing work, Tom. You can hire a couple of college students to do this for credit."

"I trust Mercy," he said.

"I'm not going to get rid of anything or change anything without your approval. Violet's got a great system. There's no reason for me to reinvent anybody's wheel. But we can't be efficient if we're unorganized."

"Hmm," Violet snorted. "Well, it seems to me this is a colossal waste of your talents, Mercy. You'd be better off at his side when your father goes to court."

"I don't need a damn babysitter," he said. "And we have nothing scheduled for a while. I just closed the Pomphrey case. We don't have oral arguments on Whitfield until November. Mercy will be long gone by then."

Violet shot me a look. Why hadn't I told my father I'd dropped out of law school yet? I made a shooing gesture.

"All right," I said. "I'm sure both of you have other work to do. No offense, but you'll just get in my way."

I didn't wait for the answers. Instead, I just walked up to the door and closed it on them. I heard Violet's soft laughter as she forced Dad back down the hallway.

Grabbing my earbuds, I put them in and turned on a deep work playlist from my focus app. Then I dove into Dad's disorganized files.

Violet really had an ingenious system. Everything was tabbed and color-coded in a way that made sense to my ADHD brain. Also, most of my Dad's files were closed. His active ones had little happening. He'd done some basic estate planning. A closing here and there. That was new for him. These were the things Uncle Lloyd would have taken care of. I felt a small pang of anger. Uncle Lloyd should have reached out to me well before things got this bad.

The bulk of my father's cases had been criminal trials. But he'd been selective, traveling all over the state. After maybe two hours, I found the files I'd been after from the moment I decided to come back here. The Jeremy Holt files. They took up five large boxes and were the most disorganized. He had probably five hundred colored sticky notes covering pleadings, partial transcripts, trial notes, and witness statements. I found his trial brief and picked a bare spot on the floor. I leaned against the wall and started reading.

The victim was Savannah Holt. She'd been ten years old when she went missing from her own backyard, not that far from where I was sitting. The case had made national news and imploded my parents' marriage. Dad had promised my mother he would not take any more murder trials. But then Jeremy Holt came along. My mother filed for divorce before the case went to trial.

CHAPTER FOUR

There'd been a massive search for Savannah. Dive teams went into the bay. After two weeks, her body was recovered by a fisherman in an inland lake near the Running Bear Dunes. Eerily, the place was called Deadwater Lake on account of three centuries old, petrified oak trees rising out of the water on its north end. Savannah was in a garbage bag, weighted down with cinder blocks. One rope had snapped, allowing her to float to the surface.

I flipped through the autopsy report. I'd seen crime scene photos before, but these were horrible to look at. Submerged as she was, the girl was barely recognizable. The coroner listed her cause of death as blunt force trauma to the back of her head. Part of her skull was missing. There'd been no sign of sexual assault, but the ME couldn't conclusively rule it out because of the length of time she'd been in the water. Her pajama bottoms were missing though, so everyone assumed.

Dad had newspaper clippings in the file. A chronology of events from the day she went missing, all from the local paper, *The Daily Caller*. Her parents had attended a lavish event for one of the town scions, Hollis Branch. Someone had snapped a picture of Steven and Olivia Holt in formal wear, beaming at the camera, holding champagne, oblivious of how their world would change when they went home.

The event itself made the front page that morning. Hollis Branch owned the paper. It seemed the whole town attended his party at the yacht club. I found a picture of my father standing next to the mayor.

One article published not long after Savannah's body had been found showed her now grief-stricken parents standing next to the sheriff, thanking the search teams for all their efforts. I focused on Savannah's mother, Olivia Holt.

"She's so young," I whispered. Olivia didn't look very much older than I was now. Her husband, Steven, had to be at least twenty years older than his wife.

Trophy wife, I thought. It felt familiar. Diane Benning, Jeremy's mother, had been Steven's first wife. Jeremy had been convicted of killing his own half-sister.

I pulled Jeremy's letter out again, adding it to the pile of papers in front of me.

The last Friday of every month for fifteen years. One hundred and eight visits. Jeremy Holt had more of a relationship with my father than I did. It was a bitter pill to swallow. And yet...

I startled at a knock on the door. I'd been at this for almost four hours. My back kinked up and I stretched out as Violet came in holding a brown paper bag that smelled delicious.

"How do you feel about an avocado turkey bagel and some tomato bisque?"

"Right now, that sounds like a religious experience."

Violet put the food on the barest spot she could find on the Archive table. She pulled a water bottle out of her pocket and set everything up.

"Thank you," I said. "And not just for lunch. I've always known how invaluable you were to Dad. But lately..."

She waved me off. "We're stuck with each other at this point. He can't live without me and life's too boring for me to retire. My son's been on me to move down to Fort Myers to be near them."

"Are you going?"

"Your father's practice has been my convenient excuse not to. I love seeing my grandkids. But my daughter-in-law? Yeah. Not so much.

I think we'd drive each other crazy. Plus, who wants to worry about hurricanes?"

"He would understand," I said. "It'd be hard. But he'd understand."

"I know. And trust me. If I change my mind, there won't be any stopping me. For now, we're stuck with each other. You sure I can't help you with this?"

"I'm okay. Oh, but there is something else you can help me with. A friend of mine from law school offered to come up here this summer and spend some time with me."

Violet smiled. "A male friend?"

"Yes, but not like that. Just a friend. A good one. I promised to help him find a summer rental. Do you have any ideas where I could send him?"

"Maybe. I can talk to Marian Greenbaum. She's an old friend. She's got some rentals just down the street in the garden district. They're lovely."

"I would really appreciate that."

My bones creaked as I hoisted myself up off the floor. Violet had her own lunch and took the seat next to me at the table. The bagel sandwich tasted just as heavenly as it smelled.

"You're in the Holt file?" she asked.

"Yeah. I think maybe you better tie a rope around my waist."

She laughed. "It has a way of sucking you in. Trust me. I know."

"So much tragedy," I said. "For that little girl, of course. But the family."

"Oh, it was horrific. Killed Steve Holt just as sure as his daughter. Olivia, her mother, never forgave him for bringing Jeremy into the world. Or into their home."

"He was living with them at the time?"

Violet shook her head. "No. As I remember it, Jeremy lived with Diane, his mom. But he was nineteen. She couldn't control him. He fell in with a rough crowd. She kicked him out. He came up here to live with his dad but that didn't last long either. Steve had a new family with Olivia and Savannah. Jeremy was disruptive. So, they kicked him out, too. I think he was living with some friends. They were doing drugs."

"Do you think he did it?"

Violet shrugged. "I don't know. They found her bloody pajama bottoms in the trunk of Jeremy's car. He lied about where he was the night she went missing. An eyewitness saw him with Savannah that night. She testified the girl was upset. Crying. Didn't seem like she wanted to be with Jeremy, and he grabbed her, forced her into the backseat of his car."

"All that came out at trial?" I asked.

"Yes. And there was nobody else. In the early days, Steve Holt was a suspect. That tore him up too just as much as anything else."

"He had an alibi," I said, pulling the newspaper out showing the Holts at the retirement party.

Violet looked sideways at it. "That was quite a to-do."

"You said Jeremy lied about where he was that night. That's what Diane was talking about when I met with her. She said she doesn't understand why Dad wasn't doing more to run down her son's alibi witness. I don't see any testimony about that other than the brief interview Jeremy gave to the police before Dad got involved."

"I don't know," she said. "Jeremy wasn't credible as far as the police were concerned. The people he was living with were bad news. Junkies. Jeremy didn't have a record, but he was a junkie too. He said he was with his friend that night. Another junkie. That's not exactly the most solid alibi."

"If it was corroborated, that shouldn't matter."

"It wasn't. They put the other kid on the stand, and he said he hadn't seen Jeremy that night. Hadn't seen him in a few days. His landlord said the same thing. Figured he was hiding out somewhere because he was late with his rent. It was just a mess."

"Was there ever a plea deal on the table?"

Violet nodded as she took a swig of her diet pop. "There was. Second Degree. Jeremy admitted he was probably high that night, so the prosecutor was willing to deal on premeditation."

"Dad wouldn't hear of it?"

"You'd have to ask him. I just know that entire case...Mercy...it took pieces of him. In the same way that...well...I honestly hadn't seen your dad that invested in a case, or that haunted by it since he represented your Aunt Viveca."

I put my water down. Aunt Viv. My mother rarely talked about her. But she was the reason I existed at all. Viveca Baldwin had been a B-movie actress accused of killing her abusive husband. That case, too, had made national headlines. My father had been one of the first defense attorneys to successfully use the battered woman's defense. Aunt Viv was acquitted, but the case took its toll. She took her own life a few years after that. All before I was born. Her funeral reconnected my mother and father. They were married about a year later.

"He lost," I said. "He never loses."

"You asked me if I think Jeremy Holt did it. If I'm honest, yes. I think Jeremy killed that little girl. Why? I can't tell you. Was he sick, depraved, molesting her? I don't know. Nobody ever witnessed anything like that. But there was a lot of jealousy and dysfunction. I think Jeremy looked at Savannah as the person who blew up his own parents' marriage."

"But to kill her for that?"

"He was a mess. Not a good kid. I know his mother swears he's innocent, but that's what mothers do, right?"

"Maybe. But why didn't Dad talk to this alibi witness she mentioned? I don't see any notes in these files that he interviewed her. That's not like him not to run down every lead."

"Have you asked him?"

"Do you think it'll upset him if I do?"

"I don't know. It gets harder to predict what's going to set him off. This case has always been triggering for your dad. It's one reason I try to keep Diane Benning away from him. It's not good for him to ruminate on things he can't control. He did his best for Jeremy Holt."

His best. I couldn't help thinking about whether his best at the time was the best he could do. My father was sick. How long had it been going on? Could there have been signs of mental decline even back then? I didn't notice them myself, but I had been just thirteen years old. My mother certainly wouldn't be a reliable source. It would just give her another reason to bash dad.

"Violet...back then. Was he..."

The look she gave me raised more questions. Worry lines creased her forehead. She was on the verge of telling me something, but my father appeared in the doorway.

"Violet, did you tell Hollis Branch I was going to be there tomorrow?"

Violet snapped her attention away from me and to my dad. Whatever she wanted to say to me was gone. The moment passed.

"What's tomorrow night? Hollis Branch?" I asked, looking back at the pictures from the man's retirement party sixteen years ago.

"I've got his social secretary calling me, asking me if I'm bringing someone to this goddamn gala tomorrow night. Violet, if you got me into this, by God, you're going with me."

"Oh, no," she said. "Count me out. This is all you, Tom. You're the one who told Hollis you'd be there. My fingerprints aren't anywhere near this. Besides, now you've got a built-in plus-one. Mercy, did you pack anything fancy to wear in that luggage of yours?"

"What?"

My father's face lit up with mysterious mischief. "Brilliant," he said. "It's decided then. Clear your dance card, Mercy. You're coming to a party. It'll be good for you to meet everyone who's important in Helene."

"I thought you said you were the only person important in Helene," Violet joked.

"I am. But now I get to show off my little girl. Go see Dalia down the street if you don't have a dress."

"He's got a point," Violet said, taking on the role of my father's co-conspirator. "I'll give Dalia a call right now."

"It's okay," I said. "I packed something."

They decided everything for me, and I had the distinct impression that tomorrow night would be everything I hated.

CHAPTER *Five*

"Wow."

My father stood at the bottom of the stairs in his tux and a crisp white dress shirt. His bow tie hung down around his collar. I descended the stairs. Even in heels, I only came up to his shoulder.

At nearly eighty years old, E. Thomas Gale still cut a dashing figure. His rigid posture came from his years as a military man, but also the debilitating back injury that ended his Navy career when he was forced to bail out into the South China Sea after his F4 Phantom was struck down by a surface-to-air missile.

He held an arm out for me. "We clean up good, kiddo," he said.

"Let me fix this," I said. I climbed back to the second to lowest step and fixed my father's tie. He taught me to do it when I was eight years old. He also taught me how to properly shine shoes. I could remember his deep baritone and the patience he took with me that day as I messed both things up at least a dozen times before I got them right.

"I wish I knew more practical things to teach a girl," he'd said. "But you never know what'll come in handy when you need it."

Tonight, I was happy he'd done it. My father walked over to the circular mirror he'd hung by the door. The frame looked like an old-fashioned ship's wheel. "Not bad," he said, impressed with my skills.

I wore a floor-length black halter dress that used to belong to my Aunt Viveca. It was a Halston and worth more money than I wanted to think about. It was my go-to. Not that I had very many occasions to go anywhere.

"I'll try to keep the wind to a minimum," Dad said. "I didn't think about your hair. It's been a while since there's been anybody besides me in that boat. We could have gotten dressed at the office."

"It'll be fine," I said. I pinned my hair up and sprayed the hell out of it. The short boat ride from Dad's island to town shouldn't do any permanent damage. Besides, I wasn't like my mother. I didn't really care if it did.

Fifteen minutes later, we were docked and walking up the steep steps to the Helene Yacht Club at the south end of the bay. Twinkling white lights lit the path.

"We don't have to stay long," Dad said. "Just gotta make an appearance. I like to stay on Hollis Branch's good side. It's like they say, you never wanna pick a fight with someone who buys ink by the barrel."

"I don't think anybody buys ink by the barrel anymore, Dad. Everything's online."

"Well, that's even worse."

CHAPTER FIVE

We walked into the ballroom. I didn't recognize a soul but everyone knew who my father was, of course. He turned on the charm, shaking hands, delivering his warm smile, asking personal but shallow and polite questions of everyone who came up to him.

"How's your daughter doing, Mrs. Feinstein? Tell her congratulations on that scholarship she got from the Lions Club. Those things add up."

"You're looking great, Paul. With that titanium hip, you'll be kicking my ass on the tennis court next month."

"You still play tennis?" I whispered to my dad.

"I still do a lot of things," he said.

"Tom!" A man at least as old as my father cut through the crowd holding a martini glass. His tux jacket strained a little around his midsection. He had a few fine wisps of white hair carefully combed and sprayed to the side. He flashed an expensive set of veneers as he held out his hand to shake my dad's.

"Hollis," Dad said. "This is quite a shindig you're throwing tonight."

"I hope you brought your checkbook," Hollis said through his smile. He'd aged a bit from the picture I'd seen in the old newspaper clippings.

Dad clutched his heart as if the statement were causing him palpitations. Hollis Branch laughed. A moment later, a younger man came to join our little group. He looked agitated, peering back at the podium.

"Hollis, I'd like to introduce you to my daughter, Mercy," Dad said. I held out my hand. Hollis eyed me and it felt almost predatory. Then his smile widened.

"You look just like your mother," he said.

"It's nice to meet you," I said.

"And this," Dad said, gesturing toward the other man who'd joined us, "is Beau Godfrey."

"We call him the architect," Hollis said. Beau Godfrey gave me a smile and shook my hand.

"Nice to meet you," Godfrey said. He was nice looking, with reddish-gold hair and kind eyes. I pegged him at about forty.

"Beau's running Adam's campaign," Dad explained.

"I heard you were planning on following in your father's footsteps," Hollis Branch said. "Star of your law school class. That's good to hear. If you're half as good as your father, we could use you in Helene County."

"Mercy's going to forge whatever path suits her," Dad said.

"Or maybe she's more interested in politics," Beau said. "I can't tell you how many times I tried to get your father to run for local government. He would have been a lock for township supervisor."

"Who needs it," Dad said. "I'll leave that viper pit to you two and Adam. I hear the latest polling has been kind to him."

It was the right thing to say. Hollis Branch beamed. His cheeks flushed and he raised his glass. "Shh. Don't jinx it. There are still fifteen months until the election. That's a lifetime."

"Well, you know he's got my support."

Hollis looked at me. "Mercy, I hope you don't mind if we steal your father for a few minutes. I promise, it's for something entirely boring."

"More like entirely expensive," Dad joked.

"I'm fine," I said. "Go do your thing."

CHAPTER FIVE

I felt a hand on my elbow. "Mercy?"

I turned. Lloyd Murphy, my father's former law partner and best friend, gave me a wide smile.

"Uncle Lloyd! Dad didn't say we were going to run into you!"

Though I told my father I didn't mind him ditching me so early, I was happy to see a familiar face.

"Can you keep him out of trouble while I'm gone?" Dad asked.

"Go," I said. "I told you. I'll be fine."

Dad, Beau Godfrey and Hollis Branch disappeared into a back room while Lloyd led me over to his table near the bar. I asked for a white wine. Lloyd got it for me, then joined me at the table along with a small plate of shrimp.

"When did you get into town?" Lloyd asked.

"A couple of days ago. I was hoping I'd get a chance to talk to you."

Lloyd's expression darkened. "It's good to see you. Your dad misses you. He may not say it, but it means a lot to him you're here."

"Did he tell you I was coming?"

Lloyd wasn't looking at me. He kept his eyes on the podium set up at the front of the room. A few men in suits gathered around it, adjusting the microphone and scurrying as if something important was about to happen.

"He hoped you were coming. But Tom and I don't...well...we don't keep in touch as much as I'd like to anymore. Part of that's my fault. I've got a house in Palm Springs now. I'm working on moving down there full-time. Carole just can't take the winters up here anymore."

"I hope I get to see Aunt Carole too while I'm in town," I said. "Lloyd, why didn't you call and tell me what's going on with Dad?"

Lloyd pursed his lips. He took a healthy swig of his gin and tonic, bracing himself for what he knew I had to say.

"He's struggling," I said. "And it's worse than anybody told me."

"He's just old."

"He's not just old. Something's wrong. He's forgetting things. And the other day, he was totally altered in Judge Homer's courtroom. Everybody's worried about him but nobody bothered to reach out to me. Not Violet, and not you."

"He asked me not to."

"He shouldn't be the one calling all the shots anymore, Uncle Lloyd. And he's not just some old man puttering around in his garden. He's still taking clients. Still trying to hold down that practice."

"That's his choice."

"It's not that simple."

"Do you think I could get your dad to do anything he didn't want to do? You know him."

"Not as well as you do."

"You know him well enough. And he's not incompetent, Mercy. He has some bad days. We all do at our age. He's capable of managing his practice."

"What about Diane Benning?" I asked. "Did you know she's threatening to turn him into the grievance commission?"

Lloyd's face darkened. "You talked to Diane Benning?"

"Briefly. She made an appointment for next week. I promised her I'd look into things for her."

"You shouldn't have done that. Violet shouldn't have let you do that."

"Violet wasn't there! Nobody was. That's my point. Dad was all alone. I did what I thought I should to protect him."

"Talking to Diane Benning won't protect him. Jeremy Holt is a lost cause."

"She doesn't think so. And the thing is, I can't even tell you if I agree with her. Because Dad's files were strewn all over the office like a paper bomb had gone off. Everything is a mess over there. I got him to agree to let me organize things. I have no idea what I'm going to find. I'm *scared* of what I'm going to find." For a brief second, I debated telling him that Jeremy Holt was worried about Dad, too. But I wasn't yet ready to let him know Holt had reached out to me. That Holt was half the reason I was here. I couldn't trust that Lloyd wouldn't tell Dad behind my back.

Lloyd let out a hard breath. "I didn't know that."

"How could you? You aren't there."

"All right," he said. "I'll stop by. If your dad will let me, I'll check in. And if you need help placating Diane Benning, I'll talk to her with you if you think it'll help. Tom's got a soft spot for her. It's done him no damn good over the years. He did right by Jeremy Holt."

"You think he killed his little sister?"

A high-pitched screech from the microphone cut through the air.

"Sorry about that, folks," one man at the podium said.

"We can talk later," Lloyd said. "How long are you going to be in town?"

"I don't know," I said.

"Well, I meant what I said. I'll stop by. We can continue this conversation then. I promise. And don't worry so much about your dad."

"Ladies and gentlemen," the man at the microphone said. "Thanks for your patience. We've got Simply Swingtime warming up here in a few minutes and we'll get you back to your food, drinks and conversations. For now, let me introduce the man of the hour, our favorite son, Adam Branch."

The crowd applauded. I politely joined in.

"I'll catch up to you in a little while," Lloyd said. Then, before I could protest, he got up and disappeared into another group gathered near the bandstand.

"Coward," I muttered. My drink was almost empty. Since I didn't have to drive, I decided I'd have another glass of wine and maybe one more after that. I made my way to the bar and ordered a chardonnay. Then I found a quiet corner near a potted plant and watched as the guest of honor took the podium.

He was good looking. No. That's not the right way to describe what he was. Adam Branch had a thick head of black hair and dazzling blue eyes that penetrated all the way across the room. He raised his hand to the crowd and waved.

"Thank you," he said. "I'll try to make this short and minimally boring. This next year will be one of the toughest ones of my life. I'm facing an uphill battle against a political machine that has swallowed greater men than me. But I believe in our message. I believe that the future of Michigan will be brighter than its recent past. And I am so grateful to be here with all of you tonight. Helene is the hidden gem of this state. It's not just because of the bay or our pristine white beaches. It's because of the people in this room and what you've built. I hope to give something back to you. I hope to..."

"Blah, blah blah." A voice startled me. I never heard the man come up next to me. He'd picked a spot on the wall on the opposite side of the fern.

"You don't like what you're hearing?" I asked.

He sipped his cocktail and gave me a mischievous smirk. "He's not saying anything. He says nothing and they all just lap it up."

I turned to face him. He looked to be my age, which made him stand out from everyone else here. Tall but lanky. He had an unruly head of dark blond hair in dire need of a trim. He sported two days' worth of scruff that lent him a rakish appearance. But his tux was just as crisp as my father's and the gold watch on his wrist wasn't cheap.

"Isn't that what all politicians do?" I asked. "The good ones anyway."

"Oh, he's good. He might even win."

"You don't think that's good for Helene? Having their, what did they call him, favorite son in the governor's mansion?"

He pushed himself off the wall with his shoulder and extended his hand. "Sorry. I'm bad at this. My name is Liam."

"Liam. Well, I'm Mercy."

"Mercy Gale," he said. "Oh, I know who you are. Everybody in town knows who you are. Your dad likes to brag."

"Does that annoy you?"

Liam nearly spit out his drink. "No! I didn't mean any offense by that. It's nice to have a father proud of you and all. Everybody's just glad you're here. For Tom."

"How do you know my father? I mean other than the obvious."

"Right. Yeah. Of course, everybody knows Tom Gale. He's well-loved around here. When's the last time you came up to Helene?"

"It's been a long time. Not since I was a kid. What about you? I mean...how long have you lived in Helene?"

"My whole life. I barely ever leave."

"So, what do you do that makes you so cynical?"

Liam smiled. He really was cute in that troublemaking sort of way. "Was I being cynical? Sorry. I've just been dragged to enough of these things. I thought I could spot a kindred spirit."

"Well, I've been dragged to quite a few of these things, too. Just not recently. So, are you not planning on voting for Adam Branch?"

Liam raised a brow. "I suppose that depends. Like he says, it's a long time between now and next November. Who knows, maybe he's got some hidden family secret."

"He's a Branch," I said. "Doesn't their family own the media around here?"

"Fair point."

"So what do you do, Liam from Helene?"

He laughed. "I have my own graphic design firm. What about you? Planning to follow in your father's footsteps?"

"Just trying to get the lay of the land," I said, dodging the question.

"Tell me what you want to know? Or who you want to know?"

Liam came around to my side of the fern. Still holding his glass, he pointed with his index finger across the room. "Over there? That's Steve Anspaugh. He's been on the zoning board practically since birth. We don't like new development here in little old Helene. So if you wanna open a Chick-Fil-A, you better take it down to Harbor Springs. And that couple over there? That's Judy and Bob McLanathan. Bob owns the hardware store at the edge of town. He's hiding a secret though. He's thinking about selling out to one of the big chain stores. Oh...and over there right next to the exit sign? That's Beverly Tiernan. She owns the bridal store four doors down from your dad's office. If you wanna know anything about anyone, she's the one you want to endear yourself to."

"People like to gossip while they're trying on wedding dresses, do they?"

"Like crazy."

"Thanks for the tip. Maybe I need to pay her a visit. Or maybe you could just tell me what they're saying about my dad."

I don't know why I said that. I meant it as a joke but immediately regretted it. Liam's smile faltered just for a second. It was enough to show there was plenty of gossip flying around where Dad was concerned.

"Everyone loves your dad, Mercy."

"That's good to hear."

"Your dad is a great man. A lot of people wish he was the one who had run for governor or some other state office."

"He never wanted to," I said. Though that wasn't exactly true. Long ago, Uncle Lloyd had told me Dad had ambitions to run for

Congress. Something stopped him. When I asked, Lloyd changed the subject.

"Well, I can understand that. And he's done a lot of good right where he is."

"I appreciate you saying that."

The crowd erupted in applause as Adam Branch finished his speech. He started shaking hands, but scanned the room. I don't know how he saw me all the way back here in the corner and under the shadow of the fern. But he focused those piercing blue eyes straight at me. His mouth curved up in a smirk. I'm not proud to admit it, but it sent a little thrill of heat through me.

"Oh, boy," Liam said. "Not you too."

"What?"

"You're fresh meat, Mercy Gale."

"I beg your pardon?"

Liam laughed. "I just mean Adam Branch hasn't had a chance to woo your vote. Trust me, he'll be after it."

"Thanks for the warning," I said.

Liam finished his cocktail. He shook the ice at the bottom of his glass. "Well, it was nice to meet you finally. I'll see you around town."

My father reappeared, free from the clutches of Hollis Branch. Liam quickly excused himself. I made my way back to the table. My father met me there.

"What did you think?" he asked.

"About the speech?"

CHAPTER FIVE 63

"I'm curious too." A deep voice came to my right. I turned and nearly ran smack dab into the wall of muscle that was Adam Branch.

"Adam," my father said. "This is my daughter, Mercy."

"Pleasure to meet you," Adam said. He held out a hand and shook mine with just the right amount of firmness. "Your dad has told me a lot about you over the years. I hope you're planning on staying for a while."

"A while," I answered.

"Sorry, Adam," my dad said. "She's registered to vote in Florida like her mother."

Adam's smile widened. "Your dad is a real comedian."

"He knows," I said.

"Adam!" Hollis Branch shouted to his son from the other side of the room. He motioned to him. Hollis stood among an important group of donors, no doubt. Adam touched my arm.

"It was nice to meet you, Mercy. I'll try to stop by the office in a few days so we can have a proper conversation away from all this ridiculous fanfare. And whatever my brother told you about me, I promise it's not true."

"Your brother?"

Adam's expression faltered just a bit. "Liam," he said. "I saw he cornered you over there."

I stopped myself from saying what was in my mind to say. Liam is your brother? Somehow, I didn't want to give Adam Branch any sign that I was gullible. I tried to keep the anger out of my eyes.

"He was harmless," I said. "Mostly."

"Mostly," Adam laughed. "Anyway, it was good to meet you and I really hope to see you around."

Then Adam left us. My dad took the last sip of his bourbon. "We can go if you want," he said. "I made Hollis happy. We watched Adam's speech and made our appearance. The food at these things always sucks. How about we head down the boardwalk and get some pizza?"

I pulled my shawl around me and grabbed my purse. "Ready whenever you are, Dad," I said. He held his arm out for me and I took it.

From the other end of the room, Liam Branch emerged again. He caught my eye and gave me a devilish wink.

CHAPTER *Six*

"You sure you wanna do this?" Violet stirred her coffee. She sat in the chair opposite me in my new office. I'd commandeered one of the empty rooms across from the conference room. There wasn't much in it. My dad's old desk. A couple of green leather chairs. Dad's weather-beaten, dog-eared law school textbooks from over fifty years ago. But Violet had brought in some cheerful plants and a bouquet of fake flowers that didn't look like it.

"I don't see that I have much choice. Do you feel comfortable having Dad meet with her by himself?"

"No. Absolutely not. And not for any of the reasons you're worried about. But Diane Benning has a way of making people go off on tangents for her. He can't afford that right now. His billings are way down. He's spending money we don't have. The rent on this place alone...well...it's more than my house payment."

"Why do you still have house payments, Violet?"

"Honey, that's a whole other story."

The bell over Dad's front door chimed. I checked my phone. It was ten o'clock on the dot. Dad didn't have any other appointments scheduled for the day. I booked Diane Benning when I knew he'd conveniently be out of the office on a golf outing with Lloyd.

"Well, call me if you need me," Violet said, rising out of her chair. "And if she doesn't let you up for air within forty-five minutes, I'll buzz you with a fake emergency. I'll tell you Mr. Garland is here for his eleven o'clock."

"Who's Mr. Garland?"

"Inside joke between your dad and me. That's his code for get me out of this. It comes in handy."

"Noted." I straightened my suit jacket. Violet gave me a thumbs-up and went back to the lobby. I heard the muffled sound of her conversation. A minute later, she came back with Diane Benning.

"Just let me know if I can get you anything, Mrs. Benning," Violet said, shooting me a wink behind Diane's shoulder.

Diane looked different from the other day. She dressed more formally in a white blouse and long black skirt. She held a leather portfolio in front of her.

"Have a seat," I said. "And thanks for coming back out."

"You said you needed a week to settle in," she said. "It's been nine days."

"It has." I gestured toward the green chairs in front of my desk. Diane kept that portfolio clutched in front of her as she sat in the chair on the left.

"You sure I can't get you anything? Coffee? Water?"

"No. I don't want to take up a lot of your time. Is your father going to be joining us?"

"Not this morning," I said. "But we can..."

"I will not be pawned off, Ms. Gale."

"You're not being pawned off. We want to make sure you're getting more attention, not less."

"Fine," she said, surprising me. She put her portfolio on my desk and ran a flat hand over it.

"I've spent some time looking through Jeremy's case file..."

"He didn't do it."

"I understand..."

"I don't think you do. If there was a death penalty in Michigan, Jeremy would already be dead. That haunts me too. I'm not insensitive to what happened to Savannah. Neither is my son."

"I cannot imagine how difficult this has been for your family. Sixteen years is a long time. But what I'm trying to understand is what more we can do for you. I know that's blunt."

"I don't mind blunt," she said. "Ms. Gale..."

"Mercy. Please call me Mercy."

"Fine. Mercy. We're running out of time. The appellate court denied all of Jeremy's appeals. I lost my house paying for all of that. What keeps me up at night is what happens after I drop dead. There won't be anybody left to advocate for my son. Your father is what, almost eighty? Jeremy will be alone. Every time I see him, there is less of him. Like tiny bits of his soul just being chipped away by time and hopelessness."

"You said you didn't mind blunt. Okay. I looked through your son's case file. I know this is hard to hear, but there wasn't a lack of evidence against Jeremy."

"You don't even know him."

"No. I don't. And I don't really know you. But you came in here accusing my father. Threatening to file a grievance against him. I know you want to protect your son. Of course, I want to protect my father. Maybe you can tell me what you think we should do for you that we're not."

She sat back and picked a piece of lint off her skirt. Then she laser-focused on me and answered the question I hadn't yet dared ask with one of her own.

"So why haven't you told your father that Jeremy wrote to you?"

Was it a trap? If I admitted I'd kept that from him, she would continue to demand to know why.

Was she calling my bluff? How did she know I hadn't told him? So I rejected the premise of her question entirely.

"Ms. Benning, what is it you and your son think I can do for you?"

She seemed to settle. "Your father makes promises and doesn't keep them. This town? It's cursed. I wish Jeremy had never come back here. That part is my fault. I will regret the choices I made when my son was a teenager for the rest of my life. If I'd tried harder or been more patient. If I hadn't kicked him out, he would have been with me. After his father and I split up, I tried to start over. I thought getting away from my hometown would make things better. I got a job at Cabela's and moved to Dundee a year after the divorce. Jeremy hated it there. He missed his friends. It made it harder for him to see his father. I was being vindictive. But when things got hard with Jeremy, I never should have kicked him out and sent him to Steven. I should have kept him with me. None of this would have happened. Savannah would still be dead. But Jeremy wouldn't have been caught up in it."

"You can't blame yourself for that. We all just do the best we can, don't we?"

"You don't have children of your own, do you?"

"No."

"I hope someday you will. You'll understand better what it is to be a mother. There's joy in it. Like you never realize that you didn't know what pure love is until you have a child. But you also realize you never knew what pure hell is either."

I waited a beat. She tilted her head slightly to the right as if she were working something out for herself. Could she trust me? Would I really listen to what she had to say?

"Jeremy didn't kill Savannah. That isn't just me as his mother, wishing for it to be true."

"Okay."

"I know who my son is. The psychologists said he had oppositional defiant disorder. A lot of it came from how things were between Steven and me. He came from a volatile home. There was never any physical violence. But Steve and I argued a lot. I wasn't a good wife. But towards the end of our marriage, Steven was cheating on me. Jeremy took the divorce hard and blamed me for a lot. And he hated that I made him move to the other end of the state. I fractured his relationship with Steven. Steven moved on so quickly. He married Olivia and they had Savannah. After that, Steven stopped honoring his parenting time. He just kind of gave up on Jeremy. I'm not saying it was all Steven's fault. Jeremy was a difficult kid. And by the time he was fifteen, he got mixed up with drugs."

"That had to have been tough for you to deal with."

"I tried everything. Got him into counseling. Enrolled him in a special school. He was being bullied at the regular high school. And for a while, it seemed like all that was working. Then he graduated and he was just lost. He started hanging out with a rough crowd again and I couldn't take it. It came to a head when a group of his so-called friends broke into my house. They stole my credit cards, all my jewelry, cash, computers, the TVs. Anything they could sell. That's when I finally kicked Jeremy out."

"And he came straight back here?"

She nodded. "A few months after his eighteenth birthday. Steven finally agreed to help out. It caused serious trouble in his marriage. Savannah was seven or eight years old. And Olivia had to deal with this eighteen-year-old, resentful young man in her home who, in her mind, wasn't the best influence on Savannah. Jeremy resented her but he would never have hurt that little girl. Finally, it just got to be too much. I think Olivia gave Steven an ultimatum. Jeremy wasn't living up to the conditions Steven set when he moved in. He was supposed to have a job or enroll in college. And he wasn't permitted to use drugs of any kind. Olivia found a blunt in Jeremy's room and that was that."

"Where did he go?"

"He was living out of his car for a little while. He begged me to let him come back to Dundee. I think a lot about what might have happened if I'd just said yes. I'd just been so run down by all of it. I was finally sleeping soundly again and finding some joy in my life. I wasn't ready to get back into it with Jeremy. He was nineteen at that point. So, I turned him down. I moved back here to support him during the trial and all of that. And I just stayed. I realized I missed my old friends, too. I needed them. I haven't left since. I was born in Helene. I'll die here. I don't know. Maybe I'm wrong. Maybe if we'd never left, he would have had an easier time. I just don't know. He probably would have fallen in with the same crowd anyway."

"The witnesses indicated he was living in a drug den of sorts?"

Diane nodded. "He was mixed up with some not so nice people again. Falling into old habits. He's never denied that and neither have I. And then...Savannah went missing and everything just fell apart."

"Diane," I said. "They found Savannah's bloody clothes in your son's car. He lied to the police about where he was the night she went missing."

"He didn't lie. The cops just said they couldn't corroborate it. That's not the same thing."

She reached for her portfolio. "This is what I've been trying to get your father to look into."

She pulled out a thick envelope and handed it to me. "Jeremy was with two people the night Savannah went missing and that entire weekend. Alicia Tate and Dustin Bolton."

"Bolton was questioned," I said, recalling what I'd read in the file. "He denied seeing Jeremy that night. The jury found him credible."

"He was lying. Jeremy has said that all along. And I know what it looks like. Bolton was a thug. A low-level drug dealer. He was probably high most of that weekend just like Jeremy was. If that's all I ever knew, I might just throw my hands up and tell my son to just make the best of his life as it is right now. He's tried. He got a college degree. He's done a lot of work on himself. He's not perfect. But he's not the same kid he was back then. And he deserves a second chance."

She certainly hadn't convinced me her son hadn't bludgeoned his little sister to death with just her story. She opened the envelope. It contained a Xerox copy of a letter written on notebook paper.

"Alicia Tate sent me this a year ago," she said. "Mercy, she says Jeremy was telling the truth. That the three of them were together that weekend. She wrote everything out and sent it to your father. Alicia's gotten herself clean. She's trying to make amends. I asked your father to look into this. I don't know what made her lie all those years ago. I don't know why she's changed her mind about it all now. I just know she has."

I picked up the copied notebook pages. They were filled with line after line of tight cursive written with a purple pen. The words "I'm sorry" were written many times. But as I flipped through, the story Diane told was essentially what was written on the pages. She dated it next to her signature. If this was accurate, the letter was sixteen years old.

A woman claiming to be Alicia Tate insisted that she'd lied to the police sixteen years ago. That she was with Jeremy Holt the weekend Savannah Holt disappeared. She believed he was innocent.

"Diane, how do you know for sure Alicia Tate wrote these when she said she did?"

"What reason would she have to lie?" she said. "Alicia was never called to testify, only Dustin Bolton was."

"There are a lot of sick people in the world. You gave interviews. It wouldn't be that hard for someone to find your address and send this stuff just as some sick joke."

"You could be right," she said, surprising me. "But what if you're wrong? What harm could it do to talk to her? You keep those, Mercy. You read through them and take your time. Alicia Tate isn't just saying she lied sixteen years ago. She's been trying to tell her story for a long time but nobody will talk to her. Nobody will take her seriously. Including your father. Now why do you think that is?"

"I don't..."

"I'm taking a risk coming here," she said. "If your father won't pursue this, then I will. And if I find out his apathy or his incompetence kept my son in prison, even a moment longer than he needed to be...I can promise you one thing. I will cut down anybody who didn't help when they could have. That includes your father."

"I'll look into it," I said. "But if my father didn't feel Alicia Tate's story was credible, you're going to have to prepare yourself for that."

Diane Benning rose. "Mercy? You don't understand. I've already lived through one of the worst things a mother can. I'm not afraid of the truth. And I'm not afraid of E. Thomas Gale or you."

I stood with her. "I'll do what I can."

"Please see that you do." She picked up her now empty portfolio and clasped it to her breast. Violet had come to the door, probably ready to tell me Mr. Garland was waiting.

She didn't get the chance. Diane Benning brushed past her. I picked up the letters she'd left.

"Anything I can do?" Violet asked.

"No," I said. "But I need to have a conversation with my father. Soon."

CHAPTER Seven

I STARED at Alicia Tate's letter. The date at the top burned into my brain. She sent it two months after Savanna Holt's body was found. After Jeremy Holt's arrest. She could have fabricated the whole thing, of course. This might just be the desperate attempt of a woman who now felt guilty for whatever part she'd played in all of this sixteen years ago.

But why?

She could have just stayed faded into the woodwork. Why stir up trouble and upset Diane Benning now?

I sat on the edge of my bed in the pink and green bedroom. So much about the Holt case had been unknown to me all those years ago. I only knew what my mother told me. That Dad had cared more about his clients than he did about his family.

I heard him stirring downstairs. I learned he liked to make himself a peanut butter sandwich as a late-night snack. I folded the letter, put it in the pocket of my pajama bottoms, and went downstairs to join him.

"Violet keeps telling me I should switch to natural peanut butter," he said. "That no sugar added kind. I figure a couple of extra teaspoons of sugar in my damn peanut butter isn't gonna be the thing that kills me."

"Probably not," I said, sliding onto one of the bar stools Dad had at the kitchen island.

"You're up late," he said. It was almost midnight.

"There's something I wanted to talk to you about."

He took a bite of his sandwich. "Want one?"

I was about to say no. But then the smell of peanut butter hit me. I reached over, grabbed the knife he had sticking out of the jar and the loaf of bread.

"Dad," I said. "I want to talk to you about Jeremy Holt."

Dad froze mid chew. He raised an inquisitive brow, then pulled up a stool of his own.

"I know you met with Diane Benning," he said. "You wanna tell me about that?"

I tried not to react.

"I did see Diane Benning yesterday. I thought maybe I could sort her out for you. Get her to understand there's nothing more you can do for her or for her son."

"How'd that go?" He reached over and grabbed a can of grape soda.

"The sugar in the peanut butter might not kill you," I said. "But how about switching to a glass of water?"

"I survived the Viet Cong. I can handle it. And what about Diane Benning?"

CHAPTER SEVEN

"Not like I expected. You know she's ready to grieve you."

He waved a dismissive hand. "She's been threatening that for years. If she was serious, she'd have done it already."

"I think she's serious. But that's not what I really wanted to talk to you about. She's been in communication with Alicia Tate. Did you know that?"

His face was unreadable. He put the second half of his sandwich down.

"Do you know who she is?" I asked.

"A dead end."

"What do you remember about her?"

"She's a junkie. I'm surprised she's still alive."

"Diane says she's sober now. Dad, she says she's willing to corroborate Jeremy's alibi now. And she says she's tried to reach out to you."

"Then she's still lying."

"Are you sure? It's been a really long time. Sixteen years. You could…"

"I know how long it's been!" he snapped. He hopped off his stool and grabbed a kitchen towel off the stove handle and wiped his hands. Then he tossed the towel in the sink.

"Dad. I'm not trying to make you angry. But Alicia says she tried to reach out to you sixteen years ago, too. She was willing to testify. Violet and Uncle Lloyd have been worried about you."

"They can all mind their own business. Alicia Tate is a drug addict. She's not credible now and she wasn't credible then. I told Jeremy that. I knew if his whole story hinged on somebody like her and that boyfriend of hers, he was going to prison. Look who was right."

"Okay. Only you never called her. She never took the stand. If she was willing to testify and her story lined up with Jeremy's, why not call her?"

"You're questioning my trial strategy?"

"No. I'm...I'm just asking why. That's all."

"Alicia Tate changed her story more times than people change their underwear. She was a no-show. A dead end. I don't know why she's whispering in Diane Benning's ear now but it's not my problem."

"Diane Benning *is* a problem though, Dad. She's asking questions that could make things difficult. If she goes to the AGC and they decide to open up a case, you could be investigated."

He leaned against the island on his elbows. "So? I'm not afraid of those pencil heads."

"Dad, if those pencil heads start snooping around, talking to your clients or other people here in town...I just don't want..."

"What?" He gave me a laser stare. "Is there something you need to say?"

"I'm saying it! I'm worried."

"Well, don't be. I've got nothing to hide."

He wasn't getting it. Maybe he never would. I tried a different approach.

"All right. I think I placated Mrs. Benning for the moment."

"What did you promise her?"

"Nothing. I told her I'd look into it. That I'd maybe talk to Alicia Tate myself if she's willing."

"If you can find her."

"Would you be okay with me doing a little digging? Let me get Diane Benning off your back."

"Suit yourself. But I'm telling you. It's a dead end."

"You're probably right. There was something else I was meaning to talk to you about anyway.

Do you remember me telling you about my friend, Christian Foley? My law school classmate? He's planning a trip up here in a few days. Would you be okay if I had him help me out at the office organizing and archiving your files?"

"I'm not paying for that."

"You don't have to. Christian's doing it as a favor to me. If you like him, maybe you'd write him a reference letter. But no pressure."

Dad eyed me, but he didn't say no. I'd take it as a victory for now. I finished the rest of my sandwich. My father settled. He poured himself a glass of water and sat back down.

"It'll kill ya," he said.

"The water?"

"The Holts. Once you get into it, it's hard to crawl back out."

"I can handle it."

He rubbed his eyes. "I told myself the same thing. Just ask a few questions. Get a read. Then, before you know it, you've got the kid's life in your hands."

"Dad, do you think he did it?"

"I don't know anymore." He sat back on his stool and took the knife out of the peanut butter jar, ran his finger down the blade, and licked it off. "He was a troubled kid. And I knew Steve Holt a little. God, he loved that little girl. I saw him out and about with her a few times. She was...just special. I could always understand where Jeremy was coming from. That kid just got shoved aside. Steven started a whole new family and left him behind. Diane did the best she could. But teenage boys are a whole different thing. Anyway...you asked me if I think he did it. No. Not then. He kept doing things to screw up his life. Getting in his own way just to spite his father. But killing that little girl? No. He wasn't the type. I've sat across from stone-cold killers, Mercy. Jeremy Holt wasn't one of them."

"If Jeremy viewed her as the thing that took his dad away from him, there had to have been a lot of resentment. You mix that with his substance abuse problem. You don't think he could have just snapped one night?"

"He wasn't violent. That kid was like a lost puppy. He never got angry when I knew him. It's hard to explain. It's just...no. I don't think he had killing in him. I'll never believe he killed his own sister. But everyone else thinks like you think."

"I don't think anything. Not yet."

"If you say so." Dad got up off the stool and put the peanut butter and bread away. He dropped the knife into the dishwasher.

"It's late, kiddo. Time to get some shuteye. I'll see you in the morning. You good with leaving around eight? And maybe tomorrow afternoon, I'll teach you how to drive the jet ski. There might be some days I don't feel like leaving the house and don't want you to feel trapped here."

"Thanks," I said. "I know how to drive a jet ski. I just didn't think yours was working."

"Hmm. Maybe it isn't."

He came around the island and kissed me on the forehead. Yawning, he headed down the hall into his bedroom.

I should have been tired too. I wasn't though. My brain just kept buzzing about Jeremy Holt. Was Dad right? Was the guy truly innocent?

I went to the sink and pulled out the kitchen towel dad tossed in it. Wetting it, I wiped down the countertops. After I finished, I went into Dad's study. He had a stunning view here. The moon shone over the lake. The stars hit the waves, making them shimmer like diamonds.

I slid into the huge leather chair Dad kept in the corner. He had an Afghan thrown over it and I pulled it around my shoulders. I should sleep. Come at the Holt/Benning problem with a fresh, well-rested brain. I couldn't though. Dad had me too worried.

I pulled my phone out of my pocket along with the letter from Alicia Tate. I punched in Christian's number. He answered immediately.

"Mercy! Your ears must be burning. I was just thinking about you."

"How's Ohio?"

"Ugh. Putrid. How is it there? How's your dad?"

"I don't know. Stubborn."

"Merce, you know that's not what I mean. How's his mind?"

"I don't know," I said. "Sometimes good. I talked to him about you doing some work for him when you get here. He's open to it. And he's open to me poking around a little more on the Holt case.

There's a witness Diane Benning wants me to talk to. One she claims can give Jeremy a solid alibi."

I heard a hard exhale from Christian. "Is she credible?"

"No idea. My dad doesn't think so. But he didn't seem to recall much, if anything about her."

"You think he just forgot?"

"I don't know. I feel like I'm betraying him by talking to her."

"But he knows," Christian said. "You said your dad is okay with you poking around in the case a little."

"I know. I'm just..."

"You're afraid of what you might find."

"Yeah," I said. "But, I don't know. I'll feel better when you're here, too. You can be more objective than I can."

"Fantastic. I just need to finish up a few things here. I can be there by the beginning of next week. Is that soon enough?"

I didn't answer at first. I kept staring at Alicia Tate's letter. Christian must have sensed something about my silence.

"Are you okay?"

"Yes. I just feel guilty."

"Mercy, if your dad's got diminished mental capacity, don't you think you've got a duty to do something?"

"I didn't say that. That's not what this is. I'm just saying...God. I don't even know. One minute I sit here and I don't know what I was thinking of coming up here..."

"Good, that makes two of us."

"But the next, I'm absolutely convinced that he needs me."

Christian laughed. "Didn't you tell me that's exactly what your mom used to say? You said she told you he was cold until he wasn't. Something like that."

"I suppose."

"Have you told her you're planning on staying? Have you told either one of them your crazy-ass plan to not come back to law school?"

"No."

"What's he gonna think in a few weeks when you don't come back for the fall term?"

"I haven't thought that far ahead."

"I have. It's not too late. You can still do late enrollment."

"I have to see this through," I blurted. As soon as I did, I wasn't sure what I meant. The Holt case or my father? Maybe both.

"I'll be there next week," he said. "Whatever is going on with the Holt case, we can figure it out together. But if he's really in cognitive decline, you're gonna get into a situation where you'll have to say something. What if you're called to testify if somebody files a grievance? Mercy, if you're trying to cover for him, you could be implicated."

"I've got to go."

"Mercy!"

"I mean it. It's late. I should have waited to call you until tomorrow. I'm sorry."

"Fine. Okay. I'm sorry too. I'm not trying to add to your stress. I'm just saying you know I'm here for you. You can tell me anything and you know it won't go any further."

"I know," I said. "I love you for that. And I think I've found a place for you to rent."

"Great. Send me a link. Maybe you can check it out for me and make sure it's not some rat trap."

"Okay," I said, already feeling better. We said our goodbyes.

It would be good to have Christian here. He was one of the smartest people I knew next to my dad. I trusted his mind. But, as I sat there staring at the moonlight, I knew what I needed to do. I needed to know for myself. I needed to talk to Jeremy Holt in person.

CHAPTER *Eight*

I'D ONLY SEEN pictures of Jeremy Holt from the weeks and months after Savannah Holt's murder. He'd been nineteen then. Skinny with long stringy hair. I watched a news clip of him being led into the courthouse in handcuffs. Slouching with a shuffling gait, he walked beside my father. Dad kept a hand on Jeremy's back and whispered something in his ear that made Jeremy stand up straighter. But he was a scared kid.

That was not the person who sat across from me behind bulletproof glass today. This Jeremy had put on probably sixty pounds of solid muscle. His acne cleared, leaving deep scars on his cheeks. His clear eyes blazed through me as he picked up the phone receiver from its cradle on the wall.

"Mercedes," he said, before I could say anything. "I pictured you as just a kid."

"That's how I pictured you."

He was only thirty-five years old. Just seven years older than me. But his eyes held hard wisdom. He looked dangerous. Terrible in a way. Prison tattoos decorated the biceps he'd earned over years of rough time. Jeremy Holt had been convicted of killing a little girl. It was the kind of offense that could get you killed on the inside. But here he was, surviving. Willing to talk to me. Reaching out to me because he was worried about the man he viewed as a father figure.

"Thank you for agreeing to meet with me," I said.

Jeremy shrugged. "I'm glad you came. I'm glad you read my letter. How is your dad?"

I didn't want to answer. Despite how Jeremy felt about him, Tom Gale was my father, not his. I knew it was petty of me to resent the time my father spent with him. But I think I did.

"You know your mom came to see me? You know she's still fighting for you."

"She shouldn't."

"Well, she's your mother."

"She's sick," Jeremy said. There was almost no emotion in his voice.

"What do you mean?"

"She has lung cancer. Never smoked a day in her life, but she's got it. It's spread to her lymph nodes. Her liver. She's been through two rounds of chemo. This second one is just supposed to keep her going. It won't cure her. She's dying. That's why she keeps coming after your dad."

"I'm so sorry to hear that. I didn't know."

"She thinks nobody does. She doesn't even think I do. But my aunt told me. She wrote me a letter."

"Wow. Jeremy, I don't know what to say."

"She thinks she's got to spend the rest of her short life trying to get me out of here. I want her to just have some peace."

I didn't know what else to say. I couldn't imagine what Diane was feeling, let alone Jeremy.

"You didn't answer my questions about your dad," Jeremy said. "Have you seen him?"

"Yes."

"So then, you know. He's not...himself."

"He's fine," I said. Jeremy narrowed his eyes. Then his face settled into a resigned grin. Tom Gale was *my* father. Not his.

"He still talks about you all the time. When he still came to see me. And back then. You were just a kid. I think he thought he could relate to me that way. Because you had parents who split up too. Like it was the same."

"No," I said. "We're not the same."

"I bet I have more of a relationship with your dad than you do," he said. There was something malevolent about the way he said it. As if he were trying to get some reaction out of me.

"You'd win that bet," I said. I felt like Jeremy Holt was testing me. Seeing how much bullshit I would take.

"You know," I said. "You're indirectly responsible for my parents getting divorced."

No reaction. He just kept his gaze locked with mine.

"My mother gave him an ultimatum. He promised her he wasn't going to take any more murder trials. She was pretty much a married single mom my entire childhood. But my father promised her he was going to semi-retire. Spend more time with us. Take her on the vacations he'd always put off. And then..."

"Me," he said.

"Yes. I remember them arguing about it. I didn't know who you were. He didn't tell me anything about you or your case. But he told my mother he was going to take one last murder client. That was the last straw for her. We moved back to St. Petersburg where she's from. That was that. I only saw my dad sporadically after that."

"Sounds awful," Jeremy said, his voice dripping with sarcasm.

"I'm not trying to compare my situation with yours. And I don't know why I even told you that at all. Somehow it felt like something you should know."

"Fine. Now I know it. What else?"

"My father doesn't believe you killed your sister."

"You wanna hear me say it out loud? Look me in the eye while I say it? See if you can tell if I'm lying?"

I hesitated. Still, Jeremy Holt hadn't broken his stare. He looked me dead in the eyes. Unflinching.

"No," I said. "I don't think I am. You're a loose end I'd like to help him tie up."

"There's no loose end. You can tell my mother she's not welcome across your doorstep anymore."

"Is that what you did? Tell her she's not welcome here? Did she finally get the hint?"

"Mercy, does your dad know you're here?"

"No. He knows I've taken an interest in your case."

"How's your mom feel about that?"

"She hates it." I was honest in so far as what I chose to tell him. "She wants me to come back to Florida and work for her."

"Well, now that you've shared your family history with me, you wanna tell me why you really came?"

"You're the one who reached out to me, remember?"

"Because there's something wrong with your old man. You want to protect him. Okay. Fine. So I guess I was wrong. You weren't the person I should have reached out to. Maybe I should just let my mom file the grievance she wants to file. Tell the State Bar your dad is mentally incompetent."

"My dad's not your enemy."

"Isn't he? Maybe he's been playing me all these years. Because I didn't kill Savannah. That's what you came here to hear me say. Somebody wanted to make damn sure the world believes I did. I trusted your father once. Maybe that was my biggest mistake. Maybe he's not the man you think he is. Maybe I was wrong about Tom the whole time. Maybe he never wanted to help me prove my innocence."

I stared Jeremy Holt down. My father's words echoed in my mind. He said Jeremy didn't have murder in him. I didn't have any sixth sense about it. I'd never sat across from murderers before. But I sensed one thing. Holt was bluffing.

"If you believed that, you wouldn't have written me that letter. You wouldn't care if there's something wrong with my dad."

"I don't owe you answers."

"You want to know why I'm here? Why I care about what happens to you? Your case affected my life as much as yours. And that's not me comparing myself to you. If you're truly innocent and you're sitting in here for the rest of your life serving time for a murder you didn't commit…well…I can't think of too many things more awful. For me? I think helping you might make some of the collateral damage in my life make more sense. So that's it."

He sat back, assuming a more casual posture as he gripped that phone and stared at me. "Nice speech. But it's not all the way true, is it?"

Maybe I should have told him to go to hell. I felt like it.

"You're threatened by me," he said.

"What?"

"You resent me. I get that. I've had more of a relationship with your father than you have."

"You're right. And I'm sorry that pisses me off. It shouldn't."

"Sure, it should. I'd be pissed too."

"It pisses me off. I didn't know he visited you that often. That I don't know a lot of things about him."

And that maybe now I was losing him. Goddammit. Jeremy Holt had more of my father than I did. He knew it. He was trapped in this prison for the rest of his life. I wasn't. And yet here I was, jealous of him for that.

"My dad believes you're innocent," I said.

"You're gonna tell me that's enough for you to believe it, too?"

"No. The one thing that's got me the most concerned. It was the thing that stuck with the jury. What were your sister's bloody pajama bottoms doing in the trunk of your car, Jeremy?"

His face went hard. For the first time since I sat down, he looked away from me.

"How did they get there?" I asked.

"I don't know."

"If you didn't kill her, then maybe someone associated with you did. Someone who had access to your car. You've been sitting in here for sixteen years. Are you going to tell me you haven't come up with a theory?"

His eyes snapped back to mine. "You really wanna ask me that?"

"Yes."

"Somebody put them there. It wasn't me."

"What about Hannah McLain? She testified she saw you with Savannah that night. She was wearing those pajamas. She was crying. You were angry with her."

"She's lying. I don't know why. I don't know who put her up to it. But I wasn't there. I didn't kill my sister."

"So, who did?"

"My curiosity's been satisfied, Mercy. I told you what I think you needed to hear about your dad. Time for you to go."

"Do you want my help?"

"I didn't ask for it."

"You're the one who reached out to me. Don't pretend it was only out of some concern for my dad. I won't stand for your mother's threats."

"I don't control my mother. In case you haven't noticed, I'm kind of powerless here."

"You're not powerless."

"You're asking me to call my mother off?"

"Yes. That's what I want you to do for me. In exchange, I'll take a fresh look at your case. Your mother's been in contact with Alicia Tate. Did she tell you that?"

Jeremy shook his head. "Alicia's a lost cause. And she can go to hell for stirring up my mother."

"What if she'll go to the police on your behalf now?"

"You don't get it. Alicia Tate could be a nun now. It won't matter. Nobody's gonna believe her. Nobody's going to believe Hannah McLain lied when she said she saw me with Savannah. Just like nobody will ever believe me I didn't put those bloody clothes in my car. Why the hell would I do that?"

"It doesn't make sense to me either. So, who put them there, Jeremy?"

"You're asking the wrong person," he said. "Somebody set me up, you get it?"

"You've had a long time to think about that. Who would have wanted to hurt you?"

"Go home," he said. "Because if you stick around long enough, you might get answers you don't like."

"It doesn't matter if I like them as long as they're the truth."

A tremor went through Jeremy Holt's jaw. If I didn't know better, it read like fear.

"What if your answers lead you to somebody *you* care about?" he said.

"Who? My Dad? You think he sabotaged you? Why would you reach out to *me* if you thought that?"

"Maybe he's just been...not right...for longer than you think," he said.

Anger simmered through me. I bit back what I wanted to say. God. What if Jeremy was right? Had my dad's confusion been going on far longer than I knew? Had he bungled this case?

"I think we're done talking," Jeremy said.

He slammed down the phone. I called after him, but he couldn't hear me anymore. He rose and called the guards.

It left me stunned. Shaken. He didn't come out and say it directly. But the implication was clear. Jeremy Holt thought my father might have something to do with what happened to him.

That was crazy. Delusional. And yet there was something in Jeremy Holt's eyes that sent a chill of fear through me.

CHAPTER Nine

I CAME BACK to an empty office. Violet left a note on the reception desk saying that she had a doctor's appointment. I texted my father but got no response. That alone wasn't enough to trigger anything suspicious. The man hated his smartphone, carrying it only because Violet forced him to.

I walked into the small office I'd been using as my own. Most of my dad's files were under control. My system was working. The Holt files took up a third of the space. I went to them. Two boxes contained copies of the intangible evidence against Jeremy. Crime scene photos. Witness statements. Photographs of every piece of physical evidence cataloged by the police.

I took out the photographs taken of Jeremy's car. He drove a beat-up Toyota Celica. One of the wheel wells was jagged with rust. I looked at the images taken of the trunk interior. Savannah's pink striped pajama pants were wadded up in one corner. The next photo showed them laid out on a table. Droplets of blood were clearly visible down one leg.

It was a haunting image. Easy to imagine little Savannah wearing these pants. They came with a matching top with cartoon unicorns on it. The prosecution had found an identical pair at a local department store to show the jury.

I ran my hand over the image. The coroner determined the blood on her pants most likely came from the deep gash on Savannah's head. She'd been hit with something. Probably a rock. It had caved in the back of her skull, causing the blood to run down her back and onto her pants.

I couldn't imagine anyone being so cold-blooded to do something like that to her. To anyone. I heard my father's voice echoing through my mind. He didn't believe Jeremy had it in him. Jeremy swore he was innocent. But could drugs and jealousy have turned him into a monster that one night?

I jumped when my phone rang in my pocket. It was my mother's ringtone.

"Mercedes," she said, breathless. "What are you doing right now?"

I couldn't tell her. The woman seemed to have some sort of sixth sense to ask me that while I was staring at crime scene photographs. She didn't want to know this. I didn't want her to know this.

"I'm just organizing a few things in Dad's office."

"Is he helping you? Is he there right now?"

"No. It's just me."

"Good. Don't tell him I called."

"What does it matter if he knows you called? He knows I am talking to you. You're my mother."

"I don't want to hear it. And he doesn't need to know what I do or don't do."

I couldn't hide the irritation in my voice. "Mom, I can't do this. I don't want to talk about Dad with you. Is everything else okay?"

"It will be as soon as you tell me you're on a flight back to Florida."

"Not today."

"Not today you're not flying? Or not today you don't want to talk about it?"

"Both. Neither. Ugh. Just don't worry about it. I'm fine. I'll see you soon."

"What are you working on?"

"I told you. Just helping Dad organize some things in his office."

I heard the front door open and close.

"I hope he appreciates it," Mom said.

"He does. And we're talking about him again. I said let's not."

Violet came around the corner. She waved. I gestured toward the phone and mouthed, "My mom." Violet's face dropped. I quickly muted my end while my mom kept talking.

"Where's Dad?" I asked Violet.

"Lloyd took him golfing again. They'll be back in a little while."

"Thanks," I said. I unmuted my end of the phone. Violet backed out and put a finger to her lips.

"Fine," Mom said. "But I can't help being concerned. I don't want him taking advantage of you. He's not your responsibility. He gets you to take care of things. It starts out little by little and before you know it, you're sucked in. The longer you stay out there, the harder it's going to be for you to break away. It's not good for you, Mercy. He's just going to break your heart."

"Are you talking about you or me?" I asked, and instantly regretted it.

"Don't joke. Don't you dare joke."

"I wasn't. Look, Mom. Was there something specific you called me about or were you just checking in? Things are fine. I'm fine. Nobody's taking advantage of me."

"Well, I need you too. Magda quit. I'm short-handed this summer. I could really use you in the shop."

The thought of selling handbags for the rest of the summer made me want to vomit. "Mom, hire someone."

"I'm not looking for free labor like your father is."

"I'm not doing this for free."

"Really? How much has he paid you so far? I already know. Zero. He made you a promise. What did I tell you about his promises?"

"Mom. Stop. Really. It'll be a few weeks at least before I leave here. When I do...well...I'm not sure I'm coming back to Florida. Not right away."

"Where are you going?"

"I don't...I'm not sure. I'm just saying, don't rely on me to be your summer help. Hire someone permanently. You wanted to fire Magda anyway. You've been saying that for a year."

My mother's breath caught. I knew how this would go. In another minute, she'd start crying. Start telling me how much she missed me and needed me. She became so childlike sometimes. My whole life, I'd stepped in to take care of her. To manage her emotions. To reassure her. The urge to do it now was strong.

"Look," I said. "How about I check in in a couple of days? I'll have a better idea then what my plans are. But like I said, I'm not going to be back in Florida for a while. You need a more permanent solution for your shop."

"It's your shop too, Mercedes. It's ours. I always thought we'd run it together. I thought that's what you wanted."

I resisted the urge to remind her she'd never asked me. She'd only assumed.

"Can we not do this right now? I really have to go. I promise I'll call you in a couple of days."

It hurt to set that boundary. It felt so much easier to give her a definite date when I'd return. It would make her happy and take the worry out of her voice.

"Mercedes..."

"I'll call you in a few days. I love you, Mom."

I could not tell her what I was working on. The mere mention of the Jeremy Holt case would send her into a meltdown. As I held the phone against my ear while looking at the Holt file, I knew she'd view it as a betrayal. Maybe it was.

I didn't give my mother a chance to pull any more of my strings. I said goodbye and clicked off the call. I waited a beat, expecting her to call me right back even more upset. I counted to ten. At eight, my phone rang, making me jump.

"Dammit," I muttered. Then I checked the caller ID. Relief flooded through me. It wasn't Mom.

"Christian!" I said, clicking the speaker button. "Thank God. I thought for sure you'd be my mother."

"How's Sandra holding up?" His cheerful voice made me breathe easier.

"She's not. She just tried to guilt me into flying back to Florida and manning the store with her for the rest of the summer."

"Sounds fun. Did you stick to your guns?"

"I did."

"You don't sound like it. You actually sound awful. What happened?"

"Nothing happened. I told you. I just got off the phone with Sandra."

"Hmmm. Well, congratulations, I guess. You've avoided purse purgatory. Though I'm not sure Hell Island is much better."

"Helene," I said. "Don't pretend you don't know."

"What are you doing right now? I mean right now specifically."

"Right now? I'm elbow deep in case files. But earlier today I got to take a field trip."

"Oooh, tell me all about it." I wanted to. But I didn't want Violet to know I'd been to see Jeremy yet and the walls were thin.

"How about I tell you when you get here? How soon will that be?"

"Well, I wanted to talk to you about that. Have you gone over to check my rental?"

I felt like an ass. I'd had a one-track mind on the Holt case. I'd forgotten to make an appointment with the landlady. "It's on my to-do list. I'll make an appointment with Mrs. Greenbaum as soon as I get off the phone with you. What day do you want to check in?"

"I've got a few things to finish up here. But I wanted to hit the road this weekend. If I leave early enough on Saturday, I should be there by the evening."

"Perfect. I'll make plans for us for dinner or something on Saturday evening. But you know you don't have to stay at a rental when you get here. There's plenty of room at my dad's. I don't think he'll mind."

"Nah. I'd mind. You and your dad need to figure stuff out without a third party around the corner."

"Nice try," I said. "You're a chicken. You're afraid of him."

"Okay. The idea of him scares the shit out of me. I'll admit it. Just...go check out the space. If it's good, maybe it wouldn't be the worst idea for you to crash with *me*. Or at least have the option."

"Thanks. Okay. I'll get over there as soon as I can. I'm heading down to Big Rapids in the morning."

"What's a big rabbit?"

"Big Rapids. And you heard me. Diane Benning gave me the address where Alicia Tate was living. I'm going to try talking to her."

"You shouldn't be going over there by yourself."

"It's fine."

"Mercy, I'll be there the day after tomorrow. Wait for me and I'll go with you. It'll give me something to look forward to. A bona fide caper."

"There will be plenty for you to look forward to," I said. "This is just a conversation. Diane set this all up. I don't want to spook the woman."

"Fine. But where exactly? Drop me a pin. So I can give it to the police."

"Nothing's going to happen. It's broad daylight. I'll park on a public street. I looked up the Google street view already. The house is on a corner. Two doors over from a gas station and across the street from a U-Haul center."

"Lovely. Whatever. I guess you're right. Plus, the only white women who get murdered are the ones who light up a room. You're sour and judgmental and never smile. You'll be fine. I mean it. Drop me a pin. Somebody should know where you are."

"Fine," I said, sending him the pin. "I miss you. Hurry up and get here."

"I know. Just be careful. If Jeremy Holt didn't kill Savannah, somebody else did."

"Drive safe," I told him. "I'll get the stuff to make margaritas. We'll celebrate as soon as you get here."

"Get extra tequila," Christian said.

"On it." I clicked off.

After I hung up, I felt lighter than I had in days. I needed another brain on the Holt case. Jeremy had to be wrong. Whatever happened during his trial. Whatever was going on with Alicia Tate. I didn't want to believe my father wasn't at the root. But I wasn't naïve enough to think I could be objective. Christian could. Now I just had to convince my dad to let him in on the case.

Violet walked back around the corner. "You okay?"

"What? Oh, no. You mean Mom? That was...it's all fine."

Violet gave me a tight-lipped smile. "Sure. Fine. You sound like your dad. I'm sorry those two put you in the middle all the time. I know it's been like that since you were little."

It was in me to deflect. Say it was fine again. I just matched Violet's smile and she mercifully didn't ask me to elaborate.

"Anything I can help you with, honey?" she asked.

I was about to tell her no. Then I picked up my phone. "Actually, yes. That was my friend Christian. The one who's coming down to hang out with me this summer. He's asked me to go check out the rental place you recommended. I thought tomorrow afternoon I could..."

"I'll call Marian right now. I'll tell her to meet you there after what, four? She spent a lot of time and money restoring that place. She loves to show it off. She's a trip, that one. Kind of crusty at first, but she'll like you."

"I really appreciate it."

Violet frowned. Alicia Tate's letter sat on my desk. She picked it up. "Does he know you're getting into this?"

"Not completely. And I'm not *completely* into it yet." A lie. I felt bad about it. But something made me want to hold back.

"Mercy..." I wasn't fooling Violet. "What did you do, honey?"

"Nothing. I'm just placating Diane Benning. That's it. I'll get her off Dad's back."

"Are you going to go see this one?" Violet put the letter down.

I took a breath. "Yes," I said.

"Well, good."

"Good?"

"Yes. Good. Better you than Tom. You can be more objective. Tom just...well...he has too much trouble letting go. So go see her. Then maybe things can start getting back to normal around here. And I'll tell Marian to expect you after work tomorrow."

I thanked Violet, then picked up the desk phone and called Diane Benning. She answered right away but sounded weak, breathless. I wondered if I'd woken her up.

"Diane," I said. "It's Mercy Gale. I want to make arrangements to meet with Alicia Tate. Tomorrow morning. Can you let her know to expect me?"

"Of course," she asked, her voice gaining strength. "Alicia works afternoons. If you can get there first thing in the morning, I'll tell her you're coming. Mercy...thank you. You don't know how much this means."

I wanted to tell her I did. I wanted to tell her I'd seen Jeremy. I wanted to tell her I believed her son was innocent and that my father had truly done all he could. Only I didn't yet know which of those things was true.

CHAPTER Ten

I sat behind the wheel of Dad's Cadillac CTS-V. It took me a few tries to get in the groove of the manual transmission again, but once I did, I remembered how much I liked the feel of it. It took me just under two hours to get to Alicia Tate's address. Now that I had, I started to doubt whether I'd made a mistake.

In the ten minutes I'd been sitting outside 426 Draper St. in Big Rapids, I'd watched half a dozen people walk by. Moms with strollers mostly. There was a public park four blocks over and Draper seemed like a cut through.

A blue Honda Accord was parked in the driveway but the brick bungalow looked dark inside. I slipped my phone into the outer compartment of my purse and stepped outside. Steeling myself to have a door slammed in my face, I walked up the sidewalk and onto Alicia Tate's front porch.

The doorbell didn't work. I knocked lightly on the screen door and waited. I heard a dog bark inside. It sounded small. A Yorkie or something.

"Alicia?" I peered through the window at the front of the house.

I took a step off the porch and walked around to the side of the house. I saw a door there too when I parked. Maybe she was somewhere where she couldn't hear me knocking on the door. Though she should have been able to hear the dog barking. I think the entire neighborhood could hear that.

I knocked on the side door and pissed the dog off even more. I could hear it scratching furiously on the other side.

There was no point waiting any longer. I started back down the driveway. Another car pulled up, parking at an angle right behind the blue Honda. A muscle-bound young man got out. He narrowed his eyes with menace as he walked up to me. I took a step back.

"You're on private property," he yelled.

"I'm hoping to speak to Alicia Tate. I was told she was expecting me."

The man got in my personal space. He towered over me. "Who the hell are you?"

"Mercy Gale," I said, putting my hands on my hips. "I work for Tom Gale. And Alicia is expecting me. We have a mutual acquaintance, Diane Benning."

He reared back like I'd slapped him. "Yeah. You need to keep right on walking, lady. Get in your car and get the hell away from here. Alicia doesn't need to be talking to you or that whack job Diane Benning ever again. Tell her I said that."

"Who are you?"

"None of your damn business. So get moving before I kick your ass down the damn sidewalk."

CHAPTER TEN

Two stroller moms were right across the street. They saw everything that was going on. This guy couldn't be crazy enough to assault me in front of witnesses. I could hear Christian's voice in my head. "Do you really want to take the chance?"

"Fine," I said. "You tell Alicia I was here. Mercy Gale. She can figure out how to get a hold of me again if she wants to."

I suffered no illusions that this jerk would deliver any messages from me. It made me feel better not to back down though.

I pushed past him and marched back to my car.

"You show your face here again, you'll regret it," he yelled.

"I'm sure I will," I muttered. The stroller moms picked up their speed and kept their heads down.

I slipped behind the wheel and put the car in gear, intending to peel away from the curb. Instead, I popped the clutch. The car sputtered and stalled. So much for trying to appear intimidating. I took a breath, took my time, and got the car into first gear.

As I made my way to the main highway, I tried to call Diane Benning. My call went straight to voicemail.

"Perfect," I said, slamming an annoyed hand against the wheel. A half a day wasted. I should have listened to Christian and waited for him to get here. At least then the two of us could go find some fantastic hole-in-the-wall lunch place on the way back to Hell...er...Helene.

I HAD an unexpected visitor waiting for me when I finally made it back to my father's office. Dad was standing in the reception area with a dazzling smile on his face. Full-on Charming Tom as my mother used to describe him.

Standing in front of him was someone tall, fit, with a full head of black hair. Liam Branch turned around and smiled just as brightly as my father.

"There she is," Dad said. "How was your trip, Mercy?"

"Uneventful," I said. "My appointment got canceled." My father gave me a quizzical look. But that was as much detail as I wanted to divulge.

"I was hoping I could borrow you for lunch," Liam said. He looked worlds different than he had the other night at the yacht club. Today, he dressed casually in a pair of faded blue jeans and a black tee shirt.

"I'll get out of your way," my father said. He shot Liam a conspiratorial wink. It was weird of him. It seemed something more like my mother would have done when she found out how much Liam's family was worth. Dad disappeared back down the hall into his own office.

"You owe me an apology," I said to Liam as soon as my father was out of earshot.

Liam raised a brow. "I'm offering to buy you lunch. Does that count? Also...what am I sorry for exactly?"

"Withholding information," I said. "You should have told me Adam Branch was your brother."

Liam rolled his eyes. "I try to forget. Usually, nobody else ever lets me. Please don't tell me you're one of those."

"One of those?"

"Adam worshipers," he said. "I've spent enough of my life being Adam's brother. Or the other son. It never occurred to me to mention it. Everybody else already does."

"Hmm," I said. I had another haughty retort in mind, but my growling stomach spoke for me. I never bothered to eat breakfast before I headed out for my wasted trip to see Alicia Tate. I put a hand over my belly button.

"Come on," he said. "It's Friday. That means food trucks at the pier. Nothing fancy. You've gotta try Taco Hut. Best shredded chicken tacos you'll ever taste."

It sounded delicious. I'd seen the trucks he spoke of lining up as I drove back in. Slinging my purse back over my shoulder, I walked out the door Liam held open for me.

Fifteen minutes later, Liam was proven right. The shredded tacos practically melted in my mouth. We found an empty bench facing the water. I should have thought about bringing my floppy hat. My sunglasses weren't quite enough to fully shield my eyes.

"So," he said. "How are you liking Helene so far?"

"I'd say these tacos are a definite highlight."

"Told ya. But other than that?"

"Other than what?"

"You think you'll move here permanently?"

"I haven't thought that far ahead. I mean...no. Not permanently."

"Hmm. You know, there's been some speculation."

A jolt of anxiety speared through me.

"Who's been speculating? About what?"

"Oh, just how long it'll take Gale Force to scare you off."

"Gale Force?" I smiled. I hadn't heard that nickname used for my father in a long time. I didn't think anyone other than his Navy buddies knew it. There weren't very many of them left alive.

"All bluster," he said. "I don't know how Violet puts up with it."

"They've been together a long time. Hell, longer than both of his marriages."

Liam polished off the last of his taco. He wadded up the foil wrapper it came in and expertly tossed it in the wastebasket next to us.

"I'm not sure I'm comfortable with you or anyone else speculating about me."

Liam smiled. "Well, then you really have come to the wrong town. Everybody knows everybody else's business here."

"So, what else have people been speculating about?"

Liam looked out at the water. In the distance, a pair of freighters made their way north.

"He's a good man, your dad. People can see he seems happier now that you're here. It's good for him. He's less...blustery."

"Gale Force," I repeated.

"Yeah."

"It's complicated. I'm not from here."

"I suppose it's not easy being an outsider."

"Everybody knows everybody. Nobody knows me. So they speculate. Is that why you wanted to take me to lunch? So you could report back to the town peanut gallery?"

He laughed. "No. If there were such a thing, I'm not part of it. That's all my brother. The schmoozing. The politics. I'm the shiftless Branch brother, don't you know? The one who refuses to fall in line."

"Ah. I can relate to that."

"You're shiftless too?"

"Refuses to fall in line," I said. "My dad thinks I should be a lawyer like him. My mother wants me to help run her custom handbag shop in Florida. No. That's not entirely true. She wants me to act like a true nepo baby and become a social media influencer so I can drum up attention for her handbag shop."

Liam laughed. "I don't even know what any of that means."

"Consider yourself lucky."

We sat in companionable silence for a moment. Then I turned to him. "So you refused to work for the family firm too? You said you had your own graphic design business?"

He wiped his hands on his napkin and balled it up. "I do all right for myself. Logos. Branding. That kind of thing. But there isn't a whole lot of use for it in my family. Let's just say the Branches are already pretty well branded."

"Maybe I should hook you up with my mother. She's *all* about branding."

"So, you don't wanna be a lawyer like your father?"

"To be honest? This is supposed to be the summer where I find myself."

Liam stared at me. A moment passed, then we both burst into simultaneous laughter.

"Well," Liam said. "Here's to bucking family expectations."

He lifted his plastic soft drink cup and touched it to mine.

"Touché," I said. Things were easy between us then. I decided not to hold the other night against him. It had been his brother's big night. I couldn't blame him for not wanting to be introduced to me as Hollis Branch's "other son."

"I better get back," he said. "It was good talking to you, Mercy. I hope you stick around a little while. I have a feeling you're gonna make things interesting in Helene."

"Interesting? How will I do that?"

Liam didn't answer. Instead, he shot me that same wink I'd seen him share with my father. Odd. But friendly. I waved goodbye and turned to watch the freighters.

I got a text just as I was about to head back to the office. It was Christian.

> Did you die?

I answered back.

> Almost. But it was a dead end. I'll tell you when I see you tomorrow. I'll head over to your rental first thing in the morning to pick up the keys. I'll let you know if I find any cockroaches.

> Don't even joke.

> Drive safe

> THERE BETTER BE LOTS OF TEQUILA IN HELL

> Helene

> Same thing.

> You don't have to come, you know.

I was joking. But for a moment my breath caught, hoping I hadn't just given Christian an excuse to abandon me. I stared at three gray, blinking dots. Maybe Christian was thinking twice as well.

> Yes, I do. I know when you need back-up.

I wanted to hug him right through the phone. He was right. Until that second, I hadn't realized how alone I really felt.

CHAPTER
Eleven

THE NEXT MORNING, Christian called just after nine to let me know he was hitting the road. It would take him five or six hours to get here. I couldn't pick up his key until after lunch. After about my tenth promise to Christian to check out his rental, I clicked off. The morning flew by as I busied myself archiving the last of Dad's closed files. When noon finally hit, I poked my head through his door, but Dad was immersed in paperwork, barely looking up. I left him to it, but stopped by Violet's desk.

"I'm heading out to Mrs. Greenbaum's rental to pick up the keys for my friend. I shouldn't be long."

"He's coming today?"

"This afternoon. Yes."

"Well, take your time, honey. I'll keep your dad occupied. Tell Marian I said hello."

"I will." It was a nice enough day that I walked. The house was only ten minutes away on foot.

In person, the house was everything it looked like in the online listing. Known as the Garden House, it was a Victorian-era townhouse, complete with a white picket fence and pink and yellow rose bushes lining the sidewalk; it had been split into a duplex. One door had been painted bright yellow, the other sky blue. Christian rented the yellow unit. He'd have a small patio and yard in the back. From the front porch, he had a clear view of the bay.

I texted him.

> You're gonna love it. It looks even better than online.

> Fantastic. See if you can get her to let you in. Warn me if there's any cat smell. I'm making good time.

I sat on a white, wrought-iron bench just outside the fence. Mrs. Greenbaum was ten minutes late for our planned meeting.

I texted Christian.

> I'll see what I can do.

A moment later, Mrs. Greenbaum appeared. She walked with purpose down the sidewalk, stabbing a jeweled-hilt purple cane in front of her.

"You're Mercy," she said. It wasn't a question.

"I am. Thanks for coming out. I would have been happy to come to you. I..."

She waved the cane in the air. "I like to get eyes on the people renting from me. If I didn't know your family, I wouldn't have agreed to this rental. As long as you're vouching for Mr. Foley."

"I am," I said. I extended my hand to Mrs. Greenbaum. She was a formidably sized woman. Broad shoulders, tight white curls, blazing green eyes. Violet said she'd just celebrated her seventy-fifth birthday at the yacht club.

"I also don't like to rent to people under forty. But apparently that's against the law now. Which I find ridiculous."

"Well, I'm sure you'll find Christian to be the perfect tenant. He's here to help me at my father's office. He's a law student."

"Like you?"

"Er...yes. Like me."

"Well, all right then. But you're young too. What are you, twenty-three?"

"Twenty-eight," I said.

"Hmm. That might even be worse. It's in the lease, no guests here without my permission. That means you and your friend, under no circumstances, can throw any loud parties. If I get even a whiff of anything like that, he'll forfeit his deposit and I can evict him immediately."

She couldn't. *That* was against the law. But I decided the wisest course was not to point that out.

"I can assure you, there won't be anything like that going on."

"You say that now. But..."

"Oh, relax, Marian!" A deep voice came from my left, over my shoulder. Marian startled. Then her face split into a wide grin.

Adam Branch strode up the walk wearing an expensive, tailored black suit. He had a big smile on his face, showing his deep dimples. He towered over Marian Greenbaum as he came to her and leaned in to kiss her cheek. She blushed.

"Adam!" she said. "You look so handsome. It just takes my breath away."

"Is she giving you a hard time, Mercy?" Adam said. He put an arm around Mrs. Greenbaum. "Don't let it get to you. She's like this with everyone until you get to know her."

"She's just being a smart businesswoman," I said. "My friend is going to be renting one of the townhouses for the rest of the summer. I'm picking up the keys for him."

Adam's smile didn't falter, but his eyes twinkled. "Well, then, your friend has good taste. Marian's done an amazing job renovating all her historic homes. She was even featured in the lifestyle section of the *Record Eagle*. What was it? The Hidden Gem of Lake Michigan rentals?"

"The Crown Jewel of Lake Michigan Getaways. That article upped my revenue fifty percent. I've been booked solid for almost three years because of it. I know I've got your father to thank for that."

Adam waved her off. "You've got yourself to thank for that. You've got impeccable taste and the Garden House is one of the gems of Helene."

Marian Greenbaum couldn't stop blushing. She reached into the pocket of her dress and pulled out two keys. "One's for the front door. One's for the back. They're labeled." She handed them to me.

"Thank you," I said. "Christian will take care of your property as if it was his own. Do you mind if I take a peek inside?"

"I don't mind," she said.

"Allow me," Adam said. He walked up to the gate and opened it. He held it for me.

"I'll let you two get to it," Mrs. Greenbaum said. "I'm late for a doctor's appointment."

"You're not sick, I hope," Adam said.

"Oh, no. Just a routine thing. Dr. Munn has me come in every six months to make sure all systems are a go."

"Good. You tell Dr. Munn I said hello. And that he better keep on taking care of you. The Garden House is one of our jewels, but you're another, Marian. I've known this lady for as long as I can remember. Did she tell you that?"

"We didn't get that far," I said.

"Marian worked for my family for decades. This woman turns everything she touches into gold. She was a photojournalist. One of the best. All those beautiful photos you found online of this place? Marian took them herself."

"You have a great eye," I said.

Her hand fluttered to her throat. Mrs. Greenbaum said goodbye again and walked down the street with her head held high.

"Sorry about that," Adam said, still holding the gate open. "She's always been skeptical of people she doesn't know very well. Your father's been a resident for, what, twenty years? She still views him as a newcomer. If it weren't for the fact he's famous, she'd still be looking down her nose at him. To Marian Greenbaum, the great E. Thomas Gale is new money."

I laughed. "I didn't realize they still made people like that."

"She's a dying breed. But...I wasn't kidding about what I said. She did a fantastic job renovating this house. It's one of my favorites. And she did brilliant work for my father back in her prime."

"I was just going to take a quick look inside for my friend. Make sure there aren't any surprises."

"I'll leave you to it," he said.

"You know, my father seems to think you've got a real shot at winning the governorship next year."

"Your father's good opinion is something I don't take lightly. We care about him in this town."

Adam hesitated. His expression darkened in the way I'd grown familiar with from some people in town.

"I'm glad of that. He's lived alone for a long time."

"It's good that you're here. Tom's been so isolated out there. I know that's what he likes, but…"

"It is." My words came out sharper than I intended. Defensive.

"I'm sorry," Adam quickly said, picking up on it. "I didn't mean to step into your business. It's just…Tom's…well…Of course I've noticed some changes."

We weren't alone. Mrs. Greenbaum's townhouse was on a fairly populated section of the street. The main drag into downtown.

I turned, unlocked the front door and gestured for Adam to follow me. "Why don't we continue this conversation inside?"

"Of course. I didn't mean to be indiscreet."

I walked into the foyer. The house took my breath away. An ornate crystal chandelier hung above me with the original sculpted plaster ceiling. I couldn't see a speck of dust anywhere. The oak floors gleamed, highlighting a starburst inlaid pattern.

"Christian's going to love this," I said. It smelled clean, freshly scrubbed.

"I told you," Adam said. "A crown jewel."

I left the key to the back door on a small table in the foyer and pocketed the front door key. I'd give it to Christian when he got in.

"I'm sorry," I said, turning to him. "I'm glad my father has people looking out for him."

"He does," Adam said. "He has nothing but friends in this town. But I won't pretend I'm not worried about him. He's stubborn. But...he's not the same, is he?"

I didn't want to answer. It felt like a betrayal. Maybe Adam saw something in my eyes.

"Mercy," he said. "I'm on Tom's side. He's supported my career for over a decade. He's actually one of the first people who encouraged me to run for higher office. I value his counsel. He can trust me. So can you."

God, he was good. Adam Branch had a way of speaking. A way of moving that just made you want to unburden yourself. He carried himself tall and straight. He seemed genuinely caring and earnest. Was it all an act?

"I appreciate that. And my Dad's okay. He's just...almost eighty."

Adam nodded. "I get it. Anyway...I just wanted to say I'm glad you're here. For him. Also...I think maybe you're someone worth getting to know, too."

I could understand why Marian Greenbaum lost her head when Adam Branch fixed that dazzling smile on her. He did it to me now and I can't deny it heated my blood. The man had movie star good looks mixed with a certain smalltown aw-shucks charm. It could make him dangerous.

"Thanks," I said. "For your help with Mrs. Greenbaum. And for your concern for my dad."

"I suppose I've intruded on your privacy enough."

"I don't mind," I said, gushing a little.

"Tell your friend we'll be neighbors for the summer. I live on the next corner."

Adam pointed out the window to a stately white two-story Victorian with a white picket fence and a huge, wraparound porch.

"You live there?" I asked. "I guess I just assumed you lived in the Branch mansion at the top of the bluff."

Adam laughed. "I'd hardly call it a mansion. And I haven't lived with my parents since I was eighteen. I live in my great-grandparents' old house. I bought it from my dad. Restored it."

"I'd love to see it sometime," I said, then immediately blushed. I was only curious about the house itself.

"Then I'll be happy to show you. In the meantime, if I don't get a chance to meet him, tell your friend welcome to Helene for me. He must be pretty special for you to do all of this for him."

"He is," I said. "Christian's one of the good ones."

"Those are rare. I'll see you around, Mercy. And please, now that you know where to find me, reach out if you need help with anything."

Adam hesitated a moment, as if he were going to say something else, but thought the better of it. Then he let himself out the front door. I went to the window and watched him stroll down the street. He took his time, stopping to say hello and a kind word to everyone he passed.

I pulled out my phone and sent another quick text to Christian.

> Good news. No cat pee smell. Text me when you think you're a few minutes away.

Christian sent me a thumbs-up. I could hear his voice in my head. If he'd been standing here during all of this, I knew he would have told me to find a way to put myself in Adam Branch's path again.

Time got away from me that afternoon. At four o'clock, I packed my things and got ready to leave the office. Christian hadn't texted, but I expected to hear from him any minute.

"You sure you're okay if I head out?" Dad asked. "I can wait. I mean if you and your friend want to come out to the island tonight, we can have a late dinner."

"It's okay. I'll stay in town tonight. Help Christian get settled at the townhouse. Then we'll both meet you at the office in the morning."

I followed my father down to the dock. He'd be driving the boat back by himself.

"I suppose the two of you probably want some time alone to catch up."

"We do," I said, then noticed the look on Dad's face. "Oh, no. Not like that. Christian's just a friend. Not my boyfriend."

Dad laughed. "I wasn't trying to pry. It's none of my business."

"I suppose it's not. But really. He's sort of like a brother to me. A nosy, annoying brother who never shuts up or keeps his opinions to himself." I muttered the last part.

"Well, all right. But you let me know if you change your mind. I can drive back out and pick you up."

"You don't need to be driving the boat out here at night. I'm fine. I packed an overnight bag. Mrs. Greenbaum's townhouse has six bedrooms and three floors. It's huge."

Dad came up to me and kissed me on the forehead. "Well, I'll leave you to it. Are you taking your friend to dinner tonight?"

"Maybe. I don't know if he grabbed something on the road."

"If you do, you could check out Zelinski's over on Maple Street. It's a hole in the wall but they've got the best burgers in Northern Michigan. Good craft beer too if you're into that."

"I'll keep it in mind. Thanks."

My father climbed into the boat. I helped him pull off his ropes and gave him a shove. He waved as he revved the engine and roared across the bay.

He was in his element out there, I thought. Though I knew he'd rather be in the cockpit of a plane, he loved the boat almost as much. The scent of the lake filled my lungs. Crisp. Clean. I could get used to it.

I also knew Christian was going to hate it. He told me he got seasick in the bathtub. I wondered if I'd ever get him over to Dad's island while he was here.

I walked the six blocks to the Garden House. It was a cool, clear night. I sent a text to Christian, asking whether he knew his exact ETA. Three gray dots pulsed, but he didn't answer.

Using the key Mrs. Greenbaum gave me, I let myself into the Garden House. The smell of fresh lilacs filled my head. She'd put a bouquet on a table in the foyer. Turning the lights on, I walked into the kitchen. Another heavenly scent drew me. She'd left a large gift basket on the kitchen table. Jams, crackers, fresh baked bread. More fresh flowers sat in a vase on the counter. Beside that,

CHAPTER ELEVEN

she'd left a plate of homemade chocolate chip cookies. My stomach growled and I couldn't help myself. I took a cookie. It was moist, delicious, and about as big as my head. For all her gruff demeanor, Adam was right. Marian Greenbaum was a true gem.

I checked my phone. No response from Christian. I scrolled to his contact, ready to call him. But my phone rang in my hand. A number I didn't recognize.

"Hello?"

A gruff male voice answered. "Am I speaking with Mercedes Gale?"

"Yes."

"Ms. Gale. This is Detective Jack Garvey. I'm with the Michigan State Police. Ma'am. Your name was listed as the emergency contact for Christian Foley."

Outside, I heard a loud whistle, drowning out the sound of the caller's voice for a moment. But the words I heard pummeled me as if they transformed into something solid.

Sorry to inform you...accident...hospital.

My hand shook so badly, I dropped the phone to the floor at my feet. Picking it up, I ran out the front door and into the street.

CHAPTER Twelve

"Mercy."

My chest felt hollowed out. I couldn't draw air.

"Mercy!"

I looked up. My vision blurred. Why couldn't I see straight?

Strong hands gripped my shoulders, lifting me. Liam Branch's eyes filled with alarm as he put a finger under my chin, tilting my head toward his. It was then I realized I was kneeling on the lawn in front of the Garden House. I stared at my phone screen.

"Ms. Gale? Are you there?"

Liam grabbed my phone. "I'm with Ms. Gale. This is Liam Branch. I'm her...her friend."

"Liam," I said, my voice sounding far away. The detective's words hammered into my brain.

"There's been an accident. We need you to come."

Liam nodded, getting the same basic information as I had. "We'll be there," he said. "Thank you, Detective. Yes. I know where that is."

I couldn't cry. I couldn't fall apart. Christian needed me. Liam ended the call and handed me back my phone.

"Mercy, I'm so sorry. You understand they want you to come to the hospital in Cadillac? Will you let me go with you?"

"I don't...my dad's car keys are back at the office."

"Come on," Liam said. "You shouldn't be driving anyway. I'm parked in the public lot across the street. The hospital is a good hour and a half away."

"Thank you," I said. I put one foot in front of the other, following Liam to his black Bentley. He opened the passenger door for me. When he reached in to help me buckle the seatbelt, I took it from him.

"I'm okay," I said. "I just...Can we just hurry?"

"Of course." Liam got behind the wheel. He whipped the car around with the precision of a NASCAR driver and zoomed us toward the highway. I know he said it would take over an hour, but it only seemed like seconds.

This was not happening. Christian was not in some hospital in Cadillac. They had to have the wrong guy. He was on his way to Helene. We were going to spend the rest of the summer together.

Liam pulled into the valet lot at the Cadillac Hospital. He wrapped his key in a fifty-dollar bill and handed it to the attendant.

"Do you know where we can find the, uh...?" He mouthed something I couldn't see.

The attendant frowned. "You just take those elevators down one floor. There are signs."

"Thank you," I said. I ran to the elevator with Liam trailing behind. I don't know why I felt the need to hurry. That seemed absurd. I felt an out-of-place laughing fit coming on. This whole thing was ridiculous. Christian was playing some kind of awful prank on me.

Two sheriff's deputies waited in the hallway outside two steel double doors. Another man wearing a suit and a badge on a chain around his neck came out of an office door.

"Are you Detective Garvey?" I asked.

"I am," he said. He was young. He barely looked older than me. Liam had a comforting hand on the small of my back.

"I'm Mercedes Gale," I said.

"Yes. Thank you for coming down. I'm sorry it has to be under these circumstances. If you'll come with me, there's a room we can use for a little more privacy."

Garvey opened the door he'd just come out of and held it for me.

"I'll wait right out here for you," Liam said.

"Thanks." I grabbed his sleeve. "Thanks for everything. I can't..."

"It's okay. Take your time. I'll be right here."

I walked in with Detective Garvey. It was a small office with just a desk in one corner and two leather chairs on opposite sides of the room. I sat in one. Garvey sat in the other.

"What happened?" I said. "I'm trying to understand."

"A vehicle rented to Mr. Foley was found parked at a rest stop along I-31 near Cadillac. The driver had...Ms. Gale, he shot himself. We believe it was a suicide."

Shot himself? I shook my head. "Christian was on his way to visit me. He was headed up from Toledo. He rented a house for the next month. I just talked to him this morning. He was on his way. I'm sorry. I didn't...he didn't own a gun?"

"Are you sure?"

I felt as if someone had sucked all the air out of the room. "No," I heard myself say. "I don't know. He never told me he had one."

"Well, we'll sort all of that out."

"I just talked to him. He was...he was on his way to see me? We were talking all morning."

"We've retrieved his phone. But you didn't have any idea that he might have been depressed?"

"Depressed? No. Nothing like that. This can't be real. Are you sure it was him? Maybe someone just stole his wallet or something."

"That's one reason we needed you to come down in person. Ms. Gale, we couldn't find any information about next of kin. He has you listed as an emergency contact with a card we found in his wallet."

I shook my head. "Christian doesn't have any family. His parents passed away a few years ago. A car accident. No siblings. He never talked about any other family."

"How long have you known him?"

"Just...not even two years. We were law school classmates. He's from upstate New York. He's enrolled at the University of Toledo because they gave him a full ride."

I was babbling. What did Christian's scholarship have to do with anything?

"So, you've not known him that long?" Garvey said.

"I was the first person he met in Ohio," I said. "We were...close."

"Okay. Do you think you could make an identification?"

"His body? You want me to look at his body?"

"It seems there may be no one else."

I sprang to my feet. "I have to see him. Now. Please."

"You don't have to be in the room," he said. "We do it on a closed circuit monitor."

"No. I want to see him." I didn't *want* to see him. But something rose up inside of me. I had to be sure.

"All right. It's just in the next room."

The next room. Christian was lying in the next room. I don't remember walking out of that room or into the next one. I don't remember what anyone said to me. But the next thing I knew, I was standing in front of a large window. There was a gurney on the other side of it. A body under a black plastic tarp.

They only showed me part of Christian's face, keeping the tarp over part of his head. He only looked asleep. Christian was a redhead. He had dark freckles covering his cheeks and down his neck. He hated them. His eyelashes were pure blond. His eyebrows too.

My knees felt weak, but I stayed on my feet. Liam was there again. I hadn't heard him come in. He had his arm around my shoulders.

I nodded. "It's him. That's Christian Foley."

They covered him back up. I walked out into the hallway with Detective Garvey right behind me.

"What do we do now?" I asked.

"There are a few arrangements that need to be made. We'll need to know where you want us to send Mr. Foley's remains."

"Does that have to be decided right now?" Liam asked.

"No. One of the local funeral homes can..."

"He wanted to be cremated," I blurted. "We went to a funeral together last year. One of our professors lost her husband. A bunch of us went together to pay our respects. Christian said he thought the whole thing was ghoulish. The guy had cancer. He looked terrible. Christian said just put me in an urn. I don't... It's so funny that I remember that."

"Can you take care of this?" Liam said to Garvey. "Let me leave you my card. Just send whatever bill there is to me."

"Liam, I can't ask you to do that."

"Don't worry about it. We'll figure out the logistics later. Is there anything else Ms. Gale needs to do for you here? Paperwork you need her to sign?"

A woman appeared with a clipboard and a stack of papers. I went on autopilot, signing everything she put in front of me.

"What happens now?" I said to Garvey.

"That's everything I need right now. We have to do a few other things to tie up the investigation. There will be Mr. Foley's personal effects. I'll be able to release those in a couple of days. I can send them to you."

My mind raced. Christian had an apartment in downtown Toledo. There was the rental in Helene. What did any of that matter now?

CHAPTER TWELVE

"That would be fine," I said. "Thank you."

Liam reappeared.

"I am very sorry for your loss, Ms. Gale."

My loss. Christian. God. Liam had his hand on my back again. He gently ushered me toward the exit. Right before we made it to his car, I turned to him.

"Thank you," I said. "I don't know what I would have done if you hadn't come up to me. I just..."

Then he was there. Just. There. I choked out a sob and Liam pulled me into an embrace.

"Come on," he said. "Let's get you home."

Home. I was supposed to be staying at the Garden House with Christian tonight.

"My dad," I blurted. "I never called him. He doesn't know where..."

"I called him," Liam said. "I talked to him while you were in there with Detective Garvey. He's waiting at his office for you."

I nodded. "That was very sweet of you. All of this. The money... Oh. I have to..."

"Mercy, don't worry about any of that."

It doesn't matter. None of it mattered. When I closed my eyes, I could imagine them shoving poor Christian inside a cold metal drawer.

Liam put me in his car. That suffocating feeling came over me again. I almost couldn't breathe. Then, Liam reached over and took my hand. He tethered me back to earth.

CHAPTER
Thirteen

WHEN I LOOK BACK at the week following Christian's death, I can see now how numb I went. It was as if I'd forgotten how to cry or feel. I pushed my emotions into some corner of my brain and locked the door on them. And then, four days after I identified Christian's body in that morgue, Detective Garvey called me back. I braced myself when I saw the caller ID. Some part of my brain expected him to tell me it had all been a mistake.

"Ms. Gale?" he said. I sat at my desk in my father's office. For four days, I'd buried myself in his files, spending up to sixteen hours a day here. I organized his old case files. I had his back room cleared out. Closed files were digitized and archived. Active files were sorted, color coded, and put back into the oak cabinets he'd had since he first hung out his shingle.

Christian put me down as his emergency contact in his phone. I was the only one expecting him on the day he chose to take his life. He knew it would be me dealing with the fallout. I couldn't help that I hated him for that.

"Hello," I said.

"I promised you a follow-up call. I just wanted to let you know where things stand with Christian Foley's case."

"Okay."

"I'm afraid nothing's really changed from my initial findings. It's being ruled a suicide. But I am trying to track down one thing."

"What is it?"

"The gun Mr. Foley had in his possession wasn't registered to him. It was registered to an Anne Barnheiser. She had an address in Hartford, Connecticut, but we haven't been able to locate her. The phone number associated with her registration is disconnected."

"Anne Barnheiser? Christian never mentioned anyone to me with that name."

"It's certainly possible he purchased the firearm secondhand."

"You said you went through his phone. Is Ms. Barnheiser listed as a contact?"

"No," Garvey said. "Though he was communicating with someone he called Barney. Just...Barney. There's no email. No physical address. No contact picture."

"They were communicating about a gun?"

"No. The texts between them were of a more intimate nature. I believe your friend Christian was in a romantic relationship with someone he called Barney."

"And you think this Barney is Anne Barnheiser and that she gave Christian her gun?" My head spun. He never told me he was dating anyone.

"No, I can't make that leap. And the number in Mr. Foley's phone is also a dead end."

CHAPTER THIRTEEN

"How could it be a dead end?"

"It looks like it was a prepaid phone. We can't trace it. At any rate, it doesn't really affect my conclusions about what happened to Mr. Foley. He fired the gun that was used to take his own life. I was also able to speak to his primary care physician. Mr. Foley had been prescribed antidepressants some time ago. He made an attempt on his own life four years ago as well. Were you aware of that?"

"No," I said, my throat going dry. "He never told me."

"Sometimes we never really know people. Please don't blame yourself. There's nothing you could have done. Is there anything else I can try to answer for you?"

"No," I said, then changed my mind. "Yes, actually. Yes. I still don't understand what he was doing in Cadillac, or whatever town you said he was found. Was there anything about that in his phone?"

"Not really. Not his reasoning. But Mr. Foley had checked into a hotel the night before he was found."

My head felt scrambled. A hotel? What for? Where?

"He was checked into a Quality Inn about ten miles south of the rest stop where he was found."

"I don't understand. I don't know why he would have done that."

Detective Garvey sighed on the other end of the phone. "It's hard to say. As I said, he checked in the night before. He checked out a few hours before his vehicle was found at the Cadillac rest stop. Hotel manager barely remembered him. As far as we know, he didn't talk to anybody, wasn't seen with anybody, just stayed in his room. We'll never know why. But...sometimes, with suicide victims, once they make a plan they often hole up somewhere nobody knows about. So, they won't be stopped. Or so they can work up the courage. I've seen it before. More times than I'd like to remember."

"Thank you," I said, though it seemed a strange thing to express gratitude for.

"I'll be closing out the case over the next few days. I mainly wanted to let you know his personal effects are on their way to you. The tracking ID I have shows them arriving today. I wanted you to be prepared."

I felt like my brain was encased in mud. It took me a moment to answer. "I appreciate the heads-up." Though I had no idea what I'd do with any of it.

"I'm really very sorry for your loss, Ms. Gale."

"Thank you." Gavey said a few more things, but I could barely register any of it. When we hung up, I stared at the files I'd made in the office. They were the only thing I felt like I had any control over. I wished I could put Christian in his own box, filed away, just like my father's records. I felt like I really didn't know Christian at all. Why would he have stopped overnight on the way to Helene? It wasn't like he was driving cross country. The whole trip was a half a day drive. He didn't know anyone else in Michigan as far as I knew. And he lied to me. When we texted and talked that morning, he told me he was just hitting the road. He didn't tell me he'd actually left Toledo the day before. And a girlfriend? Someone he had never told me about. None of it made sense. My head throbbed as I tried to understand it. I knew I never could.

For now, I would immerse myself in all things Jeremy Holt.

My attempts to get a hold of Alicia Tate again went nowhere. The number she gave Diane Benning was now out of service. Diane wasn't even returning my calls. I decided to let that mean she was no longer a threat to my father. Whatever happened with Alicia, she wasn't interested in pursuing anything against Dad.

Dad and I settled into a good routine. I prepped him for the few hearings he had in court. Most of those were mundane. He had two criminal appeals that took up most of his time and paid most of his revenue. He was knee-deep in brief writing and I enjoyed doing some of the legwork for that. Even though Christian was supposed to be here helping me with it.

Dad was there for me the night Liam Branch brought me back to Helene. I had yet to tell my mother about any of it. I'd only known Christian for less than two years. It would be easy to just pretend I'd never met him. Less painful. But lately, I'd talked to him more than my mother. More than anyone else during my brief stint in law school. There was a hole in my life now. And none of it made any sense.

I needed air. A little early for lunch, but I grabbed my leftovers out of the office fridge and headed across the street, picking a bench overlooking the bay. I picked absently at my turkey and avocado sandwich as the seagulls gathered.

"Hey there!"

I looked up. Liam was on a bike. Helene had a bike and walking path all the way along the water.

I shielded my eyes from the sun. "You're supposed to be wearing a helmet."

Liam smiled. He climbed off the bike and parked it in a rack right next to us. "I was looking for you," he said.

"I'm not too hard to find these days."

"I didn't want to bug you. Give you some space. But...how are you?"

I wrapped the remains of my sandwich and put it in the paper bag I'd brought. "I'm okay. Keeping busy. Trying not to think too hard."

"Good plan."

"I don't know what I would have done if you hadn't been there when I got that call from Detective Garvey."

"Nobody should have to go through that alone. Have you found any of your friend's family?"

"No," I shook my head. "I really don't think he had any. I talked to his landlord down in Toledo. He had me listed as his emergency contact there, too."

"You had no idea he was having mental health issues?"

"No." I shook my head. "I didn't even know he owned a gun."

"The police ought to sort that out. They can figure out if it was registered to him pretty quickly."

"They have," I said. "It belonged to some friend of his I'd never heard of before. The police are trying to track her down."

"Wow," Liam said. "Mercy, it really sounds like Christian had this plan all along."

I stared at the water.

"I'm sorry. Listen, I wanted to let you know Adam talked to Marian Greenbaum. She wants to return Christian's rent money. She charged him everything upfront. Two thousand dollars. She's asking who she should make the check payable to. If there's an estate being opened up."

"I hadn't even thought that far. What a mess."

CHAPTER THIRTEEN

A van pulled up in front of my dad's office. A delivery driver got out. He pulled out a large brown box and looked up at the signage on the building.

"May I help you?" I asked. I quickly threw my brown lunch bag away, dusted my hands off on my pants, and walked across the street.

The driver looked at the package. "I'm looking for a Mercedes Gale. I've got this address on the package."

"Let me," Liam said, stepping forward. He took the package from the driver. The driver pulled out a small tablet.

"I need you to sign for this," he said. Liam looked at the label on the package and his face dropped.

I signed the tablet and thanked the driver. He hopped back into his van and drove away.

"Let me help you get this inside," Liam answered. "It's from the Wexford County Sheriff's Department."

A lump formed in my throat. "It's Christian's personal effects," I said. "What he had with him in that rental car. Detective Garvey said they'd be arriving today. I told his Toledo landlord to just donate whatever he found in Christian's apartment. I don't even want this."

Violet was gone for lunch. I used my key to reopen the office door. Dad had taken the day off to go fishing with Uncle Lloyd. He wouldn't be back until after four.

"Just put it in my office," I said. "I've commandeered the one on the right side of the hallway."

Liam did as I asked. He set the box on my desk.

"Are you sure you're all right? Is there somebody else I can call for you? Maybe even another friend from law school? It can't just be you dealing with all of this."

"It's fine. Really."

"Do you want...help with this?"

"No." I shook my head. "I think I just need to be alone. I'm sorry if that comes off rude. I..."

"No. I understand. I just...why don't you let me pick you up in a couple of hours? I can take you back home. I've got the boat today."

"If my dad isn't back by five, I'll take you up on that."

Liam smiled. "Just text me."

I thanked Liam. When he left, I put the closed sign on the door and locked it. Then I walked over to that awful brown box on my desk.

THERE WAS NOTHING LEFT. Barely nothing. Christian had packed a small, carry-on sized suitcase. In it were a few pairs of shorts and shirts. His usual uniform of maroon or blue polos and cargo shorts. A belt. A shaving kit. His toothbrush. Some over-the-counter medication. Detective Garvey had taken a bottle of antidepressants from this bag. The ones I never knew Christian was taking.

I laid everything out on an empty table I'd cleared of my dad's files. I pulled out two plastic baggies from the box. The police had tagged Christian's cell phone. But there was just so little here. Granted, he'd only planned to stay in Helene for a few weeks. But this looked like what you'd pack for a single weekend.

"Guys are different, I guess," I said. It just seemed so final. And so...paltry. Was there really only me left to remember who Christian Foley was?

I took his cell phone out of the baggie and I clicked it on. The thing wasn't even passcode protected. I pulled up Christian's text messaging app. It made me smile. Just like my phone, the vast majority of his texts were to me in the last few weeks.

I found a few texts to other classmates of ours. Jolie. Brian. Mindy. He knew them better than I did. I had some of their numbers in my phone. God. I should have called them.

Then I saw the texts from the person he named Barney. They had a thread going back about six months. Cordial at first. Friendly. Barney's number had a 212 area code. New York City. But I knew that didn't have to mean anything. Detective Garvey told me this was a burner number. But I also knew Christian had spent a week in New York during spring break. I'd gone to Florida to see my mother or I might have made the trip with him. The texts with Barney started right after Christian would have come back to Toledo for the rest of the spring term at UT Law.

> I'm at the coffee shop now. I got a seat by the window.

> I see you.

Then two days later.

> I miss you already. Summer can't get here soon enough.

> Same. I'll call you later.

Then there were long calls between Christian and Barney, lasting over an hour. Was she a hookup? A girlfriend? Was Barney actually

Anne Barnheiser? Christian never told me anything about her. Then, more recently, the texts got colder. Several calls from Christian to Barney that went unanswered. Then texts. Barney had ghosted Christian. No wonder he'd never told me about this person.

I pulled up his recent calls. His last incoming call from me went unanswered. It sent a spear of pain through me.

But I wasn't the last person Christian Foley called. The number didn't have a contact name. He made it just two hours before the police said his body was found.

I don't know what made me do it. I hit redial.

It rang three times, then went to voicemail. I pressed the speaker button.

"Hello, you've reached the voice mailbox of DeShawn Sims. I'm sorry I missed your call. I'll be out of the office until August 7. If you need more immediate assistance, you can call the main desk of Gossip Zone. That number is..."

I clicked off the call. I pulled out my laptop and put DeShawn Sims's name into my browser's search bar. A series of entertainment articles popped up with Sims's byline.

DeShawn Sims. Gossip Zone. Why in the ever-loving hell was Christian calling a reporter for a gossip rag?

Christian's phone rang. I jumped. The caller ID on the screen was the number I'd just called.

I hit the speaker button. "Hello?"

"You tried to call me?" The caller said.

"Mr. Sims," I said.

"Yes. This is DeShawn Sims. To whom am I speaking?"

"I'm...I was... Were you a friend of Christian Foley's?"

Silence. A breath. "Who is this?"

"How did you know Christian Foley?"

"Who is this? And why are you calling me from Christian Foley's number?"

"He's...Mr. Foley passed away. I *am* a friend of his. My name is Mercedes Gale and I..."

"Wait a minute," Sims interrupted. "You're Mercy Gale?"

"What? Yes."

"I heard about what happened. I'm sorry for your loss, Ms. Gale."

"I was...thank you. I don't mean to be rude or too direct. But...can you tell me what your business with Christian was?"

"He shot himself. Suicide. I heard."

Heard? How the hell had he heard?

"Christian never talked about you."

"Ms. Gale, your father is E. Thomas Gale. Isn't that right? You're in Helene. Christian was coming up to stay with you in Helene."

I picked up the phone. Took it off speaker even though I was the only one in the building.

"How do you know that?"

"Can we meet?"

It got hard to breathe.

"I need to know what business you had with Christian."

"I can come to you. Tomorrow. I know a diner not far from you.

It's called the Frosty Fork. It's tiny. Quiet. Right off 31 before you get to Torch Lake."

I knew the place. I should have hung up. Every instinct in me was telling me DeShawn Sims of the Gossip Zone wasn't someone I should meet with. But Christian had. They'd been communicating. I saw incoming and outgoing calls to his number. Seven of them over the last three weeks.

"Tomorrow," I said. "Ten o'clock. I'll meet you there."

Before he could say anything, I clicked off the call. Then I tossed Christian's phone back in the box and shut the lid.

CHAPTER
Fourteen

I'D TURNED BACK at least four times. I sat parked in the furthest spot away from the entrance to the Frosty Fork Diner. Slamming the car into reverse, I was about to peel out and leave whatever this was behind me.

"Mercy?"

He tapped on the window. DeShawn Sims peered in at me, smiling. He had a handsome, youthful appearance in a golf shirt and khakis. His bio told me he was fifty years old. If I pulled out now, I would run over his feet.

"Shit," I murmured, then put the car in park and pulled out the keys.

Sims stepped back, allowing me to get out. "Hi there," he said, extending his hand to mine. I shook it.

"It's about to rain," he said. "I've got a table for us. They're switching over to the lunch menu in about five minutes, but if you'd rather have breakfast items, I can talk to the cook."

"I didn't come here to eat."

Sims kept the smile on his face. I didn't wait for him, but made my way up the walk and into the restaurant.

It was like stepping through a time machine. Red leather booths with checkerboard tops. There was a gleaming, old-fashioned soda fountain behind the counter.

"We're in the back," Sims said. "It's just this way."

I got a cheery wave from the server behind the counter as I followed Sims to a table. He held a chair out for me in gentlemanly fashion.

"Thank you," I said, taking my seat. I ordered an iced tea, not wanting to be rude.

"Thanks for coming," Sims said. "I know this seems clandestine."

"How did you know Christian? How did you know I was in Helene?"

He waited as the server dropped off our drinks. He stuck with lemon water.

"I'm sorry for your loss, first off. It was a shock to hear what happened. Did you have any idea Foley was depressed?"

"Everyone keeps asking me that. Of course I didn't know."

"Again, I'm sorry."

"I'd prefer it if you just came right out and told me what this is all about."

Sims raised a brow. He was studying me. My facial expressions. My tone. Everything. I found it unsettling.

"You look a lot like your aunt. Do people tell you that?"

"I never knew my aunt," I said. "I have nothing to say about her. Certainly not to a reporter."

"I can understand that. The media wasn't fair in the way they covered your aunt's trial. She was painted as crazy by the kinder publications. The rest of them flat out called her a whore. But she wasn't either. I hope you count the Gossip Zone among the publications that were kinder to her."

"GZ wasn't particularly kind to my father," I said. "I recall a cover story calling his relationship with my mother twisted. They published photographs at my aunt's funeral."

"That was well before my time. You've clearly formed an opinion about my employers already. So why not just tell me to eff off? Why meet with me at all?"

"You were communicating with Christian. I want to know why."

Sims took a sip of his water. "Are you sure about that?"

"I'm here, aren't I? Like you said, I could have just as easily told you to go piss up a rope."

Sims smiled. "Right. Listen. Christian was worried about you."

"What?"

"You know he didn't think it was a good idea for you to uproot your whole life and move to Helene. Your mother wasn't very keen on that either, was she?"

"And what business is that of yours?"

"Christian made it my business."

"What are you talking about?"

"A couple of months ago, I got a phone call from this kid who told me I might want to look into the Jeremy Holt case again. Now, I'd never heard of it. I get phone calls like that all the time. Whackos. Dead ends. But this kid was persistent. He said he had something my paper might be interested in. You want to guess what that was?"

"I really don't."

"He said he had credible intel that legendary lawyer E. Thomas Gale might have botched one of the biggest cases of his career. Or worse...that he might have taken a deliberate dive on it."

"If that were true, why would you think I'd be interested in talking to you about it?"

"Normally, that's exactly where my head would go on something like that. Only my source had an interesting twist on the whole thing. He said he was going to provide insider details."

"Your source?" I braced myself for it. Didn't want to believe it was true. Only, I'd seen his phone. I'd seen their call history. Christian had initiated contact with Sims, not the other way around.

"You know Christian Foley was communicating with me. So, you also know he's the one who reached out to me. I didn't go looking for this."

"Then I can't help you. Christian's dead. And I have no interest in continuing with this conversation."

"Then why did you come?"

"You talked to him the day before he died. You asked me if I had any inkling that Christian was depressed. Did you?"

"We weren't friends. We were just building a rapport. I hadn't even decided whether he was a trustworthy source."

"You expect me to believe that one of my best friends was trying to sell a hit piece on my father?"

"You're asking the wrong questions. Maybe Christian Foley wasn't the friend you thought he was."

CHAPTER FOURTEEN

"I think we're done here." I rose. I felt my skin getting hot. No. This couldn't be who Christian was. He would never try to sell out my family like this.

"Your father's sick," Sims said. "The kind of sick that could get him disbarred, or worse if he had symptoms during his representation of Jeremy Holt. Or whoever he's representing now."

"You've been misinformed."

"I don't think I have. And I wouldn't be here if Christian Foley were my only source. Your mother's worried about you, too."

"What does my mother have to do with this?"

"You should ask her."

I could feel the sweat on my neck. My mother had talked to him?

"My mother isn't in the habit of talking to reporters from GZ. Your paper painted her as some kind of Lolita after my aunt died. You implied my father was sleeping with my aunt during her trial."

"He went after your mother, your aunt's lookalike baby sister as soon as she came of age. I think that's what people had questions about."

"Things must be pretty rough in the scandal rag business to sniff around about a man who's been retired from public life for over a decade."

"It's coming up on the fiftieth anniversary of the Dr. Anton Milo trial. That case made your dad's career. Did you hear they're talking about remaking *A Deadly Affair*? Julian Stone nabbed an Oscar for his portrayal of your dad. Didn't your dad get his own Oscar for co-producing that film? There's a lot of interest from some A-List actors in reprising that role."

"My father sold the rights to that story a long time ago. What the studio does with it is out of my hands."

"It's newsworthy in light of all of that. I'd think your family would want to get out in front of it. If your father is as sick as I believe he is...as Christian Foley believed...he's going to get hurt."

"Are you threatening me?"

"No. Look, I had a deal with Christian. He was a source. I know that's hard for you to hear. I get why that seems like a betrayal. But I don't think it was. He was trying to protect you. I thought you should know. That's all."

"Protect me. By spreading rumors that my father's sick? Why is that news? If he's sick, it's not anyone's business or anything he should be ashamed of in the first place. Are you trying to make people think he's been negligent?"

"You should talk to your mom. She has a different perspective. I'm giving you the opportunity to tell your side of things. Control the narrative."

"And you're full of shit." I stood. My pulse pounded in my head.

"Ms. Gale. Think about it. Give it some time."

He tossed a business card on the table in front of me. I picked it up.

"Keep it," he said. "Line your birdcage with it. It's your choice. But I'm not your enemy. There's a story coming. Running away from it won't help."

I crumpled the card in my palm.

"I think you're just as worried about the things Christian was. I think you're the one who made him worry. Are you going to deny that you've been looking into the Jeremy Holt case?"

"No comment," I said.

"Fine." Sims threw up his hands. "But if I'm asking, other people will too. If your father is sick, like I think he is, it's not his fault. I'm not looking to tar and feather a dying old man."

"My father isn't dying," I said. "You've been misinformed."

"Maybe. I hope so. But he's not going to make this go away by running away to his own island. Neither will you if you follow him there."

"Goodbye," I said. "Don't call me. You don't have permission to use my name."

"I don't need it."

I turned my back on DeShawn Sims and stormed out of the diner. My heart jack hammered in my chest. My mother talked to that creep? Christian talked to that creep?

I didn't want it to be true. But Sims knew things he shouldn't know. Was Christian using me this whole time? Was his whole plan to spend the rest of the summer in Helene as just a ruse to get dirt on my family?

It felt impossible. Except...he'd been so dead set against me coming here. He'd begged me to come back to school. Then he changed his mind on a dime and offered to come up here to help me.

I drove out of that parking lot as fast as I dared. Part of me wanted to just keep on going. Far away from Helene. From Michigan. From any part of the world that had my mother or father in it. But I knew one thing DeShawn Sims said was true.

Running was only going to make what was coming worse.

CHAPTER Fifteen

I DON'T KNOW why I wanted to be at the townhouse. Somehow, being there made me feel connected to Christian. I wanted to be angry. I wanted to be sad. Most of all, I wanted someone to talk to about everything that had happened. For the last year and a half, my someone, my confidante, had been Christian.

And now I knew that may have been the problem. He was the only person who knew Jeremy Holt wrote me a letter. He was the only person I'd shown it to.

I sat in the window seat overlooking Main Street. It was beautiful here. Helene was quiet. Clean. On a night like this, it all made sense why my father wanted to be here. I tried to imagine what it was like for him to grow up in this small town where everybody knew everybody else. His life had taken him so far from all of this. There was comfort in it. But tonight, I just felt lonely.

I picked up my phone. My mother called me twice today. DeShawn Sims's words pummeled through my brain. He knew things about me. Things Christian might have told him. But I knew in my heart that wasn't all of it.

Taking a breath to steel myself against what I knew would come, I punched in my mother's contact.

"Mercy!" she answered, breathless. "Why haven't you been returning my calls?"

I could have played the game. Apologized. Placated her. Managed her anxiety. That would be the easier path. This? This would be like walking uphill through wet cement.

I took the first step.

"I know what you've done," I said. "I met DeShawn Sims today."

I heard her take her own breath for courage.

"I don't know what you're talking about."

"Yes, you do. And you know he's a reporter for the Gossip Zone. The GZ! How many lies have they printed about you and Dad over the years? About Aunt Viv?"

"Don't talk to me about Viveca. You have no idea what you're talking about."

"You're not denying it."

"Mercy." She switched her tone, becoming softer, breathier. "Honey. I'm worried about you."

"I don't need you to worry about me. Tell me what you told Sims. He was asking a lot of questions about our family. You know what happens next. It happens every time on the anniversary of Viveca's death. Or the anniversary of Uncle Cy's death. Or whenever Dr. Milo's or any of dad's high-profile cases turns up on a true crime podcast."

"Don't call him that. He wasn't your uncle. He was a monster. Cyrus beat your Aunt Viv, almost killed her. He deserved what she did to him."

"You moved to Florida because you said you wanted your privacy. Hell, you divorced Dad for the same reason. And now you talk to a reporter for the GZ?"

"Mercy, everything I do, I do to protect you. Until you have children of your own, you'll never be able to understand."

"How is giving that vulture raw meat going to protect me? You know what he's after. He wants to tear Dad down. He could do real damage, Mom. If the Attorney Grievance Commission gets a hold of this. If Dad's clients get a hold of this..."

"I knew it," she screamed. "You've been there, what, a month? It's what he does, Mercy. He makes you feel sorry for him. Sucks you in. And before you know it, you've lost yourself. You make choices that aren't good for you. They're only good for him. I can hear it in your voice. You need to get on a plane and go far away. If you don't want to come back to Florida, fine. God, if you want to go back to Toledo of all places, fine. Don't take on his problems. They'll destroy you. Believe me, I know what this is."

I squeezed my eyes shut. "Mom, you haven't even asked me. You don't even know what's going on."

"What are you talking about?"

"DeShawn Sims. Do you know why he called me?"

"He promised me he wouldn't."

"Since when have you trusted the media?"

"He was supposed to talk to me only."

"You and my friend. He told you about Christian Foley, didn't he?"

"He said he had a source. Someone that could confirm your father is sick."

"And you were okay with that. Look, whatever your problems are with Dad, with your marriage, stop putting me in the middle of it."

"You put yourself in the middle of it."

"He's dead!" I blurted.

"What?"

"Christian Foley. He shot himself. After he talked to DeShawn Sims. That's why Sims reached out to me. Because Christian's dead and so his source dried up. He thought I'd be upset enough to pick up where you and Christian left off."

"Oh, honey. I'm sorry. I didn't know. Oh...baby. Please, just come home. That place? It's bad luck. It's cursed. Just leave. We'll figure it all out together. I promise."

For a moment, I was eight years old again. My parents had just had a screaming argument. The kind where my mother would lock herself in the bedroom and not come out for a day. And all I wanted to do was comfort her. Make sure she was okay.

"I have to go," I said. "I'm done talking about this. But I hope you're done talking to people like Sims. Because if some story shows up in the Gossip Zone or somewhere else...you won't hear from me again. I'll go no contact."

"You're just like him," she spat.

"Goodbye, Mom."

"Mercy, don't. I'm sorry. Okay. I won't talk to anybody. Just promise me you'll come home."

Before she could say anything else, I clicked off the call.

God. How could she do it? Neither of my parents could ever seem to understand that when they hurt each other, I was the one in the crossfire.

I slipped my phone in my back pocket and walked to the kitchen. I felt the urge to call Christian. We would commiserate about my narcissistic parents. Again, I felt the sting of betrayal. Every conversation I'd ever had with him. Every secret I shared. Had it all been fodder? Tiny treasures he could store away and use against me for what? A few dollars?

A loud bang drew my attention. It sounded like something crashed to the ground at the back of the house. I heard the back door rattle.

"Hello?" I called out.

No one should be here. It was almost nine o'clock. It would be fully dark in another twenty minutes. Mrs. Greenbaum's construction crew working on the other side of the duplex had left hours ago. The small backyard was fenced off. And yet...somebody was out there.

I moved away from the big picture window in the dining room. Fear snaked up my spine. Was the front door locked?

I saw movement. A shadow. The large hedge in the backyard swayed wildly to one side as if someone had pushed their way past it. Then, slowly, the knob on the back kitchen door turned.

"Shit," I whispered.

The door was locked. Whoever it was jiggled the knob. The door had a stained-glass pane at the center. One punch and it would shatter, allowing the intruder to bust his or her way in.

Adrenaline fueled me, and I ran to the front of the house. I'd left my small cross-body bag on the window seat. Grabbing it, I raced out the front door and into the street.

Instinct took over. I saw Adam Branch's townhouse down the street. He'd pointed it out just that once. It was a large, white Victorian on the corner lot. I ran for it.

A pair of cyclists passed by me as I pushed through Adam's gate. He was just coming out his front door as I ran up.

"Mercy?" he said. "Are you okay?"

"I...uh...well...you said if ..."

"What's wrong?" he said. He took me by the elbows.

"I was just at Mrs. Greenbaum's place. Somebody was trying to break in the back door."

Adam looked over my shoulder. His expression was fierce. "Are you hurt?"

"No. I feel a little silly. It's just...the backyard is closed off with a fence. Nobody should be back there."

"They most certainly should not. Did you call the police?"

"No. I just ran."

"Good. You did the right thing. Are you staying there? Liam told me about your friend. I'm so sorry."

"Thank you."

A rush of embarrassment went through me. I hadn't imagined the person in the backyard. But it seemed once again, I needed one of the Branch brothers to come to my rescue.

"Wait here," he said. "I'll go check it out."

"You shouldn't go alone."

"I won't," he said. Adam pulled out his cell phone. He punched in a number.

"Hey, Wade. Adam Branch. Can you send a crew over to Main and Waters? We think there might have been a prowler in the backyard of the Garden House. Marian Greenbaum's rental."

Adam pulled the phone away from his ear. "Did you get a description?"

"No. It was too dark. I just saw a shadow. I think it was a man. But I'm not sure."

"It's fine," Adam said. He clicked off. "Crew will be here in less than five minutes. They'll make sure everything's secure over there. They might have been trying to get into the other unit. She's got copper plumbing in there. I've been telling her for years to put in a security system. She's worried it'll conflict with the aesthetic."

A few minutes later, a Helene County Sheriff's cruiser pulled up. Two deputies got out. They introduced themselves as Pete Hackett and Drew Lohman. I explained to them what I'd seen and offered to walk back over to the house with them.

"We'll take care of it," Deputy Lohman said. "Thanks for calling it in."

"Do you need Mercy anymore?" Adam asked.

The deputies exchanged a look. "We can call you if we have any other questions. We know where to find you, Ms. Gale. Just try to have a good rest of your night."

I thanked them.

"Come on," Adam said. "You weren't planning on spending the night over there were you?"

"Not now," I said. "I think I just want to go home. To my dad's house."

Adam pulled out his phone again. He sent a quick text. "Come on," he said. "I'll walk you up to the pier. Liam can run you over in the Scarab. He's across the street at Dooley's."

"I hate to put him out. Or you."

"Mercy." Adam put his hands on my shoulders. "I told you to call me if you ever needed anything. Making arrangements to get you home safely is not putting me out."

"Thanks," I said.

We started walking. It really was a beautiful night. The moonlight shimmered off the water. The township had strung white fairy lights on all the bushes lining the sidewalks.

"Are you sure you're okay?" Adam asked. "You've had a hell of a week. Was Mr. Foley a very close friend of yours?"

"I thought so," I said. "Now I'm not sure."

Adam nodded. "I suppose we never can really know what's going on in someone's head."

"Everyone keeps asking me if I knew he was depressed."

"Mercy, even if you had, I'm not sure it would have mattered. If Mr. Foley made a decision…well…you know what they say. Depression lies. I'm just…it doesn't feel adequate. But I'm sorry."

As we reached the pier, Liam was already waiting, alarm on his face.

"Are you okay?" he said. Liam's gaze went from me to Adam, then darkened.

"I'm fine," I said.

"Someone might have been trying to break into Marian Greenbaum's rental."

"I've told her to install alarms on that house," Liam said, echoing his brother.

"It's being taken care of," Adam said. "Sheriff Gentry sent Hackett and Lohman. They're going to call me after they've done a sweep. But I imagine whoever it was is long gone by now."

"Probably," Liam said. He walked up the pier. His Scarab jet boat was moored in the first slip.

"Thanks again," I said to Adam. "I'm sorry if I disrupted your evening. Both of you, actually."

"And I said anytime. I mean it, Mercy." He stared at me with that intense, blue-eyed gaze. It could make a person feel like they were the only one in the world. He squeezed my hand, looked at his brother over my shoulder, then said goodbye.

Liam was vigorously untying the ropes on the Scarab. I went to help him. He held out his hand and helped me into the boat. He hopped in beside me and shoved off.

"If you're cold," he said, "there's a blanket under the seat." His tone was harsh and clipped.

"Thanks," I said. Liam revved the engine and pulled away from the dock.

"Are you sure you're okay?" he asked.

"Yes," I said, raising my voice over the engine. "But are you?"

He steered around the cove and gave me a pointed expression. "What do you mean?"

"You seem a little off. Um...pissed. I'm sorry. I should have just stayed at the office tonight. I really didn't want to bother you."

"I said I'd take you back tonight. I was waiting for your call."

"Oh." And then. "Liam, what is it?"

He shook his head. "Nothing."

"It doesn't seem like nothing. Did I do something?"

"*You* didn't do anything. It's just..."

"What?"

Liam slowed the engine, making things a lot quieter. He turned to me. "Mercy, I need you to be careful around my brother."

"Your brother? Why?"

Liam shook his head. He sped up again. My father's dock was within sight.

"Just nothing," Liam shouted over the engine.

He pulled alongside the dock. I reached over and grabbed one of the dock poles, helping bring the boat parallel. Liam cut the engine and grabbed a rope.

"What's got you miffed?" I said.

"Nothing. Honestly. I shouldn't have said anything."

"But you did."

"It's just...Adam likes you."

I reared back a bit. "Is that a bad thing?"

"Adam's complicated, okay? And he's always got an angle. You just need to know that. I really should have just kept my mouth shut. Forget it."

"Liam," I said, putting a hand on his shoulder. He went rigid beneath my touch. I'd spent enough of my life managing other people's emotions enough to know I shouldn't pry further.

"Thank you," I said. "It seems like I keep having reasons to do that. Thank you. You're a good friend, Liam. And I'm in sore need of those at the moment."

He met my eyes. Up the hill, I saw the front door open. Dad came out onto the porch. He waved down. Liam waved back, then he turned to me.

"I am your friend, Mercy. I'm glad you know that. Are you coming back into town tomorrow?"

"I'm sure I will," I said.

"Good. Maybe I'll catch you for lunch if you're not busy."

"I'd like that."

Things were easy between us again. Liam smiled. It lit his whole face. I reached down and unwound the rope from the pole. As Liam got back behind the wheel and started the engine, I shoved him off. He was still smiling as he sped away.

CHAPTER Sixteen

"She called you."

My father stood in the doorway of my office. He'd been unusually quiet this morning on the boat ride in. Normally, I would have tried to carry the conversation, draw him out. But today, I didn't have it in me.

"What?" I sat immersed in the last files I needed to archive. The Jeremy Holt boxes towered behind me. Sometimes it felt like they had a presence of their own. Staring at me. Judging me. Calling to me.

"Your mother," he said. "She called you. I'm sorry."

"Did she call you?"

"She sent me a text. Mercy, maybe she has a point. Maybe spending the summer here isn't the best thing for you. I don't need you to take care of me. I don't want to be the thing that holds you back."

"You're not."

"I'm sorry about your friend. You know you could have called me."

"It's handled. I had...Liam."

His expression didn't change. "He's had a tough time of it."

"Liam? Why?"

"It's maybe not so easy growing up in the shadow of someone else."

Was he talking about Liam or me?

"It took him a long time to find his own way. He's a talented graphic artist. But there wasn't much call for that in the family business. Hollis had a path laid out for him. I've been telling him for years to just let the boy make something for himself. Follow his own dreams. Save his scheming for Adam. He has a real chance to rise high in national politics. I don't think he knows it yet, but he's going to win next year. I can feel it in my bones. He does at least one term as governor, then he could go even higher. Hell, he might be president one day. Hollis just needs everyone in the family to be pulling in the same direction."

"How does Liam having his own business pull focus from Adam?"

My dad shrugged. "That family is just complicated."

"It is. But Adam and Liam have been good friends to me since I came to Helene. Liam said something last night though. He said... he told me to be careful of Adam. That he has his own agenda. I suppose maybe that's what you're talking about too. That it's been hard for Liam to step outside Adam's shadow."

"Yes," Dad said. "But you always do that."

"Do what?"

"Change the subject. I'm sorry about your mother and me. Sorry you're still getting caught up in our...issues."

"I didn't change the subject. You did."

He smiled. "You sure about that?"

Dad had always been easier to talk to in his own way. I'd never worried about his volatile moods. His narcissism was less overt, but still equally toxic.

"I'd like to get through the rest of these files today. Maybe I'll take the day off tomorrow if you don't mind."

"I don't mind. I want you to be happy here, Mercy."

"I know, Dad."

He stood there, watching me for a moment. Staying silent felt like betrayal. I couldn't tell him about DeShawn Sims. Not yet. Couldn't tell him that someone I believed was a friend might have sold him out to the Gossip Zone. There was a reason this man lived on a literal island. I didn't want to be like that. And yet...I understood the desire.

"Let me know if you want to grab lunch later," he said.

"What are you working on?"

"You worried I'm going to forget something?"

"No. I'm just...I'm here if you need any help. That's all."

"I've been a lawyer for a long time, Mercy. It's the only thing I know."

I'd heard him tell my mother that a thousand times. He knocked his ring against the door, smiled and walked back down the hall.

His ring. They'd been divorced for over a decade, and yet my father still wore his wedding ring.

When I went to look for my father for lunch a few hours later, he was gone.

"One of his old clients, Walt Sabo, called," Violet said. She was packing up her purse, heading down to the bistro at the corner. "He's buying up some property in Charlevoix. He wants your dad to come look at it."

"He's not a real estate lawyer," I said.

"Yeah, but he's the only person Walt trusts. See, that's the thing about all his active clients. They'll only talk to your dad. It's why I've wanted him to bring on a new partner for years. Help with the transition whenever he eventually retires."

"He's never going to retire," I said. "Not willingly. I'm just trying to make sure the decision isn't taken out of his hands."

"Honey, you do too much." Violet smiled. "Why don't you walk down with me? I'm heading over to Tina's Luncheonette. Tina's got her chicken salad croissants on special. They're delicious."

I was about to accept her invitation. Then my phone rang. I looked at the caller ID and immediately turned the screen so Violet couldn't see it.

"You go on ahead," I said. "I'm going to take this call. I've got a sandwich in the fridge. I was thinking of working through lunch and cutting out a little early today."

"Suit yourself," she said. Violet grabbed her purse and walked around the desk past me. I waited for the front door to shut before answering the call.

"Diane?" I said.

I was met with a hacking round of coughs. "Mercy," she said. "Can you meet this afternoon?"

"Diane, I can't go on anymore wild-goose chases. I know you want..."

"Please," she said. "It's just one more thing. I promise. Just an hour of your time. Then you won't hear from me again."

Her coughing got louder.

An hour. Dad would probably be gone at least that long. Violet too. I'd be back before either of them.

"I'll give you half an hour," I said.

"Come to my house," she said. "I'll text you the address."

I looked across the street. Luckily, Walt Sabo must have picked Dad up. The car was still parked in its usual spot next to the gazebo at the public park.

I grabbed the keys off the hook on the wall. "I'll be there in ten minutes," I said, checking Diane's address.

She clicked off instead of saying goodbye. Every instinct in me screamed this was another lost cause. A dead end. But I was determined to make good on what I'd told her. This would be the last time.

～

DIANE MET me at the door. She lived in a small, two-bedroom, one-bathroom ranch just outside of Helene in Ellsworth. There wasn't much out here. Another car was parked in her driveway, a beat-up Toyota Corolla with its back passenger door almost rusted out.

As I got to the front door, Diane called out through the screen. "It's open. We're in the back!"

We?

I walked through the house. Diane's small galley kitchen had green cabinets and butcher block countertops. With some fresh paint and a little sprucing up, it would be a mid-century modern gem. She had a shoebox on the counter filled with pill bottles. I saw Diane sitting with another woman on patio chairs outside.

I opened the slider. As my eyes adjusted to the bright sunlight, I recognized the other woman from her social media profile, and it stopped me in my tracks. Alicia Tate.

"What is this?" I said.

"Please sit down," Diane said. Her voice was hoarse. She sat with a woolen navy blanket wrapped around her legs. Her head was wrapped in a paisley scarf. She looked as if she'd lost weight since the last time I saw her.

I took the empty patio chair opposite the two women. Alicia Tate had yet to meet my eyes. She sat with her hands folded. She was slim. Pretty. She had toned and tanned arms and legs that looked like she spent an unhealthy amount of time in a tanning booth. She wore a red halter top and shorts with matching flip-flops. I couldn't help that my gaze went to her arms. I saw no tracks there.

"Alicia," I said. "You know I stopped by your house?"

Finally, she looked at me. "I wasn't home."

"I think you were."

"Alicia wants to talk to you," Diane said. "She has some questions of her own first."

"What about your boyfriend?" I asked. "You know he threatened me?"

"I'm not with Danny anymore," she said. "He's gone back to Phoenix where he's from."

"I'm going to leave the two of you alone," Diane said. Before I could stop her, She threw off her blanket, heaved herself out of her chair, clutched her stomach and started walking toward the slider.

"Diane," I said, rising. "Let me help you get..."

She lifted her hand. "I'm fine. I can still get where I need to go. I'll be in the living room. I like to nap in the recliner out there. It's easier on my lungs if I'm upright. If I'm asleep when you leave, please just show yourself out. Both of you."

"But..." Alicia started. Then she stopped herself. We waited until Diane was safely back in the house, then I turned to Alicia.

"Why are you doing this to her?"

The question seemed to startle her. "To her?"

"Yes. She seems to think you've got some story to tell. One that could change her son's situation. But that's not true."

Alicia stared at me, slack jawed.

"Look," I said. "I'm sorry about whatever your life has been. You've been mixed up with a lot of men who didn't treat you well. You probably could have used a friend. But right now, you're not helping Diane. This isn't bringing her peace."

"You think I'm lying?" she asked.

"I don't know you."

"Your father didn't either," she spat.

"What's that supposed to mean?"

"I'm used to people dismissing me. Treating me like I'm nothing. Just some junkie or crack whore or whatever you have to tell yourself to make yourself feel better about what your dad did."

"What did he do, exactly?"

"I don't need this. Believe me, if I could go back and change things, I never would have agreed to let Jeremy Holt stay in my spare bedroom. I wish I'd never met him. I wish I'd never met Diane. But I did. And I saw what I saw."

"What did you see?"

She looked down. "Jeremy didn't hurt that little girl. At least he didn't hurt her that weekend. He couldn't have hurt anybody. He was too gorked out of his mind on a bad batch of meth. If it weren't for me, he'd be dead. So would Dustin."

"Dustin," I said. "You mean Dustin Bolton? He testified against Jeremy. Told the cops he wasn't with him like Jeremy said he was."

"Yes. We were going together. Another of my biggest mistakes. Before him, I was only smoking pot sometimes. He got me hooked on the hard stuff. But that came later. Much later. Sixteen years ago, I was still pretty straight."

"Alicia, I think you better start from the beginning. What happened that weekend sixteen years ago when Savannah Holt disappeared?"

"They said Jeremy took that girl from her bedroom, spent time with her out in the woods. Killed her. Then strapped her to cement and threw her in Deadwater Lake. But that weekend? He wasn't even in Helene. We were staying in an apartment I rented just outside of Boyne City. Tiny little nothing town. Underwood.

It was me, Dustin, and Jeremy. Dustin scored some good stuff and the two of them got wasted. They were shooting off fireworks in the backyard. I thought they were going to light their stupid asses on fire."

"Fireworks. You had neighbors? Didn't anyone else report hearing anything?"

"No. Have you ever been out to Underwood?"

"No."

"It's different now. Re-gentrified or whatever you call it. I saw the other day the house two doors down from where I used to live went for over two hundred grand. But back then, nobody around there would have wanted to cooperate with cops. I don't think anybody was ever questioned. But Dustin and Jeremy never left the house. I found them both passed out. Jeremy would have choked on his own vomit if I hadn't turned him over. I'm the one who got them awake. Got them to throw up the rest of what they took. I've seen more people OD than you'd believe. Those boys would be dead if I hadn't been there. And none of them were capable of hurting a spider, let alone that little girl."

"Okay," I said.

"Nobody would listen to me. They thought I was garbage. I was a mess. Dustin was worse. And Jeremy? I think if he hadn't been arrested for killing Savannah, he'd have been dead himself inside a year. In a way, this whole thing saved his life. But for what though?"

"Alicia, I want to believe you. If you'd have come forward sixteen years ago..."

"We tried to. Dustin was going to go to the cops. He promised Jeremy he would. I was there. I heard him. Dustin hated cops. But he liked Jeremy. He didn't have a lot of friends and in his mind, he and Jeremy were brothers."

"You should have gone to my father. He was on Jeremy's side."

"Tell her what you told me," Diane said. I hadn't even heard her come back. She stood in the doorway, scowling at Alicia.

"I did go to your father. I wrote him that letter telling him everything I remembered about that weekend," Alicia said. "Dustin didn't want me to do that. He was too scared after what happened to him. But I thought maybe your dad could do something. But…he wasn't interested in what I had to say."

"What do you mean he wasn't interested?"

"I never heard from him. Then he sent me a letter saying he appreciated me reaching out but that he couldn't use me. He said because I'd been using, that the prosecutor would tear me up in court. He said he'd call me if he needed me, but I never heard from him."

"Do you have a copy of the letter he sent you?" I asked. "I'm familiar with his file. I saw nothing like that in it."

"You think I'm lying?" she said. "Why would I stick my neck out like this if I were lying?"

"I'm not saying you're lying. I'm just trying to understand the chronology here."

"I didn't keep the letter he sent," she said. "I tore it up after I read it."

It seemed too convenient. At the same time, I couldn't figure out her angle if she were lying about it. I didn't want to believe my father would just brush her off like that. It didn't sound like my dad. But as I sat there, I realized I really couldn't know.

"So, what about the police?" I asked. "You said Dustin was going to go to them."

She shook her head. "He was. Then he didn't. He talked to his own lawyer who told him he didn't have to. But he went to your dad and told him the truth. He was going to testify. Your dad promised he'd keep him safe. All I know is not long before the trial, one night Dustin didn't come home. For a week, I didn't know where he was. I looked everywhere for him. He was just gone. And the other guys in his crew. Remy. Blackie. Jerome. They just all went to ground or something after Jeremy got arrested. I don't know if they were all afraid Jeremy was going to cut some deal by ratting them out for something. But when Dustin finally showed up, everything changed. He said he wasn't going to help Jeremy anymore."

"Why?"

She held up her left hand and spread out her fingers. She curled a fist around her ring finger and pinky. "Because when he came back, somebody had cut these two fingers off with a meat cleaver. And his chest was melted. It had these rings on it. Somebody had held him against the burners on an electric stove."

It made my stomach turn, imagining what that might have been like. "Who did that?"

She shook her head. "He wouldn't say. And he wouldn't tell me where he and the other guys had been hiding out all that time. But he said Jeremy was on his own and we were getting farther away."

"You're saying someone tortured Dustin to lie about Jeremy's alibi under oath? Dustin told you that?"

She nodded. "Just that one time. Then he never talked about it again. If I tried to ask questions, he'd hit me. That went on for a long time. I stayed with Dustin for a few months. Then finally, I was the one who OD'd. I woke up in the hospital and Dustin never came for me. My brother did. I went home to Midland, and I stayed there."

"Did you know Dustin was going to perjure himself against Jeremy?"

"I thought he might. But by then, there was no need for me to stick around. I didn't want to end up like Dustin. I tried to do the right thing. Your dad didn't want my help. And I was way too deep into my own problems. It took me a lot of years to really turn myself around. In some ways, I'm still trying. But this thing with Jeremy is wrong. He didn't kill his sister. Now, I have a son of my own. He's with his dad right now down in Ohio. But Diane's dying. Jeremy is her son. I just...I have to tell the truth. How can I teach my son to do the right thing if I'm not willing to do it myself?"

"Why now?" I asked. "Why come forward now, after all this time?"

"Because of Ms. Benning. It's like I said, I want to set an example for my son. I want to make up for all the people I hurt because of my addiction. I'm working my steps. And if I can help give Diane her son back before she leaves this earth, that's worth doing."

It was a lot to take in. But the thing was, I think I believed her. There was no reason for Alicia Tate to pursue this on some whim. She could be wrong. She'd admitted she was using. Who's to say she didn't have her weekends messed up?

"I kept these," she said. Alicia pulled out her phone. She clicked it open and swiped up. She handed it to me.

I wasn't prepared for what I saw. It was a young man with stringy brown hair. He had these burns on his chest. It was awful. The circular patterns she described, like the rings on an electric stove.

"That's what they did to him," she said. "Dustin wasn't a good guy. But not even he deserved something like that. And he was just trying to tell the truth."

"So why stick your neck out?" I said. I took my phone out and snapped pictures of the ones on her phone. "Where is Dustin now?"

"Just outside of Detroit," she said. "Last I heard anyway. But I think he'll talk to you. He was working at a body shop in Highland Park. I can write the name. I just can't live like this anymore. Knowing there's a guy in jail for something he didn't do."

She took her phone back and grabbed a scrap of paper on the table beside her. She wrote a number and handed it to me.

"So why didn't you come to the door that day when I came to your house?" I asked.

She stared at me. "You really don't know, do you?"

"No."

"Somebody was following you. Danny chased him down the street after you left."

Followed. My heart raced. Someone had tried to break into the townhouse last night.

"Did Danny get a description? Call the police?"

"Danny doesn't like talking to the cops, either. But he got this."

Alicia swiped her phone's screen again and handed it back to me. The air went out of my lungs. It was a grainy picture. The guy was sitting behind the wheel of his car. His face was contorted in rage as he turned to the camera. If someone didn't know him as well as I thought I did, they might not have recognized him. But I did.

"This was the man following me?" I asked. "You're sure?"

"Yep. Danny caught him at the stop sign right after he told you to leave. He'd been circling my house for about ten minutes before you got there."

I looked down at the phone again. There, staring up at me, was Christian.

CHAPTER
Seventeen

Dad was back in the office when I got there. He had a far-off look on his face. He didn't even seem to hear me when I knocked on the door to his office.

"Dad?"

He startled, snapping to attention. Then he found a smile for me. "Mercy! I don't know where my head was. Come in. I was looking for you before. I wanted to see if you felt like going to court with me in the morning."

"You have nothing scheduled," I said. "You have oral arguments on the Chaney appeal but that's not for another week."

He frowned. "Maybe you're right."

I came fully into the office. "Violet set up that new daily calendar for you. It's on your desk blotter. Here."

I moved a mess of papers he'd spread out on the top of his desk. Violet's bold pink lettering marked off the days of the month. She had the Chaney appeal date circled for late next week.

"I was looking for you," he said.

"I'm here. I went to Diane Benning's house. She's not doing very well, Dad. They've suspended her chemo treatments. It's hard to put an expiration date on somebody, but she probably won't survive to the end of the year."

"I'll have to see Jeremy," he said.

"He knows."

Dad nodded. Violet came to the doorway holding a cup of coffee in one hand and a bagel on a plate in the other.

"Tom," she said. "You skipped lunch. I brought this back from the bakery. Fresh baked this morning. Just cream cheese."

"You should eat," I said to my father. He looked at the two of us like we'd sprouted horns. Undeterred, Violet put my dad's lunch in front of him.

"Dad, I saw Diane Benning today." He looked at me, unfocused and I knew he'd already lost what I told him before.

"It's harder when he hasn't eaten," Violet said. "Tom, eat."

My father grabbed the bagel and took an angry bite out of it. "Happy?" he said while chewing.

"Be nice," I said. "You'd be screwed without Violet."

"Hmmm. Tell me about Diane Benning."

"Tom, I've told her a thousand times. That's a rabbit hole that never ends. What did she rope you into this time?"

"Nothing," I said. "She had a visitor. Alicia Tate was there."

No recognition on my dad's face.

"Alicia Tate," I repeated. "Dad, we've got to talk about her. She told me a disturbing story about the weekend Savannah Holt went missing. She corroborates Jeremy's alibi."

"So why didn't she come forward sixteen years ago?" Violet said. She took a seat beside me in front of my dad's desk. I know she wanted to make sure Dad ate his entire bagel.

"She said she tried to. She sent you a letter detailing everything she knew. Dad, she said you sent her a letter to discourage her. Do you know why you would have done that?"

My dad gave me another blank stare.

Violet gave me a pained look.

"But Alicia Tate specifically," I said. "I couldn't find a single note in your files about her. You were meticulous. You wrote the dates and times of every witness you spoke with. I couldn't find her name. I couldn't find these letters she's talking about. Not the one she wrote you or the one she claims you wrote her."

"Then she's lying that she sent one. Mercy, it was a long time ago. Are you accusing me of something?" Dad asked.

"No. I'm just trying to understand. Alicia said...she showed me some disturbing photographs on her phone. Her boyfriend was Dustin Bolton. Do you remember that name?"

"Of course I do. That's the piece of crap Jeremy was crashing with. He went south on Jeremy. Backed up Jeremy's alibi at first. Then he turned on him. Claimed Jeremy asked him to lie for him on the witness stand. That, more than anything, is why we lost that case. He changed his whole story."

"That's right. Only...these photographs. Didn't you ever wonder why? Alicia said somebody got to Dustin. He was tortured. They cut off two of his fingers and held his chest to a hot stove. Alicia says that's why he changed his story."

"Well, that sounds pretty convenient."

"Dad, Alicia says she can put me in touch with Dustin Bolton now. She knows where to find him."

"To what end?" Violet said. "Mercy, even if these two will swear to Jeremy's alibi, they have credibility issues. They did then. Now... sixteen years later?"

"Don't you think it's at least worth asking some questions?" I said.

"She really got to you, didn't she?" Dad said. "Mercy, Jeremy doesn't want this. He doesn't want to put his mother through any more heartache."

"He doesn't want to spend the rest of his life in prison for something he didn't do. Dad, Jeremy, has literally nothing left to lose. I know you believe he's innocent. What if he is?"

Maybe I should have told him about Christian's involvement in all of this. But something made me stop. I wanted to believe everything my father told me. That he'd pursued every lead. Tried to track down Dustin and Alicia. That my father hadn't blown her off when she tried to tell her story. Or that she'd been lying all along. But the simple fact was DeShawn Sims believed my father had taken a dive during Jeremy Holt's trial. And I couldn't trust that Dad was accurately remembering what happened.

"What do you want me to say, Mercy?"

"I want to pursue this. I want to talk to Dustin Bolton. And it has to be me. Her reasons may be without merit, but Alicia Tate doesn't trust you. Diane Benning still does. So let me be the middleman. Let me chase down this last lead so Diane Benning can die knowing we truly did everything we could for her son."

CHAPTER SEVENTEEN

"No," my father said.

"No?" Violet and I said it together.

"No," he repeated. "Mercy, you don't know these people. You've lived a pretty sheltered life. Your mother and I have protected you. But this guy? Dustin Bolton? You can't go see him. You can't get yourself on his radar. And you certainly can't talk to him by yourself. It's too dangerous."

"I'm not stupid. I'm not naïve, and I'm not sheltered like you think I am. This isn't my first murder case, either. I interned for the Maumee County prosecutor's office last summer. I helped prosecute a major murder trial."

"One case?" Dad said. "Mercy..."

"Enough. Like it or not, Alicia Tate only wants to talk to me. I'm going to talk to Dustin Bolton. If his story holds up, we can decide what to do about it. But if he was beaten to change his story or keep silent, the prosecutor's office needs to know that. If he's willing to testify now..."

"It'll be too late," Dad said.

"Maybe not. And I'm not asking for your permission."

I rose out of my chair. My father's face turned purple. But he didn't yell. I turned on my heel and left the office, not giving him the chance to say anything else.

I went back to my office and pulled out my phone. I sent a text to Alicia Tate.

> If you can reach out to Dustin, tell him I'm coming down to talk to him. It's going to be okay, Alicia. You can trust me.

I hit send. I had two unread texts on my phone. One was from DeShawn Sims. The other from Liam Branch. I hovered my finger over the text from Sims. Then I pulled up his contact number and blocked it.

Violet knocked on my door. "You got a second?"

"I've got all day."

"Mercy, are you sure you know what you're doing?"

"What do you mean?"

"He's not gonna let you see it, but this whole thing, dredging up the Holt case, it's very upsetting for your dad. He felt that loss deeply. Mercy, it almost destroyed him."

"It didn't just destroy him," I said. "Violet, you know the Holt case is the reason my parents got divorced?"

She came into my office and took a seat. "No, it wasn't."

"Yes, it was. He promised my mother he wouldn't take any more murder trials. He was an absent father because of his job, Violet. My mother had had enough. But when Jeremy got arrested, my father couldn't say no. He chose this case over our family. And it was the last straw. She filed for divorce the same day he filed his appearance as Jeremy's lawyer."

"Well, that's a neat little story you've told yourself. But it's not true. Your parents decided they were done trying a long time before the Holt case came along. And look, I'm not taking sides here. Your father would have been a hard man to be married to. But it takes two people to make a marriage work. And it takes two people to fail at it."

"Violet, I have to talk to this guy. Those pictures Alicia showed me? It's one of the worst things I've ever seen."

"And you're absolutely one hundred percent sure that was to do with his testimony on Holt? Or is that just what Dustin Bolton wanted Alicia to believe?"

"I don't know," I said. "But I'm going to meet with him. That's all."

"Oh, honey. You're just like him. I think that's the part that's been hardest for your mother. You're not like her. You're him. Driven. Singular focus. And I know it's pointless to try to change your mind. So be careful."

"I am."

"Your father thinks Jeremy's innocent. When you're done talking to Bolton, maybe it would be good for you to talk to someone who believes he's guilty. Someone who knows this case as well as your dad."

"Who do you mean?"

"You should talk to Mac Henderson. The detective who worked this case. He'll give you a different perspective. He's a good man. Just like your dad."

"Maybe I will."

"Just make sure you really understand why you're doing this." Violet rose, not giving me the chance to ask her what she meant. She closed the door behind her.

Make sure you really understand why you're doing this. Why was I doing this?

My phone rang. Liam.

"Hi," I said, hitting the speaker button.

"I'm sorry if I'm bothering you. I wanted to swing by and grab lunch with you if you were free, but you'd already left the office."

"I'm back now. But I'll take a rain check on lunch."

"I figured you could use some fresh air."

"I could. How about tomorrow?"

"Well...actually...things have changed a bit. I was kind of hoping you'd be willing to upgrade."

"Upgrade?"

"Tomorrow night. I'm getting roped into another fundraising event for my brother. I just don't think I can stomach another one of these by myself. So, I was hoping you'd do me a huge favor and be my plus-one."

I laughed. "Boy, you're not really selling me."

"Come on," he said. "Consider this me calling in the favor you said you owed me."

"I don't recall saying any such thing," I smiled. Though we both knew I owed Liam big time.

"You're just going to sit by the window on that dreary little island like some princess locked in a tower. So, I'm asking you. Rapunzel, let down your hair. For one night anyway. We'll make an appearance. Cut out early. Then I'll take you anywhere else you'd rather go."

"Liam, are you asking me out on a date?" I meant it half-jokingly. But the second I said it, things felt more serious. I felt a little flutter of heat through my core.

"I think maybe I am," he said.

"Well, then I think maybe I'm saying yes."

"Perfect. Then I'm hanging up before you have a chance to change your mind."

"Is this a black-tie affair?"

"Slightly less formal. But I suppose I'll have to show up in a suit and tie. I'll pick you up at seven at your Dad's boat slip on the island. The event's at one of the yacht clubs on Beaver Island."

"So, we're traveling by water," I said.

"Unless you're an excellent swimmer," he teased.

"All right. Seven."

"See you then," he said. I clicked off.

The urge to text Christian nearly overwhelmed me. For an instant, it was hard to catch my breath. I pulled up the last picture I'd taken of him on my phone. It was a shot of the two of us. We'd gone to a baseball game in Toledo a few months ago before school let out. He was laughing. The local team's mascot, some sort of chicken, had its arm around Christian.

We were happy. Laughing. Now, I knew all of it had been a lie.

CHAPTER
Eighteen

I WORE the other nice dress I packed when I came to Helene. A black halter that hit just at the knee. I fussed about my shoes but settled on a pair of red sandals. I grabbed a wrap and headed downstairs. Violet had made a tuna casserole for Dad. The buzzer went off in the oven. He'd been in his study for the last hour.

"Dad?" I called out. I slid my hand into an oven mitt and pulled out the glass dish. It smelled good. Everything Violet made was delicious. Not healthy, but delicious. I grabbed a wooden spoon from the drawer and pulled out a plate and fork.

"Dad?" I called again. "Your dinner's ready. Liam's going to be here in a few minutes. Do you want a tossed salad or anything to go with this?"

I heard him grumble. Something fell to the floor in the study.

"Dad?" I rushed to the hallway. Dad came out looking disheveled.

"Damn lamp. The ceramic cracked. I tried to glue it last fall, but it didn't hold."

"Are you okay?"

My father walked into the hallway, meeting me halfway. He shook his right hand and popped his index finger into his mouth.

"Did you cut yourself?"

He mumbled something unintelligible and walked with me into the light of the kitchen. I reached for his hand, wanting to see how bad the damage was. He jerked it away.

"I'm not a toddler. It's just a scratch."

"I'm just trying to help."

He plopped himself on one of the stools at the island. I grabbed the First Aid kit he kept under the sink. When I turned around, my father's face fell. His eyes seemed to go in and out of focus. I took a step toward him. I put the First Aid kit on the counter.

"Doesn't look like you're going to bleed out at least," I said. "Let me get that cleaned up."

I pulled a bottle of iodine out of the box and grabbed a paper towel. My father held that strange look on his face as I dabbed at his small cut.

"Ow!" He jerked it away.

"I know it stings. But quit being such a baby," I reached for him again. My father jerked his hand away with force.

"Viveca, for once in your life would you just do what I tell you?"

He jumped off the stool. There was a glass sitting on the counter next to him. Dad swiped his hand across it, sending it crashing to the tile floor and shattering it.

"Dad!"

He froze. Then he trembled.

"Dad?"

He blinked, trying to focus. I took a step toward him. He recoiled as if he were seeing a ghost. In his mind, maybe he was.

"Dad," I said, my voice soft. "You're not wearing shoes. I'm afraid you're going to cut your foot on top of everything else. Just sit at the table while I get this cleaned up."

He stared at me slack-jawed, but he did what I asked. I grabbed his broom and dustpan from the closet and cleaned up the glass. By the time I came back from the garage where he kept the trash can, my father seemed more himself.

"I'm sorry," he said. "I'm a klutz."

"It's okay. It's just broken glass." And a broken lamp. I went to his study with the broom and dustpan and cleaned up that mess, too.

As I walked back to the kitchen, there was a knock at the front door. My eyes went to the clock in the hall. It was seven fifteen. I was late. I was supposed to meet Liam down at the dock.

He was standing at the front door in a sharp black suit and red tie.

"We match," I said, smiling. His eyes went down the length of me, seeing my shoes.

"The broom's a nice touch," he said.

I smiled. "I figured I'd use my own transportation."

"Does that make you a good witch or a bad witch?"

"Mercy!" Dad called out. "Who's out there?"

"Come on in," I said, opening the door wider.

I leaned the broom and dustpan against the wall, and Liam followed me back to the kitchen.

"Wow," he said, marveling at the fieldstone fireplace that was the centerpiece of the room. "It's been years since I've been out here. Tom, you've done a hell of a job on the renovations."

"Took ten years," Dad said. "Contractors tried to gouge me. Then the township got overly involved."

"I remember," Liam said. "Did you end up suing the zoning board?"

"Almost. We worked it out on the golf course."

"Good plan," Liam said.

"Actually, your brother was helpful in that regard. Steve Anspaugh was the holdout. He didn't want me to build the boat house. Said it would mess with the historical aesthetic or something like that. Adam sweet-talked him. I think he made a campaign donation too, but I don't think I was supposed to know about that."

Liam stared up at the cathedral ceiling. The massive window, with an unobstructed view of the bay, was a stunner.

"My brother has a way of getting what he wants."

"You sure you're going to be okay?" I asked.

My father had already gotten his own bandage out of the First Aid kit and wrapped his finger. I wasn't sure I wanted to leave him on his own now. For a moment, he had looked at me and only seen my dead aunt. Dad seemed like he'd been in a different reality in his mind for that brief instant.

"I'm fine. She treats me like a baby."

"Sometimes you act like one."

My father waved a dismissive hand. Then he busied himself getting a plate and scooping himself a generous helping of Violet's tuna casserole.

"We won't be late," I said. "At least I don't think so."

"We won't," Liam answered. "To be honest, I was just thinking of making an appearance to satisfy the family. Then we can cut out and get dessert or something."

"Tell Adam my check is in the mail," Dad said, his mouth full.

"Consider yourself lucky," Liam answered. "I hate going to these things. I don't know how Adam does it. A bunch of fake people with obscene amounts of money. He turns into a different person."

"He plays the game," Dad said. "And he's good at it. I'd rather have him on my side than against it."

"It's good to have Adam on your side," Liam said. His expression grew dark though. It was the same look he had when he gave me that cryptic warning about his brother.

"Are you ready to go?" I asked.

"Whenever you are."

"Let me just figure out where I put my wrap."

"You might want to take something heavier than just a wrap," Liam said. "There's a good breeze out over the lake tonight."

"A coat," I said. "Shoot. I don't think I have a coat. Hang on."

I went to the hall closet. My father had a few things in it that still belonged to my mother. One of them was a black peacoat that no longer fit her. I'd co-opted it a few years back. Luckily, my dad saved just about everything. I found it right where I expected it.

Liam came to me and held the coat out for me as I slipped one arm through.

"Sandra!" Dad called out. I froze. Liam met my eyes and mouthed my mother's name.

"Hang on," I said. I slipped the coat back off and went into the kitchen. Dad was standing over the sink, his hand shaking. He'd ripped the bandage off his finger and blood flowed down it.

"Dad," I said. "You've opened it up again."

"I didn't mean to," he said. "Mercy was just playing in the yard. I was watching her the whole time. I never took my eyes off of her."

"Dad. It's me. I'm Mercy."

"Is he okay?" Liam said.

My father stared at me but didn't see me. He was replaying something else in his mind.

"Dad!"

He kept shaking his head. "Come on. Let's get you into your chair in the living room."

My father went with me, clinging to my arm. He sank into his recliner in front of the fireplace. "Dad," I said. "Look at me. You're tired. I should have made you dinner a while ago."

Liam stood in the kitchen. He turned and grabbed the plate of food Dad had set out for himself. He brought it and cleared a space on the end table next to my father.

"Thanks," I said. I picked up the fork. Seeing me, my father wrenched the fork out of my hand.

"I'm not a child. I can damn well feed myself."

I was on my knees in front of him. "Dad? Do you know who I am?"

He blinked. Fear filled his eyes, then anger. "Of course I know who you are. Don't be so dramatic, Mercy." He reached for the plate, stabbed his fork through some pasta noodles and ate them.

I rose. Liam stood in the entryway to the kitchen, giving us space. I went to him.

"Mercy," he said. "We don't have to go to this thing. It's not important."

My father grabbed his remote and turned on a cable news channel. He angrily stabbed his fork into the tuna casserole.

"I don't think I should leave him," I said. "Liam, I'm sorry. You went to all this trouble."

He smiled. "Are you kidding? You're giving me an excuse not to go to one of my brother's boring fundraiser dinners. I should thank you."

He pulled out his cell phone and sent a quick text, then pocketed it.

"Oh," I said. "Liam, I don't want you to…"

He put a hand up. "It's nobody's business. I just texted my father, telling him I wasn't feeling good. Something I ate."

"And you think he's gonna buy that?"

"I don't think I care."

I looked behind him. Violet had made enough tuna casserole to feed a dozen people.

"Well," I said. "I'd say we're overdressed, but how do you feel about tuna casserole?"

"What a coincidence. I had a craving."

Laughing, I grabbed two plates and two forks from the cupboard. Liam joined me on the kitchen island. We ate in friendly silence for a few minutes. My father was content in the other room. I poured Liam and myself a glass of white wine.

"I'm going to bed," Dad called out. "I'm tired. It's been a long damn day."

I slid off my stool. "Can I get you anything?"

Dad scowled at me. He waved a hand and went down the hallway to his bedroom. When I heard the door shut, I turned back to Liam.

"He just gets cranky some evenings."

"Mercy," Liam said. "Is he okay?"

"Yes, he's fine." My voice came out an octave higher than usual. I knew Liam wasn't buying it.

"It's okay if he isn't," he said. "I mean...it's something we've all been worried about. Tom...he seems to lose his bearings from time to time. Forgets where he is."

I dropped my chin. "I know."

Liam reached for me, putting a gentle hand on my forearm. "It's okay. I hope you realize I'm a friend. Tom...your dad...he matters, okay?"

I felt a rush of tears threatening to spill. I took a quick breath, pushing them back. "Thank you. He has his good days and his bad days. It seems to get worse in the evening."

"I see. Is there anything I can do?"

"You're doing it."

"This is why you came back to Helene, isn't it?"

I closed my eyes. Answering Liam's question went against everything I'd been brought up to guard against. Don't tell the family secrets. Don't trust anyone.

"Yes," I finally said. "I was worried about him. He didn't seem like himself when I talked to him."

"Yeah. And it's just you? Where's your brother in all of this?"

"We don't...Everett and I just aren't particularly close. I mean he's over twenty years older than me. He wasn't around when I was little. Different moms. Different states."

"But does he know? Regardless of how close the two of you are, Everett's Tom's son, too."

"Yeah. Well...I'm pretty sure if Everett saw my number in his phone, he wouldn't pick up."

"It's his loss. Brothers can be...complicated."

"I really am sorry I kept you away from your obligation."

"Come on," Liam said. "Why don't we get some air? It's still a nice night. Do you want to check in on your dad?"

"Can you give me just a few minutes?"

"Sure."

I walked quietly down the hall. Dad's door was shut, but I could hear him snoring already. I knocked softly with my index finger.

"Dad?"

He kept on snoring. I carefully opened the door a crack. Dad lay stretched out on his bed, the covers pulled up to his chin. But he was out. I closed the door and went back to the kitchen.

"He's fine," I said. "Sleeping like the dead." I sucked in a breath, stunned by my own poor choice of metaphor.

"Come on," Liam said, undeterred. "Let's take a walk."

I grabbed my dad's old Navy sweatshirt off a peg near the back door and put it on. As soon as we walked outside, I was glad I did. Though it was mild, there was a chill in the air.

Liam walked down the stone path toward the gazebo by the water. I slipped off my sandals and went barefoot. It was a full moon tonight. I could see the lights of two freighters in the distance.

"You know," Liam said. "When you come out here, it makes all the sense in the world why your dad wanted to buy this place."

Liam took a seat on the bench. I joined him.

"He got into a bidding war with my father for the island. It had been on the market for years. Hollis thought he had it locked up."

"I didn't know that."

"It was a sore spot between them for a while. But then when your father made his plans for the place known...my father became one of his biggest allies. Hollis just wanted to make sure nobody was going to come along and screw this place up."

"My mother was furious when he bought it. She said it was a money pit."

Liam laughed. "It was."

"But he had a vision. It was the only thing he wanted from the divorce. He gave up the house in Florida. The beach house in Monterrey. Plus, she got a huge cash settlement and monthly support for me. I could never understand it. How much money does a person need? I hated him for it for a long time. This place felt like another way for my dad to wall himself off from us."

"I can see why it would seem like that."

"Now? I'm worried. It feels like he's losing a little more of himself every day. He's trying to hold on and it's all just slipping out of his grasp."

"I'm glad you came," he said. "For your dad. But also...because I'm enjoying getting to know you."

I looked up at him. Liam really was handsome. He had a darker look than Adam. Deeper set eyes. A thicker brow that lent him an almost sinister air. But when he fixed his gaze on me, just like when Adam did it, it made me feel like I was the only other person in the world.

"I'm enjoying getting to know you, too. And it seems you have a real knack for showing up just when I need a friend the most."

He smiled. "A friend. Would it freak you out if I was hoping for something more?"

My breath caught. Maybe it was a mixture of the wine and moonlight. But just then, I wanted nothing more than to cling to this and let him be everything. Even as I knew, every time I let someone in like that, I was always the first to blink.

Liam caught my chin between his fingers and tilted my head up to meet his.

"Mercy," he whispered. Then his lips met mine. He smelled good. He tasted good. His kiss was soft at first, then grew more urgent. I sank into it. Heat flared through me. I slid my hands up, snaking my fingers through his thick, dark hair. I felt like I could drown in him.

He left me gasping as we both came up for air. Liam ran a gentle thumb over my cheekbone.

"I'm glad you're here," he said.

"Me too."

"I hope you know you can count on me. And you can trust me. Whatever is going on with your father, I want to help. I get the impression you don't let too many people do that. Help you."

"No," I said.

"Well, I care. I just want you to know that."

"Liam," I said. "Thank you. It's just...it's hard. Because you're right. I'm not used to asking people for help. I don't trust very many. Things with my parents...well...a lot of people have had motives that weren't pure when it comes to us."

Liam smiled. "Yeah. I know a little something about that. Being a Branch isn't the easiest thing in the world."

"I guess maybe you're the one person who knows exactly what I mean."

He threaded his fingers through mine. "I don't want anything from you, Mercy. I don't have an agenda. Other than wanting to be close to you. But I'm also not in a hurry. It's enough you let me onto the island tonight."

"Okay," I said.

"But I know something's going on. Something that's got you worried."

"Liam..."

He put a hand up. "You don't have to tell me what it is. But...if there's ever a time...Mercy. I just don't want you to do anything that could get you hurt. I can be there for you. No questions asked. Okay?"

The moonlight shimmered in his eyes. I badly wanted him to kiss me again. At the same time, I wasn't sure I was ready for where that could lead. Not yet.

"Okay," I said. "I appreciate that more than you know."

"Good," he said, smiling. Then, with his hand in mine, we walked back up to the dock together. He kissed me one more time. Slower. Deeper. Then he climbed in his boat and headed back to the mainland.

CHAPTER Nineteen

IF IT WEREN'T for Dustin Bolton's missing fingers, I probably wouldn't have recognized him. He was a hundred pounds heavier than the boy who stared fiercely at the camera during his most recent mugshot fifteen years ago. The receptionist at McClintock Body Shop in Highland Park absently pointed over her shoulder when I asked her if Bolton was working.

Bolton stood over the open hood of a Buick Regal.

"Dustin?" I said. He could have told me to get lost. Hell, he could have even told me I had the wrong guy, despite his name tag embroidered into his blue overalls. Instead, he straightened, wiped his hands on a shop towel and scowled at me.

"Who's asking?"

"My name is Mercy Gale," I said. "I'm sorry to bother you at work like this, but it was the only way I knew how to find you."

This got us looks from some of the other mechanics in the garage. Only one older guy in the back kept on staring as Dustin stepped away from the Buick and out into the parking lot. He hadn't told me to go to hell yet, so I followed him.

Bolton pulled a cigarette out of his front pocket and lit it.

"Mercy Gale," he said. "Am I supposed to know you?"

"No. My father is...I work for Jeremy Holt. Do you remember him?"

I realized that was a stupid question. Bolton raised a brow. "Yeah. I remember him."

"Is there someplace we can talk?"

"You have as long as I take to finish this cigarette unless you piss me off before that."

"That's fair. I work for Jeremy Holt. My father was his...*is* his lawyer. I was hoping I could ask you a few questions about the time you knew Jeremy."

"That was a long time ago. And I don't remember a lot about it."

"I was told you do."

"Let me guess, this is Alicia. She never knew when to keep her mouth shut."

"I think you already know what she told me. What she told my father. I'd like to hear your side of it."

He took another drag of his cigarette and watched the traffic going by.

"Mr. Bolton, Jeremy Holt has been in prison for almost sixteen years. He's serving a life sentence. Do you believe he killed that girl?"

"Doesn't matter what I believe. Alicia shouldn't have sent you here. In fact, Alicia should keep my name out of her mouth."

"If Jeremy was with you. If you're his alibi..."

"I'm not his alibi. You wasted both our time coming out here."

"I don't think I did. Jeremy will die in prison if I can't get the truth out."

Another drag of the cigarette. Bolton stared straight ahead.

"That's not my problem."

"Were you with him the weekend Savannah Holt disappeared? Look. Alicia showed me some pretty disturbing pictures. I know you paid a pretty heavy price for knowing what you know. You have no reason to trust me. But if I can help ensure that never happens again..."

Bolton flicked his cigarette to the ground and stubbed it out. "You? How you gonna do that?"

"I told you who my father is. He's not without resources or connections."

"Whatever, lady. You don't even know what you don't know."

"So, enlighten me."

He pushed off the wall and turned towards me. "Why don't you ask Alicia? Did she tell you the real reason she's so interested in Jeremy Holt?"

"She knows he didn't kill his sister. And she knows someone tried to keep you from talking to the police about it. What happened to you, Dustin? Who gave you those scars I know you have on your chest? Was it because someone had a vested interest in making sure Jeremy's the one who got pinned for Savannah's murder?"

"Go to hell," he said. "And tell Alicia she can go right along with you. Alicia's been obsessed with Jeremy for sixteen years. She was screwing him behind my back. I bet she didn't tell you that, did she? She'd do or say anything for that guy. How many times has she gone to see him while he's been inside?"

I couldn't answer. I tried to keep my face neutral so Bolton wouldn't see the surprise I felt. No. Alicia had not shared that little tidbit with me if it was true. Neither had Jeremy.

"It doesn't matter," I said. "That's all in the past, isn't it? Alicia hasn't been your girlfriend for a very long time. You've both moved on with your lives. Only Jeremy can't. He's still paying for what happened that weekend. He was your friend once. No matter what he and Alicia might have done behind your back, do you really want to see him rot in prison for something he didn't do?"

"We're done talking," he said. "Don't come back here. I'm not part of this."

"Dustin…"

He turned and charged me, jabbing a finger into my shoulder. "You need to keep my name out of your mouth, too. Jeremy Holt's problems aren't my problems. I've got a decent life now. A family. I'm not part of this anymore."

He pushed me back. I held my ground. But I would not chase after him. Bolton stormed off and disappeared down a hallway at the back of the shop.

I let out a breath. Though I hoped things would go differently, I can't say his reaction was a surprise. But Alicia.

I went to my car and slid behind the wheel. Pulling out my phone, I punched in Violet's cell phone number.

"What's up, Buttercup?" she answered.

"This is going to sound like a strange request, maybe. But is there any way we can find out how many times someone has visited Jeremy Holt in prison in recent years?"

"Shouldn't be too hard," she said without missing a beat. "Your dad's still his attorney of record. We can put in a request."

"Violet...I'd rather my dad not know I'm asking. Not yet."

"Oh, honey, I can sign Tom's name better than he can at this point."

"Yeah. Maybe that's not something I should know," I laughed. "But thanks."

"Might take a day or two to get an answer. Is there somebody in particular you've got a hair up your ass about?"

"Yeah. Alicia Tate."

I could hear Violet sigh through the phone. "Kiddo, that girl's like a bad penny."

"I know. That's sort of what I'm trying to figure out."

"All right," she said. "I'll make the request. Are you coming in today? Your dad's asking about you."

"How's he doing today?" Dad woke up this morning in a good mood. He seemed to have no memory of what troubled him last night.

"He's having a decent day," she said. "I just ordered him a gyro salad from Gamma's. I was just about to go pick it up. Do you want anything? Are you going to be back soon?"

A shadow crossed in front of me. The older man I'd seen at the back of the body shop stood on the passenger side of my car. He rapped on the window with his finger.

"Uh...nothing for me, thanks," I said to Violet. "I'm just doing some shopping in Traverse City. I probably won't be back until after five. Tell Dad not to wait for me. I can crash at the office."

"Okay."

I clicked off and hit the window button, opening it.

"May I help you?" I said. The old man leaned into the window.

"Don't have a lot of time. Why don't we take a ride around the block?"

"Who are you?"

He looked toward the front door of the body shop. "Dustin Bolton."

"I'm sorry?"

"Senior."

"Okaaay. Listen, your son made things clear. I didn't come here to make any trouble for anyone."

"Let's talk. Just once around the block. You're the one driving. It ain't like I'm trying to kidnap you."

"Get in," I said on impulse. The elder Mr. Bolton opened the door and climbed inside.

I started the engine and pulled out of the parking lot. There was a gas station a little down the road. I drove there and pulled into another spot.

"So, what's this about?"

"My son's been through hell," he said. "I don't care what he told you, what happened to that little girl eats at him. Dustin was a good kid most of the time. Used to get straight As in middle school. He was a pretty talented basketball player. He just fell in with the wrong crowd. I wasn't around a lot. His mother and me...we weren't very well suited for each other. I should have been more involved in that kid's life."

"Mr. Bolton, I'm sorry. But Dustin is a grown man now. And I believe he could have corroborated Jeremy Holt's alibi way back when. I believe he could still do it now."

"He won't. He's too scared. And it shouldn't have to fall to just him."

"What do you mean?"

"What makes you think he's the only one who can corroborate that kid's story?"

"I was told he, Jeremy, and Alicia Tate were living together at the time."

"Sure. They were. But there was a whole crew my son hung out with. You should talk to some of them."

"You're saying there are other witnesses who can back up Holt's alibi?"

"Ain't my job to figure that out. You said you worked for Jeremy's lawyer."

"I'm his daughter."

"Yeah? Well, good for you."

"Do you know who they were? Your son's crew?"

"Sure. They used to come to the house before I kicked Dustin out. I regret a lot of things, but not that."

I pulled out a small pad of paper Dad kept in the center console. He had a pen clipped to it.

"Who are these other guys?" I asked. "Whatever you remember could be helpful."

Without missing a beat, Bolton Sr. Took the pad of paper and wrote three names on it. He handed it back to me. I read it quickly. They were the same names Alicia Tate mentioned.

"Jeremy came from money. My boy? These others? We came from nothing. Jeremy didn't know how good he had it. And he pissed it all away. Dustin and Jeremy were followers. But these boys? They were bad news. And they knew Jeremy's dad was loaded."

"You think they tried to steal from Steven Holt?"

"I don't know that for a fact. But I know one of them went to prison for burglary a while back."

"Do you know where I can find them?"

"One of 'em's in a cemetery outside of Helene. Got shot in a drive-by maybe six or seven years ago." He pointed to one name on the paper. "Jerome Dupris. I don't know about the other two. That's up to you to figure out if you think it's worth your time."

"Thank you. But I have to ask you. You know what happened to your son. Why help me?"

"My son's got a wife. But he never had kids of his own. He's got some stepkids, but the hard part of raising them didn't fall on him. He doesn't know what it is to be a parent. I do. And I made every mistake there is. A long time ago, I was friends with Diane Benning. She was a sweet girl. She married an asshole who didn't deserve her. If her son's sitting in prison for something he didn't do, well, that's the kind of thing that eats you from the inside out."

"It is," I said. "Mr. Bolton, Diane Benning has stage IV lung cancer."

He nodded. "I heard a rumor about that. Well, then all the more reason to let you try to do right by her son. Because I heard some other rumors too. About your dad."

I went rigid.

"Mr. Bolton..."

He put a hand up. "I said all I got to say. As far as my boy, you do what he said. You leave him alone from now on. I don't wanna see you here."

Before I could answer, Bolton opened the door and slammed it shut behind him. He gave a wave to the attendant inside the booth of the gas station. Then he whistled as he walked across the street back toward the body shop.

I looked down at the note he gave me. Three names. Remy Horner, Blackie Thompson, and Jerome Dupris. I took a quick picture of the note for safekeeping. Alicia hadn't given me last names. I'd seen none of these names in the copy of the police report in my dad's files.

I had to drive by the body shop again as I headed out of town. Dustin Bolton Sr. stood in the doorway. He had a fierce look on his face as he met my eye and raised his hand in a last wave.

CHAPTER
Twenty

TWO DAYS LATER, I woke up to voices down in Dad's study. I threw on a quick pair of shorts and a tee shirt and brushed my teeth. Uncle Lloyd's unmistakable deep laughter drew me. I looked out the bay window and saw his boat moored at the dock.

"Is this a private party?" I asked, poking my head into the study.

"Mercy!" Lloyd said. "I was hoping I'd get to see you. I'm trying to convince your dad to go fishing with me this morning."

"What's to convince?" I said to my father.

"I was just gonna try to get some work done today," he said. Lloyd met my eyes.

"It's Saturday," I said. "Nothing's due this upcoming week. Go. Have a good time."

"Are you sure?" he said.

"I can find my way into town by myself if I feel the need," I said. "Seriously. Go."

"Hmmpf," he said. I could see a glint in his eye though. "You're sounding like Violet."

"Violet's right!" Lloyd and I said it together. But Dad was up out of his chair.

"Give me a few minutes to get some stuff together," he said. "I've been working on some new lures down in the shed. Been meaning to try them out anyway."

"Good," Lloyd said. "I'll meet you down at the dock."

"Did you eat?" I said. "I bought some pastries from Connie's Bakery. I can whip up some eggs or something."

Lloyd patted his stomach. "Carole made me an omelet before I left. Let's go get some air while Gale Force here takes his sweet time getting all pretty."

Lloyd brushed past me and held the door open. I grabbed a hoodie from the hook. It was still chilly this early, with the breeze coming off of the lake. I grabbed my dad's jacket as well. I'd put it in Lloyd's boat in case he forgot to bring it.

"I'm so glad you came out," I said. "He hasn't really taken a day off since I got here. His golf outings don't count. He's out there schmoozing."

"Tom's always got some wheel or another spinning."

The water was calm today in the bay. I knew Lloyd and Dad had a secret fishing spot even I didn't know about. We walked down to the end of the dock. I sat on the bench under the awning next to the boat lift. Lloyd was moored right beside it. He took the spot next to me.

"He seems better since you came, Mercy. Sharper."

"I'm glad."

CHAPTER TWENTY

"I understand you're still kicking rocks over in the Holt case. You sure that's a good idea?"

Lloyd Murphy was nothing if not direct. "Where did you hear that? Violet?"

"I understand Diane's been in town a couple of times talking to you."

"She's not doing well," I said. "She suspended her chemo treatments."

"That's rough. Are they telling her how long she has?"

"A few months. Maybe."

"Hmm. Does Tom know?"

"Yes. And Violet. Now you."

Lloyd nodded. "School starts in a few weeks?"

I smoothed an errant lock of hair away from my face. It blew right back a second later.

"I'm not going back," I said.

Lloyd let out a sigh that told me the news wasn't exactly a surprise to him. "I take it your dad doesn't know."

"It's not a secret. I just don't feel like answering a lot of questions."

"It's your life. Were your grades not good?"

"My grades were fine. I was in the top ten in my class."

"Does that mean you're planning on staying in Helene?"

"I'm just trying to figure things out as I go."

Lloyd chuckled. "I suppose we all are. I can't imagine Sandra's too happy with you right now. She called me. I probably shouldn't tell you that. She says you haven't been answering her texts."

"It's not easy being their daughter."

Lloyd nodded. "I suppose it's not. If there's something you want to bounce off me, I've got a good ear. Or come on out to the farm. Carole would love to see you."

"Soon," I said.

"He's stirred up, Mercy. Holt's always been a problem. Tom ruminates. Fixates. Then it makes him...worse."

"I talked to Dustin Bolton and Alicia Tate," I said. "Alicia is adamant that Jeremy was with them that whole weekend. She has a copy of a letter dated just after Savannah's disappearance that she claims she sent Dad. She says he told her he couldn't use her. And Dustin Bolton was going to go to the cops. Somebody got to him. He was tortured into silence."

"Well, damn," Lloyd said.

"Did you know?"

"Did I know what?"

"That he talked to Alicia. That she wrote to him. Do you remember him talking about her statement back then?"

Lloyd shook his head. "Mercy, it's been sixteen years. Your dad killed himself over that case. It cost him your mom. And you."

"He didn't lose me," I said.

"She told me she made him choose. When he said he wanted to take Holt's case to trial and move here permanently, that was it."

"Why are you telling me this?"

"Because you don't know how it was."

"Lloyd, they're my parents. I was the one living in the house with them. I know how it was."

"Survivor's guilt."

"What?"

"Survivor's guilt. When Tom came back from Vietnam, it took years for him to really come back. He doesn't talk about it much. But he left a lot of good men behind. It drove him. He channeled all that into his work. His clients substituted for the men he couldn't save in the jungle."

"No man left behind," I said.

"Yeah. Anton Milo. The Guru Killer. That NFL player, Jackson Smith. Your Aunt Viveca. Her trial damn near destroyed him. Then a few years later, when he got the call that she swallowed all those pills."

"I'm not trying to stir all that up. But I think my dad was right about Jeremy. He didn't kill his sister. I just have a lot of questions. Things he did. Things he didn't do."

"What's your question, Mercy? Your real question."

I turned to him. "Was he sick back then, too?"

Lloyd sighed and closed his eyes. "I don't know, Mercy."

"But you were concerned."

"Yes."

"Do you think he did something wrong? Because I don't understand why he didn't pursue Alicia Tate's story harder. Subpoenaed her. It could have raised reasonable doubt."

"You didn't see him in his prime. A Tom Gale cross-examination was pure art, Mercy. I don't know why that jury decided things how they did. I don't know if Jeremy Holt was guilty or not. He did the best he could."

"The best he could, not his best."

Lloyd shrugged.

"Dustin Bolton is still terrified. He's not willing to go to the police with what happened to him. But I talked to his father too, Dustin Sr. He gave me names. People his son used to hang around with during that time frame. He hinted maybe they were overly interested in the fact Jeremy Holt's father had money."

"Can you find them?" Lloyd asked.

"I don't know. But the police should have found them. Violet suggested I talk to Detective Henderson. I plan to."

"Mercy, those kids were all thugs. Users and drug dealers. They have credibility issues. Your dad made a judgment call."

"Did he? Because I think he never tried to track these people down."

"Mercy, this is dangerous. If Dustin Bolton is telling the truth, then somebody went to drastic measures to keep his mouth shut. What do you think they might do if they found out you were digging into this?"

"So, you're okay with this? If there's even the slightest chance there are witnesses out there that can exonerate Jeremy Holt, you're telling me not to pursue it? Dad has an obligation. An ethical duty. Diane Benning knows it. But he's not himself. He's forgetting things. Every day, a little more of him slips away. If he was negligent during that trial..."

"He wasn't!" Lloyd yelled. Then he took a breath, settling himself. "He wasn't. I was there. I had his back."

"His wingman. Only if you really had his back, you should have told me what was going on. You shouldn't have let it get to this point."

"He's not my family," Lloyd said. "You're his family."

"Are you judging me?"

"You're judging me. But Jeremy Holt? That case is over. It's a bottomless pit. Your dad was never the same after he lost that trial. Neither was your family. I just can't understand why you want to get mired in all of that again."

"Because it has to be worth it! What it's done to my dad. To Diane Benning. To my mother. To me! It has to be worth it. I have to know the truth."

"Ok. I can make a call. Violet's got the right idea telling you to talk to Mac Henderson. Let me call him and smooth the way for that."

"Okay. I'd really appreciate that."

"He's still with the sheriff's department. If anyone can convince you Jeremy's guilty, it's Mac."

"Did you know he's been visiting Jeremy every single month since the verdict?"

Lloyd gave me a tight-lipped smile. "I thought he cut that out years ago."

"Well, he didn't. Not until a few months ago."

"How do you know this?"

I hesitated. If I told Lloyd I'd been in communication with Jeremy before I told my father, he might think it was disloyal.

"Never mind," Lloyd said. "You can keep your secrets, Mercy. I just want to make sure you don't get hurt."

"I just want to know what happened. So I'm asking you. How long has Dad been showing these symptoms? The bouts of confusion?"

"I don't know," Lloyd said, sounding defeated. He just told me I could keep my secrets. I realized now I was asking him to tell me one of his.

"Lloyd?"

"Something happened during that trial. It was just one day. Right after opening arguments. Your dad had an episode."

"What do you mean an episode?"

"He left the courtroom. Went to the office. He was sleeping there for the duration. Not going out to the island. We had dinner. Pizza delivery. And he just got this blank look on his face. Then he was gone. It's hard to explain. But it was like his short-term memory was just zapped. He was in a loop. Couldn't remember what happened that day. Couldn't remember how we got back to the office. So, I took him to the emergency room in Traverse City. Gave him some discretion until we figured out what was going on. Well, he was fine. They tested him for everything. Couldn't find evidence of a stroke. Nothing. All they said was that his blood pressure spiked. He was *fine*. That was a Friday night. By the time he woke up the next morning, it was like nothing happened."

"Christ, Lloyd. Did you call my mother?"

"They were separated. I was with him. Carole too. We made sure he got checked out and he was fine."

"Did it happen again?"

"Not then. Not during that trial, I swear to God. But a couple of times over the next few years, he'd have these brief episodes. And he'd get over it. It was nothing."

"That doesn't sound like nothing, Lloyd."

"I'm telling you. He was fine."

"I don't want to argue about it. If you'd set up that meeting with Detective Henderson, I'd be grateful."

"Go there first thing Monday morning. I'll make sure he's available for you."

"Hey there!" My father called from behind us. He was wearing his fishing vest and lucky hat. He had his best fishing pole as he made his way down the dock.

"Better get going," I said.

"You wanna come?" Dad said as he joined us.

"Maybe next time. I'm going to work on a few things here. Maybe head into town for lunch later."

"Will you see Liam?" Dad asked.

I felt a blush creeping into my cheeks. "I don't know. I'm winging it today."

Dad leaned over and kissed me on the cheek. He looked happy. He stepped into Lloyd's boat. I went down and pulled off the ropes. As Lloyd revved his engine, I gave them a shove. Dad waved as they sped off toward their secret cove. I watched until they were nothing more than a dot on the horizon. I thought of Jeremy Holt and Diane Benning. Survivor's guilt. No man left behind. Call it generational trauma. Call it anything. But I had to find out the truth.

CHAPTER
Twenty~One

Detective Michael "Mac" Henderson had been a cop longer than I'd been alive. A fact I fully expected him to lord over me. He didn't. That wasn't the only thing that surprised me about him.

"Thanks for agreeing to meet with me," I said, shaking Henderson's hand. "I'm afraid when I tell you what it's about, you might not be so patient."

Mac smiled. He wasn't a tall man. Five foot six at best. He had a solid, muscular build and a full head of silvery hair he kept cropped short in a buzz cut. His eyes crinkled when he smiled. I knew I probably wouldn't see many of those during our conversation.

"You want to talk about the Jeremy Holt case," he said.

"Lloyd Murphy filled you in?"

"Violet Tamblyn too. I'm only a little surprised you waited so long to come see me. What's your dad think about all this?"

Henderson gestured to an empty chair in front of his desk. I sat down and pulled a small notepad out of my purse. Henderson didn't go behind his desk. Instead, he sat on a leather loveseat against the wall, facing me.

"I'm here for the summer helping him organize his office. Archive some files. He knows I've taken an interest in this case."

"But what does he think?"

"He thinks it's a rabbit hole."

"It was a tough loss for your old man. He really believed in that kid. To be honest, when I found out Tom Gale agreed to represent him, I thought, oh, shit."

"You thought he was going to get an acquittal?"

"No."

"Why not?"

"Because I knew Jeremy Holt killed that girl."

"No doubt in your mind? Ever?"

Henderson sat back, draping his arm over the back of the loveseat. He straightened his tie. "Not by the time I arrested him, no."

"You know my dad still believes Jeremy's innocent. Does that surprise you, Detective?"

"No. But I think it's unfortunate. So, what can I do for you, Mercy? Is it okay if I call you that? And I'm Mac. You know, this isn't the first time we've met. I remember you from when you were just a little girl. A couple of times, your dad let you ride the golf cart when we went on some outings."

I recalled a few weekends in the distant past where Dad took me with him to the golf course. I couldn't have been more than eight or nine years old.

"You're not angry with him? For hanging on to his beliefs about Jeremy Holt?"

Mac laughed. "It doesn't matter what he believes. I'm not one of these cops who thinks all defense attorneys are scum. Your dad is good at what he does. I respect him. He respects me. So no, I'm not mad at him for what he believes."

"That's good to hear. I'll try not to waste your time. I have some concerns about the case. A few things have come up that make me think not everything is what it seemed about that night."

Mac furrowed his brow but didn't alter his relaxed posture.

"Jeremy's lack of alibi was always a problem," I said. "But I've spoken to a girl he knew. She insists she was with Jeremy the whole weekend Savannah disappeared. She was afraid to come forward at the time."

Mac chewed his bottom lip. He regarded me for a moment, then rose from the loveseat. He went over to a large metal file cabinet in the corner. He opened the bottom drawer and pulled out a thick, ragged file. Slapping it on his desk, he took a seat and opened the file, leafing through the pages.

"I keep this one here," he said. "At least copies I made of certain things. My murder book. This thing was part of me. Is still part of me."

"It has a way of getting under your skin," I said.

"Alicia Tate?" he asked.

"She was Dustin Bolton's girlfriend," I said.

"Dead end. I tried to talk to her. Jeremy gave me her name. She left town, from what I could figure out. The girl had no interest in backing up Jeremy's lies."

"But you interviewed Bolton," I said. "What do you remember about that?"

Mac closed the file and sat back. "Bolton was always a problem. The first time I interviewed him, he was cocky. All attitude. Told me Jeremy was with him all night. Only the two of them were wasted. I personally didn't find him credible. I knew if he was going to be Tom's start witness, he'd have real problems with him. He and Jeremy were buddies. Then, a couple weeks later, Bolton came back in and changed his whole story. Said he really hadn't seen Jeremy that weekend. He swore under oath that Jeremy asked him to lie about that."

"Alicia told me something disturbing. She claims Bolton was telling the truth at first, when he corroborated Jeremy's alibi. Because the three of them *were* together that weekend. Only Bolton went missing for a few days before he gave you his official statement. When he showed up again, he'd been worked over. That's why he recanted. Because he was kidnapped and tortured into selling Jeremy out."

I pulled out my phone and brought up the pictures I'd taken off Alicia's phone. I handed it to Henderson. He put on his readers and scrolled through them.

"Alicia Tate says Dusty had two fingers chopped off his hand. And he'd been held against an electric stove. That's what those rings are on his chest."

"He wasn't injured when I spoke to him," Henderson said, handing me back my phone.

"Are you absolutely sure? Those wounds on his chest wouldn't have been visible. But what about his hand?"

Henderson opened the file again. He tabbed through it. "No," he said. "I don't have any note in here about wounds to his hand. He didn't tell me anything like that."

"Do you remember if his hand was bandaged during that second interview?" I asked.

"No."

"But that doesn't mean it wasn't. Just that you don't remember it," I said.

Mac smiled. "Is this a cross-examination?"

"No," I said. "I'm just trying to get the facts."

"You have them. I don't remember any injuries. Dustin certainly never told me about them."

"Which fits with Alicia's story now. Dusty was coerced into denying Holt's alibi."

"Look," Henderson said. "Alicia Tate and Dustin Bolton were junkies. Even if they *had* corroborated Holt's alibi, I might not have believed them. Or it wouldn't have mattered. Jeremy Holt's lack of an alibi was probably the weakest piece of evidence against him. He was seen, Mercy. I had an eyewitness who saw him put Savannah into his car. She was crying. She was wearing the pajamas she was eventually found in. The bottoms of those pajamas were found in Jeremy's car, covered in her blood. He did this. He killed her."

"There was nobody else you looked at?"

Henderson let out an exasperated sigh. But he checked himself. Folding his hands, he leveled his gaze at me.

"Holt wasn't the only suspect, no. Not initially. Steven Holt was another one. We came at him hard."

"I didn't know that," I said.

"Nobody did. Why would they? But of course, I looked at the other members of that family. But he and Olivia, Savannah's mother. They had a rock-solid alibi."

"They were at Hollis Branch's retirement party. I've seen the newspaper clippings."

"That's right. More than half the town had an alibi, Mercy. It was well documented."

"Who else did you look at?"

"The only other person of interest I had was Joe Jarret."

"Joe Jarret," I repeated, searching my memory for the names I'd read in my dad's case file. "Savannah was supposed to be at a sleepover with his daughter?"

"That's right. Only she and Lexie had some kind of argument. Savannah left right after dinner. She took off for home. I questioned Joe. I questioned the entire family. Joe was having an affair with the wife of his next-door neighbor. He was with her that night."

"None of that was in the file. You only disclosed that Joe's neighbor vouched for his whereabouts," I said. "Do you think Savannah could have seen them together?"

"No. I don't think so. And you're right. I didn't put his... indiscretion in the file. There was no point. Not after I had an eyewitness who saw Savannah with her brother. Not after we searched his car and found what we found. I wasn't gonna destroy two families."

"I'd like to talk to Joe Jarret."

"He's dead. Joe died of a heart attack about a year ago. None of it would matter anyway. Joe admitted everything to his wife. I urged him to. They got divorced not long after the trial. You need to trust me that I turned over every stone there."

"I believe Alicia Tate. She has no reason to lie now. None."

"It's just not enough. No prosecutor in the world would agree to open this back up based on somebody like Alicia Tate changing her story. Is she the only one? What about Bolton? Are you hearing this stuff about him being roughed up from him directly?"

"No. I talked to him. He wanted nothing to do with any of this. Wouldn't admit to anything. But his father took me aside and said some things that went along with Alicia's story."

I tore a sheet out of my notepad where I'd written the names Dustin Bolton Sr. gave me. "His dad says these three were the ringleaders of Dusty and Jeremy's gang. He said Jeremy and Dusty were afraid of them. And they knew Jeremy came from money. Alicia said all of them kind of disappeared right after Savannah went missing. Do you recognize any of these names?"

"Yeah," he said. "Two of them are dead. Jerome Dupris was the victim of a drive-by shooting maybe ten years ago. Blackie Thompson was an informant of mine for a while. Tried to get clean. Didn't last. He OD'd around the same time."

"What about the last one, Remy Horner?"

Henderson walked over to his desktop computer. He hit a key on his keyboard, jolting it out of sleep mode. I couldn't see his monitor from where I sat. He two-finger typed something into it. His face darkened as he read what was on the screen.

"Horner's about as bad as the others. Only…"

"Only what?"

"He's in prison down in Jackson. Burglary and assault. Then..."

"What?"

"CSC. Third degree..." he read, frowning.

"Criminal sexual conduct," I said. "Third degree? That means his victim was under sixteen? Mac..."

"I'd have to pull a report. It didn't happen here. And don't go jumping to conclusions."

"You never questioned Horner in connection with Savannah's case."

"Why would I? Just because I didn't question every random dirtbag in the state doesn't mean the right guy isn't in prison."

"No, I'm not accusing you of anything. I didn't mean to imply I was."

"Why are you really getting into this?" Mac asked.

"I told you."

"No, you said you were organizing your dad's files. But why *this* case? I know your dad hasn't asked you to. So, what are you really doing and who are you doing it for?"

In an instant, I knew I was now the target of Mac Henderson's thirty years of police interrogation skills.

"I believe I already told you. Because I believe Alicia Tate."

"Who knows why this Tate girl is changing her story now? Maybe she just wants attention. Maybe she's got some old score she's trying to settle with Bolton. How'd you connect with her in the first place?"

I hesitated, knowing how it would probably sound to him. "She reached out to Jeremy's mother."

Henderson let out a haughty laugh. "Diane? Jesus. No wonder. Has it occurred to you that girl's playing Diane? And you?"

"She hasn't asked for anything, Mac. Not a dime."

"Well, I don't know what to tell you. But it sounds like a hustle to me. You should be careful. Diane doesn't have money, but your dad does. She might be playing some kind of long game. Just because she hasn't asked to be paid yet doesn't mean she won't."

"I appreciate your insight."

He pushed his chair to the right and turned to the credenza behind him. He had a row of framed photographs. Grabbing one, he set it in front of me. It was of a little girl, maybe six or seven years old. She was sitting on top of a pony and holding an ice cream cone.

"We've talked about your dad," Henderson said. "You've had a lot to say about Jeremy Holt and Dustin Bolton and this Tate girl. But you haven't once asked me about her." I picked up the photograph. I hadn't recognized her at first. I'd only seen photographs taken closer in time to her death. But now, I saw it.

"This is Savannah," I said.

"That's right. Olivia gave me that. She wanted me to have one when she was happy. Herself. So, I could remember her this way. Not...how I found her. As if I could ever forget."

"She's beautiful," I whispered.

"She was weighted down in that water, Mercy. It was almost two weeks before we found her. That was a hot summer. We had ninety-degree days going into late September."

"I've seen the crime scene photos," I said.

"Photos are one thing. This kid didn't have an easy death. She would have been terrified. Hannah McClain saw Jeremy put her in that car. She was a sweet kid and nobody hated her. But Jeremy did. He was on drugs, but that's no excuse. I haven't lost a day's sleep over his conviction. I wasn't out for revenge. It was justice. Jeremy Holt is guilty of this. I'm not telling you to let it go. You do what you think is right. Hell, if there's an inkling of a chance somebody else was involved, I'd be the first person to thank you for figuring that out."

"Thank you," I said.

"You might want to talk to Olivia."

"Savannah's mother? I wouldn't want to upset her."

"This may sound strange, but I don't think you would. If you come at it with pure motives. If you're really just trying to honor a promise to Diane Benning and help your dad. Olivia will understand that. I know her pretty well. I'll make a call."

Mac Henderson surprised me again. "Thank you."

"I'm here for anything you need. I mean that. At least for the next two months. After that, I'm retiring."

"Congratulations," I said. "I imagine it's well earned." He walked me out. As I turned to shake his hand, I could still see Savannah Holt's smiling face from that picture on his desk.

It was a five-minute walk from the top of the bluff back down to my father's office. He was waiting for me so we could take the boat back to the island. I wanted to be as confident as Mac Henderson in Jeremy's guilt. Or as confident as my father was in his innocence. But at that moment, I flat out didn't know who to believe. I wasn't being completely honest with Mac when I told him I had faith in Alicia, though her motive for lying now wasn't clear. Mac was right. It wasn't enough.

CHAPTER TWENTY-ONE

My phone vibrated in my back pocket. It was a number I didn't recognize, but an NYC area code.

"Hello?" I said.

"Is this Mercy Gale?" a feminine voice said. "Can you talk?"

I stood at the top of the bluff, looking out at the expansive blue waters of Lake Michigan.

"Who is this?"

"You can call me Anne."

My pulse skipped. "Okay, Anne. What can I do for you?" I wanted to interrogate her. I kept my cool, not wanting to scare her off.

"Is your father there? Are you sure you're alone?"

"Yes. What about my father?"

"I work for...you know. Never mind that for now. But can we meet?"

"About what?"

The caller took a breath on the other end of the phone. "I need to talk to you about DeShawn Sims and your friend Christian Foley."

Though I guessed what this was about, the mention of Christian sent a shock of anger through me, followed quickly by grief that took my breath away.

"Who are you?" I asked.

"I think we can help each other."

"With what?"

"Please. Can we just meet? You pick the place. You pick the time."

"I'm going to need a little more to go on, Anne."

"I didn't know what else to do. Please. Christian was my friend, too. I think we can help each other. Twenty minutes of your time. You set the terms. The time and place. I'll be there."

"Why?"

She took a hard breath. "Listen...I'm...we were...Christian called me Barney."

"What's your name? Your full name."

She paused. "Anne Barnheiser."

"You know the police wanted to talk to you. You gave Christian that gun?"

"Now, will you talk to me?"

"Okay," I said. "You have my attention. Can you meet tomorrow? There's a truck stop off 31 called Bumpy's. It's an hour south of Helene. I'll be there tomorrow at eleven. Are you close enough you can be there?"

"I'm close enough," she said.

A chill went up my back. Was Anne the prowler I thought I saw out at Mrs. Greenbaum's townhouse?

"Are you stalking me?"

"No. I swear. I just want to talk. That's it."

"Fine. I'll see you tomorrow."

The call dropped. I hit redial. It rang twice, then went to an out of service message. I looked back out toward the island. Every instinct in me told me meeting this girl would be a mistake. But it would be mine to make.

CHAPTER
Twenty-Two

At eleven, Bumpy's Truck Stop should have been busier than it was. I only saw two other cars parked around the back. The next gas station was two blocks in the other direction and the parking lot abutted the woods. The road sign was perched high atop a pole, and you could see it from half a mile away.

I kept the sharp end of my keys sticking out of my fist as I made my way into the diner. The server behind the cash register gave me a cheery hello and told me to seat myself anywhere.

I picked a booth against the far wall but in the center of the dining room. The server followed me and stopped to grab a menu from the shelf she passed on the way.

"There will be two of us," I said. "I think."

She grabbed another menu. I scooted into the booth and ordered a lemonade. I really didn't want to be the first to get here. How long does one wait in these situations before leaving?

It wasn't long at all before a rakishly thin woman with light brown hair down to her waist walked in. She looked more nervous than me and that was saying something. She wore a pair of faded jeans with holes in the knees, a loose tee shirt, and carried a boho bag with rainbow-colored patches. She looked like Christian's type. Pretty, unassuming, sloppy chic.

"Ms. Gale," she said. Not waiting for me to answer, she took the booth opposite me and told the server she didn't want anything as she brought my lemonade.

"We'll order later," I told the server. She gave me an annoyed look. I felt bad about that. I'd leave a couple of twenties on the table no matter what else we did here today.

"Who are you?" I said to Anne.

"I'm just a student," she said. "An intern."

I took a guess. "For the Gossip Zone?"

"For DeShawn Sims."

I took a sip of my drink. "Does he know you're here?"

Anne's eyes got wide. "No way. And you can't let him know if you see him again."

"Do you know why I saw him in the first place? What was your part in it?"

"Christian was my friend too," Anne said. "I'm sorry for what happened to him."

"You're sorry? That was your gun they found him with."

"I didn't know it was going to get this out of hand."

"Out of hand? Christ. I think you better start from the beginning, Anne."

Anne nodded. "I was there when Christian came into DeShawn's office for the first time. That's how we met."

"How did it happen? Did Sims approach Christian?"

Anne shook her head. "Why would he? He had no idea who Christian was. Look...I'm not...this whole thing...I wouldn't even stick my neck out at all. But after what happened, somebody needs to know."

"Know what?"

"What do you know about the story Foley was trying to sell to DeShawn?"

"How much? What did Sims offer? What was the price of betraying me?"

"At first, I was surprised that DeShawn even took the meeting. He wasn't who Christian contacted in the first place. He called Kennedy Terry. But she hasn't worked for the GZ in like a year or two."

"Kennedy Terry." The name seared through me. A long time ago, Terry's name showed up on a byline to an article about my Aunt Viveca. She's the one who printed lies about Dad and Aunt Viveca having an affair during her murder trial. Christian tried to reach out to her specifically. It was another knife in the gut.

"You're sure?" I said. "It was Kennedy Terry that Christian was trying to get a hold of?"

"I'm absolutely sure. But the call got routed to DeShawn. And he asked Foley to come in and meet with him. I was in on it. DeShawn had me take notes."

"Christian was trying to sell a story about my father," I said. "About his health."

"He said he had information that E. Thomas Gale was acting erratically. That he was still representing clients and was about to get turned into the State Bar. Then, I heard him tell DeShawn that your dad might have screwed up big time on his last murder trial. He said he could prove it. That there was a witness he never called. Something like that."

My hand trembled as I picked up my glass. Everything I'd ever told in confidence to Christian about my dad, he'd turned around and tried to peddle it. I'd shown him the letter Jeremy sent me. He knew I was trying to track down Alicia Tate. That I'd met with Jeremy's mother.

"DeShawn was interested in all that," I said. "He pursued it. Sims was the last outgoing call on Christian's phone."

"I didn't understand what the hook was. I mean, no offense. But who cares about some washed-up old lawyer and a case he lost almost two decades ago?"

"Sims told me there's been some interest in a remake of *A Deadly Affair*. It's one of my father's most high-profile cases."

"Yeah. Listen, Christian wasn't who you think he was. I know it probably seems like he was trying to stab you in the back."

"Christian was trying to take money for a story that could have ruined what's left of my father's career and reputation. You can see why I'd find that a betrayal."

"Yeah." Anne took a straw from a dispenser at the center of the table. She twisted the end of the wrapper. "Except DeShawn...The GZ was never going to print that story."

"What do you mean? And what's your angle? You don't know me. What's in it for you? And you haven't answered my question about your gun. Why did you give it to Christian?"

She kept on twisting that straw. "I liked Christian. We got pretty close. And I know what it's like to feel like you have to do something because you have no other choice."

"What choice? Why would Christian feel backed into a corner if he was the one who initiated contact with the Gossip Zone?"

"He didn't want you hurt. He told me that."

"Were you sleeping with him? Did you know what he was going to do? Jesus. You helped him. Even if you didn't pull the trigger."

"It didn't get that far. We went out a few times. Texted. Talked. He was a nice guy. But after a while, you were all he wanted to talk about. He was...did you know he was in love with you?"

"He wasn't in love with me," I snapped. "We were friends. We hooked up once like a week after we met. We *both* decided it was a bad idea. We worked better as friends. At least, I thought so. Now I know he was only using me."

"No," she said. "That's not it. He cared about you. And he felt horrible about everything."

"Horrible enough to sink into a depression?"

Anne's eyes flicked up, locking with mine. "Do you believe that?"

"I don't know what to believe."

The girl looked miserable. I'd only just met her. I couldn't read her.

"He never told me about you," I said. "You were talking before I came back to Helene. Before I started looking hard into the Holt case. He confided in you after I started telling him about it. You're lying. You're the one who pedaled this story to your boss. He didn't just waltz into Sims's office, did he? You didn't just *happen* to be in some meeting between Christian and Sims. You worked on him, didn't you? You put him up to this."

Anne shook her head. "No. I swear to God. That's not how it went down."

"But you brokered the meeting between Christian and DeShawn Sims."

"No. It's like I said. I met him in DeShawn's office. After their meeting, I walked Christian down to the elevator. We hit it off. That's it. I got to know him. I knew he was strapped for money. He was about to get evicted from his apartment. He was gonna have trouble paying his tuition this upcoming term."

"He never told me," I whispered. My head pounded. I knew so much less about Christian than I realized.

"He should have. Maybe he would have. But Ms. Gale...what happened to him...If he..."

"You don't think he killed himself," I said.

"Do you?"

"Tell me about the gun," I said.

"I got it for protection a few years ago. When I moved to New York. I kept it in a box under my bed. Christian never even knew I had it. A couple of weeks ago, I had a break-in at my apartment. They took my computer. Some cash I had in a drawer. And they took the gun. But listen, this was well after the last time Christian and I talked. Things cooled off between us. I told Christian he needed to back off. Forget pursuing this stuff about your dad."

"You ghosted him."

"Yeah. I'm not proud of that. I found out some stuff that made me realize this story about your dad was not worth touching. Christian refused to listen, and I just bailed."

"Then you had a break-in?"

"Yes. And I think it was that gun they were after. I think somebody was setting something in motion. I didn't realize how dangerous this was going to get."

I stared at Anne Barnheiser. I put her at twenty-one, tops. Though I was only seven years older on a calendar, I felt ancient as I looked at her.

"You think someone staged Christian's death to make it look like a suicide? Using your gun."

"Yes."

"But why? It's like you said. Why would anyone care about a fifteen-year-old murder case involving an old lawyer who's been out of the public eye for over a decade?"

"Do you know what a catch and kill order is?"

"I think so," I said, my heart racing. "It's when someone pays to catch a news story and kill it before it goes to print or online."

"Yeah."

I fingered the rim of my glass. "What are you telling me?"

"DeShawn Sims wasn't feeling you out because he wants to run a story about your dad."

"He wanted to catch a story about my dad. Are you trying to tell me there's a catch and kill order on my father?"

Anne nodded. "Somebody's protecting him."

"Who?"

"I don't know. I only know that Christian told DeShawn he was going to get him evidence. Some woman who said she could prove Jeremy Holt's alibi."

"Alicia Tate," I said.

"He had recordings," he said. "Of...you."

"He recorded our conversations," I said, the words tasting bitter in my mouth.

"I'm sorry. If it's any consolation, I don't think he felt good about it. He felt...desperate. But DeShawn was never planning to publish any of this. He was under orders not to."

"But Christian kept calling. He made plans to move to Helene for a few weeks to help me with this case. To prove Jeremy Holt is innocent. Somebody killed him before he could. You think someone tried to make it look like he took his own life?"

She wouldn't answer. Nothing made sense. Or it made too much sense. One more person I trusted had let me down.

"What did he tell you about coming here?" I asked.

"I don't know what you mean," Anne said.

"He followed me to Big Rapids when I went to talk to Jeremy Holt's alibi witness. Then he wound up staying in Cadillac for a night. The whole time he was lying to me. Making me think he was still in Ohio. What was he doing?"

"I don't know for sure."

"For sure? But you have a guess."

She shook her head. "I don't know. Really. I told you. I'd pretty much ghosted him by the time he was ready to hit the road."

"Convenient."

Tears finally spilled down Anne Barnheiser's cheeks. "I thought you needed to know. Christian loved you."

"He had a hell of a way of showing it."

"He didn't deserve to die like that. And he wouldn't want you to be in danger either."

My brain felt stuck in syrup. Danger. Catch and kill. My father. Who would have the most vested interest in killing stories that could ruin him?

"No," I said. "I can't be here. I can't hear this."

Anne reached across the table and tried to grab my wrist. I jerked it away.

"I'm done," I said. I vaulted out of the booth. I threw two twenties on the table, then I practically ran back out to the parking lot.

I barely remember pulling out or how I got back on the highway going almost ninety in my father's car. I headed north. Back to Helene. Back to the only place left for me to go.

Only I felt sucked under by the secrets and lies swirling up around me. Christian lied to me. Maybe my father lied too. And someone out there was willing to kill to keep the truth about Jeremy Holt from coming to light.

CHAPTER
Twenty-Three

"Is he here?" I asked Violet as I walked into the office. She was sitting at her desk, sorting through mail.

"He is not. He's out with Hollis Branch today. Strategy session for Adam's campaign. Beau Godfrey picked him up. He told me to tell you he'd be back by seven but if you wanted to head back home before that, to take the boat."

I stared into space for a moment, still reeling from my meeting with Anne Barnheiser. Anne had given voice to the suspicion I'd carried with me from the moment I heard from the police. Christian wasn't suicidal. Neither of us had ever known him to own or know how to use a gun.

"Mercy?" Violet said. "You okay?"

"I don't know." I couldn't tell her about my meeting. Not yet.

"Well, you got a package delivered from the courthouse. I think it's those videos you ordered of the Holt trial. I don't know why you wanna keep picking at that scab, honey."

Violet picked up a fat envelope and lobbed it across the desk to me. I caught it against my chest.

"You're lucky," she said. "They've got a new kid working in records for the county. He's about your age. Before, Ida Swan was doing everything. I think Ida only knew how to work a VCR. Now you've got everything all fancy with a flash drive."

"Thanks," I said. "Do I have anything else on the schedule for Dad?"

"Nope. He got his appellate briefs in yesterday. There's nothing on his docket for a couple of weeks. And you're gonna head to Lansing with him for oral argument, right?"

"That's the plan," I said.

"You think he's got a snowball's chance in hell of getting the Connelly conviction overturned?"

"I don't know. But it doesn't look like the panel down there goes against the trial court judges very often on suppression hearings."

"Well, the Connellys are loaded. Tom gets paid the same either way. We need a new roof on this building."

I smiled at Violet and made my way back to my office. My head still pounded like it did as I sat across from Anne.

Catch and kill.

The one person with a vested interest *and* a bank account big enough to squash any negative stories about my father was my father himself. Was he behind whatever happened to Christian? Or had this thing just gotten so far away from him he no longer remembered what he'd done? No. I couldn't...wouldn't believe it. He wouldn't do that. Could he do that? His concern for Jeremy was real. He wouldn't have invested fifteen years of monthly visits for someone he didn't care about. Oh God. Unless it was guilt.

CHAPTER TWENTY-THREE

No. I couldn't think it. This could not be true. There had to be another explanation.

Not for the first time, I regretted ever taking that initial meeting with Diane Benning. Or opened that letter from Jeremy Holt.

I ripped open the tab on the envelope Violet gave me. It contained a single flash drive with a label printed with Jeremy Holt's lower court case number.

I pulled out my laptop and popped the drive in. A file menu immediately pulled up. Each folder was organized by date. Jeremy's trial took up five whole trial days. I clicked on the first dated folder. Each subfile had been labeled with the portion of the trial contained in it. Opening Statements first. Then the testimony of every witness called by the prosecution. My father's defense witnesses. Then closing arguments and jury instructions.

I clicked on the opening statements file. Bill Hiram had argued the case for the state. Dad said he'd suffered a massive stroke and died just a few months after the trial ended. I could see why. Hiram was grossly overweight. He huffed and puffed through his opening, dripping with sweat.

I scrolled further. When I pressed play, my heart nearly stopped. There he was. My father. Sixteen years ago. I hadn't realized how much he'd aged since then. He'd been around sixty-three during the trial. He could have passed for a man twenty years younger. He wore a tailored black suit and his signature red "trial tie." His thick dark hair was slicked back, freshly barbered.

His tone was conversational. The camera was mounted just behind the jury box so you could almost put yourself in their place. I watched as my father made eye contact with every member. For a moment, it felt like he was looking right at me.

Behind his shoulder sat Jeremy Holt. Scrawny. Wearing an ill-fitting suit like something he'd borrowed from his father's closet. He stared straight ahead most of the time, keeping his hands folded in his lap. He was a boy. Not a man. And terrified. Halfway through my father's opening, Jeremy started to silently cry.

I clicked open another file from the fourth day of the trial. This was during the last day of the prosecution's case. Hiram had called Hannah McClain to the stand. Hannah was the eyewitness who claimed to have seen Jeremy with Savannah on the day she disappeared.

I watched as Hiram methodically took her through her direct testimony.

"Hannah," Hiram said. "Can you tell me, in your own words, where you were the night of September 18?"

Hannah leaned forward, speaking close to the microphone. "I left my house around eight o'clock. There was a party out at Oak Point. A friend of mine told me about it and asked me to pick her up to take her."

"Which friend was this?"

"This was Cameron Phillips. Only when I got to her house, Cam wasn't there. So I went out to Oak Point without her. I assumed we just got our wires crossed or something. That maybe she was gonna meet me there."

"What happened when you got out there?"

"It was just a party. A lot of the kids from around town were there. I knew a few. A couple of kids I went to high school with. And I ended up finding Cam. She came with this guy she met online. She was pretty wasted so I wasn't happy. She just forgot that she told me to pick her up."

"Did you see Jeremy Holt at that party?"

"Not right away. I didn't really know Jeremy very well. He didn't go to high school here. I knew he was a friend of Dusty Bolton's. I went to high school with him too. But I don't really like hanging around with that crowd."

"Did you see Dusty Bolton at the party?"

"No."

"Why don't you like hanging around with Dusty's crowd?"

"They're just into stuff I'm not into."

"Drugs?"

"Objection," my father said. "Counsel is leading the witness."

"Overruled," Judge Raymond Whitney said. I knew he died a few years ago. It made the national news. Whitney died of a sudden heart attack right from the bench.

Hiram took a different approach. "Okay. Why don't you just tell me what you saw when Jeremy showed up?"

"I figured out pretty quick I didn't want to stay. Too many of the losers hanging around. They were passing around plastic cups with some kind of lime green drink in them. I don't know what was in them, exactly, but I didn't want to take any chances. I was going to ask Cam if she wanted a ride home. But I couldn't find her. There was this bonfire where everybody was hanging out. It was just a bad vibe. I was already in trouble with my folks from the weekend before. I got into a fender bender with my sister's car. It was a whole thing. So I left. That's when I saw Jeremy. He was standing near his car."

"What kind of car did he drive?"

"It was, I think, some kind of red Honda. It had a dent in the rear driver's side door. I was walking to my car and I saw him leaning in through the passenger window. He was yelling at somebody inside the car. And I mean like really yelling. He said the F word a few times. The person in the passenger seat tried to get out. That's when I saw it was a little girl. She had blonde hair in a ponytail. She had on these pink pajamas, which I thought was also pretty strange. She got one foot out and I saw she was barefoot. That's when Jeremy just kind of pushed her back in the car. She was crying."

I fast forwarded until my father took the lectern for his cross examination.

"Ms. McClain," he said. "I just want to understand a few things. Prior to this case, did you know who Savannah Holt was?"

"No, sir."

"You'd never met her?"

"No, sir."

"And you'd only met Jeremy Holt one or two times. That's your testimony?"

"I wouldn't even say I met him. I just knew who he was because he hung around Dustin Bolton and that crowd."

"I see. But you didn't want to have anything to do with Bolton, correct? You stated on direct, Bolton and his friends had a bad reputation. You knew they were into drugs. You weren't interested in being around that."

"Yes. That's true."

"Who were the rest of Bolton's friends that you knew of?"

"What?"

"If you can name them. Who were Dustin Bolton's associates that you were so dead set against having anything to do with?"

"I don't...I don't know who they were. Not their names. I just knew he ran around with a crew and they were all a bunch of junkies. I wasn't into that scene."

"But Cameron Phillips was, wasn't she?"

"I don't...she hung around with that crowd more than I did. Yes."

"How many times before the night of September 18 did you go to parties at Oak Point?"

"I don't know. None, I don't think."

"None. And why is that?"

"It's just a rough scene out there."

"How would you know that if you don't routinely attend parties out there?"

"Everybody knows that. The Point is a drug hangout. I'm not into that."

"But you were into it that night, isn't that right?"

"I didn't take drugs that night."

"You said everyone knows the Point is a drug hangout. But you also said you're not into that. So which is it, Ms. McClain?"

"I'm not into drugs. I didn't do drugs that night."

"You just thought it was a good idea to head out there on your own after you went to Cameron Phillips's house and claimed she'd already left without you."

"I didn't say I thought it was a good idea. I just said it's what I did."

"Right. Ms. McClain, you know that your phone records were subpoenaed in preparation for your testimony today?"

"Yes."

"How do you normally communicate with your friends when you want to get together with them on the weekends?"

"What do you mean?"

"I mean...do you call each other? Do you text?"

"We text."

"But you didn't text Cam Phillips at all the night of September 18, did you?"

"No. We didn't text."

"You didn't call her that night either, did you?"

"No."

"You went to her house, expecting to find her there. You testified she wasn't home. But you didn't call or text her when she wasn't where you expected her to be?"

"Objection," Hiram said. "Asked and answered."

"Sustained," Judge Whitney said. "Let's keep this moving, Mr. Gale."

"Fine," my father said. The tips of his ears were red. I knew that meant he was fired up. He came out from behind the lectern and paced in front of the defense table.

"Ms. McClain, you expect us to believe you just decided to go to the Point not knowing for sure whether Cam Phillips was even there? When you said yourself you don't really go to the Point because you believe it's a drug hangout."

CHAPTER TWENTY-THREE

"I just said what happened."

"Fine. So, let's talk about Jeremy Holt. You said you knew he was a friend of Dustin Bolton's, is that right?"

"Yeah. They hung out together."

"But you didn't see him with Bolton that night, did you?"

"No. I just saw him near his car, like I said."

"Did you speak to him?"

"No."

"Did you ask him who he was talking to?"

"No."

"Did you recognize who you claim he was talking to?"

"No. I just saw a little girl with a blonde ponytail."

"And the pink pajamas? Isn't that what you said?"

"Yes. She had on pink pajamas."

"Where were you standing in relation to the car?"

"I was toward the rear of it."

"On the passenger side."

"That's right."

"So, the car was parked facing north?"

"I don't know. I didn't have a compass."

"Fine. Was the car on your left or right as you passed by it?"

"It was on my left."

"On your left. And you approached it from its rear and walked alongside the passenger side?"

"Yes."

"The side you claim Holt was leaning in."

"Yes. He was leaning into the front passenger window, which was on my left."

"What did you do after you saw him?"

"I just... I left. My car was parked a bit further down the hill."

"Did you have to walk past Jeremy's car to get to it?"

"What do you mean?"

"I mean...was your car positioned ahead of Jeremy's or behind it?"

"Well, ahead of it, I guess."

"So, after you passed by him, Jeremy was behind you, correct?"

"Right."

"So, you didn't go around Jeremy's car on the other side?"

"No."

My nerves tingled. My God. It was so obvious what Dad was doing. Hannah McClain testified she spotted a dent in Jeremy's car on the driver's side rear door. Only she just committed herself to the story that she never walked around to that side of the car that night.

"Never walked by the driver's side then, right?"

"I just told you. I kept going to my car."

"Got it," Dad said. "Okay...Ms. McClain, I just want to

understand something. You called the police yourself, isn't that right? They didn't come interview you on their own."

"They came and interviewed me, Mr. Gale."

"Right, but that was after you called a Crimestoppers hotline set up for information about Savannah Holt, isn't that right?"

"They were asking if anyone had seen that little girl."

"You saw it on television?"

"Yes."

"Your Honor," Dad said. "I'd like permission to play Defense Exhibit 41."

I fast forwarded past Dad's authentication testimony. The Crimestoppers ad played on a large projection screen to the right of the jury. It was a picture of Savannah wearing a ponytail. Then a picture from a catalog of the pink pajamas she'd last been seen in. Finally, there was a picture of Jeremy Holt's red Honda. The dent in the rear driver's side door was clearly visible. It was a point of contention with the evidence. One my father exploited when cross-examining Detective Henderson. They'd issued a description of Jeremy's car based on an anonymous tip they received that Savannah was seen in it the night of her disappearance.

"You didn't call the police until almost a week after Savannah went missing, isn't that right?" Dad asked.

"I don't know the exact timeline."

"But you knew Savannah Holt was missing, didn't you? I mean it was all over the local news. There were massive search parties going on. Why didn't you call right away?"

"I called when I called," she said. "I didn't know that little girl was Savannah Holt."

I stopped the tape. Dad had her. He'd blown enough holes in Hannah McClain's testimony to give the jury reasonable doubt if they wanted it.

I sank into my desk chair. He wasn't pulling punches. What I witnessed was E. Thomas Gale at the top of his game.

So why had everything gone so horribly wrong after that?

On a whim, I pulled up Lexis/Nexis on the desk computer and logged in to Dad's account. Hannah McClain wasn't exactly an uncommon name so it took a few tries. It helped that Dad had written her date of birth in his file notes.

Hannah McClain was now Hannah Corbin. She'd been married three times in the last fifteen years and life had not been kind to her. Husband number two had been arrested four times for domestic violence before she divorced him. Hannah herself had a record. But she'd been arrested along with husband number one for solicitation.

"My God," I whispered. It appeared husband number one had turned her out. She might be worth talking to if I could ever find her. She had a slew of addresses, and it wasn't clear which one was current. This was a rabbit hole for another day.

I picked up my phone. Something Mac Henderson said stuck with me. If I wanted to know Savannah Holt. If I wanted to try to understand what might have happened that night, there was only one person who could help fill in those blanks. Hoping I wasn't making a mistake, I texted Mac Henderson.

> Were you serious about me meeting with Olivia Holt?

He answered almost immediately.

> I was. I've already talked to her. She'll see you. When do you want to set it up?

I hesitated over my phone's keyboard.

> How about tomorrow?

A moment later, he sent me Olivia Holt's pinned location.

> I trust you'll be respectful.

> Thank you.

I just prayed I was doing the right thing.

My computer screen was frozen in front of me on the image of my father as he turned away from the witness box. He had a scowl on his face. The tips of his ears were red.

CHAPTER
Twenty-Four

I SAT outside Olivia Holt's two-story brick Tudor longer than I meant to. My feet felt cemented to the floor of my car. Hers was a quiet street in one of the older neighborhoods of Helene. The lots were big, five acres apiece. The house itself had been built in the 1920s. She had no view of Lake Michigan, but the natural woods abutting her acreage made up for it.

A teenage boy cut her lawn. He didn't hear me over the sound of his riding mower and his earbuds as I finally drew the courage to get out of my car and head up Olivia Holt's front walk.

I raised my hand to use her iron door knocker. The door swung open, startling me.

"I didn't think you'd have the guts to come," she said through the screen.

"It surprised me too," I said, deciding to give her as much honesty as I could.

Olivia cocked her head to the side. I knew she was fifty-two years old. She'd been just thirty-six when Savannah died. A young mother who many people had accused of breaking up Steven Holt's marriage to Diane. Today, she was a lonely woman who had lost her family. And for some reason, she was willing to talk with me.

Olivia swung the screen door open. She kept an immaculate home. Gleaming dark oak floors, original three-inch baseboards and high arches. She led me through the living room.

"I have an appointment in a little while," she said. Olivia wore a light blue tennis dress and kept her hair swept up away from her face. You could see a little of the pretty young woman she must have been. But the years and grief had ravaged her face, leaving heavy lines in her forehead and around her eyes.

"I won't keep you long," I said.

She turned. We stood at the entrance of a sunroom, the back half of which she'd turned into a lush terrarium.

"Mac said you want to ask me about Savannah. About that weekend. Whether I think Jeremy killed my baby girl."

"Well, I wouldn't put things so bluntly. But you understand, my father believes Jeremy was innocent. There are some things that have come up. I felt like you should hear this from us."

"Us. Does Tom know you're here?"

I thought about lying. But I'd done enough of that. "No," I said. "He doesn't."

"I've heard some other things," she said. "About your dad. That maybe he's not in his right mind."

"He's almost eighty years old," I said, feeling like that was enough.

"The answer is yes," she said.

"I'm sorry?"

"Yes. Jeremy killed Savannah."

"I appreciate your directness," I said. "And I'm not here to cause you more pain."

She smiled. "Honey, you really think anything you could say would do that? I've already been through the worst thing that will ever happen to me. It's the one blessing in all of this. It's freeing in a horrible way. To be able to live your life like this. Little things just don't matter. Terrible people just don't matter."

"I'm sorry for your loss."

"I miss her," she said. "There's a moment or two. Usually, first thing in the morning when I just wake up. Before I'm even fully awake. I'm happy. Content. But then I breathe and the weight of it settles around me. Grief is like a yoke you have to carry around your neck for the rest of your life."

She stared absently out the window. A pair of colorful finches fluttered around a bird feeder.

"This way," she said. I followed her into the sunroom. She gestured to a pair of rattan chairs.

"It's a lovely view," I said. From here you could see through to the woods. The sun bathed us in a warm glow.

"This was Savannah's room," she whispered.

"Oh," I whispered.

Olivia shot me that mysterious smile again. "Were you expecting a shrine?"

"I wasn't expecting anything."

"We argued about this," she said. "Steve and me. He wanted the shrine. The day after the funeral, I took a sledgehammer to that north wall. I wanted it all gone. I didn't need a room to remind me of my baby. She's in me. The whole world is a reminder of her absence."

"Well, it's beautiful here."

"See, that was my point. Let me sit in her space but I'll make it my space. She lives in my mind, not within four walls. Steve never understood that. Nobody did. Everyone thought I was trying to erase her. And now, they're all gone and I'm the only one left who *can* remember her. Some prize, that is."

"Mrs. Holt..."

"Olivia," she said. "I changed my last name back to Jergen, my maiden name. Not because I was angry at Steve. And I know it was Savannah's name. But it's also Jeremy's name. To me, the name is cursed. It was just another reminder I didn't need."

I shouldn't have come. What the hell was I thinking? What the hell was Mac Henderson thinking?

"I really don't want to cause you more pain, Ms. Jergen."

She smiled. "Do you know why I agreed to meet with you?"

"To be honest, no. I would think I'm the enemy to you."

"You didn't kill her. You were just a kid yourself when she died. Nobody ever wants to talk about her. It's like I said. I'm the only one that holds her memory now. So why in the world would I pass up the opportunity to talk about her? Even to you? Maybe you think that sounds crazy."

"No. It doesn't make you sound crazy."

She stared through me, leaning back into her chair.

"What was she like?" I asked.

Olivia looked out at the woods. The finches flew off. "She liked the cardinals the best. When she was eight, she found a fledgling on the ground. She picked it up and built a nest for it out of a shoebox. Steve told her she shouldn't have done that. The parents were probably still around somewhere watching out for it. And now they wouldn't be able to find their baby. I thought that was so cruel of him. She was just trying to be kind. We got into such an argument that day. That was also the summer Jeremy came back. We argued all the time. That's what I remember most about that summer. Jeremy was disrespectful. He took money from my wallet. He resented Savannah. I saw the way he looked at her. Just pure contempt. Jealousy. You know...I blame Jeremy for that, too. For robbing the peace of my household that last year."

"Did they have a relationship at all?" I asked. "Jeremy and Savannah?"

She shook her head. "Not a healthy one. But Savannah loved everyone. She loved the idea of having a big brother. When he would sulk, slam doors, she would go to him. Bring him dessert from the dinner table and he'd eat it in his room. He tolerated her, at least outwardly. But they were ten years apart, and Steve and Diane weren't in a good place then. Which meant Diane and I weren't in a good place. I felt like I cried every day of that year. So much wasted time. That's the other thing Jeremy stole from me."

She leaned forward and reached for a pink, hardbound book sitting under the table in front of us. She clutched it to her breast and drew her knees up in the chair.

"This is what I kept," she said. "This is what I want to remember."

She uncurled her body and handed me the book. It was a scrapbook. I carefully opened it. There were baby pictures of Savannah. She had light, silky hair and chubby cheeks. She outgrew those by her third birthday. The next page was an 8x10 of

Savannah sitting in the yard covered in frosting as she ate her cake. A tiny brown puppy with floppy ears licked her toe. She had her head thrown back in full-throated laughter.

"That was Droopy," Olivia said. "He was some kind of beagle mix. Steve rescued it from a shelter and gave him to Savannah that day. He lived to be seventeen years old. I had him longer than both Savannah and Steve. Good old dog."

The rest of the scrapbook was filled with drawings. Sketches. Flowers. Finches just like the ones from the feeder. The front of this house. Another was an attempt at a self-portrait. A little girl with her hair in a side ponytail. She even captured the small butterfly-shaped birthmark on her left cheek.

"These are incredible," I said. "Savannah did these?"

"She was my little artist. I bought her this paint set I was going to give her when she turned ten. I think it's still in the box up in the attic. I never had the chance to give it to her. She would sit and draw for hours on end. We'd have to yell at her to come down to dinner."

I turned the page. There was another picture of Droopy as an older dog.

"She didn't like that one," Olivia said. "His nose isn't quite right. She struggled with faces. But her landscapes were really something."

Savannah had drawn a picture of the woods. This was in color. Chalk. She'd drawn the finer details of the leaves and violets on the ground.

"You could exhibit these," I said. "I think they're that good."

"So people can talk about the tragedy of her murder again? No. I think these are just for me."

I turned the page. Savannah had drawn a picture of a rustic log cabin in the woods. It had a slanted roof and a wraparound porch complete with two rockers and a whisky barrel between them.

"That's out at Deer Park," Olivia said. "Steve used to take her out there. There's a pond there on state land that they stock with fish. He bought her this pink Barbie fishing pole when she turned seven."

On another page, she'd drawn the pond itself. Lily pads floated on the surface. She'd made an attempt at a turtle sunning itself on the rocks.

I closed the book and handed it back to Olivia. "Thank you for sharing that with me."

"That's all I need," she said. "Not some room with things only a nine-year-old would like. That would just be a grim and awful time capsule. I don't want to remember Savannah as she was. I'd prefer to think of her as something more."

I don't know what I expected coming here, but I'd stepped into something sacred.

"She wanted to draw me," Olivia said. "I had this silver sparkly dress she loved. I wore it that night. We went to that stupid party at the yacht club for Steve's boss. I had my hair and makeup done. Savannah said I looked like a princess."

I remembered the photograph of Olivia and Steve Holt that appeared in the local paper. Savannah had been right. Olivia was beautiful that night.

"She tried to touch my hair and I snapped at her. I wish I hadn't done that. The Jarrets came to pick her up right after that. She tried to touch me and I batted her hand away."

"You can't blame yourself for that," I said.

"I don't. I blame Jeremy. But that's the last memory I have of my little girl."

"I'm so sorry. I should go."

"She's dying," Olivia said.

"I'm sorry?"

"Diane. She's dying, isn't she?"

"Yes."

Olivia closed her eyes. "You know, I hated her in those first few months after I lost Savannah. More than I hated Jeremy, I hated Diane. I blamed her. I was awful to her. We made amends. After Jeremy's trial, something just flipped over inside of me and then I hated myself just as much. Because I realized Diane lost her son too. Not in the same way. She can go see him. Watch him get older. And then Steve had his heart attack and somehow, I shared that loss with her. We both loved him at one time. And we both blamed him for being at the center of the thing that ruined us. I know that's not fair. Steve suffered. Those years after Savannah died. I watched my husband waste away. I wanted him to be stronger. He just couldn't. I knew he was visiting Jeremy in prison that final year."

"He was? I don't even think Diane knows that." Jeremy never mentioned it to me, either.

"We've never talked about it. I threw him out of the house for a while because of it. I was getting ready to talk to a divorce lawyer. I just couldn't carry the weight of Steve's grief and guilt along with my own."

"Most marriages don't survive the tragedy you endured."

"Then he was gone. And I was angry at him for that too."

"Of course."

"Then Diane and I were what was left. We're bonded in some odd way. I should plan to go see her."

"I think that's a good idea."

"We don't talk about Jeremy or Savannah or even Steve anymore. We just sit with each other. We've gone for walks."

"I shouldn't take up anymore of your time."

"But yes," she said, turning to me. "Jeremy killed my baby. He was vile that last year. Savannah had three hundred dollars saved in a piggy bank on her dresser. He smashed it to pieces and took every last cent to buy drugs. He didn't even bother denying it. She told me, 'Mom? He's sick. We have to help Jeremy.' She went online and printed off info sheets about rehab facilities. She was nine years old! He took a swing at Steve. I got in the way. He gave me a black eye. Savannah saw it all. She lunged at him. God, it was so awful. I thought he was going to hit her. He pushed her away from him. He looked at her with such hatred. He broke her heart. Then he took her away from all of us. Just like he said he would."

"What do you mean? Like he said he would."

"That night when Steve finally threw him out, Jeremy lashed out and told Steve he would make him sorry. He was going to make sure he took everything that mattered away from him just like Steve did to him."

"But he didn't threaten to physically harm Savannah?"

"You know they found her clothes in his trunk. I don't know what you came here to find. Maybe Jeremy is a different person now. I hope so. For Diane's sake. But sixteen years ago, he was a lost soul who blamed Steve for everything that went wrong with his life instead of looking in the mirror. And he knew Savannah was the thing Steve cared about most of all. So he did what he said and took her from him. From me. I know in my heart Jeremy did this. And that's all I have to say."

She didn't say goodbye. She didn't show me out. She just left me there alone in the sunroom as she went outside to feed the birds.

CHAPTER
Twenty-Five

Saturday night, I told my father another lie. I told him I had plans with Liam in town and that I was staying at the office. He was tired. Though he'd had a good week, he needed to decompress, and I knew him well enough to know that even having me around could overstimulate him. I waved from the dock as he cast off and went back to the island alone.

Now, I sat in the relative dark of his office feeling like a thief and a liar. But had he been lying to me all along? A catch and kill order like Anne Barnheiser described would take a lot of money. Could my father afford it? Was he capable of doing something like that? If he was, he would never tell me the truth. It would mean my mother had been right all along.

I pulled out two boxes filled with old ledgers going back twenty-five years. My father still wrote paper checks for everything. He had one set of ledger books for his lawyer's trust account, another set for the firm's business account, and a final ledger for his personal accounts.

I pored over them, looking for large transfers in or out of any of the accounts. My father had made meticulous notes for every deposit or withdrawal made from the trust account as he was required to by law. His business accounts had a pattern to them. There were settlement amounts he kept his share of. Violet's salary remained constant with yearly five percent raises. He paid her well and she deserved it. There were payments to Lloyd representing my father's buy-out of his share of the business when he retired. And Dad paid himself a modest salary that decreased over the years though he made sure to keep Violet's raises.

He paid for expert witnesses. Process servers. Court fees. Utility bills. He still had a small mortgage on the office building. He owned the house on the island outright.

Methodical. Logical. Dad.

The only hint of the cognitive decline I knew was happening was in his penmanship. Sharp, tight letters and numbers became looser, shakier, dipping below the lines of the ledger. I ran my hands over them. The smell of the paper unlocked a core memory of me sitting on Dad's lap when I was little, pretending to write checks of my own.

But there was nothing here that proved a massive payout to or from a source that made no sense. No smoking gun.

A knock on the outer door drew my attention away from Dad's books. I packed them away and put them in the boxes.

Liam stood on the sidewalk, peering in the window. His face lit up when he saw me.

"Hey, stranger," he said as I unlocked the latches and let him in.

"Sorry," I said. I promised him I'd call him when I had free time. I still owed him a rain check for the dinner we'd skipped out on the other night.

"No apologies," he said. "I was down at the pier. Saw your dad leave without you. It's eight o'clock and I figured you probably hadn't eaten dinner. Mind if I kidnap you?"

I smiled. "No. And I'm a jerk. I should have called you."

"Do you need a ride back to the island tonight?"

"I was planning to stay in town. I'm catching up on some work. Plus, we needed to give each other space."

"Island man," Liam said. "You know, he really has the perfect setup out there. People think he's an extrovert. He's not, though. He just knows how to fake it."

"I think you're one of the few people who understand that. Peopling depletes him. I'm kind of like that too. It's my mom who thrives on her social life. That was one thing that caused a lot of problems for them. He never wanted to go anywhere. Especially when he'd just finished a trial."

"That makes sense. How do burgers sound? I heard a rumor you've never been to Blimey's. If that's true, it ought to be a felony."

"Can't have that," I said. My stomach growled in agreement, loud enough for Liam to hear.

"Come on," he said. "You wanna walk or drive? It's about a good mile but further down the boardwalk."

"Let's walk," I said. "But am I dressed appropriate enough for Blimey's?"

I was wearing a pair of faded jeans and a pink tank top.

Liam laughed. "No," he said. "You have regular shoes on. Blimey's is a flip-flop kind of place. But I know the owner so I can squeak you in like you are."

I grabbed my cardigan off the coat rack and locked the doors behind us. A light breeze came off the water, and it seemed like all of Helene was out tonight. Soft laughter filled the air. The fresh scent of the lake filled my head. The setting sun cast the world in a pink and orange glow.

Somewhere in the next block, Liam found my hand and laced his fingers through mine. It warmed me through and through. Something I needed and hadn't realized.

As we walked, we got friendly smiles and waves from almost everyone who saw us. For a moment, I felt self-conscious about holding Liam's hand. It would be noted. Talked about. Maybe even judged in this tiny town. But for now, I didn't care.

Blimey's was everything Liam said it would be. A tiny little Irish pub serving nothing but draft beer and whiskey. I had a cheeseburger that practically melted in my mouth and homemade French fries that tasted like heaven.

"You wanna talk about it?" Liam asked halfway through our meal.

"About what?"

"Whatever it is you're working on that has you making that face all the time."

"What face? I didn't know I had a face."

"You do. You get this little line right between your eyes."

I reached up and smoothed my forehead. I knew what line he meant. My mother got the same one. She had Botox a few times a year to make it go away.

"Sorry," he said. "I didn't mean to make you self-conscious."

"It's okay. It's just...I feel good when I'm with you. I feel like the only time I ever really get to stop and appreciate Helene is when you're around. The rest of the time, it's just all the stuff with my dad."

Liam put a hand up. "I get it. And I'm flattered. This place has a way of growing on you. I always end up back here."

"You've traveled a lot?"

"I've been to all the usual places. New York. LA. London. Paris. Madrid. Mostly for family business. Or to make my mother happy. I don't know. This place just gets into your blood. That view out there, the lake? It's as good as anywhere else in the world."

"And your family is here," I said.

Liam let out a haughty laugh and took a drink of his beer. "My family," he said. "Yeah. Them."

"I haven't met your mother," I said.

"She's in Tuscany at the moment. She and my dad are separated but not telling anyone. They're nutty enough to think it would impact Adam's chances at the polls."

"Why would anyone care if Adam's parents are getting a divorce?"

"Oh, no. We don't say the D word. Branches don't divorce. We're too Catholic for that. You marry in, you're stuck with us for life."

He meant it as a joke, but the second Liam's words landed, his expression got dark. "Sorry," he said. "I didn't mean..."

I put a hand over his. "I get it. It's okay. I didn't take it as a proposal." Things grew easy between us again.

"What about Adam?" I said. "With that kind of old-fashioned viewpoint, I would have thought your parents would make sure he was well married before running him for governor."

A shadow crossed over Liam's face. "Adam's never found someone that suited him. My parents' attempts at matchmaking have been disastrous. Adam just...well...he's always been the family project."

"What about you? That doesn't seem fair."

"Trust me. I'm fine letting the family light shine hardest on Adam. I'm not interested in any of that. As long as I protect the family brand." He said the last part using air quotes.

"The family brand," I said. "I feel that. Mine is also... problematic. Everyone thinks my father married my mother because she looks like her dead sister that he was supposed to be having an affair with."

"Was he?"

"I've been asked that question a thousand times," I said. "But somehow, you asking is the first time I haven't wanted to hide under a rock rather than answer it."

Liam smiled. "Because I don't care. As in, your family is your family. It's not you."

"When Dad gets entrenched in a trial, it takes over his whole being. He lives, eats, sleeps, breathes it. My Aunt Viveca was just beautiful. Sexual. Everybody wanted to sleep with her. People just assume my dad was no different. He was obsessed with her, but not in the way people think. He was obsessed with defending her. So no. I don't think he was sleeping with Viveca Baldwin."

"Then he met your mom."

"No," I said. "Then Viveca died. They found each other after that."

"She killed herself," Liam said. "I'm sorry."

"Don't be," I said. "Mom said my Aunt Viv was always a chaos agent. That's what she called her. Then she got herself mixed up with a real son of a bitch who abused her. Daily. Brutally. So, Viveca did the only thing she could and killed him before he could kill her. Only it killed her too in the sense she wasn't able to live with the guilt of it. My mom thinks her acquittal was the worst thing that ever happened to her. That if she'd gone to prison, she might have been able to come to grips with how everything played out. Isn't that odd?"

"Actually, it makes a certain degree of sense."

"Yeah. Maybe it does. I don't know."

We sat in silence for a moment, finishing our drinks and listening to the band that started playing at the back of the bar. Liam found my hand again. He pulled it to his lips and kissed my wrist.

"I've never told anyone what I just told you," I said. "About my aunt and my mom and dad."

"I'll never tell anyone that you did," he said. "I've never talked about my family stuff like that with an outsider, either."

"Thank you," I said.

"Liam!" The shout cut across the rising music and the growing crowd. Adam stood a few feet away, his expression grim.

Liam dropped my hand and rose to his feet. He walked over to his brother. Adam whispered something in his ear. Liam stiffened. He closed his eyes and let out a sigh. When he opened them, he gave Adam a terse nod, then walked back to the table.

"Mercy, I'm really sorry. Something's come up. It's a family matter. I've got to go. Adam's going to walk you back to your dad's office. He can run you back to the island in the jet boat if you want."

"Family business?" I asked, rising. Liam took out a one hundred-dollar bill from his wallet and tossed it on the table. Our entire bill couldn't have cost more than fifty.

"I'll call you tomorrow," he said. "Just let Adam walk you back. It's pitch dark out there now."

"It's Helene," I said. "He doesn't have to do that."

"I'll call you tomorrow," Liam said. He gave me a quick peck on the cheek. Adam's stern expression didn't change. Not until Liam walked out of the pub. Then Adam came to me, his bright smile back in place.

"I'm really sorry," he said. "Don't hold it against my brother."

"I don't," I said, unable to hide the annoyance from my tone.

Adam's face fell. "No. I suppose you wouldn't. This is entirely my fault. But let me make it right. Let me walk with you."

I gathered my things and walked out of the pub. Liam was already long gone. He was right. The streetlights barely lit the way and it was a long way back. Adam came out. He kept his hands in his pockets as we walked down the sidewalk.

"I suppose you won't tell me what this family business was?" I asked.

"It's just...my father. I'd think you of all people might empathize with that."

"I think I don't want to talk about my father right now," I said.

"You must think I'm a complete ass."

There was something about his face. His posture. Whatever was going on, Adam seemed upset.

"I hope it's nothing serious," I said. I meant it.

We kept on walking, staying silent for another block. As we got closer to downtown, it got chillier. I put my sweater on but had trouble with one arm. Adam stepped in and helped.

"Thank you," I said.

"He likes you," Adam said. "A lot. And my brother doesn't like very many people."

"He's a good guy," I said.

Adam smiled. "He really is. I think he might be the best of us."

"That's not what he thinks."

Adam stopped walking. "You see that too?"

"I see a lot," I said.

Adam regarded me. "I guess you would. I understand you paid Olivia Holt a visit yesterday."

"How do you know that?"

We started walking again. The office was just around the corner. "My cousin lives across the street from her."

"I guess not much goes on in this town without everyone knowing about it."

"How was she?"

I shrugged. "How well do you know her?"

"She writes to me. She's been a big supporter of my campaign. So is Diane Benning. I know she's not doing well. She also writes to me. She asked me...no. She begged me. If I win the governorship, she wants me to grant her son a pardon."

"For murder? She has to know you can't do that."

"I think she knows she's running out of time. She doesn't think Jeremy will survive much longer in prison. I don't know why she thinks that. Do you believe her?"

"Diane?"

"Yes. Do you think she's right about Jeremy? Did he kill that little girl?"

"Jeremy is a client of my father's firm. You know I can't discuss that case with you."

"Right. Sorry. Gosh. It seems that's all I can really say to you tonight. Sorry."

"This is my stop," I said, giving him a half-smile. We'd reached my father's office door.

"You sure you don't want a ride over to the island? It's really no trouble."

"Not tonight," I said. "Thanks for the walk."

"Oh, I think it's the absolute least I could do. Don't you?"

"I think you always manage to show up when it's dark out. It makes me think maybe you're part vampire."

Adam laughed. "I've been called a bloodsucker before. And a lot worse."

"Goodnight," I said. "And I really hope your, uh...family matter isn't serious."

"I'm sure Liam will tell you all about it tomorrow."

"Do you not want him to?"

Adam gave me an odd look, cocking his head to the side. "I think he's been a different person since you came to town. And it's nice to see. Things have been rough for my brother for a few years."

"Why is that?"

Adam reached out. He ran a hand down my arm. "Good night, Mercy. My offer still stands. I'll be around. If you change your mind and want to go back to your dad's house, I'd be happy to take you."

"This is fine," I said.

Adam's hand lingered on my arm. Then he pulled away, turned, and crossed the street.

CHAPTER
Twenty-Six

I STARED at my phone screen longer than I should have . The caller ID read Ionia Correctional Facility. I sat outside the prison walls, staring at the razor-wire fence. But the man on the other end of this call wasn't inside these particular walls.

"Jeremy," I answered.

I could hear him breathing. The ragged sound of it filled my car when I shut off the engine.

"Where are you?" he asked.

"I saw Olivia the other day," I said, not wanting to tell him where I was right now. Not wanting to give him any false hope that Remy Horner held some answer to the hell he'd lived in for the last sixteen years.

"I wrote her letters for a long time," he said. "Most of them came back unopened."

"You know she stays in communication with your mother."

"I'm glad."

"Are you okay? Have you seen your mother? Talked to her?"

"Yes. I said goodbye. That's why I'm calling you. I need you to tell her she can't come to see me anymore. It's too much for her. It will kill her."

"She's dying anyway, Jeremy."

He went silent again. I watched as visitors lined up at the gate of the G. Robert Cotton Correctional Facility in Jackson. I was supposed to be among them. I hoped I hadn't missed my window. I didn't know if I had the courage to come down here again.

"I need you to do something for me," Jeremy said.

I resisted the urge to say "anything." Because it would be a lie. I couldn't do anything he asked. Not anymore.

"I need you to tell her you're getting me a new trial."

"Jeremy..."

"Lie to her. I know I'm never getting out of here. Give her hope. Make something up. I don't care what it is."

"I don't know if I can do that. She'll know I'm lying."

"She won't. She deserves to have some peace and hope before she dies. She's the only one who kept believing in me all these years."

"My father believes you."

"Do you?"

"Jeremy..."

"No," he said. "You don't have to say it. I'm asking you to lie to my mom, not to me."

I took a pause. It was one o'clock. I was fifteen minutes past my appointment time.

"I have to go, Jeremy. But I'll come and visit you again. I'll see your mom at least one more time. That's what I can promise."

"Okay," he said. Then, before I could say anything else, Jeremy ended the call. I squeezed my eyes shut and held my phone against my ear for a moment longer. Then I got out of the car and walked up to the visitors' entrance, hoping I wasn't too late.

REMY HORNER WASN'T what I expected. Skinny, meek looking. As they led him to the table across from me, I realized he was only an inch or two taller than I was. It was then I understood how he could make some young girl feel safe around him. Nothing about him appeared threatening or sexual at all. He just looked like a little boy.

His scrawny arms were covered in tattoos. He folded his hands on the table. Remy had thinning tufts of black hair that stuck out in all directions. His unkempt beard smelled. His left eye was puffy and yellow underneath from an old bruise.

"My name is Mercy Gale."

"They told me," he said. Remy had a high-pitched voice that barely sounded like he'd gone through puberty. Another asset for him in the commission of his crimes.

"Someone hurt you," I said.

Remy shrugged. "I walked into a door."

I knew what happened to guys like Remy in places like this. The ones who hurt kids. He had six years left on his sentence. I wondered if he'd make it.

"Do you know why I'm here?"

"If I cooperate with you, will you put a good word in for me with the parole board?"

"I don't have that kind of influence."

"Fine. Then with your dad. If I'd had a lawyer like Tom Gale, I might have gotten a plea deal or something."

"That would depend on what kind of information you have to offer," I said. I was treading carefully here. I came with no authority to make any sort of deals. But I had one card to play. Remy Horner didn't know that.

"But he'll take my case?"

I considered Remy for a moment. Beady-eyed. Strung out. Maybe it was unethical, what I was about to do. I found I no longer cared.

"He's considering it," I said. "It depends on whether you give me truthful answers to my questions."

"I ain't never lied. Not once. And I never did anything to anybody that they didn't want done."

"You're in here for raping a thirteen-year-old girl."

"She said she was nineteen. It wasn't rape."

"Okay," I said, committing to the lie. "If that's all true, then maybe my father can help you. You have to do something for him first. I know you hung around with Dustin Bolton several years ago. I know you were friends with Jeremy Holt. You know he's in prison for a murder he didn't commit."

Remy leaned back in his chair. His eyes widened. "Why you gotta bring that up?"

"Because it's been sixteen years. It's time for the truth to come out. If you want help on your case, tell me what you know."

Remy shook his head. "I haven't seen Dusty in eight or nine years. Where was he when they locked me up? He said he was my friend. He didn't show up."

"You were friends with Jeremy too though, weren't you? You were with him the weekend his little sister went missing. You. Dusty Bolton, Jerome Dupris and Blackie Thompson, Alicia Tate. But you never spoke up for Jeremy. You have a chance to put that right now. Through me."

Remy shook his head. "I need a deal on the table."

I slammed a fist. "No prosecutor gives a shit about you now, Remy. Two witnesses saw you rape that little girl, Lauren Petersen. You bragged about it. I can't promise you miracles. You're going to do most of your time. But you might be able to do it somewhere where you don't end up with black eyes. Somewhere you might actually survive to the end of it."

"You think I killed Savannah Holt? The hell with this."

"Did you?"

His eyes flashed. "No."

"I know you were all together the weekend she went missing. Alicia Tate tried to come forward, but the cops didn't believe her. Dustin Bolton tried to come forward and..."

"Naw. No way."

"You're scared," I said. "But it's been sixteen years. Do yourself some good and tell the truth."

"I'm not a dumbass like Dusty. You should have seen what they did to him for trying to do the *right thing* like you're calling it."

"I did see it. Alicia took pictures. I can offer you protection. My father might not have the power to get you out of here. But he can help make sure you don't get hurt anymore. If you tell the truth."

"I tried to!" he said. "Nobody wanted Jeremy going down for killing his kid sister. That was nuts. He was an asshole. A junkie. But he didn't kill that kid."

"What do you mean you tried to tell the truth?"

Remy leaned in. "I want it in writing. Your old man gets me some time off my sentence. And he gets me the hell out of Jackson."

"If your story checks out," I said. "You first. That's the only way this is going to work."

Remy shook his head. "You're bluffing."

"You're wasting my time," I said, gathering my things. "I'm the only person who's come to see you in, what, two years? Enjoy your solitude."

I got up. Remy grabbed my wrist. Two guards in the corner came forward. I raised a hand to wave them off.

"You can't leave," he said, desperation filling his voice.

"Then tell me what you know. You hung around Bolton for years after Jeremy's arrest and trial. You know what happened. Alicia said you were with him that week when you all disappeared after Jeremy's arrest. Did you see who jumped him? What did you see?"

Remy shook his head. "Not guys. One guy. And he showed up out of nowhere. Look, things were crazy after Jeremy got arrested. The whole town was out for blood. The cops were on a rampage. All trying to make a name for themselves off that murder. We were just trying to keep from getting dead. Or worse."

"Who was it? Who came after you?"

"Nobody was supposed to know where we were. Your old man set up an apartment for Jeremy. We crashed with him because it was supposed to be safe. But this guy showed up. Says he's there to talk to Dusty. I told him don't get in the car. Don't trust him. But the guy was wearing a suit. Dustin thought he was a cop. Like that would have made it any better. We were doing the right thing. We didn't want Jeremy going down for something he didn't do. We looked out for each other back then. Nobody else would. But Dusty went anyway. And when he came back, half his chest was melted off. And worse."

"What do you mean worse?"

Remy shook his head. "He was cut. All over. A bloody mess. And he wouldn't let us take him to the hospital. He was too scared. So, it was me and Blackie who made sure he didn't die."

"Who was it that came and picked him up? You said he looked like a cop?"

Remy nodded. "Like the FBI or something. He told Dusty he was there to take him somewhere safer. Until he had a chance to testify. But it just didn't feel right to me. I tried to warn him. But you couldn't tell Dusty anything."

"What did he look like, the guy in the suit?"

"Big muscle-head type. Looked like a bodyguard or something. That's why Dusty believed what he said. About being there to protect him. Garland."

"Garland?"

"Yeah. His name. Garland. That's what Dusty said. Mr. Garland."

"Was he old? Young? Help me out, Remy."

Remy shrugged. "I don't know. Like maybe my dad's age. Sixty? He had some gray hair and that kind of leathery face."

"White guy? Black guy?"

"White. Tanned. He looked like the Terminator. But like he had money. That's why Dusty trusted him. That's why I didn't."

"Garland," I repeated. Mr. Garland.

"Yeah. Garland. Or Garlan. Something like that."

"What else?"

"That's it. He drove up in a black Town Car. Couldn't tell you anymore about that. Didn't see plates or anything. But Dusty left with him, and we didn't see him for two days. When he came back, he was raw hamburger. You said you saw the pictures. So you know. Or you think you know."

"Thank you, Remy. This could help."

"Damn straight. So, when is your dad going to do something for me?"

"As soon as he can," I said. "But it will take some time. He'll have to file a motion with the court about your transfer."

"Not just a transfer. I want a new trial. You tell him that."

"I'll tell him that. But first, I need to check out your story."

"I'm telling the truth. I got nothing to lose."

"No," I said. "I suppose you don't. Remy, I've got to ask you something else though. Do you remember where you were the night Savannah Holt went missing?"

Remy smiled. "I was in the hospital that weekend. You can look it up. You're a smart girl. I took something I couldn't handle. They

CHAPTER TWENTY-SIX

had to pump my stomach. Jeremy was supposed to party with me that same night. I bet now he wishes he had."

"Yeah," I said.

"I got lucky."

"Lucky," I repeated. "I'll be in touch, Remy."

"I'll be waiting," he said. Then he blew me a kiss as I turned to walk away.

CHAPTER Twenty-Seven

I DROVE BACK to the office in a daze, not knowing whether I wanted my father to be there or not.

Garland. Garland. Garland.

When Remy said it, at first it didn't register. Or I hadn't wanted to. It was a common enough name. Except it wasn't. And I knew I had seen it. Had heard it.

As I passed each mile marker, the weight of it settled onto my chest.

Garland. Violet and my father used the name as their secret code when he wanted her to get him out of a meeting. She would tell him Mr. Garland was here to see him.

By the time I made the exit toward Helene, I couldn't breathe. It was past six o'clock. When I turned down the boardwalk and toward the pier, my pulse raced.

The boat was already gone. Dad was back on the island. Relief washed over me. I had to be sure. Before I asked him the question that could change everything, I needed the literal receipts.

I parked on the side street and sprinted toward the office. The tourist dinner crowd was out. I wanted to shove past every person between me and the back door of my father's office. I heard someone call my name but ignored it.

My hands trembled as I fumbled with the keys. I dropped them once. Then finally, I turned the lock and stumbled through the door.

No lights. No sounds. Violet had long since left for the day, too. Dad left a note for me on the reception desk.

"Turning in early. Call if you need a ride back. Love you."

My phone rang. Without even looking at the caller ID, I hit the side button, turning it to silent. I went back to Dad's office and closed the door.

I needed a moment. I needed to breathe. I sat in his desk chair, my hands flat on the blotter. Finally, slowly, I went to the boxes I'd stacked against the wall the other day. Tomorrow, I had planned to take all of these back into storage. Most of them could be shredded. God. If I'd done that. If I'd waited a few more days to talk to Remy, maybe I never would have had to do this at all.

I pulled down the top box and grabbed the one beneath. I'd labeled each of the stacks of check stubs by year. Thumbing through, I found the ones from the early 2010s.

I went through them one by one. My mind went still as I skimmed through Dad's looping cursive. It was there. I knew it. It was only a matter of time. I had seen the name at least a dozen times. Year by year.

John Garland.

Check after check he'd written to him. Many were small amounts. A hundred dollars here and there. Dad had written small notes in the memo lines. They corresponded with entries in the business ledgers.

Process Service - Chaney Matter

Background Checks - Delia Morgan

Process Service - Longfellow

I pulled each stub bearing John Garland's name and set it to the side. Then I pulled out my phone, swiping aside the three missed call notifications. I typed John Garland, Helene, Michigan, into my browser's search bar.

A news article from ten years ago pulled up. "John Garland, former Green Beret honored at Helene Rotary Club."

Remy's description echoed through my mind. He'd said he looked ex-military. Like a bodyguard. Like the Terminator.

The John Garland I found online was square-jawed sporting a military buzz cut. Wide shoulders. Tall. He stood next to Fred Penney, a former Helene Township Supervisor shaking his hand. Garland was a head taller.

Dad had written larger checks to him over the years. Nothing more than five hundred dollars at a time, but there were dozens of those. The payments went back twenty years, from the time my father and Lloyd Murphy set up the practice here.

Maybe Remy was wrong. Maybe Garland had only come to their hideout to talk. If Dad was paying him for process service, maybe he was there to deliver a subpoena. Remy could have confused him with someone else. He had to be wrong.

Because I could not let myself believe my father had paid a man to sabotage his own client's case. He could not be allied with someone who beat and tortured a man...even someone like Dustin Bolton...into silence.

"Mercy?"

I jumped as someone pounded on the back door. My whole body shook. Remy had to be wrong. But bits and pieces of things Jeremy said came rushing into my brain.

I trusted your father once. Maybe that was my biggest mistake.

Maybe he's not the man you think he is.

I want to believe you're not like him.

I took all the check stubs and shoved them into my bag. I closed the boxes and went to the back door.

Liam stood there. He peered through the window; his face lined with worry. When he saw me, his shoulders sank with relief and his eyes lit with a smile.

I opened the door. "Are you okay?" he asked, rushing forward. He grabbed me. "What's wrong?"

The words wouldn't come out. I couldn't tell him. I couldn't tell anyone. Not yet. Not until I understood it myself. If I ever could.

"Nothing."

"It's not nothing. Mercy, I saw you walking down the street. You looked...panicked. You didn't answer my calls. Don't tell me you're okay. I can see it in your face. Something upset you. Did someone...Mercy, who hurt you?"

His tone went from concern to something colder, more protective.

"I can't," I said. "I need to get out of here."

Liam put an arm around me. "Do you want me to take you home? The jet boat is docked at the pier. I saw your dad take off a couple of hours ago."

"No," I said, breathless. "I don't want to go back to the island. Not tonight."

"You don't want to stay here," he said.

I shook my head. I needed to go...somewhere.

Liam went rigid. "Come on," he said. "Let's get you out of here. You don't have to tell me anything if you don't want to."

In that moment, it was all I needed to hear. I grabbed my bag and dug for my keys. Liam held the door for me. I turned and locked it behind us. Then he held out his hand and I took it.

We walked down the street. The few people who recognized us, Liam deftly said our hellos and steered me away. He took me to his car, and I was grateful for the small sanctuary it provided.

I didn't have it in me to be polite. Or engage in small talk. Or answer questions. Liam seemed to understand that. He simply pulled away from the curb and drove up the steep hill to the top of the bluff. It was just a five-minute drive to Beecher Street. Liam's townhouse. It reminded me a lot of Mrs. Greenbaum's. Of Adam's. But they were four blocks away and at the bottom of the bluff.

There was a chill in the air tonight. I followed Liam up the walk. His front door was under an alcove of oak trees. Private. Inviting. He unlocked the door and invited me in.

"You've got to be starving," he said. Like a zombie, I walked into Liam's kitchen. Tastefully remodeled with cobalt blue cabinets and white stone countertops, he had a huge kitchen island with metal stools. I sat on one. Liam took a container out of the fridge and heated it up. Then he plated some spaghetti and put it in front of me. It smelled delicious. We ate in silence together and Liam poured me a glass of wine.

"Thank you," I said, as I came back to myself.

"I like having you here," he said. "I've been meaning to ask you to come. Sorry about the mismatched plates. I never really have cause to entertain anybody."

"I hadn't even noticed," I said. I was eating off a blue plate that almost matched the cabinets. Liam's had a different pattern, with yellow flowers. The forks weren't from the same set either.

"My mother has been threatening to come over here and re-outfit the entire house. What do I care if my dishes don't match?"

"My mother's the same way," I said. "Worried what people will think if they see my ottoman doesn't match the sofa."

"Do you still keep an apartment of your own?"

I shook my head. "No. I had one in Toledo. But...I let the lease go."

"You're not going back?"

I paused for a moment. Then I met Liam's eyes. "No. There's nothing left for me there."

"Will you stay here? I mean...not here, here. In Helene." The expectation in his eyes cut through me.

Will I stay here? Could I stay here?

"I'm trying," I whispered. It was the truest thing I could say. Then the events of the day just bubbled up inside of me. The lies. The secrets. The truths I wasn't sure I could bear. It went through me like a tsunami.

"Mercy," Liam said, his voice catching.

I felt like I was drowning. Instinct fueled me and I reached for him. A lifeline. The only person who truly seemed to pay attention.

CHAPTER TWENTY-SEVEN

He came to me. Gently at first. But when I gripped his arms and pulled him to me, a different kind of wave came over us both.

I kissed him. I inhaled him. He stayed so still, letting me take control. He became the rock I clung to so the current wouldn't drag me under. Then I knew I wanted it to.

"Mercy," he whispered. And I didn't know whether it was my name or a plea for it. Maybe it was both.

My hands were in his hair. His hands came around my waist, pulling me off the stool. I wanted him. Had wanted him maybe from the first time we met. I knew what he thought. What he worried about.

Adam was the one everyone thought was handsome. Desirable. But Liam was the man who seemed able to see through my soul. There was never any competition.

His kisses became more urgent. I felt starved for him. Hungry. Every cell in me cried out for more. For him. For a night, a moment, where there was nothing but what I wanted. And no one else to take care of.

We became a tangle of limbs, of raw need. Liam skimmed his hands over my hips. I fumbled with my shirt, pulling it over my head. His fingers slid up my back, finding the clasp on my bra. I reached for the button on his jeans.

He pulled off his shirt, and I couldn't stop touching him. He was beautiful. Hard muscles, a dusting of dark hair across his chest. And that night, he made everything right in my world.

He lifted me off the floor and carried me to the living room. We never made it to the bedroom. But somehow that was perfect too. He made love to me on the floor in front of his fireplace. I could see the full moon through his skylight as Liam's touch carried me up to the stars.

CHAPTER
Twenty-Eight

IT HAD BEEN a long time since I woke up next to someone. Liam slept on his stomach, his head turned away from me. I watched the rise and fall of his back.

I could leave. Quietly, grab the rest of my clothes and sneak out without waking him. It wouldn't be the first time I'd done something like that, or had it done to me. Only this didn't feel quite like a one-night stand. I hadn't yet decided whether that was good or bad.

His breath caught. Liam snorted, rolled over, and opened his eyes. It took a second for him to register where he was. But his smile melted me and stirred something deeper down. He slid his arm around my waist and pulled me closer, kissing my cheek.

"Morning," he said.

"Morning."

He propped himself up on one elbow. "I figured you'd bail."

"I was thinking about it. Thought maybe it would make things easier."

Liam rubbed the sleep out of his eyes. He had sinfully long, dark lashes. The kind that wasn't fair to the rest of us.

"You can still make a break for it. I'll pretend it was all a dream."

"Too late," I said. "You've already gotten a whiff of my morning breath."

"I wasn't gonna say anything. But you're fairly hideous." He could keep me warm with just his smile.

"You're no picnic yourself. You're a bed hog. Anybody ever told you that?"

"Believe it or not, there haven't been that many in a position to tell me."

I slid out of bed, found my pants and stabbed my legs through them. Liam rose. I watched his backside as he made his way to the bathroom. He was completely unshy, leaning over to brush his teeth.

"I've got extras in the drawer there," he said, spitting out his toothpaste.

We were comfortable with each other, putting ourselves back together. Liam's automatic coffee maker had a fresh pot brewed by the time we made our way out to the kitchen. He poured me a mug, and it tasted like heaven. He toasted some bagels and made me a plate.

"You think of everything," I said.

"I think of you."

I sipped my coffee.

"You want to talk about it yet?" he asked.

I put my mug down. "Do we have to? I don't think I'm ready for labels."

He smiled. "Not that." He gestured toward the couch. The cushions were still strewn all over from our late evening...er...romp. "I mean you. Do you want to talk about what you were so upset about?"

"Family stuff," I said.

Liam nodded. "I figured. I'm here if you need someone to listen."

"I suppose you'd know a thing or two about that."

"Family stuff? A bit, yeah. I try to compartmentalize."

"Does it work?"

He laughed. "Rarely. I suppose the difference is I've got Adam to help bear the brunt of it. When it isn't his mess, I'm trying to clean up."

"I always wondered if that would have made a difference, if my parents had another kid."

"What about Everett? Where does he fit in?"

I shrugged. "Mostly, that's between Everett and my dad."

"And Everett has no idea you're here?"

"Not from me."

Liam paused. He poured himself another cup of coffee and warmed mine. He slid onto the stool beside me. "Maybe you just need a break from all of it. I mean you're working at the office with him. When you're not there, you're on a literal island with your father. I would think after a while that would get...isolating."

I nodded. "It really does."

"Well, you have a place to hide out whenever you want it. I like having you here, Mercy. And if you just want some space to yourself, there's a guest house out back. I just finished renovating it last year. Nobody's even stayed in it yet."

"Wow, that's...Liam, that's extremely generous of you. And as much as I'd like to say everything's fine and I have things under control right now? The truth is I don't know."

"Do you want to stay here tonight? No strings. In spite of everything else, I want to be your friend."

I turned to him, put a hand on his cheek. Then I kissed him.

"Thank you. Right now, I feel like you're the only friend I really have here in Helene. It matters. I don't want to do anything to screw that up."

"You can't," he said, putting a hand over mine. "Promise."

"But I think I have to go back. This family stuff isn't going to resolve itself. And I need to talk to my dad. While I still have the courage to do it."

Liam gave me a puzzled look, but he didn't ask any more questions. I was grateful for that.

"Come on," he said. "I'll drive you to the office. If he's not there, I'll take you out to the island. And I can wait for you if you don't want to stay. I can be whatever you need."

"Thanks," I said. I found my purse and my shoes. Liam grabbed his keys. Then we headed down to the docks.

~

MY FATHER SAT on his fishing bench next to the pier. He wore his New Balance tennis shoes and lucky purple fishing socks. It made me smile. My mother hated those things and tried to throw them away. Dad cast his line as Liam pulled his boat alongside. I stood at the bow, ready to catch the dock pole and guide him in.

Dad looked up. He cocked an inquisitive head our way and raised his hand. Liam waved back.

"Do you want me to wait for you?" Liam asked.

I felt the weight of the check stubs I'd taken from Dad's office in the bag slung over my shoulder. Liam gave me a hand as I stepped off the boat and onto the dock.

"No," I said. "It doesn't look like he's going anywhere today. If I want to vote myself off the island later, I can leave under my own power."

Liam nodded, satisfied that I had a suitable escape plan. "How about dinner tonight? You can meet me in town or I'm happy to come out here for you."

I looked back at Dad. He kept his eye on his fishing pole, but I knew his face. He was very much focused on Liam and me more than the fish.

"I'll text you," I said. Liam moved toward me, then froze, reading my body language. I wasn't ready to answer any questions from my father. Let him think Liam was just a good friend offering me a ride.

I gave Liam a tight-lipped smile and pushed him off. He called out. "Hope you have better luck with the walleye than I've been having, Tom."

Dad pulled up his line and recast. "You just can't be in a hurry," he yelled. Liam tapped the horn on his boat and sped away. Wind whipped my hair around my face as I made my way up the dock toward my father. With each step I took, I felt my adrenaline rise.

"Thought you were coming back last night," Dad said. "I was worried."

"I'm an adult," I said. "And I've lived on my own for a long time. Before I was even an adult."

I don't know why I said that. It was picking a fight. But maybe today I wanted to. Maybe today I didn't care.

"Maybe so," Dad said. He reeled in his line and stuck his pole in a metal holder he had soldered to the dock. "But I'm allowed to worry."

I sat beside him for a moment, trying to figure out how to even have this conversation. So much had happened in the last thirty-six hours. I didn't think I could stomach a lie from him. I wasn't sure I could stomach the truth.

"So, what is it?" he said. "What's got you making that face?"

"What face?"

"I know my way around Baldwin women, Mercy. You've got a damned ravine between your eyes. You're clenching your jaw so hard you're gonna ruin about six grand worth of orthodontics I forked over for your smile. I wouldn't mind seeing it once in a while. You haven't done a lot of that since you came to Helene."

"Maybe I shouldn't have," I said. My words came out biting. But they rang true.

"Maybe so. But you did. You're here. And I'm too damned old to play guessing games. Why are you pissed at me now?"

I kept my hand on my bag, feeling the outline of the stacks of paper.

"We need to have a conversation I've been avoiding for a few weeks now, Dad. I went to visit Remy Horner yesterday. Do you know that name?"

He squinted. The sun poked out of the clouds. "No," he said. "Should I?"

"Remy Horner. He was one of Dustin Bolton's crew. He says he was with him and Jeremy Holt around the time Savannah disappeared."

"Stop," he said. "You're wasting your time chasing ghosts. I should have told Diane Benning she wasn't welcome in the office anymore. I'm sorry she's sick. But that's not my fault."

"Is what happened to Bolton your fault?"

He turned sharply toward me. "What the hell are you talking about?"

"About a month after Savannah's murder, he was beaten. Tortured. You knew that. Didn't you?"

"No, I didn't know that. He was a junkie. His whole life was playing with fire. What does any of that have to do with me?"

"Remy told me who did it," I said. "He said a man came to their hideout. The place nobody was supposed to know about. But you knew. Bolton was your witness. You arranged for him to have a safe place to stay. And Remy gave me the name of the man who came and took Bolton. Threw him into the back of his car. When he came back, he was missing two fingers and his chest was half burned off. Then he went to the cops and changed his story. He perjured himself at Jeremy's trial. He refused to back up Jeremy's alibi. Because he knew the same man would come back and kill him if he did."

"If Remy Horner was Bolton's crony, then he was a crackhead too. How does this help anything?"

"Horner's in prison, Dad. Did you know that? He raped a thirteen-year-old girl. He ran around with Jeremy and Dustin during the time Savannah went missing. But nobody questioned him. Not even you. Horner should have been a person of interest in Savannah's murder."

"I'm not a cop, Mercy."

"No. Mac Henderson was. I talked to him too. He didn't know about Horner, either. He didn't know Horner was in prison for raping a minor until I had him look into it. And he didn't know Dustin Bolton had been roughed up and threatened before he gave his story to the police. Dad, you've had the means to reopen Jeremy's case all along."

"You don't think I've done everything I could for that kid?"

"John Garland," I said. I reached into my bag and pulled out the stack of check stubs. Dad barely looked at them.

"What about him?"

Something about his tone. He seemed so cavalier. So irritated with me. I was done. It was everything. The last few weeks. The past sixteen years. Lloyd told me this case got under my skin because my mother thought it ended my parents' marriage. Maybe they were all right. My anger bubbled up and exploded out of me.

"John Garland! That's who came and took Dustin Bolton. Who beat and tortured him within an inch of his life. John Garland. That's who Remy named. He described him. I've seen pictures."

"He's full of crap," Dad said.

"Garland was on your payroll!" I yelled. I ripped off one paystub and shoved it at my father.

He took it. Without his readers, he had to squint to read it.

"What is this?" he asked.

"Who was he? Who was Garland to you?"

"Johnny? He was a friend. Ex-Green Beret. My mother...your grandmother...was friends with Johnny's mother. His dad, Bart, served in Korea. When I enlisted in the Navy, Bart Garland came over to mentor me. When Johnny came of age, his mother asked me to do the same thing. But she was hoping I'd talk him out of it. He went through some rough stuff overseas. Served in Beirut during the eighties. When he got out, I gave him work. Process service. Then some private investigations. Background checks. I haven't seen him in years."

"I don't believe you."

"The truth is the truth."

"You knew where Bolton was holed up. You sent Johnny Garland after him. That's what Remy told me."

"Fine. Believe him over your own father. God, you sound just like your mother."

"Don't. Do not bring her into this."

"Mercy, I don't know what you want me to tell you. I didn't sabotage my own case. Christ. I'm the only one who still believes in Jeremy Holt besides his mother. Why in the hell would I take a dive on Holt?"

He was saying things that made sense. And yet, the trail to John Garland was clear. Why would Remy have made it up?

Then there was Christian. The minute he tried to go to the press and stir up questions about the Holt case and Dad, he ended up dead. Who else would have had something to gain by silencing him, but Dad himself?

It was in me to tell him about Anne Barnheiser. About the so-called catch and kill. But something stopped me. Could I trust he was telling me the truth about John Garland? Or that he was even remembering correctly?

He crumpled the check stub I'd given him and let go of it. It was quickly carried off by the wind.

"Is this why you've been visiting Jeremy once a month for fifteen years?"

"What?"

"Was it guilt? Or were you just trying to make sure Jeremy wasn't piecing things together the way I am?"

"Mercy, what is this? How the hell do you know how often I've visited Jeremy Holt?"

"He wrote me," I said. "Jeremy Holt wrote me letters. He said he was worried about you. You stopped coming to see him. And before that, he said you weren't yourself. He thought I should know. He thought..."

"He went behind my back? And what business is it of yours how often I talk to former clients? Since when have you taken any interest in that, Sandra?"

"I'm not Sandra. I'm Mercy."

"Mercy!" he yelled. "Christ. You think I don't know my own daughter's name?"

"And yet you've spent more time with a convicted murderer than you have with me."

I hated the way my voice sounded. I hated that my throat felt thick. That I could feel tears stinging my eyes.

"Jeremy shouldn't have involved you."

"No, but you should have. Dad, what's going on? Tell me. Make me understand why a man on your payroll beat up Jeremy Holt's alibi witness and scared him into lying to the cops?"

"I have no idea. Odds are Horner's lying."

"How would he just pull John Garland's name out of thin air? Or give me an accurate physical description?"

"I don't know! You want to play this game? How about you? How about the lies you've been telling me since the second you got here?"

I clamped my mouth shut.

"I know you dropped out of school. Why?"

"That's none of your business. You weren't paying my way."

"That's another thing your mother blames me for. Instead of being proud of you for choosing a smaller school you could afford on your own, she was angry I didn't pull strings to get you into somewhere more prestigious. That's when she wasn't blaming me for pressuring you into law school in the first place."

"Don't put me in the middle of your issues with her. This is about you. You and me."

"Why did you come here?" he asked. His tone was stinging, accusatory.

"Because I was worried. Because it wasn't just Jeremy Holt you ghosted. You stopped taking my calls, too."

"You wanted to check up on me. *Spy* on me."

"No. Not spy. I'm your daughter. The things I was hearing had me concerned that you weren't doing okay. And if I didn't come out here, who would?"

"I didn't need you to. Nobody asked you to uproot your life."

"You should have! Maybe you should have made a point of spending time with *me* every month instead of Jeremy Holt."

He dropped his chin to his chest. "You're messing with things you don't understand."

"So, enlighten me. Let me help you."

"I don't need any help."

"Yes, you do! Dammit. Yes, you do!"

Something changed in my father's face. The fury went out of it. His eyes went wide with what looked like fear. He grabbed my hand.

"What," I said. "Dad, what? What is it?"

"I don't know," he said. "I just don't know. I don't remember, okay? I don't remember what I had Garland doing. Lots of things. I told you. And I...I don't remember Remy Horner."

His voice softened to a whisper. It was as if I could *see* his brain struggling to capture the silken strands of memory as they slipped away from him.

"Dad," I said, softer. "Tell me the truth. Please. Did you know that John Garland tortured Dustin Bolton to force him into lying in court?"

He shook his head. "I can't. I don't. No. I don't believe that. I would never do that. I could never do that."

"But you don't remember?" It hurt to watch him. Physically hurt. He didn't even trust his own mind. But my whole life, I could say many things about my father. He was gruff. Sometimes cold. Rarely affectionate. Brilliant. Fierce. But something else as well. He was staunchly moral. The kind of man who would march me back to a cashier if I'd been given even a dime more change than I should have. The kind of man who forced the court to understand that my poor, battered aunt was a victim, not a killer.

"Did I?" he asked. His eyes stayed wide and red with terror. Before he could answer, he shook his head with the vigor of a dog emerging from water. "No. No, Mercy. I did everything I could for Jeremy and I still am."

"I know, Dad," I said. And I wanted to. His fear turned quickly to indignation.

"I'm done talking about this," he said. He got up and stormed off toward the house, muttering as he went.

I wanted to smash something. I still had more questions than answers and the one man who could put it all to rest had just walked away.

I watched the water for a while as it crashed against the sea wall. Walls. Walls and lies. I was surrounded by them. There was one person left who had to stop lying. If I couldn't convince her to trust me, I would have to make her fear me. She was easier to find than I expected her to be. A simple Google search. Simple. If I could find it so easily, anyone could have. Anyone who knew why she was important to Jeremy Holt's case. As I read the name of the town where she lived, my heart turned to stone.

Cadillac.

CHAPTER
Twenty-Nine

Beads of sweat dotted my forehead as I sat in the parking lot of a Used Car lot in Cadillac, Michigan. It couldn't be a coincidence. Of course it couldn't.

Then I saw her.

The years had changed her. She was heavier. She dyed her hair a purplish red instead of the wispy blonde she'd worn when I saw her on the witness stand in that grainy footage from sixteen years ago. She'd changed her name as well. Dropping her maiden name. Now she was Hannah Corbin.

For nearly two months since I'd come to Helene, I'd tried to find out who my father was, but I kept myself distant from his name. With Remy Horner, I had traded on it. I would have to do it one more time. Her probation officer had been eager to confirm what I suspected about Hannah. Cooperating with law enforcement had been a condition of her release. She'd done eight months of a two-year sentence for solicitation.

I checked myself in the visor mirror, smoothing an errant hair over my head where I'd all but shellacked it back. I wore a black suit and heels. I looked like my mother. No. I looked like my aunt. Viveca Baldwin. The Black Widow. Killer of men. As some wanted to believe.

A tap on my window startled me. But somehow, I managed not to jump.

"Can we help you?" A smarmy salesman with bad veneers peered in.

Waving him off, I stepped out of the car. "I'm just looking," I said. "If you don't mind, I'd like to walk into the showroom but not have you hover. Just give me your card and I promise you'll be the one I ask for if I see something I like. Er...Brad." He wore a name tag.

Brad looked put off, but he was smart enough not to piss off a potential sale. He gave me his card and a wide berth. I walked into the showroom.

Hannah sat at the reception desk. She gave me a bright smile. "Can I help you with something?"

I pulled a card out of my purse and slid it across the desk. It took her a moment to register the name on my father's business card. When she did, she lost a bit of the color in her cheeks.

I felt my blood drain from my head. I don't know what I was expecting. Exactly this, I suppose. Still, part of me hoped she would have no reaction at all.

"Can you take a break?" I asked, keeping my voice low. "I only need a few minutes."

"I don't see what good that will do."

"Just a couple of minutes. I'm not here to ruin your day." Except I was.

Hannah looked to her left. Another woman stood in the doorway to the inner office filled with cubicles. Hannah grabbed her purse.

"I'm gonna take my break a few minutes early. Do you mind covering?"

The other woman smiled and nodded. She said something to the man she'd been conversing with at his cubicle.

"This way," Hannah said. She led me out the side door. There was a small alley between the showroom and the body shop. By the ashtrays propped against the wall, this had to be where employees took their smoke breaks. For now, there was nobody else around.

"What do you want?" she said.

"My name is Mercedes Gale," I said. "Tom Gale is my father. And I work for him now."

"You another lawyer?"

"Sort of," I said. "You know why I'm here?"

She stared upward, then leaned against the wall. "I can't do this anymore. You said you only need a few minutes. I'd say your first minute is up. This is a good job. I don't need you people here messing things up for me again."

Again. Of course, again.

"I'm not the first to come here asking you questions this month, am I?"

"You tell me," she spat.

Trying to keep my hands from shaking, I took out my phone. I pulled up a photo of Christian and showed it to her. "Was it him? This man? Did he come to see you?"

She glanced at the photo, but registered no recognition, just a cold stare. But she didn't have to admit it. I knew. Christian had been in Cadillac because he wanted to talk to Hannah McClain. And days before that, he'd been on my heels when I tried to talk to Alicia Tate.

"I just wanted to check in on you. Make sure you're doing all right, Hannah."

"Yeah," she snapped. "I'm doing just fine. Happy now?"

She tried to brush past me. I grabbed her forearm. She went rigid. The fear in her eyes was real. She was afraid of me. No. Not me. Of who she thought I represented. My heart turned to ash. I'd never wanted to be more wrong about something in my life.

"There have been some developments," I said. "Questions are being asked about the Jeremy Holt case. By the wrong people. But you already know that. So I need to know what you told the man who came to see you."

She jerked away from me. "Are you stupid or something? You come marching in here, plain as day. Throwing this around?"

She still held my father's card. She flung it to the ground.

"Would you rather I send Mr. Garland out here to talk to you again?" I snapped.

She took a step backward, her eyes widening. "You need to leave."

"Alicia Tate is talking," I said.

"I don't know her."

"You know enough."

She jabbed a finger at me. "I am done. I am not part of whatever you think this is. This is harassment. Or witness tampering. I told the other guy the same thing."

CHAPTER TWENTY-NINE

"Except we both know you're not a witness," I said. "Not really. Perjury is a crime, Hannah."

"Go to hell. I guess you really are an idiot. I did my duty." She spat out the word duty.

"Good," I said. "That's what I wanted to hear."

"You shouldn't have come here," she said. "If any of you try again, I'm going to get a restraining order."

"We're just having a conversation," I said.

"Right," she said. "Well, next time you better bring somebody bigger and scarier than you. I have a life now. I'm not going backward. I'm done."

"You're done when you're no longer useful," I said, hating myself for it. "But right now? We need to talk about revising the terms of your deal."

"There it is," she said. "What deal? There was no deal. There were just threats and violence. And I'm not afraid of you people anymore."

People. God. What people? I needed her to slip up. Name names. So far, she'd done nothing to make it seem like she didn't think my father was behind her lies.

"I've done everything I was asked to do," she said. "I'm not part of this. Not anymore. You need to get the hell away from me."

I wanted to ask her. Make her admit that her testimony in Jeremy's trial was all a lie. She never saw him with Savannah. She'd been put up to it. Threatened with violence just like Dustin Bolton.

"Dusty Bolton sends his regards," I said, taking one more shot.

She froze. Tears sprang to her eyes. Her bottom lip quivered. My God. She was terrified. Bolton.

"You're sick," she said. "You wouldn't bring Dusty up to me if you were a decent human being. And if he's dumb enough to talk to you? You tell him. You tell him I can still smell it. I have nightmares about it." She put a hand to her chest in the very place where I'd seen Dustin Bolton's scars. She could still smell it. They'd made her watch.

I didn't feel decent. I felt awful.

"You lied on the stand," I said. It just came out of me. Of course, I knew it was true. And she believed my father was partially behind it. Was he?

"Go away," she said. "You don't even know what you're asking me."

"Hannah?" Brad poked his head out the door. Hannah stiffened. She plastered on a fake smile.

"I'm coming," she said. She flashed a final angry look my way. Squaring her shoulders, she wiped her face, hiding her tears.

She left me alone in that alley. I was shaking. She hadn't admitted to lying. She didn't have to. Her fear spoke volumes. And Christian came here before me. Someone must have seen him. Did he pay for that mistake with his life?

Someone set Jeremy Holt up to take the fall for Savannah's murder. Who? Why? She was just a little girl. Who else would have wanted her dead? Or who else would have gone to these lengths to conceal her real killer?

I took a step. My shoe landed on my father's business card. With a trembling hand, I picked it up. Then I crumpled it and threw it in the dumpster at the end of the alley.

CHAPTER *Thirty*

I MEANT TO DRIVE HOME. I wasn't sure where that even was anymore. The island? Florida with my mom? Toledo?

I kept on driving past the pier. My father's boat wasn't docked. He'd gone back to the house. I could sleep at the office again. I could call Liam. I wanted to escape to his townhouse, crawl under the covers, and be with him. Let the pleasure of him blot out everything that was becoming true.

A man on my father's payroll had brutally beaten Dustin Bolton into silence. He had made Hannah McClain watch. She hadn't said the words. But her implication was clear. Hannah had perjured herself on the stand and made the jury believe she had seen Savannah Holt with Jeremy the day she disappeared.

I hadn't consciously planned to come here. But an hour before sunset, I parked on a desolate county road near the trail marker down to Deadwater Lake.

This wasn't where the tourists came, but the view was even better. I got out of the car, climbed over the guardrail, and made my way down the trail.

The Running Bear Dunes were to the right of me. The wooded nature preserve on one end of the lake was straight ahead. I took the path, minding my footing.

I didn't know exactly where to look. Never expected the place to be marked after all these years. But a tiny metal cross with faded plastic flowers tied to it was staked into the ground at the eastern shore of the lake. An old satin bow hung from the bottom of the cross, its ragged ends swaying in the breeze.

This was where they found her. Weighted down and wrapped in a plastic garbage bag. Discarded. Thrown away. She had only been nine years old.

I said a prayer for Savannah Holt that day. I hoped she'd found peace. I hoped she suffered no pain. But there was no way to know. There was no closure for Olivia Holt. And none for Diane Benning.

It was beautiful here. The fading rays of sunlight poked through the maple trees, dappling the still waters of the lake. I closed my eyes and inhaled the scent of sap and the hint of Lake Michigan to the west of me.

My ringtone shattered the peace, startling me. The caller ID read Ionia Correctional Facility. It seemed fitting that he would call me now. I answered.

"Jeremy," I said. He didn't speak at first. I could just hear the faint sound of him breathing.

"I haven't heard from you in a while," he finally said. "Are you still working on my case?"

What could I say? That I now believed his mother had been right all along? That my father may have been paid by someone to make sure Jeremy went to prison regardless of his guilt? I was close to proving it. I was close to destroying everything he built and everything I believed about him.

"I am," I said. "I've hit a snag. Be patient. I need more time."

He laughed. "I have all the time in the world. But she doesn't."

"She?"

"I got a call. They've brought hospice in for my mom. I spoke to the nurse. She doesn't think it'll be more than a week. She doesn't eat anymore. She barely drinks. They started her on morphine this morning."

"Jeremy, I'm so sorry."

"Will you go see her for me?"

"Will they let you talk to her on the phone?"

I rose, stepping away from the small, tattered memorial someone had placed for Savannah. I couldn't tell Jeremy where I was. I didn't think I could tell anyone.

"She doesn't really say anything. But maybe if you were there, you could make sure she hears me."

"I don't know, Jeremy. I'm not your mother's favorite person."

"It doesn't matter. She knows you'll do what I ask. Will you?"

I kept on walking along the shoreline. On the opposite shore, I could see the tall, haunting petrified oak trees that gave Deadwater Lake its name. Some said they'd been there a thousand years. I came to the tree line. This part of the woods should run into the Running Bear Wildlife Center. My dad brought me here once when I was thirteen years old. They had an "ambassador" possum in a pen near the Welcome Center. His name was Wilbur.

"I can try," I said. "I'll reach out. But I can't promise anything."

"You made me the one. You said you'd get answers for me."

I squeezed my eyes shut for a moment. I would regret making that promise for the rest of my life. It would haunt me for at least that long.

"Jeremy, I never promised you they would be ones you'd like."

"I know. After Mom dies, it will just be me. No one else will ever want to believe the truth. Except maybe for you."

"I have to go," I said. "I'll try to reach out tomorrow."

I kept on walking. A trail split through the woods. It really was beautiful here. There was a small clearing up ahead. This wasn't state land anymore. I passed a private property sign and realized I'd gotten turned around. The trees were tall here. The sun still poked through, so I knew what direction I was heading. I was about to turn around and come back the way I came, but something caught my eye. The sun gleamed off something metal.

A roof. I made my way through the thicker brush, then found the clearing. A small cabin was nestled between two black walnut trees. One window was broken out near the front door. Its copper roof drew my eye as the sun reflected off of it.

I stopped. I knew this place. Had seen it somewhere before. The sagging slope of the roof with the red chimney in the center.

Savannah's drawing. Olivia's words replayed in my mind. Her father used to bring her out here to fish in the lake. But this wasn't right. This wasn't the angle of what she'd drawn.

I walked around to the back. The woodpile she'd drawn was still there, though much smaller and the cords weren't neatly stacked. Some had fallen over and rotted. An ax leaned against the wall of the house. I looked behind me. Savannah had drawn her picture from a greater distance. From above.

CHAPTER THIRTY

I walked that way. My need to see through Savannah's eyes, if only for a moment, burned through me. It didn't look like anyone had been here for years. Birds nested in the sagging gutters. Another window was broken out in the back. There was no telling what manner of critters had taken up residence inside.

I walked up a small hill at the back of the property. A few trees ahead of me seemed likely candidates for Savannah's perch. I looked up through the leaves for solid branches that might have supported her weight. One tree in particular, an ancient oak, had thick knots at the bottom. Perfect for a small girl to find a handhold and foothold.

I thought about climbing up then came to my senses. If I fell, if I broke something, I was out in the middle of nowhere and nobody knew.

I looked back at the cabin. Even from this vantage point, I could see inside. It might have been cozy once. Just one room with a fireplace in the center. I saw a kitchen off to one side with a wood-burning stove. A few copper pots still hung on hooks, but the countertops were covered with rodent droppings. Squirrels or mice. Racoons, maybe.

But I felt her. Savannah. The widest part of the lake was right behind me. This had to be near where her father had brought her to fish. Did they have permission from the property owner? Had anyone bothered to ask?

That had been a theory at one point. That Jeremy had lured her out here under the guise of going fishing. Because it was an area she was familiar with. But there had been no physical evidence found anywhere in the woods. There was no mention of this cabin or Olivia's drawings in Henderson's report. It might not have been something he would have naturally asked for. Or that Olivia would have thought to mention.

"What happened out here, Savannah?" I whispered.

The trees rustled in response but held onto their secrets. I ran my hand along the knotted bark. Walnuts and acorns littered the ground. A squirrel's paradise.

I walked back down to the cabin and peered into the broken window.

"Ugh." I covered my nose with my forearm. Something had died inside, for sure. Recently. Even as I thought it, a chipmunk skittered out from under the foundation.

I walked around to the front. A small yellow piece of paper was tacked to the front door. Most of the words on it had faded. The paper itself almost turned into a paste from countless rain storms soaking through. But the bold red lettering at the top was still legible.

Notice of Condemnation.

I took my phone out and snapped a quick picture of the notice. When I got to the office in the morning, I wanted to find out who owned this place. Nobody had ever spoken to them in conjunction with Savannah's murder investigation as far as I knew. Maybe it didn't matter. But this place had been important enough for that little girl to sketch.

My phone rang again. It surprised me the reception was still good enough. It was Liam. Warmth spread through me.

I took a step back and snapped a quick picture of the cabin before answering his call.

"Hey," he said. "I was getting worried. I drove by the office and you weren't there. Violet said nobody's seen you all day. You're not trying to make a clean getaway, are you?"

CHAPTER THIRTY

I laughed. "No. I just needed to take care of a few things out of town. I'm finished now."

"Good. Are you hungry? I'm making dinner."

"You cook? I'm impressed."

"I didn't say I cooked well. I am pretty good with the grill. You up for barbecued chicken?"

My stomach growled in response. "Yeah, actually. That sounds perfect."

"Where are you?" he asked. "Sounds like you're outside."

I turned my back on the cabin and started walking toward the trail. "Just needed a little exercise."

Liam laughed. "I can maybe help with that. Er...if you're..."

"Yes," I said, faster than I should have. But nothing sounded better than running to him right now. Away from the ghost of Savannah Holt. Away from my father. Away from my mother's expectations.

Even as I thought it, part of me knew it wasn't fair. Liam didn't deserve to be the thing I used to escape. He deserved something more. I didn't know if I could be that. Would I ever be capable?

It was as if he could read my mind. "Mercy," he said. "Just get here."

A moment later, I ran down the trail.

CHAPTER
Thirty-One

"You don't have to tell me if you don't want to," Liam said. I stood on his back porch, sipping coffee. A pair of finches had swooped down, landing on a feeder he kept on a hook.

"Tell you what?" I said.

"Why you're avoiding your dad."

"I'm not avoiding my dad," I lied.

"Mercy, you stayed here last night. Which makes me happy. Thrilled. But as far as I know, you didn't tell him. And now it's ten o'clock and you haven't once said anything about going into the office. In the short time I've known you, that's out of character. Did something happen?"

"Nothing happened. Living with my father can be...a lot."

He came up behind me, snaking an arm around my waist. He pulled me back so I leaned against the solid muscles of his chest. As he kissed the space between my earlobe and my neck, goosebumps went down my spine. That familiar warmth settled low in my core.

I liked this. Liked waking up with him. Being with him. Maybe even more than I wanted to admit. But he was right about something. This was a way for me to escape. So I wasn't being fair.

"I'll head to the office later today. I want to finish a few research projects I've got going on. I'm heading over to township hall."

"Anything I can help you with?"

"I don't think so. Pretty mundane property tax research."

"Ohh," he said. "I love it when you talk dirty."

I turned to face him, sliding my hands up his chest. I kissed him. "But maybe we can meet for dinner later. You're right about something. I need to check in with Dad. At this rate, he'll probably file a police report about his missing car."

Liam laughed. "I doubt it. He barely drives the thing as it is. I think he's happy you're getting use of it. Tom Gale prefers to travel by air and sea as far as I know."

"You're probably right."

"I'm always right. Haven't you figured that out yet?"

"Mmm." I kissed him again, then went into the kitchen to rinse out my coffee mug. I put it in the top rack of his dishwasher. Liam leaned against the doorframe leading out to the patio, smiling at me.

"What is it?" I asked.

"I just like watching you."

"Fill your dishwasher? That's what gets you off?"

He gave me a wicked grin that sent heat shooting down to my toes. "Oh, never mind," I teased.

"No. I just like that you're comfortable here. I like that you know where I keep the coffee mugs. There aren't many other people who know where I keep my coffee mugs, you know?"

My breath caught. Something heavier settled between us at the implication he maybe didn't mean to make. Liam's face fell as he realized it. Then he quickly recovered and put his own dirty cup in the dishwasher.

"Liam..."

"I've got a full day myself," he said. "Only slightly more interesting than property tax searching. I'm working on a logo for Fletcher Realty. It's very exciting."

"Sounds like it," I laughed. "I'll leave you to it. But I'll text you later. We can figure out dinner."

"Are you ready to go out somewhere? Or would you rather stay in hiding? I'm down for it either way."

"I'm not hiding," I said.

"Oh, you're hiding. I don't mind. You're not ready to answer questions."

"Liam, I'm not hiding. Honest. I just...are *you* ready to answer questions?"

He let out a breath. "Honestly? No. I'd rather just keep you to myself. Plus, I'm not too keen on getting the death stare from Gale Force."

I laughed. "I still can't believe you know about Gale Force?"

"Everybody knows about Gale Force. I fully expect to find your dad sitting on that bench by the dock with a shotgun across his knee next time."

"He's not that bad." As I said it, I prayed it was true.

"Have you met your dad?"

I rolled my eyes. "Fine. I'll come here. But let me bring dinner. You shouldn't have to cook for me all the time."

"I like cooking for you. Though, we're getting close to the end of my repertoire."

"Good. That settles it. You let me figure out dinner."

"As long as you don't mind eating late. Does eight work for you?"

"It works perfectly."

He came to me again, pulling me into his arms. It felt good there. Too good. We kissed and I grabbed my purse and keys off the counter.

"Good luck on your logo," I said. "Will you be working here all day?"

"Yeah. That's why the late dinner. When I get knee-deep in a project, I'm no good to the outside world."

"I get it," I said. "I'll leave you to it then."

I said a last goodbye and headed out. As I did, Adam pulled into Liam's driveway. I froze. Liam came up behind me, holding the door open. Adam frowned as he saw us together, but quickly recovered. He plastered on a smile as he got out of his car.

"So much for hiding," I muttered.

Liam reached for me. He pulled me back and gave me a kiss on the cheek. It made me uncomfortable. As if he were pissing a circle around me for his brother's benefit. It seemed out of character for him.

"Sorry to interrupt," Adam said, his tone cheery enough. He looked from me to Liam.

"I was just leaving," I said. "Good to see you, Adam."

"It's always good to see you too," he said. "Your father was asking about you though. I just saw him at the office. He was asking Violet if you'd checked in. Mercy, he looked a bit frazzled."

"Thank you," I blurted.

"I didn't mean to pry," Adam said.

"You're not. Thanks for checking up on him."

"I wasn't checking up. I was just walking by and saw him at the front desk through the window. He was...well...disheveled. I'm sorry. But I know Tom well enough to know when he's having a bad day."

"I appreciate it. And like I said, I'll check in."

"Come on in if you're coming in," Liam said, his expression gruff. "That is if you're done telling Mercy her business. How about we stick to our own family drama and leave hers alone?"

Adam's face flashed with anger, but he said nothing. He found that rehearsed smile once more and moved past his brother to go inside.

"Sorry," Liam mouthed. I held a hand up, gesturing that it was all right. Then Liam turned and went inside.

He was right about one thing. I wanted to leave them to their own family drama and have them stay out of mine. At the same time, if he was right about Dad, it could be a long day.

I sent a quick text to Violet.

> Heading to township hall for a few things. Is Dad all set with his schedule for the day?

She responded almost immediately.

> No worries. He was asking about you, so thanks for checking in. I'll hold the fort down over here.

I sent her a thumbs-up and got in the car. It was only a ten-minute drive to township hall further up the bluff. It was one of the oldest buildings in Helene, built in 1881. It had been a church at one time. The bell tower still existed, making it one of the most recognizable landmarks on Helene's skyline.

I parked in the small lot across the street and headed over. Township hall shared a lot with the Helene Public Library. A young mother and her two preschoolers walked in carrying armfuls of books. It was story time. I politely waved and went into the government building.

One long counter had signs marking the different departments. Assessor. Zoning and Planning. Township Supervisor. Records. Two clerks in cubicles behind it served all the departments. I walked over to records. One clerk, Jennifer Pohler, smiled and came to help me.

"Hello, Mercy! It's good to see you. Tom was in here just the other day talking about what a help you've been to him this summer. We're sure glad he's letting you."

The other clerk, Gloria Willis, gave me a knowing but polite smile.

"It's good to see you, too."

"Are you going to stay here permanently?" Jennifer asked.

"I'm here for now," I answered. It was the most honest thing I could say.

"Well, what can I help you with today?"

CHAPTER THIRTY-ONE

"I was hoping you could give me some information about this abandoned property out at Deadwater Lake. It abuts one of the county parks out by the dunes."

I pulled out my phone and queued up the image I'd taken of the condemnation notice I'd found on the cabin door yesterday.

"I don't know the address," I said.

There was a large township zoning map on the wall next to us. I set my phone down where Jennifer could see the image. I walked over to the map and traced a line down until I found the approximate area where the cabin sat along the northern shore of Deadwood Lake. A large portion of the area was shaded in green, designating it as protected wetlands. But along the western shore, there were a handful of rental properties.

Jennifer frowned as she looked at the image on my phone. "Oh, I think I know which property you mean."

"Is it for sale or in foreclosure or anything? The notice on the door was pretty faded. I couldn't read the dates."

"Let me check," she said. "That property has changed hands a few times. It used to belong to the Bing family. Way, way back. It's not there anymore, but one of the last pioneer cabins was out there."

"The cabin I saw didn't look that old," I said.

"No. The original log cabin burned down in the 1960s. Before my time even. I think there's a newspaper article about that somewhere. Big, big fire. Started by some careless kids. Made the national news, I think because the original cabin had been built in the early 1700s. Such a shame."

She went over to her computer and punched in a search.

"Yeah," Gloria chimed in. "The Bings sold all that property off in the seventies. A brother-in-law of mine looked at it once. He wanted to build out there but the zoning board wouldn't let him. I was kind of glad about that."

"Oh, it's been bought and sold tons of times since then," Jennifer said. "Here we go. Beau Godfrey. That's who's on the rolls now. Hmm."

"What is it?"

"The taxes are delinquent on it. Looks like the condemnation order was signed almost two years ago."

"What happened? Why hasn't it been torn down?" The name Beau Godfrey sounded familiar, but I couldn't immediately place it.

"Things move kind of slow around here sometimes. Looks like Godfrey appealed it. It'll wind its way through the court if the thing doesn't fall down on its own. Anyway, that's who owns it now. I've gotta talk to our assessor. He should have filed a lien on the place. Things just kind of fell through the cracks during the pandemic."

"I can imagine. Can I get a copy of that? The tax page?"

"Sure," she said.

"Why do I know Beau Godfrey?" I asked. "Does he live in Helene?"

"No," Jennifer answered. She went to the printer and pulled up the pages she'd just sent over. She walked them to the counter and handed them to me.

Beau Godfrey was listed as the owner. He had a Lansing address.

"What's a guy who lives all the way down in Lansing doing, owning property up in Helene that he's let go to pot?"

"Good question. I hate to sound so negative or...parochial. But I sure hate when out-of-towners buy property in Helene. This is the reason."

"Well, I appreciate this," I said.

"Mind if I ask why you're interested in that property? Not many people go out that way. It's too swampy to camp. And...well... there's a rumor that it's a little bit haunted. You know, on account of where they found...um...Savannah Holt. Isn't that right near there?"

"Yes," I said.

"Dear Lord," Jennifer said. "I hate to even think about that. You know that case really destroyed your dad. After the verdict came in, we didn't see him around town for weeks. Lloyd Murphy and Hollis Branch finally went out there to make sure he was all right. He was out of his mind. I heard he ran them off with a shotgun."

"Jen!" Gloria barked. "Don't be such a gossip. That was a million years ago. Mercy, don't pay any attention to her. You know we all love your dad."

"I know," I said. "And it's nothing to worry about. Thanks again for this." I waved the papers. "What do I owe you?"

"For that? Oh, honey, nothing," Jennifer said. "It's public record. You shouldn't even have to come down here to get it. Just about every other county in the state has their property info online. Not us though. God forbid the township would allocate funds for that."

"It's fine," I said. "Gave me a chance to say hello."

I thanked Jennifer again and left her and Gloria to their chitchat. I could hear Gloria continuing to scold her coworker as the door shut behind me.

Beau Godfrey. I knew the name. I was certain of it. As I got behind the wheel, I plugged it into my phone's browser.

Beau Godfrey. His picture pulled up under a news article. A rush went through me. I'd met him. The first weekend I was in town at Adam Branch's fundraiser. The night I met Liam.

Beau Godfrey was Adam Branch's campaign manager. The man everyone believed would get him elected governor in fourteen months.

He owned the cabin that Savannah Holt had sketched from her perch in the trees. An odd thing, that. According to the tax rolls, he'd owned it for over twenty years.

I knew I needed to talk to him. Find out if he knew who had been staying there. Had he ever lived in it? Rented it?

I pulled out my phone. I didn't know if Adam would still be at Liam's. I hoped not. It could have been awkward if he answered a call from me while he was there.

Finally, I decided I was just being paranoid. I punched in Adam's cell phone number and left him a message.

"Hi, it's Mercy Gale. Look, I was hoping to talk to you about something if you're going to be in your office tomorrow. I know it's short notice. If you'd rather I call your scheduling secretary, I understand. Just shoot me a text."

I clicked off. As I started the drive back to my father's office, a text came through from Adam. I punched the option to hear it read back.

> I'd like to talk to you about something, too.
> Come by my office at nine tomorrow morning.
> Looking forward to it.

A pleasant enough response. But I dreaded the meeting.

CHAPTER
Thirty-Two

Adam Branch kept his district office in Charlevoix, just a few miles west of Helene. It was beautiful here. A similar lake coastal vibe, but Charlevoix had more tourist traffic. Adam's office took up the top floor of an old clock tower. He had a magnificent view of the South Pier Lighthouse.

I arrived just before nine the next morning. His receptionist, Bailey, informed me he'd taken a breakfast meeting and would be back at any moment.

"Congressman Branch asked me to have you wait in his office," Bailey said. She was pleasant, attractive, dressed professionally in a sharp, eggplant-colored suit. She told me she'd started out as an unpaid intern when Adam ran for the statehouse for the first time, ten years ago.

"Hopefully," she said, "we'll be making a move to Lansing by the end of next year."

"I hear the governor keeps a house on Mackinac Island, too."

"Oh, it's beautiful," she said. "I can't wait." Then her face fell. "No. I mean...I shouldn't jinx us."

"His chances are good," I said. "Everyone says the governorship is ripe for a party change. Fresh blood. He's polling double digits ahead of the competition."

"Still," Bailey said. "It's good to be superstitious. His office is just through here. Is there anything I can get you? Coffee? We have fresh pastries in the conference room."

I put a hand up. "Thanks. I'm fine."

Bailey smiled. "He'll just be a few minutes. Please make yourself at home. I'm just outside this door if you change your mind and I can get you something."

I thanked her. It really was a lovely office. The building was at least a hundred years old. A chandelier hung above my head with a beautiful medallion plaster design surrounding it. The six-paneled oak doors looked original, standing eight feet high with stained-glass windows above them.

I went to the window. A corner office, Adam had a view of the bay on one side, the quaint downtown area on the other. The only wall without a window had a massive built-in bookshelf. Adam kept a copy of the Michigan Compiled Laws in it along with various other treatises. Another shelf housed framed photographs of Adam shaking hands with various bipartisan movers and shakers.

I spotted a picture of him with both the current and former presidents, sports heroes, even the pope. His picture shelf reminded me a lot of the one my dad had in his study. A few of Adam's pictures with actors were autographed, just like my father's.

"Mercy!"

I jumped a little, not hearing him come in.

"Good morning," I said, clasping my hands behind my back. I turned to face him.

"Sorry to keep you waiting. I was meeting with some members of the UAW. A bunch of talkers. I didn't want to be rude."

"Of course not," I said. "I feel guilty tearing you away from something like that."

"Trust me, you did me a favor. Have a seat. Did Bailey offer you something to drink?" He went to the door and shouted her name.

"No," I said. "I mean yes. She offered me refreshments. I really don't need anything. I don't want to take up much of your time."

Adam waved Bailey off and shut the door. He gestured for me to take a seat at one of the overstuffed leather chairs in the corner rather than in front of his desk. He had a cozy seating area on the bay side. He joined me, taking the opposite chair.

"So, how's it going at the Gale Law Firm?"

"It's going well."

"Do you enjoy working with your father?"

"It's been interesting," I said.

"I'll bet. I didn't think Tom was taking on too many new clients. Has that changed?"

"Not really. He's mostly just finishing up with his existing clients. I'm trying to get him to wind things down. Enjoy his retirement."

Adam laughed. "I don't see E. Thomas Gale packing away his shingle anytime soon. But it's good that you're there keeping an eye on him. I have to tell you; he's been on my mind a lot lately."

"I appreciate that."

"Mercy," Adam said, letting his tone drop an octave. "Forgive me for being blunt. I have a lot going on this morning. And as much as I'd love to spend all of it with you, Bailey's going to come in here in about fifteen minutes to hustle me to my next appointment. But...I'm in a precarious position. The Branch family and your father go way back. In a way, I consider him part of my family. Or at least my father does. There was a time when Tom's endorsement could make or break somebody like me. But now..."

I was confused. I had no intention of making this meeting about my father.

"Adam...I..."

"Don't get me wrong," he said. "I will stand by Tom Gale to his dying breath. I owe him a lot. His early support of me was the tipping point in my first congressional election. I won't forget that. It's just...things are more nuanced now. I'd like for your father to enjoy the sunset of his life without the spotlight a gubernatorial election might bring. But I also don't want him to feel like he's being shoved aside. Like I said, his support is important to me."

"So, you want his money, but you don't want him in any pictures with you," I said.

Adam's face fell. "I didn't mean..."

I smiled. "I know what you meant."

"I'm not doing a very good job of this. The last thing I want to do is offend you. I was hoping you and I could come to an understanding. About your father...but also about a lot of other things."

Adam shifted in his seat, closing the gap between us so his knee was almost touching mine.

CHAPTER THIRTY-TWO

"You and my brother," he said. "You've gotten close. I have to admit, it's not a match I saw coming. And it's like I told you. Your father is like family to me. Which means you're like family to me. Do you understand what I'm trying to say?"

He reached out and actually touched my knee then. It made me uncomfortable. As if he were trying to take up all the space between us.

"I don't think I do," I said.

"Liam is complicated. I just want to make sure you know what you're getting into."

"I appreciate your concern. But I don't really feel comfortable talking about Liam with you just yet."

"He cares about you. My brother can be very charming. Very disarming. At first."

Oddly, it felt like he was describing himself more than Liam.

"I didn't come here to talk about Liam. I said I didn't want to waste your time. I'm actually looking into some property near the Running Bear Nature Preserve. There's a cabin that's been condemned by the township. I did a little research into the owner and it's someone you're familiar with. Beau Godfrey."

Adam's face didn't change or register any alarm or recognition.

"Do you know the property? I was out there the other day and kind of stumbled upon the cabin. It's beautiful there, but incredibly rundown. I was hoping to talk to Mr. Godfrey about it. I understand he's worked as your campaign manager. The contact information the township has isn't current."

"Beau is out of the country," Adam said. "He has property in Italy. His wife has family there. I don't imagine he'll be back for a couple of weeks."

"But he works for you."

"Yes."

"I'm curious why he's still holding on to property here. The township wants to tear that cabin down."

"Are you looking for an investment opportunity?"

"Maybe," I lied. "Do you think you could get a message to him I'd like to talk to him?"

Adam kept a plastic smile on his face. It unsettled me. "Of course," he finally said. "I can text him right now." He took out his phone, swiped up, then punched in something.

"There. Though I can't promise when he'll respond. It's late afternoon Tuscany time. I wouldn't expect to hear from him until maybe tomorrow."

"I appreciate that," I said. "I won't take up anymore of your time."

"Don't go. Not yet. I feel as if I've said something to make you uncomfortable. That wasn't my intention."

"I'm not uncomfortable."

"You are. Look, I've made a mess of this. It's just...Liam and I are very close. The Branch family isn't the easiest to belong to. We've always looked out for each other. I know he's harbored some jealous feelings. It can't be easy being my brother. I've never wanted him to feel like he has to live in my shadow. But I know he does. It's just...this is going to be a very challenging year leading up to the election. It's important, Mercy. For me. For my family. And whether you realize it, it's important for you and your father, too."

"I'll be happy to take a yard sign," I said, trying to lighten the mood.

"I'll take you up on that. Honestly, I'm going to need all the help I can get. My opponent is going to play dirty. Try to uncover every family skeleton. I have nothing to hide, but that doesn't mean people can't find things to twist, you know what I mean?"

I didn't. I didn't want to. I just wanted to leave.

"I've heard nothing but good things about you as a politician, Adam. I know my father thinks the world of you. He also thinks you're going to win."

"That's high praise. But what about your opinion of me?"

"What do you mean?"

He moved even closer to me. Unsettlingly close. Adam reached up and smoothed my hair behind one ear. I flinched.

"You're special, Mercy. I'd like to get to know you better. I mean, if you're truly getting serious about my brother."

I moved away from him, sliding out of the chair. I went over to the bookshelf to look at his pictures again. My gaze settled on one where he was wearing a tux. My father stood next to him, a martini in one hand, his other arm around Adam's shoulder.

"That was the night I won my election to the state house. It was an upset. I'd been down in the polls for two weeks leading up to Election Day. But your father...he told me the polls were wrong. He bet me a hundred dollars I would win. I took that bet. The day I was sworn in I gave him a hundred-dollar bill in a frame. I think he keeps it in his office. Have you seen it?"

"I'm not sure," I said. "Dad has a lot of memorabilia scattered everywhere."

"He's lived a long, colorful life."

My father appeared in another photograph in a tuxedo. Adam looked younger in this one. I felt as if I'd seen the photograph before. Adam had his arm around a pretty brunette in a red dress. Why was it so familiar?

"That was my father's first retirement party," Adam said, reading my mind. "It was bittersweet. Dad really hoped Liam would take over the newspaper from him. But Liam marches to the beat of his own drum. Dad came out of retirement about a year after that."

I felt the icy fingers of fear snaking down my spine. I remembered where I'd seen this photograph before. I'd read the local newspaper from the night Savannah Holt disappeared. This picture was in the same edition of *The Daily Caller*. It was the same weekend. But that wasn't what made every hair on my neck stand on end.

Adam posed for the camera. The pretty brunette was off to the side almost as if she were trying to get out of frame. Another man had an arm around Adam. He held a rocks glass, toasting him, a big smile on his face. I recognized him.

"His first retirement party," I said, almost absently. "My goodness. It looks like the whole town was there."

"I think they were. Shut the whole yacht club down. The governor came. It was an embarrassment."

"Why?"

"Because it was supposed to be Liam's coming out party as much as my father's going away party. Dad was handing him the keys to the kingdom. Liam agreed to step in and take over the entire company from my father. He'd been planning for it for years."

I kept my eyes transfixed on one photograph. I tried not to make it obvious.

"Liam didn't last a year. That's an ongoing problem with my brother. He can't commit to anything long-term. It's good you know that."

"Running a local newspaper isn't Liam's passion," I said. A younger version of Adam stared back at me. My heart thundered as I studied the man standing beside him.

Hollis Branch's retirement party had been the event of the season. Everyone who was anyone in the state attended. My father was there. And it was the last night Steven and Olivia Holt saw their daughter alive. They, too, had been at this party.

On the night of Savannah Holt's disappearance, Adam Branch had been at his father's grand retirement party. And the man standing so close to him in the picture I now gazed at, drinking with him, slapping him on the back was none other than John Garland. The man who had beaten Dustin Bolton into silence and made Hannah McClain watch.

CHAPTER
Thirty-Three

JOHN GARLAND. Every twist this case took, the road led to John Garland.

I don't remember what clumsy thing I said to get me out of that office. Adam was polite. He hugged me and I tried not to recoil. I tried not to sprint back to the parking lot. I could feel Adam watching me from that second-floor window with the full view of downtown.

Sweat poured down my back as I got behind the wheel. I peeled out of the parking lot and drove until I couldn't see Adam's building in my rearview mirror.

I pulled into the first parking lot I saw. It belonged to a small, quirky pottery shop run by a local artist selling her own creations. I pulled out my phone and punched in the number Anne Barnheiser gave me, not knowing if she'd answer.

She did.

"It's Mercy," I said, breathless. "We need to meet."

I heard her exhale. "I don't think that's a good idea."

"Barney, you made Christian a promise. We both have to see it through. I need to know who ordered that catch and kill. It matters."

"You have to stop," she said. "Things are getting out of hand."

"What things? Stop what?"

"Just...stop."

"You don't want me to. You knew that the minute you picked up the phone and called me. I never would have known who you were or what Christian was to you. I think you loved Christian. So did I. I may never forgive him for lying to me, but I loved him."

"Mercy, you don't understand. People know what you've been up to. You've made too many waves."

"What waves? What people?"

"You did it out in the open. You used your real name. It's been noticed."

"By whom? DeShawn Sims?"

"Yes..." she hissed. "That girl you talked to. Hannah. She must have called someone after you showed up at her work. What did you think was going to happen?"

"Who did she call? How did it get back to Sims? You know who's behind all of this. Christian thought it was my father. I need to know the truth. It's the only way we're going to find out who killed that little girl."

"It's not on me."

"Yes, it is. It was the second you involved me. The second you involved Christian. You were looking for some scoop. You used me as much as Christian did."

"I want to help you. I do. But DeShawn? He's not somebody whose bad side I want to be on."

"It's too late for that. Christian's dead. It wasn't that hard for me to figure out your relationship with him. You don't think Sims could? You're in it up to your neck. I'm the only chance you have of not ending up like Christian. You know he visited Hannah McClain before I did. He tried to get Alicia Tate to talk to him. Why?"

She went silent. "No," she finally said. "I had no idea he was going so far as to track down witnesses. I would have begged him not to."

"But you know why he did it," I said.

Anne sighed. "He either wanted to prove your father tanked that case or solve it. Either way, he thought there'd be a paycheck."

"You hung him out to dry," I said. "You knew it was dangerous for him to meddle in this. So, you're warning *me* now. But you ghosted Christian."

"What do you want from me?"

"You have access to Sims. You can find out who paid him off so he wouldn't run what Christian had."

"You don't even know what you don't know."

"Yeah? That's what Hannah McClain said to me. I have a name, Anne. I know who abducted Dustin Bolton and beat him to a pulp, so he'd change his story on Jeremy Hunt's alibi. But he has deeper connections to someone besides my dad."

"Who?"

"No," I said. "I'm not showing you mine until you show me yours."

"Goddammit, Mercy. Sims isn't stupid. He's protected."

"By whom?"

"Not by whom. By what. Sims has dirt on powerful people. That's how he keeps his job. That's why he has value to the Gossip Zone. And that's why he's untouchable."

"He's got a burn file," I said. "You need to find it."

"I'll do what I can."

"Twenty-four hours," I said. "Then you need to get the hell out of there, Anne. If people know I've been snooping around, it's not safe for you there."

"You're asking me to give up everything I've worked for."

"You're working for the devil."

"You can't protect me."

"No. I can't. There's only one way to do that. You're going to go public with this. You're going to have the scoop of the century if I'm right about this. And I know I am."

"God."

"I need proof."

Silence on the other end. Only the second counter on my phone let me know Anne hadn't hung up.

"All right," she said. "I'll be in touch."

Something about the tone of her voice. It was like a door swung open in my mind.

"You already know," I said.

"What?"

"You know who ordered the catch and kill."

"Mercy…"

I had the name in mind. A breath. A beat. Would she say it? Would she confirm my suspicion?

"You know," I repeated. "Did Christian? Did you tell him?" If she had, Christian's betrayal ran even deeper than I thought.

"No!" she shouted through the phone. "God. No. I swear. I tried to make him stop this quest of his. I begged him to leave it alone. I thought he had. I had no idea he was traipsing all over Michigan looking for witnesses. By the time I found out, Christian was already dead. I knew why. I've been trying to make this right ever since."

"You can make it right by telling me everything. All of it. Who did this, Anne?"

"I need some time," she said. "Not over the damn phone. Give me some time."

"Come now," I said.

"I said I need a little time. I have to make some arrangements first."

"Where are you?" I said. "I'll come to you. Let me help you."

So many memories flooded through me. This was just like my last conversation with Christian. He said he would meet me tomorrow. He said he would be alone. No. No. No.

"I know what I'm doing," Anne said.

"I need to know you're safe."

She laughed. "You have no idea what you're asking."

"Yes, I do. Don't come to Helene. Meet me at Petoskey State Park."

"Tomorrow," she said. "I'll be there by noon. But Mercy, you need to lie low until then. Don't rattle any more cages on the Holt case. Don't talk to any more witnesses. Just...don't do anything."

"Okay," I said. "I won't talk to anyone until I see you."

Then I heard the two quick tones indicating she'd ended the call. I stared at my smartphone screen for a moment. I knew if I pressed redial, I'd get an automated message telling me the number wasn't in service. She'd likely used a burner and just pulled the battery out. She was playing it smart.

Maybe I should have done the same.

A pair of tourists pulled into the spot beside me. Young women looking for souvenirs of their trip up north. Giggling, they walked into the pottery studio. The building itself was dome-shaped and painted purple. I thought about going in. Hoping it would ground me somehow. Instead, I started the car and headed back to Helene.

Violet greeted me with a smirk as I walked into the office. "He's back there stewing," she said, pointing over her shoulder toward my father's office.

"About what?" I asked.

"Beats me. It's been one of his bad days. He thought...I mean I got him sorted...but he thought he was in trial this afternoon."

"Lord," I said.

"Relax. I was able to head him off and keep him from marching down to the courthouse. Now he's just agitated and barking orders."

"I'll check in on him," I said. "Thanks for everything, Violet."

"You okay?" she asked. "You look a little peaked yourself, honey."

"I'm fine. Just working a few things out."

Violet raised a brow, but didn't ask me any other questions. Steeling myself for what I'd find when I got there, I walked down the hall toward my father.

When I opened his office door, my heart sank. He'd taken all the boxes of files I'd organized and dumped them out onto the floor and every other surface in the room.

"Dad?" I said. "What are you looking for?"

He was sweating. He ran a hand through his disheveled hair. "I can't find my notes," he said. "My yellow notebook. It was right here. Now it's gone. Violet hides things on me."

"I'm sure she didn't," I said. "But I'd be happy to help you look. What case are you working on?"

He looked at me as if I'd grown a third eye. "Yours, Viveca. Same as I have been."

He blinked then. His eyes went in and out of focus. Then recognition seemed to dawn on him. "Mercy," he said. "I mean Mercy."

"It's okay, Dad," I said. "I'm here now. Why don't we head back to the island? You have nothing on your schedule. Neither do I. We can take the day off. I'll make BLTs. I picked some fresh strawberries. I can whip up some shortcakes, too."

He nodded. I thought he would argue. But he didn't. He came to me then. He pulled me into a hug.

"I love you, Mercy," he said.

"I love you too." I barely got the words out, my throat got so thick. This was my dad. My real dad. Whatever happened with Jeremy

Holt, I knew in my soul I could believe him. He tried to do everything he could for Jeremy Holt.

"Mercy," he murmured my name over and over, as if it was the thing grounding him to now. I realized then that it was.

He pulled away. I took my father's hand and together we walked down to the pier.

CHAPTER
Thirty-Four

ANNE BARNHEISER'S warning echoed in my mind as I stood outside Marian Greenbaum's house in the garden district. Adam Branch lived just four blocks over. They were friendly. Marian had spent forty years in the employ of Adam's father. And she had been the one to take every photograph that appeared in *The Daily Caller* the night of Hollis Branch's infamous retirement party sixteen years ago.

"I really appreciate this," I said. Marian swung her door wide open. The Hosta lilies lining her slate-paved sidewalk were in full bloom. Two tiny toads darted across my path and took refuge under the leafiest branch.

"Oh, honey," she said. "I should have insisted on you staying over at the townhouse all summer. The tenant I have in there now just isn't working out."

"I'm sorry to hear that," I said. Marian took a step back, allowing me into her foyer. She decorated her home in bright hues. Hot pink, black and yellow. It gave it the vibe of a candy store. Two cats, one white, one black, sat perched atop her curio cabinets in the dining room as she led me through to the kitchen.

"One of these days, I need to hire somebody to digitize all of this," she said. She had cardboard boxes open on the kitchen table. A small portion of her life's work. When I called and told her what I was looking for, she invited me over without hesitation.

She had taken a few photographs out and laid them on a counter. One was an 11x17 color blow-up of Hollis and Paulina Branch embracing on a dance floor. Paulina looked radiant in a white beaded gown. Hollis cut a dashing figure in his tux. I picked the photo up.

"This is wonderful," I said. Paulina had her head thrown back, laughing.

"I thought you'd like that one," she said. "That was their fortieth wedding anniversary. Gosh, they just had their fiftieth."

"You didn't photograph that one?"

She frowned. "I haven't taken pictures for the Branch family in about five years. Not officially anyway. Paulie asked me a few times to do it as a favor. I just don't have the taste for it."

"Well, I know how big of a favor I'm asking of you. I hope you had someone help you bring these down."

"Oh, you bet I did. My grandnephew, Wade. He does some work around the house for me. He's fifteen. Doesn't drive yet. You know, I can't figure these young kids out. I got my license just as soon as I could. Anyway, I pay him a hundred bucks a week and he helps me with odds and ends. Carrying stuff in I can't. Putting away my groceries. Doing the trimming and edging outside. I've got a lawn care service but they miss some things."

"That's nice," I said. I went over to the boxes she had on the table. Each was stuffed with labeled yellow file folders bearing dates and event names.

"Wow." I pulled out a random file. Marian had photographed a ribbon-cutting ceremony for the medical plaza out on Carey Road. Hollis and Paulina Branch stood side by side, holding a pair of oversized gold scissors.

"I didn't know what all you wanted," she said.

"Just some highlights," I said. "So I can put together a collage for Liam. And I appreciate you keeping it to yourself. I want it to be a surprise."

"Oh, he'll love it. If you want more historical photographs, there's a good collection at the library. Hollis's great-great-grandparents helped found Helene."

"I may just have to check that out. I was specifically looking for photographs you might have taken at Hollis's retirement party sixteen years ago. Liam has talked about how much he enjoyed that night. It was before things started getting ramped up with Adam's political career."

Marian sat down at the table. She flipped a lid off one box. Licking her finger, she flicked through some files.

"That'd be right here," she said. She pulled out four fat file folders and laid them on top of the box.

"Oh, my," I said. "You really are organized."

"I used to make a pretty good living selling candids from different events I covered for the paper. I made a lot of money off that night. The whole town was there."

Detective Henderson's words echoed in my mind. The whole town had an alibi the night Savannah Holt disappeared.

I sat across from Marian and took the files she laid out. There were photographs of couple after couple on the dance floor. I found one of my father, standing at the bar holding a bourbon. He was frowning, but he had a twinkle in his eye. He looked so handsome in his tux.

"You should keep that one," Marian said. "Your father was a mercurial subject to say the least. But oh, lordy, was he handsome. He still is. I had such a crush on him way back when. And he was a flirt."

I smiled. "My mom used to say that, too."

"Well, you take your time, honey," she said. "Just lay aside whatever you think you want to take."

"Thank you," I said. "And I hope you know I'm expecting to pay for these."

She waved a dismissive hand. "I won't take your money. But maybe you could carry these boxes back to the den when you're through. Wade's not coming for a couple of days and I'm going to need my table back."

"Absolutely," I said as I flipped through more photographs.

It really seemed as if the entire town had attended Hollis Branch's retirement party. I even found more shots Marian had taken of Steven and Olivia Holt. She was blushing as Steven had a hand around her waist. It struck me how happy they looked. And I knew it was the last time. Just a few hours later, their world would implode.

I found shots of Liam, and my pulse quickened. He stood off to the side near the bar, watching everyone else having fun. But he had a pensive expression on his face.

"It was supposed to be his big night too," Marian said, looking over my shoulder. "Hollis made a grand speech about how Liam would carry on the Branch Publishing tradition. Continuity. That was the theme."

She pulled another photograph, showing Hollis holding a microphone and speaking to the crowd. Liam stood at his right, a forced smile on his face.

"He looks miserable," I said.

"He was terrible at it," Marian said. "I'm sorry. You two are close or you wouldn't be doing this for him. But I've never seen someone so ill-suited for a job as Liam was to run that paper. Thankfully, Hollis eventually realized it too and let that boy have his own life. It's just too bad it almost destroyed the paper in the process."

"You were let go?" I asked.

She nodded. "A lot of us were. And I can't say all of it was Liam's fault. Physical newspapers are a thing of the past. Hollis expected too much of Liam."

"How long did Hollis's retirement last?"

"Under a year. It was kind of the joke of the town for a while. This big hoop-dee-doo retirement party, then Hollis turns around and goes back to work. Though I imagine Paulina was fine with that. She told me he was driving her crazy being home all the time in those few months."

I found pictures of Adam next. He had a knack for finding the camera and angling himself in the most flattering light. He seemed to be everywhere that night.

I kept flipping through. My pulse skipped as I found what I was looking for. He was so tall, John Garland was easy to spot in the crowd. I tried not to draw too much attention to those photographs. But there he was, talking to Hollis. To Adam. To my father. To Judge Vince Homer.

"Did you know him?" I asked, showing Marian a photo of Garland with the mayor.

"Not really," she said. "He was some kind of bodyguard for Adam. Somebody his dad hired."

I flipped to another picture. This was one of the rare ones where Adam didn't seem to realize the camera was on him. He had his hand on the waist of a woman in a backless red silk dress. There were several more like it. The two of them speaking with their foreheads close. She was blushing in one. Laughing in another.

"She's beautiful, isn't she?" Marian said. She'd captured a photograph of her facing the camera. Tall. Brunette. Sleek long hair brushed to one side. And the dress was a showstopper. It hugged her every curve and had a plunging neckline.

"Who is she?"

"Ah..." Marian picked up the file the photo came out of. "Audra. Audra Lambrix. I made a point of getting names for everybody I planned to print in the paper."

"I've not seen her though," I said. "I looked at the edition covering this party."

Marian frowned. "Hollis didn't want me to use any of them. I got the impression he didn't approve of the woman. She seemed delightful to me. And Adam was getting serious about her, I thought. Anyway...Audra Lambrix didn't last long."

"He was?" I said.

"She was a stunner the night of Hollis's party," Marian said. "Oh, everybody was looking at her. The two of them looked like Ken and Barbie or something. I didn't agree with Hollis that we shouldn't print any of these. I just wasn't in a position to argue."

"Hmm," I said.

"All summer, Adam was causing a stir. Paulina was beside herself. I think Hollis feels he needs to be married if he wants to go beyond the governor's mansion. And believe me, Hollis wants him to go higher than that. But boy, Audra looked like Jackie Kennedy to me. Don't you see it? I mean trashier, don't get me wrong. They looked so good together. And it seemed like she made him happy. But he just dropped her like a hot potato. I didn't see her again after that party."

It could be nothing. It probably was. But just then, there was nobody I wanted to talk to more than the mysterious Audra Lambrix.

"Hollis specifically told you not to print any of these?"

"Oh, Hollis was furious about those photos the next day when he saw the layout we wanted to run. Chewed me out in front of the rest of the staff."

"The next day? But he was retiring? Why wasn't Liam the one with the final say of what went into the next edition?"

"Hollis wanted his hands in for that last spread," she said. "Between you and me, none of us really believed he'd be able to let go all the way. That's why I think he had Liam set up for failure from the get-go. But some of these old guys just don't know when to step off, ride off into the sunset. You know."

"Sure," I said. Then Marian's face fell.

"Oh, honey. I didn't mean like with your dad."

I smiled. "I didn't think you did."

I flipped through the last of Marian's photographs from Hollis Branch's retirement party. There were more of Audra Lambrix. She was easy to pick out with that red dress. In one, she was standing next to John Garland. The air in my lungs turned cold.

"Well," Marian said. "If I were you, I'd just stick to pictures with Hollis and Paulina. There's one in there of the four of them Liam might like."

"Right," I said absently.

"Here, let me get you an envelope for the ones you wanna take."

She left and rounded the corner. I put a few shots of Audra under a stack I'd collected, showing Liam's parents. Then one shot of Adam, Liam, Hollis and Paulina. When Marian brought me the envelope, I slipped the ones of John Garland and Audra Lambrix in behind it before she could see.

"Thank you," I said. "These are just what I had in mind."

"Oh, don't forget this one," Marian said. She grabbed a photograph of Hollis holding a plaque with Liam on one side of him and Paulina on the other.

"Isn't that funny," Marian said. "The old fool had his own plaque made to commemorate his retirement. A lot of us had a good laugh about that. We all signed this big card for him. But he commissioned his own stupid plaque. Then he hung it in the hallway of the Branch offices."

"This is a good photo," I said. "But Adam's not in it."

Marian peered at it. "Hmm. He probably left by then."

"He didn't stay the whole night?"

She shook her head. "No. There was some drama. You know? Come to think of it, maybe it was about that girl. I don't know.

But Adam left early. I remember that because Paulina asked me to get a shot of the four of them. When I told her Adam was gone, she was livid."

"Is there any way to know what time this picture was taken?" I asked.

Marian frowned. "The exact time? No. I didn't use a digital camera with a timestamp or anything. But...this was before they brought the cake out."

"The cake?"

"Here," she said. She showed me another picture of a giant cake decorated like a newspaper. Hollis and Paulina cut it together like a wedding cake. Liam stood beside his parents. Adam was nowhere to be found.

Adam was gone. The entire town was at the yacht club, but Adam Branch and Audra Lambrix were gone.

"These really are fantastic. I can't thank you enough."

Marian beamed. I helped her rebox the rest of the photos then carried them down the hall into her study.

She offered me lemonade when we got back to the kitchen. I knew the least I could do was sit and chat with her for a few minutes.

"You know," I said. "That party. It occurs to me it was also the night Savannah Holt went missing."

Marian's face fell. "It was? Gosh. I guess I forgot about that."

"I saw there were some pictures you took of the Holts that night. Savannah was supposed to be staying with a friend."

She nodded. "Poor Lexie Jarret. Her name is Valletta now. I heard she moved with her husband down near Ann Arbor."

"It's just hard to reconcile all those people having so much fun and celebrating. Then the next morning..."

"It tore the town apart," she said. "That poor family. Yes. I guess I'd blocked out that it happened that night."

"A lot of people did. Marian...did the police ever ask you to show them any of your photographs of that night?"

"Why would they?"

"It's just...well you've documented where most of the people in town were on the night Savannah went missing. It just seems like useful information."

"Honey," she said, reaching across the table to me. "You sound like your father. I know it's hard to believe Jeremy Holt could have done that to his own sister. But he did. I believe that in my soul."

"Did you know him? Jeremy? Or Savannah?"

She shook her head. "I knew Steven and Olivia. Mostly Steven. He did the computers..."

"IT," I said.

"Right. So, he was in the office a lot. Friendly. Good guy. But he was never the same after his little girl died. We all know it killed him, too."

"I know," I said. "Well, I don't want to keep you."

"You come and see me anytime, honey."

I promised her I would. Then I tucked my envelope under my arm and said goodbye. As I headed down the street, my heart raced.

John Garland was in town the night Savannah went missing. Marian believed he was there as Adam's bodyguard. It might lead nowhere. I had to talk to Audra Lambrix. If I could find her.

CHAPTER
Thirty-Five

I SAT on the bench overlooking the beach at Petoskey State Park. In my lap, I held a small box that had just been delivered to the office this morning. It felt like fate. I ran my hand over the label. Fowler Funeral Home. Inside the box were Christian Foley's ashes. I could feel him today, in spirit, and now physically.

Maybe Anne wouldn't come. Maybe something had happened to her like it had to Christian. I tried not to let my mind run too wild with catastrophic scenarios. We'd been careful, hadn't we? Christian had been too trusting.

Then, a shadow crossed in front of me as Anne walked up behind me. I didn't turn. She sat down beside me and for a moment, neither of us said a word. We just stared out at the water watching the gentle waves come in.

I spoke first. "There's someone else I need to find. A woman who might know something about what happened the night Savannah Holt disappeared. Are you good at that too? Finding people?"

Anne smiled. "I found you, didn't I?"

I knew what she was going to tell me. There was only one answer to the question that made everything fit. One answer, but so far, no proof.

Anne didn't ask about the box in my lap or the large envelope beside me.

"Where will you go after this?" I asked her. If she had what I needed, she couldn't go back to the Gossip Zone. I think that was why she'd waited this long to finish what she and Christian had started.

"Mercy," she said. "Are you sure any of this will matter? These people are used to getting what they want."

"They just never thought anyone else would start asking questions. And my father...they know nobody will find him credible anymore."

"Do you?"

I turned to her. "Yes."

"Christian said I could trust you."

"You can. I wish he had."

"You think it would have made a difference?"

"I don't know," I said. "But it would have made a difference to me."

Anne brushed a lock of hair away from her eyes. Then she reached into the back pocket of her jeans and pulled out a flash drive and a burner phone.

"DeShawn Sims's cell phone records are on here," she said.

"Do I want to know how you got them?"

"Probably not. But if you get to the point of subpoenaing them, he won't be able to alter anything now."

She put the flash drive into my hand.

"Christian called him on his personal cell," Anne continued. "You also have the call logs from Christian's phone. But every time he got a call from Christian, he made an outgoing call to the same number."

"A burner?"

Anne shook her head. "No."

"Does Sims know you have his phone records?"

"No."

"Barney, are you safe?"

She shook her head. "No. But I don't think you are either."

"What else is on this flash drive?"

"I started recording my conversations with DeShawn maybe five or six months ago. Right after Christian came to me with copies of the letter you got from Jeremy Holt."

"You gave a copy of that letter to DeShawn?"

She nodded.

"He's the one who told you about the catch and kill. You didn't just stumble onto it."

"No," she said. "Mercy, I'm sorry."

"Why didn't you tell Christian about it?"

"I was afraid. I was trying to protect him. I thought he'd eventually just quit asking questions. I told him DeShawn wasn't interested in the story after all."

"He was though. He was contacting Christian up until the day he died."

"I didn't know that," she said. "I swear."

"You've sworn to a lot."

"It was a mistake. The whole thing. I wish I could go back in time and do it differently. I was trying to make a name for myself too. I wanted to impress DeShawn. I thought it would be good for my career. But I had real feelings for Christian. And I didn't know what kind of a hornet's nest this was. How deep it went. How dangerous it would become."

"So, make things right. Go to the police with me. It's the only way to make sure the truth about these people comes out."

"I won't make it that far."

"Yes, you will! Nobody knows you've been talking to me. If you've been careful."

"I've been careful."

"How much were they paying Sims to keep quiet about the Holt story and my dad?"

"I don't know the full amount. But it was tens of thousands of dollars every time DeShawn made a phone call after Christian contacted him. It won't look like anything. Nobody would think anything of two news outlets transacting with each other."

"No," I said. "It wouldn't. But you recorded your conversations with DeShawn." I held up the flash drive. "Is this the only copy?"

"No. I have two others. One is in a safe deposit box. A third is somewhere nobody but me will ever know."

"What's on here?" I knew. But I needed her to say it.

"DeShawn told me what to tell Christian. What to ask for. And he told me to put a tracking app on Christian's phone. That was the line I wouldn't cross. I told him no. He almost fired me on the spot."

It felt like an anvil sitting on my chest. "But Christian reported to you about my conversations with him. What was happening with my dad. What happened at the courthouse the first day I came back to Helene. He told you all that?"

She nodded.

"How do I know you're not recording us now?"

"You don't," she said. "Except why would I give you copies of everything?"

"Say it," I said. "Who is behind the catch and kill order, Anne? Who wants to keep the truth about what really happened to Savannah Holt from getting out?"

She took a breath. "The order came from Branch Publications. DeShawn was taking calls from Hollis Branch."

"Does he know who really killed Savannah?" I asked.

Anne shook her head. "They never even talked about Savannah. DeShawn just told me Branch felt rehashing that story would bring a negative light to Helene."

"That's bullshit. It's not the town's image he's trying to protect. But you're telling me Sims was specific with you on these recordings?"

"Yes. I'd already be dead if he knew I had these. I signed an affidavit too. And taped a confession. All the files are on that drive. If anything happens to me, you know what to do."

"You think I'm your insurance policy?"

"You're all I've got."

"I should hate you both. You and Christian."

"If you really believe your father had nothing to do with the cover-up, then I should be your best friend, Mercy. Those recordings prove nothing. Not about who really killed Savannah Holt if it wasn't her brother. You don't have enough. As far as the world is concerned, all Branch did was kill a story about your dad having dementia. Or that maybe he was incompetent during a trial sixteen years ago."

"He wasn't incompetent. He fought for Holt. He put on a solid defense."

"Mercy...you're not seeing what's right in front of your face. This is what Christian was worried about. He believed you wouldn't be able to look at your dad objectively. Sure, maybe E. Thomas Gale put on a hell of a show in front of that jury. But behind the scenes, he was paying John Garland to intimidate witnesses."

"I don't believe that," I said. Or was it really that I refused to believe it? My gut was telling me I was right. I had to be right.

"You'd better start. For your own sake."

"How did someone find Christian? Who knew where he was traveling and why?"

"I don't know," she whispered. "I've been trying to figure that out myself. Christian didn't tell me he was planning to come stay with you in Helene. He knows I would have been angry about that. Jealous, probably. And toward the end, I was doing everything I could to warn him to drop this whole thing. I should have kept trying. I shouldn't have ghosted him."

"I need to know how to get a hold of you," I said. "When I call you, I need you to answer."

"That's what the burner is for," she said. "There's one number saved in contacts. That's how you get a hold of me."

"Okay."

"You asked me if I was good at finding people. Who is it you need me to find?"

When I came here today, I intended to tell her about Audra Lambrix. Now, I knew I couldn't. Barney had laid herself open to me if she told me the truth about the flash drive's contents. But I couldn't risk Audra's safety if my suspicions were true about what she knew. I tucked the envelope I'd brought under my arm.

"No one," I said. "For the rest of this, I need to be on my own. I assume the burner works both ways. If you need to get a hold of me, you'll call it."

"Yeah."

"All right. Then stay safe. You can't go back home. Not if getting justice for Christian really matters to you. You understand?"

I couldn't feel sorry for her. She lied to me. She'd known about Branch's involvement in this from the beginning.

"I wish I'd told you sooner," she said, as if reading my mind.

"Me too. But there's something else you can help me with." I handed her the box. She held my gaze for a moment, then looked down and read the mailing label. It took a second, but her eyes filled with understanding.

"I think he cared about you," I said. "And I don't think he'd want to spend eternity in a box somewhere in Michigan. So take it. Do whatever you think is best for him."

"Mercy..." she said, her voice catching. Anne clutched the box to her chest and tears fell down her cheeks. She could have been lying to me about everything else, but her emotions were real. Whatever else happened, she had loved Christian.

"Thank you," she whispered. "Please don't judge Christian too harshly. I know it's going to be difficult for you not to. Yes. He betrayed you. But he paid for it with his life. And he really did believe your father could have hurt you. And he loved you. More than he wanted to admit to me. But I knew. And I knew I could never be you. Good luck, Mercy."

"You're the one who needs it now, Barney. Not me."

Before she could respond, I rose, turned my back on her, and left her staring at the water.

CHAPTER
Thirty-Six

"Ms. Lambrix is looking forward to your meeting."

I'd just finished signing my name into the guest book at the reception desk. I'd used Mercedes Baldwin, taking my mother's maiden name. It wouldn't take much for Audra Lambrix to put two and two together if she did background research on new clients.

Ms. Lambrix's assistant looked to be about forty but was fighting hard against it. He had fresh, rosy cheeks and a mop of blond hair he pulled back into a bun.

"Are you new to the area?" he asked. He'd introduced himself as Topher, letting me know it wasn't short for anything.

"I have family in Northern Michigan."

"Well, Traverse City is wonderful," Topher said. "There are several properties Ms. Lambrix is excited to show you."

"Oh...I wasn't thinking we'd do any actual showings today. I was booked in as a consult."

"If you choose to work with her, she can set things up. You know, that's what Audra's good at. She has a sixth sense, I swear. She's a master at matching people to their dream properties. Before they even realized they *had* the dream."

"I'm excited," I said.

Audra Lambrix had been almost too easy to find. A quick browser search pulled up her company name. Premier Real Estate. She was a broker now with her own real estate firm. She specialized in luxury properties along Lake Michigan.

A bit more digging told me she'd been married and divorced since her last encounter with Adam Branch. By the look of the office, she was doing very well for herself. She owned this building. A prime location right along the shore in the downtown Traverse City area. She'd bought it for half a million dollars fifteen years ago and renovated it. Similar properties were now going for four times that.

Topher led me to a corner office overlooking the lake. I took a seat in a chair in front of Audra Lambrix's acrylic desk. She'd decorated her office in pinks and golds. A crystal chandelier hung in the center of the room.

"Sorry I'm late!" I turned in my seat. Audra Lambrix looked more or less the same as in the photographs Marian Greenbaum captured the night of Hollis Branch's retirement party. Today, instead of her plunging red ball gown, she wore a pink suit in a shade that matched her wallpaper.

I rose and extended my hand. "Thanks for agreeing to meet with me on such short notice."

Audra carried a portfolio. She set it on the desk after she shook my hand. Instead of taking her seat behind it, she sat in the chair next to mine.

"Can I get either of you anything?" Topher asked.

"No, thank you," I said.

Audra gave Topher a pleasant smile as he excused himself.

"Well," Audra said. "Tell me how I can help you. In your online booking, you said you were looking for investment space. You're thinking vacation rentals? Do you want turnkey or are you willing to do a little renovation?"

"Ms. Lambrix," I said. "I don't want to waste any more of your time. But I was afraid you wouldn't meet with me if I told you the real reason I'm here."

Her smile didn't falter, but her eyes narrowed in curiosity.

"I'm...I am new to the area. I've been staying with family in Helene, actually."

The smile dropped.

"This is difficult for me to talk about," I said. "I have every expectation that you may end up throwing me out. I was hoping you'd talk to me about your time in Helene."

"I've never lived in Helene," she said. "I don't have any listings there. If that's the area you're interested in purchasing, I'm sure I can refer you to a colleague. I just don't..."

"Over the last few months," I interrupted. "I've become close with Adam Branch."

The smile faded for good. She got out of her chair and walked around her desk, taking her seat behind it. A shield, it seemed.

"Will you talk to me about him?"

"I haven't seen Adam Branch in several years. I'm not sure who gave you my name."

"You were seeing him. I know it was serious. And I know it ended abruptly the night of September 18, sixteen years ago."

A gamble. But by the flicker in her eyes, I knew I'd struck gold. If she didn't do what I expected and throw me right out.

"I'm not sure what business any of that is of yours."

"You have every reason *not* to trust me, seeing as how I booked your time under false pretenses. It's just...sixteen years is a very long time. And I believe something happened that night that you might be ready to talk about."

I pulled a file folder out of my bag and set it on her desk. Audra flipped it open. I'd brought one of the more stunning pictures Marian took that night. A full-length shot of Audra, in profile. Adam had his arm around her, whispering into her ear. Her body was angled away from him. They hadn't been the focus of that image. Marian had actually been trying to capture Hollis as he raised his glass to toast. But I'd cropped and blown up this part of the frame. Adam clearly hadn't realized the camera was trained on him.

"Who sent you here?" Audra said, slamming the file folder shut.

"No one. And no one knows I came."

"You're right. I probably should just throw you out."

"Is he dangerous?"

"What?"

"Is he dangerous? He's very charming. And he has a way of just being there when you need him. Competent. Capable. People in the know think he's going to be our next governor."

"Well, good for him. I'm not one of those people. The ones in the know."

"I think you are. I think something happened that night. Something you were told not to talk about."

"You need to leave."

"If I were your friend. If I called you and told you Adam Branch had asked me out, is there any reason you'd tell me to steer clear?"

"But we're not friends."

"What happened the night of Hollis Branch's retirement party?"

"I need you to leave."

I took another file folder out of my bag. This one had a copy of one of the newspaper articles reporting on the search for Savannah Holt. I put the article in front of her and kept my eyes on her face.

It was almost imperceptible, but a tremor went through Audra Lambrix.

"Who are you protecting?" I asked.

"Me!" The answer came out as a whip crack.

"I know who these people are," I said. "Hollis Branch. John Garland. I know what they did to keep people silent after that night."

"Who are you? A reporter?"

"No. This is...for me, this is a family matter."

"Do you think Adam's in love with you?"

Could she read my face as well as I thought I could read hers?

"No," I said. "Not in love. I believe Adam's family wants him to find a wife. They're laboring under the impression that he'll need one if he wants to seek higher office beyond the governorship."

"Do you think you're in love with him?"

"I don't...I don't know. But there have been whispers. I know he's done something in his past. The kind of thing that has kept him single."

"Well, I guess you need to follow your heart."

"What happened that night, Audra? You disappeared. You and Adam were serious. I've asked around. Nobody will talk."

"Did you ask Adam?"

"No."

"Then I have nothing else to say. It's none of your business. People change. Relationships end. How would you feel if someone just showed up out of the blue and started asking about a painful breakup you had sixteen years ago?"

"We're not friends. But woman to woman, is there any reason I should stay away from Adam Branch?"

"Just get out. Please."

I rose. I stood by the doorway. Audra picked up the article on Savannah's disappearance. She flung it at me and missed. It landed in the hallway at my feet.

"Tell me the truth. Nobody else will," I pleaded. I had to rattle her. Make her angry if that's what it took. I played the last card I had. It came from a search of her financial records when she bought the property fifteen years ago. Audra Lambrix had just been starting out as a real estate agent. She didn't have the clientele to afford the mortgage on this place and the deed showed it had been purchased with cash.

"This building," I said. "This was the price of your silence, wasn't it?"

"Get. Out."

CHAPTER THIRTY-SIX

"I have the proof," I bluffed. "I have copies of the bank transactions. The Branches bought this building, and you put it in your name. That's not a thing someone does for a woman he broke up with."

"We're done here," she said. "If I see you on this property again, I'll get a protection order against you."

"He told me you were crazy," I said. "I didn't want to act jealous. We're just getting to know each other. But he said you were insane. And he said you tried to trap him."

She let out a haughty laugh. "Good luck, Ms. Baldwin. I'm sure you and Adam will be very happy together. Sure. I'm crazy. You just go on ahead and believe that."

I stood my ground just outside her door. I had one last card to play. "Audra," I said. "Tell me what happens if I let Adam take me to the cabin. He asked me to go with him this weekend."

Her face flushed instantly red. She had trouble catching her breath. She took a halting step backward then slammed the door in my face. The echo of it shot through me like gunfire.

My instincts were right.

I thought about pounding on her door. Demanding she explain what had her so scared. The cabin. The cabin.

I turned on my heel and walked toward the lobby. I made it halfway to my car before someone called my name. It was Topher. Gone was his pleasant smile and affable demeanor.

"You can't just come here and stir all that up," he said, his tone flat. "She's been through enough."

"How much of that did you hear?" I asked.

"Enough."

"How long have you worked with her?"

"Twenty years," he said. "She's my cousin."

"So, then you understand what I'm asking. I know Adam Branch did something to her. And I know she was paid off to stay quiet about it."

"Paid off?" Topher's face fell. "What, you mean money?"

"He bought her the building. Look, if you care about Audra, then you need to know I can't protect her. I'm going to expose Adam for what he is. He's running for governor. He and his father...I know they've done things. Things voters have the right to know."

"You're working for his opponent?"

I opened my mouth to deny it, then changed strategies. "Yes."

"Good," Topher said. "I hope you're good at your job."

"I am," I said. "But that doesn't mean I don't need help. Topher, Adam's cabin. What happened there?"

"She's right. You better leave."

"He hurt her," I said. "I know it. I've seen things. Flashes of his temper. Is that where it happened? The cabin?"

"Look, she won't talk. She's too scared. But yeah. Adam hurt her. He put her in the hospital. I was the one that stayed with her for days on end. They had to wire her jaw shut. If I hadn't known the shape of her hands, her fingers, I wouldn't have believed it was her."

"Where? What hospital? In Helene?"

Topher shook his head. "Here. I drove her. She was puking blood in the back seat the whole way."

"Did she tell you it was Adam?"

CHAPTER THIRTY-SIX

"She didn't have to."

"How can I prove it if she won't admit any of this? Topher, I can get a subpoena. We can go to the police."

"No. We can't. You can't be arrested for something like that sixteen years later."

"He doesn't have to be arrested. He just has to lose an election."

Topher smiled. "Good luck, Ms. Baldwin. You'll need it. Don't come back here."

And don't go to the cabin. Except as I climbed behind the wheel, I knew that's exactly where I needed to go.

CHAPTER Thirty-Seven

I FELT her in the woods with me that evening. I had six missed calls. Four from Liam. Two from my father. I texted each of them, telling them I'd check in later.

It was ghosts I was chasing tonight. I parked on the bike path and walked down to the cabin from the same path I'd taken the other day. Past the shoreline where they'd found Savannah's little body, weighed down with concrete blocks.

Audra Lambrix's face when I mentioned the cabin seared into my brain. She was afraid. What did she think I knew?

I went to the oak tree, choosing the thick, low branches a child could have climbed. I knew in my heart Savannah *had* climbed them. I knew what she might have thought. The cabin looked like somewhere the fairies could have lived with its moss-covered roof, the back door having once been painted bright pink.

As I made my way up to the second branch, I felt as if I were seeing the world through her eyes. And this was always the point.

There was supposed to be no one around. Coming from the north as she had, they would have seen no footprints. No disruption in the brush. They would be alone. Secluded. The perfect place for him to carry out the horrors that had gripped him that night.

They had to wire her jaw shut. If I hadn't known the shape of her hands, her fingers, I wouldn't have believed it was her.

Adam had brought Audra to this remote cabin and done unspeakable things to her. Savannah must have seen. She must have been terrified. Maybe she'd cried out. Screamed. Or fallen from the branch. The coroner said her left wrist was broken. The kind of injury ER doctors see a thousand times every summer when kids fall out of swing sets. Or trees.

She had seen. And there had been nobody else out here to protect her.

"God," I whispered. "For what?" Audra was already afraid of Adam and Hollis Branch. In all these years, she never talked about what happened. She had taken Adam's money and quietly disappeared. They might not have even believed Savannah. She was nine years old and if she'd gone to her parents or the police with what she'd seen, the grown-ups would have denied it. Why kill her?

I felt hot tears on my face. So many lies. So many lives ruined. Savannah and Jeremy were at the center, but the spokes of Adam Branch's wheel of terror touched so many others. Olivia and Steven Holt. Diane Benning. Dustin Bolton. Hannah McClain. Audra Lambrix.

My father and I.

I climbed down from the tree. My phone started buzzing as I walked back toward the road and the signal grew stronger.

I didn't want to go back to the island. I didn't want to go

anywhere. But Savannah had tried to run away that night. I could not do the same.

LIAM WAS WAITING for me on the porch. I wiped my face. Reapplied my makeup. I hoped he wouldn't see any trace of my tears.

"Dinner's cold," he said. "But I can heat it up."

"I'm sorry."

I didn't want to go inside. I took a seat beside him on the wrought-iron bench. We were shielded from the street by four massive hydrangea bushes. Their brilliant red dinner plate blooms swayed in the breeze.

"I've been worried about you," he said. "You've been blowing me off all day."

"I know."

Liam took my hand and held it in his lap. We watched as a few families walked by. It was a nice night for a stroll. The sun had just dipped below the horizon. It cast the lake in a brilliant amber glow.

"Am I losing you?" Liam finally said.

I turned to him. "I don't know."

He squeezed my hand a little tighter.

"You can tell me anything," he said. "You know that, right?"

"I hope so. I thought I could. But this? What if it's a path you can't follow me down?"

We hadn't said I love you. I felt safe with him. Like he saw me in a way nobody else had in a very long time.

"Mercy, I know you went to see Adam the other day. Did he..."

I turned to him. "Did he what? Hurt me? This is the path. The one you may not want to go down with me. Are you sure you want me to ask you the question?"

A muscle jumped in his jaw. He let go of my hand.

"Right here," I said. "Right now. This is your chance. Because I have to say some things."

He let out a hard breath. "I know."

"Your brother...he's not a good man."

Liam's face went hard. "Did he hurt you?" His voice became impossibly low.

"What is he capable of?"

No answer. Liam just kept that dark stare.

"Adam hurts women, doesn't he?"

Liam's head snapped up. He put his arms firmly on my shoulders and drew me to him. His eyes flashed with primal anger. His voice became a predatory growl. "Did he touch you? Did he lay his hands on you? Did he hurt you?" He shook me once, hard. "Tell me what he's done to you."

"You tell me. I won't ask you again. This is the secret. This is the thing everyone, including you, has tried to warn me about. Don't get close to Adam. He's not who people think he is. The truth, Liam. Adam can be violent. Is that it? Is that what you meant when you told me to watch out for him? Why you've been so angry when he's around me?"

He let me go and dropped his head to his chest.

"Mercy..."

"Are you going to protect him? Because I'm going to find out. I'm too far in. Are you with me?"

"I don't...I can't...Mercy, it's complicated."

"It's simple. If Adam has hurt someone, then he has to be held accountable."

Liam's shoulders dropped.

"In the end, you're going to close ranks with your family," I whispered.

"So will you!"

"Don't sit there and try to pretend it's the same. My father has tried to get to the truth."

"Are you sure about that?"

"Yes!" I hissed.

He'd turned to stone. "I care about you. But you can't win this. Adam always wins. He always gets what he wants."

I stood up. "I don't accept that."

Liam gave me a sad smile. "It won't matter."

"Are you in danger?" I asked. "Does Adam have something on you?"

I wanted to tell him. I wanted to throw it in his face. Everything I'd learned so far. That John Garland was on his family's payroll, too. That his own father had ordered the catch and kill about the Holt story. That Audra Lambrix had all but confirmed that Adam had beaten the crap out of her the night Savannah Holt disappeared. She'd seen. I couldn't prove it. Not yet. But she'd seen!

I said none of those things. I wanted to trust him. I couldn't. But I would not stop until I knew the truth. If it meant I had to destroy Adam Branch, it was a price I was willing to pay.

For Savannah.

CHAPTER
Thirty-Eight

LIAM ASKED ME TO STAY. I knew I couldn't. I wanted to go to my father. I couldn't. The Chris-Craft was moored at the pier as I drove by it. I pulled into the parking lot behind Dad's office and cut the engine.

It was after four. I wasn't sure if I could face Dad's questions. As I made my way into the office, I passed by his door. He wasn't at his desk. I couldn't hear his booming voice, only Violet's cheerful humming in the lobby.

"Mercy?" She called out. "Is that you, honey?"

Violet had ears like a bat. The woman could probably echolocate her way through dark caves.

"I'm here," I said, coming down the hallway. She was sitting at the reception desk sorting through Dad's mail.

"I didn't think we'd see you today," she said.

"Where is he? The boat's moored at the dock."

Violet looked out the window. "Lloyd picked him up after lunch. I think he's got another hairbrained real estate scheme he wanted your dad's opinion on. They were gonna head out to Beaver Island. Lloyd promised he'd get him home safely. I'm sure he's already back by now."

"I'm glad Lloyd's doing more things with him. Dad won't say it, but he's missed him."

Violet put the stack of mail down. "You're right that your dad would never admit it. He took Lloyd's retirement a lot harder than he let on. It was becoming pretty tense between them. But since you've been working with him, that's stopped. Now they're just friends again. So…that's my roundabout way of saying you can't ever leave us, Mercy."

Violet smiled. I couldn't give her the answer she wanted. I couldn't even answer it for myself.

"You okay?"

I found a smile. "Just have some things I need to finish up before I call it a weekend."

Violet put the rest of the mail in her desk drawer. "I'll leave you to it. But don't hang around here for too long. You should go out. Do something fun. I'm sure Liam Branch would be up for that too."

She gave me a mischievous wink. She gathered her purse and said goodbye.

I stood there for a moment after I heard the back door close. A million thoughts swirled in my head. The things I now knew to be true in my soul. And the ones I couldn't prove.

Adam was involved with Savannah Holt's death somehow. He had no alibi the night she disappeared. Audra Lambrix had all but

CHAPTER THIRTY-EIGHT

confirmed the two of them had been out at the cabin that night. That he'd done something to her. Brutalized her. It was bad enough Topher had to take her to a hospital away from Helene.

Savannah Holt had run away from her friend Lexie Jarret's house that night. She hadn't gone home. She'd gone to the place she used to hide. Her tree fort by the cabin. She could have seen what happened.

John Garland was a part of it. Dustin Bolton's father and Alicia Tate confirmed Garland was the one who beat Dustin into silence. Hannah McLain had been made to watch so that she knew what would happen if she didn't tell the police exactly what Garland wanted her to.

She lied about seeing Jeremy with Savannah. And Hollis Branch had paid for a catch and kill order for any stories relating to my father and the Holt murder.

Then there was Christian's part in all of this. God. If I'd never told him my concerns about my dad's mental state. If I'd kept my mouth shut about the letters Jeremy sent me. Or if he'd been honest with me about his relationship with Anne Barnheiser. Maybe things would have been different. But maybe I would have never known the truth about who really killed Savannah Holt.

I felt my heart thump harder. My pulse raced. There was an answer somewhere. Proof.

Christian. Anne swore he hadn't told her he was coming to Helene. I'd never told anyone either. Not Liam. Not my father. Only Mrs. Greenbaum knew. Could she have told someone? She worked for Branch Publications at one time, too. She was angry with Hollis for letting her go. So why would she work with him now? And as far as I knew, she would have had no idea Christian was communicating with the Gossip Zone or had anything to do with the Holt case.

I found myself in my father's conference room. The Holt files were still in their boxes where I'd put them. Dustin Bolton's false statements to the police. The transcripts and videos of the trial itself. My father's blistering cross examination of Hannah McClain. It was all there. He'd worked his ass off for Jeremy. Had it all been a front?

Not once since I'd come to Helene had my father tried to seriously dissuade me from looking into the case. He said he was convinced of Jeremy's innocence even now. And yet...he was one of the only ones who knew where Dustin Bolton was staying after he gave his first statement to the police.

I felt a trickle of sweat roll down between my shoulder blades.

One of the only ones who knew.

I was the only one who knew when Christian was planning to come to Helene. I closed my eyes. That last phone call. I sat in my office. Was my father here that day?

My eyes snapped open.

He'd been golfing with Hollis Branch, miles away from the office. But I hadn't been alone.

Like a zombie, I walked back out to the lobby. I rounded the corner and sat at Violet's desk. She left the key to the middle drawer sticking out of the lock. I opened it.

The stack of mail she'd been holding was right there on the top. Bills, mostly. The electric bill. The cell phone bill was underneath it. Two lines. The one my father used and the one he gave to Violet.

No. Just. No.

I ran my finger down the line of calls. Most were to the courthouse or county numbers. She'd circled the outgoing calls my father

CHAPTER THIRTY-EIGHT

made to various clients. He was terrible about logging those into his billable hours. Violet did it for him.

I fired up her computer. She didn't keep it password protected because my father used it. I went into her bookmarks. She had the cell phone carrier saved along with all the other utility companies. I opened up her billing software.

I pulled open the call lists from the prior statement. More of the same. Calls to county government numbers. More clients.

JULY 20.

Holding my breath, I scrolled down. My fingers shook on the mouse, making the cursor jump. I pulled out my phone. July 20. I'd last spoken to Christian at nine thirty-two am. It had been an eight-minute call.

I looked at Violet's call list for the same timeframe. At 9:43 a.m., she'd made an outgoing call lasting four minutes. A local number. She'd made no notations in her time slip.

I picked up the receiver on the desk phone. I punched in the number on Violet's call list. She hadn't called from this line. But I knew the caller ID would show up as Gale Law Offices on the other end.

It rang four times, then went to his voicemail. "You've reached Adam Branch. Please leave a message."

I hung up. Scrolling through my phone, I looked at eight other calls I'd had with Christian. I couldn't recall how many I'd made while sitting in my office here. Three or four, maybe. I checked the dates and time stamps against Violet's outgoing calls. Three more times, she'd made calls to Adam's number from her cell phone either right after or during the time I was on the phone with Christian.

My God. It had been Violet who suggested I get a hold of Marian Greenbaum about her rental property. I'd said it was for a friend who might come to visit. But she'd overheard me talking to him.

She knew where Dustin Bolton was staying all those years ago. If I could pull call records as far back as sixteen years ago, I knew what I would find. There would be calls from Violet's number to John Garland. She hadn't even bothered to use a burner phone. No one would have thought twice about her making calls to a process server on my father's payroll.

But why? What did Violet get out of helping Adam or Hollis Branch cover up the truth about what happened to Savannah Holt?

Was it enough? Would Detective Henderson finally agree to help me get the investigation reopened? Could I get my father to believe the woman he thought was loyal to him had betrayed him to the highest bidder?

He'd been generous with her over the years. When his practice had been the most lucrative, he'd given her bonuses. But Violet Tamblyn and her family had lived in Helene as long as my father. Even longer. I did not know how far back her ties to the Branch family went.

Violet had access to my father's files on Jeremy Holt. She always had. If Alicia Tate sent a letter all those years ago, backing up Jeremy's story, Violet would have opened it first. She could have shredded it on the spot and my father would have been none the wiser. And Violet had been signing my father's correspondence for years. Of course, she had access to his letterhead. She could have easily been the one to send Alicia Tate a bogus letter from my father telling her she wasn't needed as a witness.

I went to the county Register of Deeds site and pulled up Violet's home address. She lived on fourteen acres right at the edge of the

CHAPTER THIRTY-EIGHT

township. My father said she had access to the lake but never used it as it was a steep slope down the dunes.

Her deed was recorded twenty-two years ago. She was married then. Bronny Tamblyn, her husband, had died about ten years ago of lung cancer. My father once told me he'd left her in some financial distress having racked up gambling debts she didn't know about. They'd purchased the property for almost half a million dollars back then.

There was a mortgage discharge on file. My heart flipped when I saw the date on it. February 14. Two days after Jeremy Holt had been convicted of killing his little sister. She'd paid almost four hundred thousand dollars. It wasn't a refinance. It was a total payoff. But then, two years ago, she'd taken out a second mortgage for another half a million dollars.

But she'd come into a large sum of money to pay off her house right after Jeremy Holt was convicted of a murder he didn't commit.

I turned off Violet's computer. The air felt thick around me.

I slipped my phone into my pocket and raced out the back door.

CHAPTER
Thirty-Nine

"Dad?"

I called out as I finished tying off the boat. He hadn't answered his phone or texted me back. It was getting dark though. Violet said she expected he was already home by now.

Violet. God.

I walked to Dad's study. The room was dark. Freshly dusted. I could smell the faint woodsy scent of my father's aftershave. I went to his bookshelves, scanning all the items he'd carefully placed there. Proof of a life that had taken him all over the world.

He had a framed, autographed copy of the script for *A Deadly Affair*. Next to it, the certificate that had gone along with his Oscar for producing the Best Picture of the year. So much of my father happened before I was born.

There was a photograph I knew he treasured. Everyone said I was the spitting image of my Aunt Viveca. But as I pulled the photo of dad in uniform next to his F4 Phantom, I saw a little of me in him. I ran a finger across the face staring back at me.

"I miss you, Dad," I whispered. I had the power to shatter the life he'd built.

I pulled out my phone and called him again. It went straight to voicemail. It was after eight o'clock.

"Dad?" I called out. I walked out of his office and past his bedroom door. I knocked softly, but no one answered. I couldn't hear the shower running.

How could I tell him what I suspected? Violet had been the one to tell John Garland where to find Dustin Bolton. She could have fed information to Hollis or Adam Branch about what Hannah McClain should say. She knew the timeline. She was privy to all the evidence the police had against Jeremy Holt because she had access to my father's case file.

I walked out the sliding door to the back porch and gardens. He thought this would be my mother's favorite place. Her sanctuary if she had only agreed to move here with him.

I went to the white wrought-iron bench he kept next to the rose trellis my mother was supposed to love. It would feel good to stare out at the water as the sun set.

That's when I saw it. It took a moment for my brain to catch up to my eyes.

A foot. A white sneaker with its blue New Balance logo. He was wearing his lucky purple fishing socks.

"Dad!" My heart went into my throat. I dove to the ground beside him.

My father lay on his side in a loose fetal position. There was blood pouring out of a gash on his head.

"Dad!" I pressed two fingers to the pulse in his neck and felt nothing.

CHAPTER THIRTY-NINE

There was so much blood. I felt around his hair to try to figure out where it was coming from.

I reached for my phone in my back pocket. It wasn't there. I left it on the desk in my father's study.

"Dad," I said. "I'm going to get help."

I didn't know if he could hear me. I scrambled to my feet and ran to the back slider. I couldn't seem to make my fingers work. The door wouldn't open. Then finally, I threw it open and ran down the hallway toward the study.

My phone wasn't there. Where had I left it? I ran back to the kitchen, scanning the counters.

"Goddammit!" I yelled. I started back toward the slider. I had to find his phone if I couldn't lay hands on mine.

"Mercy?"

I froze. Liam stood in the front hallway; his expression filled with alarm. Relief flooded me. I ran to him. Liam put his arms up and pulled me into an embrace.

"My dad," I choked the words out. "He's hurt. He fell or something. I c-can't find my phone."

"Shhh," Liam said, kissing the top of my head. "We'll take care of everything."

I pulled away from him. Grabbed his arm. Why wasn't he moving?

"Let's go! Call 911. Make sure they know it's for my dad. They have to send a life flight. They can land on the west side."

Still, Liam didn't move.

"Liam!"

He had an odd expression on his face. Concern. Yes. But something else. Pity?

I took a step back. There was something on the floor, staining the slate tile in the foyer. It was only a moment. An instant. But in my mind, it seemed time had come to a halt.

Blood dripped from Liam's right hand. His arm was covered in it.

"Liam? What happened?"

I went to him. Pulled his arm out in front of him. But there was no cut. He wasn't hurt.

"It's going to be okay," he said. "I'll take care of everything."

The first icy tendrils of panic crept up my spine. Why was Liam here? I looked out the window toward the dock. Only Dad's boat was moored where I'd left it. I hadn't looked on the north side of the island. I turned my gaze out the bay window near the kitchen sink. From there, I could see Liam's jet boat beached next to the oak trees.

He'd been here when I arrived. He'd been here with my father.

"Liam," I said, my throat dry as sandpaper.

Adam. Hollis Branch.

"I'll make everything okay. It's my job."

His job. A million thoughts flooded my brain.

As long as I protect the family brand.

"He hurts women," I whispered. "You knew what Adam was capable of."

"Mercy..."

"He went too far that night. He took Audra Lambrix to the cabin out near Deadwater Lake. The one Beau Godfrey owns. It was supposed to be a safe place for him. That's why Godfrey bought it. That's why it couldn't be in the Branch family name. Just in case, right?"

"Mercy, you're upset. Let's take care of your father."

I shook my head. Adrenaline poured through me. I needed to run. But where? My father wanted seclusion. Freedom. Now we were both trapped.

"He went too far. My God. That little girl. She saw. She saw what Adam did to Audra Lambrix. And they saw her."

Liam took a step toward me. I staggered backward. He had something in his hand. Some sort of hard stick. With renewed terror, I recognized it for what it was. He held a retractable billy club. Slowly, without taking his eyes off of me, he extended it.

"You take care of things," I whispered. "Adam asked you to take care of things."

Liam smiled.

"One of the first days we spent together. You told me you always take care of things. You protect the family brand. Adam got to be the golden boy, and you had to do the dirty work. Savannah Holt saw what he did to Audra that night. And the family couldn't take the chance that she might tell someone. She was nine years old! You didn't have to kill her!"

Then Liam's face changed. Gone was the calm smile. In its place, something evil took over.

"Yes...I always take care of things. Always cleaning up Adam's messes. But *you* made me do this one. Jeremy Holt is scum. He's where he belongs. He was always going to end up behind bars.

He's a junkie. A thief. And Adam is...he's going to make things better. It's his destiny."

I shook my head. "Is that how you killed her? Did you hit her with that club?"

He rocked his head. "I didn't hurt her. She didn't *hurt*. I promise. I was merciful. Mercy. Do you hear that? Mercy. That's what I showed her. It was quick. Savannah felt no pain. I'm not a monster. She was only scared for a second. I swear."

A wave of hysteria bubbled up inside me. Liam's words thundered through me. He always took care of things. Violet had made a call to Adam after she knew Christian's travel plans. She knew when I was going to talk to Alicia Tate in Big Rapids that first time. She knew I'd told Christian all of that, too. Liam had been right there when I took the call from the sheriff informing me of his death. It wasn't a coincidence.

"You took care of Christian Foley too," I said.

"You think he was your friend? He sold you out, Mercy. I protected you from him."

"By putting a bullet in his head? You stood there while I had to look at him like that. My God! How long have you been watching me?"

"Christian was going to hurt you. He was lying to you. Stabbing you in the back. Don't you get it? I've been protecting you, too. Because you're mine."

All of Liam's lies hit me like waves hitting the rocks just outside that window. The minute Christian contacted DeShawn Sims, Liam's family had to have tracked him. Christian fed every conversation I had with him to either Barney or Sims. Sims fed it to Liam. Violet funneled what she knew to him, too. He used it. Planned Christian's murder to the second. He was cunning enough to break into Anne Barnheiser's apartment and use her gun. Every second I spent with Liam was a lie.

I moved to the right toward the slider. Liam moved with me. I faked left. He lunged at me. I threw myself to the right as hard as I could. He grabbed the sleeve of my shirt, but my momentum was too great. I slipped out of his grasp and ran down the hallway.

Liam was right behind me. I could feel his breath. I ran into Dad's study and slammed the door behind me. My fingers trembled as I tried to engage the lock.

Click. Boom!

Liam pounded on the door. I backed myself up against the desk. There was only one way out.

Bam! Liam slammed the billy club against the door. It wouldn't hold. In another few seconds, he would barge his way in.

I raced to the window and unlocked it. If I could get it open. If I could slide out and into the garden. My only chance was to hide.

Until what? No one was coming. My phone was gone. I knew now he must have grabbed it. I know I'd left it on my father's desk.

I got the lock unlatched but the window wouldn't budge. The wood frame had expanded in the heat and now it was stuck. I looked for something to smash through the glass.

BAM!

The door splintered.

I needed a weapon. Maybe I could stun him long enough to run past him. Dad had a crystal paperweight on the desk.

Two choices. Try to smash Liam's skull or the window.

BAM!

"Mercy! There's nowhere to go. It's just you and me. I promise I'll take care of you."

Panic gave way to anger. He may have killed my father. He murdered that poor little girl and destroyed the Holt family. Killed Christian. For what? So Adam could run for governor? So he could hurt more women if the mood struck him?

"You're not a killer, Liam," I said, changing tactics. I pulled at the window, grunting when it wouldn't move. I picked up the paperweight.

"Liam, I know you were just trying to protect your family. It's okay. I understand. We can figure this all out. You and me."

Liam laughed. "It's too late for that."

"It's never too late. As long as we're both alive."

He stopped banging on the door. I heard him gasp on the other side of it. "I love you, Mercy," he said. "I've been in love with you since the second I saw you."

I felt like I was going to throw up. But I needed time. It was the only weapon I had.

"I love you too," I lied. "I still do, Liam."

BAM!

"It's..." BAM! "Too..." BAM! "Late..." BAM. BAM! "For that!!!!"

I smashed through the window with the crystal paperweight. The pane shattered into three large pieces. I grabbed a letter opener off the desk and swung at the jagged pieces of glass, clearing them out of my way.

As the door smashed open, I vaulted through the window, twisting my ankle on the way over. My foot was tangled in vines. I ripped it free and kept going.

The anger was gone. The panic was gone.

Run. Hide. Get to the boat!

Had I left the keys in it? Could I be fast enough? Would anyone hear me scream?

I expected Liam to come through the window. He knew there was only one clear way off this island. I could get to the dock. Or I could try to beat him to the jet boat.

I ran for the woods. I could hide there. Get up in a tree. Find something else to hit him with. Unless he had a gun. I hadn't seen one. But he'd come here to kill.

"Mercy!" He shouted. "It's you and me. You're right. We can figure this out together."

He was close. Too close. But I could tell from the direction of his voice he was heading toward the dock.

I tore through the woods. Thorns scraped my legs. I stumbled. Pulled myself up, then kept on running. I could see the clearing up ahead. Liam's jet boat was there. *Please let the keys be in it.*

My legs burned as I hit the sand. I had to get off the island. But my father. If he wasn't already dead, Liam couldn't leave him alive. I was his one chance at making it out of this.

I could hear Dad's voice in my head. I knew what Tom Gale would want me to do.

Live, Mercy!

I was almost there. I could see the silver gleam of the key in the jet boat's ignition. Air felt like fire in my lungs. I was just a few feet away. I reached out for the handle.

Then something jerked me back. He had a hold of my hair. My neck snapped violently. Liam threw me to the ground.

"I'm sorry," he said as he straddled me. "I really do love you, Mercy." He brought his face close to mine. He crushed his lips to mine, giving me death's kiss. I let out a muffled scream.

"I love you. I'm sorry I couldn't protect you too," he whispered.

He raised the billy club. There was nothing. There was only Liam. His body blocked out what was left of the fading sunlight.

I heard an explosive crack.

"Mercy! Mercy!"

Rasping, wheezing, he stood over me, his old Navy service weapon held low and to his side. Liam lay beside me. His eyes were vacant, staring out at the water. The bullet had passed through his temple.

My father took a staggering step backward, then sank to his knees in the sand.

CHAPTER Forty

"He's coming around."

He had two IVs in his arm. Oxygen under his nose pumped in a low, rhythmic hiss. There were other tubes and wires too. The steady drip of the fluids into his veins would echo in my dreams for weeks.

"Dad?" I said. Someone had thrown a light blanket over me. I'd slept in a chair in the corner since they brought him back from surgery. He had a broken cheekbone they'd wired together. The laceration on his head took ten staples to close. He had a mild concussion and some bruises. But E. Thomas Gale...Gale Force had survived much worse.

My father opened one swollen eye. I knew the smile he gave me hurt him. But my heart burst and I went to him, kissing him gently on his good cheek.

"Welcome back," I said. A nurse checked his vitals, then reset something on his IV machine.

"You gave us a little bit of a scare there," she said. Her name was Amy. She'd been on since seven this morning. It was past noon now. "You've got some visitors outside. Do you think you're up for it? They'll want to talk to you, too."

Dad gave Nurse Amy a thumbs-up. Then Detective Mac Henderson walked in, a deputy sheriff in tow.

"Tom," Mac said. "You feel up to answering a few questions?"

Dad coughed a little. Amy adjusted his bed so he was sitting upright. I could tell the effort of it hurt him. But he gave us both another thumbs-up.

"Liam Branch is dead," Mac said. "Can you tell me what happened?"

I'd already filled Mac in on the bulk of it. Liam had assaulted my father. He'd come there to kill me, too. He had confessed to killing Savannah Holt in order to keep her from going to the police about what she saw out at the cabin that night sixteen years ago. He'd killed Christian Foley, too.

"I don't have to tell you," my dad said. "Got the whole thing on video."

"What?" Mac and I said it together.

"Bastard tripped the silent alarm," Dad said. "I had just enough time to turn on the cameras before he conked me in the damn head. Where's my phone?"

I went to the other chair in the corner and picked up the plastic bag a nurse had given us. I found Dad's phone and brought it to him.

"Code's..." he coughed. "0115." January 15. My birthday. I punched it in and handed the phone to my father. He pecked at it with his right index finger. The medical tape got in his way. He

CHAPTER FORTY

pulled up the app connected to his alarm system and handed the phone to Detective Henderson. I stood over his shoulder as he watched the playback.

Liam had come through the back door. Two different cameras picked him up as he headed down the hallway. He stopped in the kitchen. Dad was already out on the patio by the time Liam got there. Liam went out through the slider. One of Dad's cameras was placed behind a hanging plant on the patio. It gave a clear shot of the back of the house.

Dad turned to face Liam. Dad asked him what he was doing there. Liam asked where I was. Dad was watering plants. He turned his back to put down the watering can. That's when Liam struck him with his billy club. I knew how this turned out. It still cut through me to see him in pain.

Mac fast forwarded the tape. A few minutes later, I came home. The camera picked me up, looking through the house. Then my confrontation with Liam. Mac clicked the volume button on Dad's phone. The microphones in the hallway picked everything up.

Liam Branch confessed to killing Savannah Holt to me. He confessed to killing Christian Foley. It was all there. I sank into the chair beside my father and took his hand in mine. I watched as Liam chased me down the hall. I heard the glass break in my father's study as I tried to make my escape. Then, a few agonizing minutes later, my father reentered the house. Staggering. Gripping the wall. Leaving a bloody trail in his wake, he walked into the study. A moment later, he walked out, holding his service weapon. If he'd been a few seconds later, we'd both be dead.

"I should have listened to you," Dad whispered. "I could have prevented this."

"You couldn't," I said. "Liam didn't act alone. Detective, that's what you need to know. That's what's not on that tape. There were other people involved."

I explained everything I knew. Hollis Branch's catch and kill order. John Garland's role in intimidating the witnesses at Jeremy's trial. With Liam gone and his confession recorded, I hoped Dustin Bolton and Hannah McClain would finally admit their role in all of this.

My father hung his head. It was a lot for him to take in. But there was one more bomb I had to drop.

"Dad," I said. "I believe it was Violet. She was feeding information to the Branch family the whole time. John Garland was on their payroll, too. She's the one who told Garland where you had Dustin Bolton hiding out before he testified. He picked him up. Remy Horner can confirm that. And Garland coerced Hannah McLain to lie on the witness stand. He made her watch him torture Bolton."

"You have proof of this?" Mac asked, his face ghostly white.

"I have cell phone records," I said. "I believe Violet Tamblyn was communicating with the Branch family about conversations I had with Christian Foley and Jeremy Holt over the last two months. Violet knew where Christian Foley was. She fed that information to the Branches. Christian was communicating with a woman named Anne Barnheiser, an intern working for the Gossip Zone. He was trying to sell a story about my family. About my Dad. I have records of Christian's communications with the reporter covering the story. I have proof the Branch family was trying to kill the story. At first, I thought they were killing it to protect my father. But they were trying to protect Adam and Liam and their part in Savannah Holt's murder. I can't prove this part, but I believe someone might have been recording Christian's phone calls

CHAPTER FORTY

to Anne. Liam knew more than just casual things about her. Somehow, he knew she owned a gun. Liam broke into Barnheiser's apartment. Stole her laptop and her gun. The same gun used to kill Christian Foley. Liam tried to make it look like a suicide. Dustin Bolton, Remy Horner, Hannah McClain, Alicia Tate. They can corroborate Jeremy Hunt's alibi and how John Garland intimidated them into lying or staying silent sixteen years ago."

I said the words. But it felt like I was hearing them being spoken by someone else. Later, they would sink in. Later, I would crawl into bed in my pink and green room and cry for the friend I had lost. I would cry for Savannah Holt and all the wreckage her death left behind. And yes, I would cry for Liam Branch, the man I believed I could love.

CHAPTER
Forty-One

EARLY THE NEXT MORNING, Detective Henderson brought Violet into custody. He interviewed her for over eight hours. I hadn't slept in almost two days by then. I stayed by my father's side. That next evening, Henderson asked me to come down to the sheriff's office.

Somewhere along the way, I changed my clothes. Marian Greenbaum had brought them over. She got Lloyd Murphy to take her over to the island so she could grab some things for me. There were a thousand little kindnesses like that by the people of Helene over the next few days.

Henderson brought me into his office. He had a tablet on the desk. Lucas Braunlin, the Helene County Prosecutor sat in the chair in front of Mac's desk. I took the other. Savannah Holt's picture drew my eye.

"Violet Tamblyn's cooperating," Mac said. "She admitted to almost everything you said."

"In exchange for partial immunity," Braunlin said. "She wanted full, but I won't do it. She's too deep into this."

"She admitted it?" I said, incredulous.

"She claims she had no idea Savannah Holt would be killed. Or Christian Foley. She claims she only contacted Liam about the investigation you were launching into Savannah's murder. She told him about Foley. He asked her to call him whenever she heard you talking to him. She doesn't know how Liam tracked Foley specifically on the day he died, but she told him what she knew from you about his travel plans. She admits to contacting John Garland after Savannah's disappearance and telling him where Dustin Bolton was staying. But she refuses to implicate anyone else. Just Garland and Liam Branch."

"The two people you can't arrest," I said. "Nobody's seen John Garland in over fifteen years."

"She gave him up," Mac said. "It was part of her proffer. She gave us an address in Sarasota. I've been in contact with the local authorities down there. Garland is in a nursing home. He's got end stage pancreatic cancer. It doesn't look like he's got more than a few weeks left to go. He's corroborating Violet's story. But he's also claiming Liam Branch was the only member of the family he ever had any contact with."

"They're protecting him," I said. "Even now, they're protecting Adam. He didn't kill Savannah or Christian. I believe that was Liam, just like he said. But you can't tell me Hollis and Adam Branch weren't pulling the strings."

"We can't prove it," Braunlin said. "I can charge Garland with accessory after the fact on the Holt murder. Obstruction. Witness tampering. Assault and attempted murder on Dustin Bolton."

"But he'll be dead before it gets to trial," I said bitterly.

"Bolton's also talking," Mac said. "One of my deputies just finished his interview with him. Bolton admitted Garland was the one who roughed him up all those years ago. I suspect once we catch up with her, Hannah McClain will recant her testimony, too."

"Jeremy," I said, turning to Braunlin. "You have to get a judge to get him out of prison. His mother isn't going to make it much longer. We have to make sure Jeremy is by her side. We owe him that. And we cannot let Adam Branch off the hook."

"I don't want to," Henderson said. "I believe everything you said. Liam wasn't acting alone. Garland was all too ready to spill once the Sarasota cops got to him."

Mac took his tablet and pulled something up on the screen. It was a video in freeze frame. An elderly man sat in a wheelchair hooked up to an oxygen tank. He was a husk of his former self, but I immediately recognized John Garland.

Mac pressed play. Garland took a sip of water with a shaky hand that turned almost black from all the bruising from his IV.

"I never would have let it happen like that. I never would have hurt that little girl. It could have been managed. Liam was trying to be some kind of big shot. I told Hollis for years that kid was a loose cannon. That he was gonna do something that couldn't be undone."

"What did you do, John?" a deputy asked him off camera.

"Liam called me in a panic. I could barely understand him. Said he needed my help. Told me to meet him out by the cabin."

"You knew what he meant by that? The cabin?"

Garland looked uncomfortable. "Yeah. I knew."

"What did you find when you got there, John?"

"She was already dead. That's what you gotta understand. She was already dead. Poor kid. I *never* would have agreed to that. Never. But it was done. She was gone. Liam made a mess of it."

"What about Adam?" the deputy asked.

John Garland lifted his chin in defiance. "What about him?"

"Was he there?"

"Nope. Never saw him."

"He's lying," I said. "He's still protecting Adam." Beside me, Mac Henderson looked as if he were made of granite.

"What did you do then, John?" the deputy asked in the video.

"Took care of it. Cleaned up the cabin. Wiped every trace of anyone having been there. I did the best I could. I put Savannah in the water."

"You put her in the water. You did more than that, didn't you? She was wrapped in plastic. Weighed down. Half her clothes were missing, John."

"I only did what Liam paid me to do," John said, then folded over into racking coughs. It took him a moment to recover.

"You framed Jeremy Holt," the deputy said. "Tell me about that, John."

Garland shook his head. "The kid was a junkie. He was headed for prison one way or another. His old man asked me to talk to him. Try to straighten him out. See if he'd enlist in the Army. Heh. As if they'd have him."

"He was an easy target," the deputy off-screen said.

Garland looked mean. Even now.

CHAPTER FORTY-ONE

"You planted her clothes in Jeremy's car?"

Garland nodded. I couldn't listen to it anymore. I hit pause on the screen.

"He admits to taking the girl's body and weighing it down in the river. I think that's the only thing he really screwed up. Garland was hoping her body would never be found. Jeremy Holt was just supposed to be an insurance policy in case they ever found her." Mac spoke in a monotone. I knew he grappled with his own guilt and demons over all these lost years.

"God," I said. "Mac, Jeremy's been in prison for almost sixteen years. Savannah's mother believes he killed her baby. I think his own father died believing it. Getting him out of there...giving him back his freedom. It just doesn't even seem like enough."

"It's a start," Mac said. The shock of the last few hours seemed to have aged Mac Henderson. I couldn't imagine what he was feeling.

"I'll file an emergency motion," Braunlin said. "I'll do everything in my power to get Jeremy out of that cell by this time tomorrow."

I just prayed it would be in time.

"There's something else," Mac said. "I didn't want to ask you. And if it makes you feel uncomfortable, forget it. It's not happening."

"Mac, what?"

"It's Violet. She wants to see you. She wants to try to explain why she did what she did. And I'm telling you. You don't have to see her. You aren't part of her deal. That woman has an answer for everything. An excuse. A way to keep herself in denial that she's not part of the reason Savannah Holt's murder was covered up. If she truly wants this deal, she's going to have to stand up in court and admit her part. But she asked me to ask you. That's all."

"It's okay," I said. "I'll see her. I want her to look me in the eye and tell *me* what she did. It's the least of what she owes me."

"Okay," Mac said. "But you can change your mind."

"When?" I asked. "When can I see her?"

Mac's face went cold as he looked at me. "Today," he said. "How about now?"

CHAPTER
Forty-Two

BETRAYAL IS A FUNNY THING. Your head feels it far before your heart does. So when a Helene County Deputy led Violet Tamblyn in to see me wearing an orange jumpsuit. It jarred me.

The moment she saw me, she started to cry. My shock turned to anger. She sat down.

"Mercy," she said. "Is he...Tom. Is he okay?"

"That's what you're asking? Is okay? No. He's not okay, Violet. He nearly had his skull caved in. Lucky for all of us, he's tough to kill. And he saved my life. Liam Branch was about to beat me to death."

"No," she said. "Just no. Please don't tell me anymore."

"Fine," I said. "So you tell me. Why? How could you do this?"

"I don't. I can't...I thought I knew what I was going to say when you came. But now, I know there are no words that will satisfy you."

"Try."

"You don't have children yet. Someday when you do, you'll better understand."

"Like Olivia Holt?" I said. "She had a child. And your actions helped take that child away from her. Diane Benning has a child. For sixteen years, she'd watched him rot in prison for something she knew in her soul he hadn't done. She watched him become the most hated man in Helene. She watched his own father turn against him, then die from the grief of it. Steven Holt went to his grave wondering whether one of his children murdered the other."

"Don't you think I know that? But I didn't know Liam killed Savannah. I swear I didn't. And I didn't know he was going to kill your friend. I didn't know he was capable of that. You may not believe me, but it's the truth."

"What about John Garland," I asked. "You knew what he was capable of."

"It's complicated," she said. "Johnny and I were close. He...I...I loved him. He was good to me. I'm not proud to say it. I was married, I know that. It didn't last long, but it happened."

"Was it money? I mean I know it was money. I know the Branches gave you what, a half a million dollars to feed Dustin Bolton's hideout to your Johnny? He tortured him, Violet. I saw the photographs. His fingers were sliced off at the knuckle. They held his chest to a hot electric stove. Hannah McClain says she can still smell his skin as it charred. Dustin Bolton's also someone's child."

"No," she said. "No. I didn't betray your father. Not like that. But I'm not blameless. I looked the other way. When Johnny came to the office asking where the Holt files were, I let him in. I walked away. I thought...see no evil, hear no evil. And I know that makes me just as culpable. I've owned up to it. I'm willing to pay for my sins."

"You let my father think he made a mistake. You withheld Alicia Tate's letter from him."

"No," she said. "Johnny did that. I swear it. All I did was give him access to the file."

"All you did," I repeated.

"Enough," she said. "I'm not trying to justify anything I did. Not like that. I told you. I'm ready to take responsibility for my part in this. I just need you to know that I love you. I love your father."

"You can keep your love, Violet. You almost destroyed my dad."

"I've kept that man going!" she shouted. "Before you came, how do you think he was managing? You're here. You know now how it is with him. I'm the one who has protected him when his own family abandoned him."

"Got it," I said. "You're a saint. You want me to thank you."

"No," she said, her expression pained. "Oh, Mercy. This is coming out all wrong. Please, just give me a chance to explain."

I said nothing.

"I told you when you sat down," she said. "You don't know what it's like to be a parent. Especially one with a child who struggles. You know about Glen, my youngest. My son who lives in Denver. Mercy, he has demons. He's gotten involved with things he shouldn't. He's so much like his father. He's gambled away everything. More than once. I've tried to get him help. But when his life is threatened, how can I turn my back?"

I remembered all the times my father told me Violet's kids were losers. Deadbeats. Always coming to her with their hands out. I never pried. I never felt it was my business.

"I needed the money to help Glen," she said. "And Hollis helped me. It seemed such a minor request. Let Johnny see a file. Tell Liam about your friend. Liam cared about you. At least he convinced me he did. He told me your friend was bad news. A con artist. He was trying to protect you. He said your father asked him to look out for you. I asked Tom about it. But when he said he didn't remember or know what I was talking about, why would I think that was unusual?"

"If you needed help with Glen," I said. "You could have asked my father!"

Her anguished expression melted into anger. She sat straighter. "I tried. I begged him. Has he told you? One day, I got on my knees in front of Tom. Not figuratively. On my actual knees. The people Glen owed money to were going to kill him. It was sixteen years ago. And your father turned his back on me. He said Glen was a grown man. He was twenty-five! But the great Tom Gale, father-of-the-year, tried to tell me how to handle my son. I had no choice. So I went to Hollis, and he helped me. He gave me the money. More than I needed."

"You used the extra to pay off your mortgage," I said. "But it wasn't enough. Glen got into trouble again and again. So you took out a second mortgage. You bailed Glen out."

"You do whatever you have to to get between your children and disaster."

I nodded. "So does Hollis Branch, apparently."

"Oh Mercy, you're being flippant. But you shouldn't be. This is the other reason I wanted so desperately to see you. You've run

Hollis off for now. But Tom killed his son. You need to be very careful about going after Adam. Adam Branch is made of Teflon. He'll survive us all. And he'll probably align himself with even darker people going forward. You've made an enemy of the Branches. Please don't forget that. Please be careful."

"I appreciate you looking out for me," I said bitterly. I'd heard enough.

"Mercy, please," she said. "Try to understand."

"I do," I said. "Detective Henderson is right. He said you had an answer for everything. I'm sorry for your pain. I truly am. But it doesn't justify what you did. I could even forgive you for betraying my dad. But I can't forgive you for Savannah or Jeremy or Christian. Their blood is on your hands. That's what you have to answer for. It's not even about my dad. Do you get that?"

She wept. The thing was, I believed *she* really believed she had good reasons for her choices. There was still a part of me that would always remember her as Aunt Violet, the woman who left casseroles for my dad in the fridge. The woman who could sign my father's signature better than he could. She would sign his name to my permission slips when both my parents were too busy to remember. But that would never make up for the rest.

As I left her there, crying, I prayed someday she could truly understand the hurt she caused so many people. That was the only way she could ever hope to make amends.

∽

TWO DAYS LATER, Jeremy walked out of the Ionia Correctional Facility a free man. He came out carrying one small bag. It contained a change of clothes and a few hundred dollars.

It was strange seeing him like this. Not behind glass or bars or a table. He was free. But he was still broken. I just prayed he could find a path in life that would bring him some measure of peace.

"Thank you," he said as he stood in front of me. I leaned against my father's car. I hadn't come alone.

"I'm sorry," I said. "We failed you."

He shook his head. "You believed me. Your old man believed me. I just wish mine had."

I wanted to tell him everything would be okay. But I knew it might never be.

"Your mother's waiting for you."

Jeremy choked back a sob. "Thank you. You gave her back to me. I know she's dying. But you gave her back to me."

I put a hand on Jeremy's arm. "You gave my father back to me too, Jeremy."

Our eyes locked. There would never be the right words for either of us to express what our new friendship had done for each other.

"Come on," I said. "Your mother's waiting for you. So is someone else."

Olivia Holt got out of the car. She had tears streaming down her face as she walked up to Jeremy.

"Jeremy," she said, her voice shaking. "I'm so sorry."

She threw her arms around him. Jeremy went rigid. They were the survivors. They had both lost Savannah, Steven, and now they would lose Diane together. Maybe it would help them form a different bond. Maybe Olivia could help parent Jeremy in a way he never got.

Maybe.

But I knew they both had a long way to go.

∼

JOHN GARLAND WOULD NEVER SEE the inside of a prison. He never even saw the inside of a courtroom. He died the evening before he was set to be arraigned for accessory after the fact. He would have faced up to twenty years in prison.

Violet Tamblyn *would* see the inside of a courtroom. She pled guilty to two counts of obstruction of justice. She would serve five years in prison. I knew the Branch family would protect her though. I had every belief that she would get a big payday when she saw the light of day again.

She was a good soldier, after all. She protected the family brand.

But I didn't.

One week after Liam Branch's death, a news story broke in the National Tattler, a rival to the Gossip Zone. Audra Lambrix told her story. Topher Smith backed it up with photographs of the beating she had taken at Adam Branch's hands. Anne Barnheiser had the byline. She would present an exclusive interview of Audra to air on the Tattler's streaming network. The day the Tattler story ran, I received a dozen red roses with a simple card.

"I found the perfect spot for Christian in the park near my apartment. He'll be with me every day. Thank you. Love, Barney."

Hollis Branch hopped a private flight bound for Indonesia before the police could question him.

Audra wouldn't press charges. The statute of limitations on assault had long passed. Adam would not go to jail for his part in the murder of Savannah Holt. Or for what he'd done to Audra. The prosecutor couldn't prove rape or that he intended to kill her.

But his political career was finished, for now. There was justice in that, I supposed. There had to be. Only I knew my father and I had made a powerful enemy. One that could afford to lie in wait.

I was powerful, too. And I had something John Garland, Diane Benning or even Hollis Branch didn't. Time.

CHAPTER
Forty-Three

"I THINK IT LOOKS PRETTY GOOD," Dad said. We stood outside the office, staring at the new sign. "Gale and Gale."

"Are you sure about this?" Dad asked. He'd already asked me about that a dozen times. We walked across the street to see the sign from there. We sat on a bench underneath the streetlamp. An hour ago, Lloyd Murphy came over with the paperwork Dad asked him to prepare. He named me his power of attorney if he ever became disabled. I signed them with my own conditions.

"I'm sure, Dad. We're going to help a lot of people."

"I'm not sure you realize how many, Mercy. As soon as Jeremy's story hits the news, the phone won't stop ringing."

"That's the idea," I said. "Those are the people I think I can help."

That had been one of my conditions. We would reinvent Dad's practice, focusing on assisting clients who'd been wrongfully accused of crimes they hadn't committed.

"Come on," he said. "I have another surprise."

We walked across the street and went into the office. Dad let me hire a designer. That was another of my conditions. We'd brightened up the place with fresh paint. New furniture. A cozy waiting room where Violet's desk used to be. I took the office right next to his down the hall. He put his arm around me and turned me to face the opposite wall.

"Dad!" I smiled. He'd reframed his law degree. Beside it, he'd hung my freshly minted private investigator license.

"We look good together," he said. He kissed me on the cheek. "I'm proud of you, kiddo."

"I'm proud of you too, Dad. Now let me call Dr. Munn. Let's get you that neurology referral." That had been my last condition.

His face grew serious. "I was hoping we could just have today. But come on."

I followed him down the hallway to his office. He picked up a large envelope from his desk and handed it to me. The label on the corner read "Michigan Medicine, Department of Neurology."

"When did you do this?" I asked, my throat going dry.

"A year ago," he answered.

"Why didn't you..." I let my voice trail off. The answer didn't matter anymore.

I took a beat. "What is it?" Part of me didn't want to know. Didn't want to read the words. And yet, I didn't want my father to carry it alone anymore.

"Chronic microvascular ischemic changes. Mixed with a side of what they suspect is the early stages of Alzheimer's, honey. You can read the report. It would be fascinating if they weren't talking about my damn brain."

"Okay," I said. "Okay. So, we know. We don't have to be afraid of it. There can be some treatments. There can..."

"No, honey. That's why I want you to be sure. You're my patient advocate now. But I still get to decide."

"It's early though," I said. "You're okay, Dad."

He smiled. "I will be. But if this ever gets too much for you. If you ever want out..."

"We'll figure it out together, Dad. Promise."

"I trust you," he said.

"I trust you too."

So many people we thought we could rely on had betrayed us. Violet. Liam. Even Christian. I rested my head on my father's strong shoulder. I would have his back. He would have mine. We could save each other's lives. We had time. He knew who I was. He had good days and bad days. It's all any of us can ask for.

"Your mother isn't gonna be happy," Dad said.

"I know," I said. I hadn't told her my plans yet.

"But you're sure?"

"I'm sure." I took my father's hand. We walked out the front door together.

"Looks good, Tom!" A neighbor waved as he walked his little bichon frisé on a leash.

His neighbors. My neighbors now too. I hadn't decided if I was going to live on the island with Dad or take the apartment above the office. But Jeremy Holt wasn't the only one with years to make up for.

"It's getting harder," my father said. He looked straight ahead. The breeze from the lake picked up. It would get dark soon.

"I'm forgetting things, Mercy."

"I know, Dad."

"I'm going to need help keeping track of it all."

"I know that too. And I'm going to help you."

He laughed. "They all say that. And then I drive them away. My first wife, Loretta. Everett. Your mother. Maybe even Violet."

"Maybe you'll drive me away someday too. Or I'll drive you away. But not today. Okay, Dad?"

He smiled and brought my hand up to his lips. He kissed me. "Okay. Not today. Today I'll just be proud of my little girl. I love you, Mercy. No matter what happens. Don't forget that."

I looked at my father. He had more lines in his face. His hair was pure white and thinning a bit in the back. But he was still my father. Still Gale Force, ready to take on the world. For now, I would take it on with him. Whatever came around the next corner.

"I love you too, Dad," I said.

And I did.

∼

CHAPTER FORTY-THREE

Up next for Mercy Gale…

Ten years ago, five friends went to Deadwater Lake for one last weekend together.

By sunrise, four were gone.

When the sole survivor of a mass murder comes to Mercy Gale for help, she claims she's met a man who spoke the killer's final words—words no one else alive should know. The revelation pulls Mercy into a decades-old nightmare of secrets, lies, and blood. Was the wrong man executed for the crime? How does a stranger know what only the dead could? As Mercy digs deeper, she realizes someone is watching her… someone who remembers that night all too well—and is determined to finish what was started.

Don't miss **Blacker than Midnight** by Robin James

https://www.robinjamesbooks.com/btmback

For more information about the next book in the Mercy Gale Series, please sign up for Robin's newsletter. Turn the page to learn more about what you'll receive for subscribing. https://www.robinjamesbooks.com/subscribe/

Newsletter Sign Up

Sign up to get notified about Robin James's latest book releases, discounts, and author news. You'll also get *Crown of Thorne* an exclusive FREE bonus prologue to the Cass Leary Legal Thriller Series just for joining.

Click to Sign Up

https://www.robinjamesbooks.com/subscribe/

Afterword

I conceived the basic plot of this book years ago. Mercy and her father popped into my brain nearly fully formed one morning on a quiet kayak ride. But it has taken me almost five years to bring this story to fruition. I wasn't quite sure why. Now I know.

The struggles and rewards of dealing with aging parents is an experience most of us know or will soon know all too well. My mother, a lifelong avid reader, was one of my biggest fans and eagerly devoured everything I wrote. In the last years of her life, she struggled with Alzheimer's. Over time, it became too difficult for her to read novels. She tried for so long to hold on to it, scribbling notes in the margins so she could keep track of plot threads and characters. But eventually, this horrible disease stole that from her. After she passed, we found tiny notes hidden all over the house. Dates, memories, names. Things she tried to hold on to that she knew were slipping away.

So I could not quite make myself finish this book. In part because I knew it was the first series of mine she would never be able to read. In part, because we needed to finish her story before I could write

Mercy and Tom Gale's in the way I need to tell it. I needed my mother to show me the way.

If someone you care about suffers from this horrible disease, you're not alone. For help finding resources in your community, please reach out to the Alzheimer's Association. https://www.alz.org/local_resources/find_your_local_chapter

This book is for my mother.

About the Author

Robin James is an attorney and former law professor. She's worked on a wide range of civil, criminal and family law cases in her twenty-five year legal career. She also spent over a decade as supervising attorney for a Michigan legal clinic assisting thousands of people who could not otherwise afford access to justice.

Robin now lives on a lake in southern Michigan with her husband, two children, and one lazy dog. Her favorite, pure Michigan writing spot is stretched out on the back of a pontoon watching the faster boats go by.

Sign up for Robin James's Legal Thriller Newsletter to get all the latest updates on her new releases and get a prequel novella Robin's bestselling Cass Leary Legal Thriller Series. https://www.robinjamesbooks.com/subscribe/

Also By Robin James

For the most up to date Booklist, visit

https://www.robinjamesbooks.com/books/

Mercy Gale Mystery Thrillers

Thicker than Water

Blacker than Midnight

With more to come...

Mara Brent Legal Thriller Series

Time of Justice

Price of Justice

Hand of Justice

Mark of Justice

Path of Justice

Vow of Justice

Web of Justice

Shadow of Justice

Edge of Justice

With more to come...

Cass Leary Legal Thriller Series

Burden of Truth

Silent Witness

Devil's Bargain

Stolen Justice

Blood Evidence

Imminent Harm

First Degree

Mercy Kill

Guilty Acts

Cold Evidence

Dead Law

The Client List

Deadly Defense

Code of Secrets

With more to come...

Made in the USA
Monee, IL
16 November 2025